After
She
Falls

After She Falls

CARMEN SCHOBER

BETHANYHOUSE

a division of Baker Publishing Group
Minneapolis, Minnesota

© 2021 by Carmen Schober

Published by Bethany House Publishers
11400 Hampshire Avenue South
Bloomington, Minnesota 55438
www.bethanyhouse.com

Bethany House Publishers is a division of
Baker Publishing Group, Grand Rapids, Michigan

Printed in the United States of America

Library of Congress Cataloging-in-Publication Data
Names: Schober, Carmen, author.
Title: After she falls / Carmen Schober.
Description: Minneapolis, Minnesota : Bethany House Publishers, a division of
    Baker Publishing Group, [2021]
Identifiers: LCCN 2021023574 | ISBN 9780764239298 | ISBN 9780764239458
    (casebound) | ISBN 9781493433698 (ebook)
Subjects: LCSH: Mixed martial arts—Fiction. | Self-actualization (Psychology) in
    women—Fiction. | GSAFD: Christian fiction. | LCGFT: Christian fiction.
Classification: LCC PS3619.C449256 A69 2021 | DDC 813/.6—dc23
LC record available at https://lccn.loc.gov/2021023574

Scripture quotations are from The Holy Bible, English Standard Version® (ESV®),
copyright © 2001 by Crossway, a publishing ministry of Good News Publishers. Used
by permission. All rights reserved. ESV Text Edition: 2016

Cover design by Paul Higdon and Faceout Studios, Tim Green
Cover photography by BRAIN2HANDS

Author is represented by Golden Wheat Literary Agency.

Baker Publishing Group publications use paper produced from sustainable forestry
practices and post-consumer waste whenever possible.

21 22 23 24 25 26 27   7 6 5 4 3 2 1

To my younger, fear-filled self:
You will fall sometimes, and it will hurt.
But God is fighting alongside you.
Trust Him.

1

ADRI DOESN'T TURN ON THE RADIO or pull up Eva's playlist on her phone. For once, she drives in silence. Past crumbling apartment buildings and palm trees and the ice cream parlor with the pink neon sign. She drives until everything becomes less familiar.

Adri circles the old limestone chapel and tells herself not to go in. She and Eva aren't dressed right. They don't know anyone who goes to the church. They'll mess up the hymns. Adri hasn't been inside a church in years, and Owen's voice reminds her that she's never been a very good Catholic.

Still, she parks the car. She takes her daughter's hand, and they walk inside. They're late, but there are plenty of empty pews facing the heavy wooden pulpit. Eva watches curiously as a woman plays a slow song on the organ. A man appears, dressed in a black robe. He reads from the Bible. Eva's face scrunches in confusion, but Adri listens.

"And King David, a warrior poet, cried out to God, 'Out of my distress I called on the Lord; the Lord answered me and set me free.'"

Tears burn the corners of her eyes. She fights back thoughts of Owen—his eyes, his hands, his voice, the rare times when he was gentle. Even then, she never felt free.

"It's time to go, Mama."

Adri blinks when Eva tugs on her arm. Around them, people talk. A few smile at Adri, but she and Eva quickly slip out. The sunlight is bright, even though it's a dreary December morning in Miami.

Adri's mind races as she drives in circles again. In the back seat, Eva studies a coloring page she was handed by one of the greeters.

"Mama, why does Jesus carry the lamb around his head? Doesn't it itch his neck?"

"I don't know, butterfly. Maybe the lamb likes being carried like that?"

Eva colors in silence, leaving Adri alone to war with her strange feelings. She felt a temporary calm inside the church, but her fears are returning. Owen walked out two nights ago, saying he needed space, or time, or air—she can't keep track anymore—so he won't be back for another day or two. Part of her wants him to come back.

She hates that part.

She parks, ignoring the knot in her stomach, and she and Eva climb the stairs to their apartment. Adri finds her key and opens the door, expecting Rocky, her old German Shepherd, to greet them with his usual low bark, but he doesn't. She flips on the light.

"Rocky?"

She suddenly hears whimpering. Alarmed, she tells Eva to stay put and follows the sound. Her heart stops when she opens the bathroom door.

Water pools on the yellow linoleum as Owen kneels by the tub, his body hunched over as he forces Rocky's head underwater. Rocky fights wildly, but Owen holds him down.

When he sees Adri in the doorway, his face darkens. "I hate this dog."

Instinctively, she shoves him, barely knocking him back, but it gives Rocky just enough time to burst from the water. Owen wraps his hands around her neck.

"Where have you been? Where did you go?"

She tries to wrench his wet fingers from her neck, but her hands slip over his.

"Eva . . ." she says, choking. "Eva will see."

He lets go, and she gasps for air as he rushes from the bathroom. She tries to follow him, but Rocky blocks the way, determined to protect her.

"Come on, boy," she whispers, her throat stinging. "Come with me." She pulls him with her and finds Owen in the living room with his arm around Eva. His voice is cheerful, but Eva looks afraid as she glances between a shaken Adri and a soaked Rocky.

"Why is Rocky all wet?"

"I was giving him a bath," Owen says smoothly, ushering her into the kitchen. "Are you hungry? Where did you and Mama go this morning?"

Shaking, Adri waits as Owen makes Eva a grilled cheese. He's dressed in clean clothes, and his sandy hair is slicked back, but there's a fresh cut under his eye. She listens as Eva tells him about the church service. He pretends to be interested, but when he looks at her again, his eyes are full of fury.

God, please. Help me.

"Why don't you go to Minnie's apartment for a few minutes?" he says when she is finished. "I need to talk to Mama."

Adri watches helplessly as he walks Eva to their neighbor's apartment, and Minnie happily invites Eva in and turns on the television. Minnie is charmed by Owen, like most people are. As soon as her door closes, he charges back inside and grabs Adri's arm, pulling her toward the bedroom.

"Ouch!"

"We have one stupid fight, and you go running to church—"

"That hurts, Owen."

He tightens his grip.

"I said that hurts!"

Rocky growls and bares his fangs.

Owen looks at the dog with narrowed eyes. "I should've killed you a long time ago."

9

"Don't hurt him!"

"Shut up! Why are you screaming?" Owen snaps, his own voice dropping to a whisper. "Lower your voice." He glances at the door. Rocky tries to move closer, but Owen kicks him, making him yelp.

"Rocky, stay," she pleads, forcing herself to whisper. "Please, boy. Stay there—"

"Shut up about the dog, Adri."

She falls silent. Thankfully, Rocky lowers his head in defeat.

Owen grabs her chin and yanks her face toward his. "I came home wanting to make up with you, and you're off at church."

She braces herself. He's wearing cologne, but it doesn't hide the alcohol.

"Instead, I come home to him." Owen jerks his head toward Rocky. "Growling and barking like an idiot."

Adri stays silent, repeating her prayer.

"You broke your promise, Adri."

"I thou—"

He slaps her. Rocky growls as Owen grabs her chin again.

"You don't just disappear like that. I apologized, didn't I? You're not perfect either, even though I know you like to think you are."

She bites her tongue. He *apologized*? More like she discovered his latest affair and cussed him out as he mumbled some lame excuse. He'd almost hit her, but then he stormed out instead.

Now, she wants to wrench his hand from her face, but she forces herself to be still. She's fought back too many times before. Owen knows all her weaknesses.

"Out of my distress I called on the Lord; the Lord answered me and set me free."

Owen's eyes move over her and settle on the marks on her neck where he grabbed her in the bathroom. His blue eyes darken like heavy storm clouds.

"I don't want to see this, Adri," he says, motioning toward the flooded bathroom, then her neck. "You make me do this stuff, and I hate it." His eyes move to Rocky again, who defiantly meets his gaze. "And I don't want *him* anywhere near me. Do you understand? I want him gone, or I—"

"I'll clean up the bathroom, and I'll take care of the dog," she says quickly, making her voice reassuring as she looks up at him, willing her face to hide her emotions. "I'll take care of all of it, okay?"

He glares at her, tortured, and she knows he wants to hit her.

"I need air," he says finally.

Keep nodding, she tells herself. *Don't stop. Nod. Nod. Nod. Let him disappear. Let him, Adri. Let him go.*

Moments later, when the door slams behind him, she breathes again. She kneels to hug Rocky, who licks away her tears as it hits her all at once. Owen Anders, the man she fell in love with when she was eighteen years old, is just like her father, and she's just like her mother. She knows this because Owen's absence hurts more than his hands.

What's even worse is she knows he isn't going to disappear. He always comes back, and she always lets him. She leans against Rocky.

Please, God. Set me free.

Hands shaking, Adri dials the almost-forgotten number, reciting the words she practiced.

"Hello?"

Adri hesitates. It's a woman's voice.

"Hello?" the woman repeats. Her voice is soft and familiar, almost like her aunt's—but her aunt is dead.

"Hello," Adri says, forcing herself to speak. "Is . . . Roman Rivera available?"

"Who's this?"

"It's . . . Adri."

Silence.

"Adri Rivera?" the woman asks.

"Yes."

She gasps. "Adri? It's Yvonne, honey. Yvonne Turner. Oh my goodness. What are you . . . what's going on, dear?"

Adri feels like crying all over again. Yvonne Turner, her Aunt Dalila's best friend and old business partner. Adri wants to tell Yvonne everything but doesn't. Instead, she asks the question she should've asked five years ago—the *first* time Owen hit her.

"Can I come home?"

"You mean . . . come back to Sparta?" Yvonne can't keep the shock out of her voice.

Adri closes her eyes. She promised herself she'd never go back and stare her failures in the face, but what choice does she have? Her life is a nightmare. "If Uncle Roman will have me." Her heart races as new tears fall. "And my daughter. Eva." Her uncle has never met Eva. He'd tried, but Adri always made up an excuse because she didn't want him to see her with Owen. One look at Adri's face, and he'd know how weak she really was.

"Of course you can come home, honey." Yvonne's voice breaks through her thoughts. "I'll tell Roman to call you as soon as he gets back from the church."

When Yvonne hangs up, Adri sinks into her bed, her thoughts racing haphazardly. At least she and Eva have somewhere to go, and it's far away from Owen, tucked away in the mountains of Pennsylvania, just a few hours outside of Philadelphia. That's something, right? There is so much more she'll have to figure out, but, for now, there is Sparta. She wipes her tears away as nostalgia hits her like a kick to the chest.

For years, she'd told herself that she didn't miss what she left behind, convincing herself that what she and Owen had was imperfect but still less suffocating than Sparta. Owen, too, frequently reminded her of her humble, boring beginnings. But she did miss Sparta and its smallness, its jagged blue mountains, her uncle and aunt, Yvonne, and . . . more.

Most of all, she missed her freedom.

"Are we going on a vacation?" Eva asks as they walk to the train.

Adri thinks fast and makes her voice steady. "We're going to visit someone. He lives by the mountains."

Eva's eyes light up. They're light blue, just like Owen's. "Is Daddy coming?"

Adri tucks a strand of dark hair behind her daughter's ear and fights back tears. Eva's only four. "No, butterfly. Just us."

They step onto the train and settle into a booth. Rocky snuggles against Eva, but he keeps his eyes fixed on Adri with a look of fatherly concern. When the train starts moving, Adri's heart finally slows down a little. She watches the city blur into the falling darkness, and her thoughts drift into dangerous territory.

Owen is her most powerful addiction, and distance between them strengthens her withdrawal. She knows he'll be furious when he realizes they're gone, and there's no limit to what he's willing to do when he's angry. Her stomach tightens with fear, but she decides to pray again. That seems to help.

God, please keep us safe. Please help Eva understand. Please let me be free.

She waits for some kind of clear answer but doesn't get one. The train just keeps moving as the changing world beyond her window turns wilder and more unknown.

Ivan the Terrible watches as Roman cleans Adri's old bedroom. It is cluttered with forgotten boxes and coated with dust, but Roman works fast and hums Sinatra. He still can't quite believe that Adri called him. He'd resigned himself to the idea that she was just a memory now, like most of the people he loved—until he saw her message saying she was on her way.

Thank you, Lord.

He moves another box and finds forgotten photographs. He pauses to flip through a few and sees himself and Dalila, back when they both had thick black hair and no wrinkles. One picture is at a fancy seafood restaurant, another at the beach, another in their backyard. Roman stares at it. Eighteen-year-old Adri smiles shyly for the camera, wearing a gold cap and gown.

Curious now, Roman finds more photos of Adri. Little Adri in grass-stained white dresses, teenage Adri wrestling, Adri smiling next to a handsome boy with a shy smile, both of them wearing worn red boxing gloves. He finds one of Adri at prom with the same young man, and Roman smiles. Her prom dress—long, black, and cut by Yvonne to show off her back and shoulders—had caused a small-town scandal.

Toward the back of the stack, he finds a photo of Adri with a different man. "The Hammer," people called him. Owen Anders. He's years older than Adri and handsome in a severe kind of way, with sharp angles and light hair. Roman scowls. He's only met him twice.

The next photo is Adri again—barely twenty—in a hospital, holding a tiny black-haired baby in her arms. Roman stares at that one for a long time. Next, Adri and Owen standing in a courthouse. Adri holds white lilies and smiles, but it looks tight and small.

That's the last picture she ever sent him.

"All that time and all that money, wasted," people always said when they found out she wasn't fighting anymore. *"She wasted everyone's time, Roman. Especially yours."*

Roman stayed silent whenever Spartans complained about Adri. He wasn't annoyed like they were. He was in mourning. The time he spent training Adri wasn't time he wanted back.

He finds another photo of Dalila in the back of the stack. She smiles from a hospital bed, cheerful despite the tubes and wires connected to her heart and wrists. Roman misses that smile more than all the other memories combined. He tosses the photos in a box, suddenly tired.

"Time for coffee. Come on, Ivan."

The old chihuahua follows Roman to the kitchen and watches him grind coffee beans. Roman looks down at the dog, who stares back at him with a woeful expression.

"Cheer up, buddy." He stoops to pat Ivan's head. "You'll survive a couple guests. It'll be good for you in your old age."

Ivan closes his eyes wearily.

Roman finishes the coffee and busies himself with more preparations. He grabs a lemon candy from the breadbox, pours the coffee into two thermoses, and checks the clock on the wall again, anxious to see his niece and meet her daughter. Maybe Eva looks like Adri, or maybe she favors her father. Roman smiles faintly. It's hard to imagine Adri as a mother, but he imagines she's a fiercely good one. Mostly, he's just ready to learn why, after so many years of asking, God is finally answering his most repeated prayer.

Adri is coming home.

Adri jolts awake. After hours of restlessness, she fell into a deep sleep, and she'd been dreaming about Owen's fingers—first caressing her, then closing around her throat, pressing her into darkness—when the train came to a sharp stop. Her heart thuds as she reorients herself, but then reality slowly sinks in. Owen is more than a thousand miles away, and that makes her feel safe and terrible at the same time.

The sun has barely risen outside. Eva and Rocky snooze in the booth across from hers, using their bags as makeshift pillows. Nervous, she glances at her phone and exhales. Nothing but a text from Roman asking how close they are. Owen must be drinking, and for once she's thankful for that.

She stands to stretch as the train rumbles into motion again but stops when she hears the rustle of a newspaper a few booths ahead. A stooped elderly man—the only other passenger—is reading the sports section of the *Pittsburgh Post-Gazette*. Sensing her gaze, he looks up. She turns away but feels his eyes linger.

"I know you, don't I?"

Surprised, Adri turns back to him. "Sorry?"

He squints. "You're Roman Rivera's girl."

Heat floods Adri's face.

"That's it. *La Tormenta*," he says. "I used to read about you, all your tournaments. You still fighting?" His cloudy eyes move over her, and Adri senses his skepticism. Her body is still lean and athletic, but age and motherhood have softened her.

She shakes her head. "Not anymore."

He frowns and returns to his paper. "Too bad."

Adri sits down again and faces the window, her pride stinging. Even though six years have passed since she left Sparta, the unexpected reminder of her failure still hurts. She tried, but she hasn't forgotten who she used to be—a local legend in mixed martial arts, a professional fighter in the making. She closes her eyes, trying to remember and forget at the same time.

Her uncle started training her when she was just eight years old, a few months after her mother dropped her off on his porch. She was always smaller than other girls her age, but Roman turned her into a fierce fighter, despite her petite frame. He's the one who said Adri moved like a storm, sealing her nickname—La Tormenta.

"I knew you were a fighter the moment I saw you," he told her, after she won her first tournament. *"When your mom left, you didn't say a single word to me or your aunt for three months, but I saw the fire in you. You're a Rivera. You were born to fight."*

For years, he and Adri had the same dream—that she would become a professional and fight in front of the whole world, not just Sparta. They worked tirelessly for that dream, and it was within Adri's reach. And then . . .

She met Owen.

The train starts to slow, making her glance up. Her heart skips as she realizes that they're close. The man with the folded newspaper gives her a quick wave before he ambles off, and Eva stirs a moment later, waking Rocky with her. Adri digs through her duffel bag and finds two granola bars. She gives one to Eva and splits the other with Rocky. He crunches his half noisily.

"Are we there, Mama?" Eva asks sleepily.

"Almost."

"I want to see a mountain lion."

Adri smiles. She points out the window at Mount Minsi in the distance. "There might be one up there." Mountain lions and memories—some she'd like to forget.

The train screeches to a stop in Sparta, and Adri steels herself. She's not ready to face her past yet, but she has no choice.

———

Adri and Eva approach Roman, Rocky trailing behind them. The station is empty, besides a yawning security guard huddled on a bench. Roman moves to embrace her, but she extends her hand. He shakes it before pulling her into a tight, long hug. She stiffens at first, but then she relaxes in his arms.

"Hi, Adri."

"Hi, Uncle Roman," she says quietly against his coat. She breathes in the familiar smell of Aladdin cologne and cinnamon gum, and tears almost rise to the surface.

When he finally releases her, he wipes his eyes quickly and studies her while she studies him. He's still trim and well-dressed—she'd never seen him leave the house in anything less than a pressed button-down and slacks—and he still sports a neatly trimmed mustache, but he looks startlingly old. She frowns as it sinks in just how long she's been gone.

She watches his gaze move to the finger-shaped bruises on her neck, and his brows crease. Adri's heart races, but, thankfully, he doesn't press her for information. Not yet. Instead, he turns his attention to Eva. She stares back at him from behind Rocky.

Adri nudges her. "Eva, say hello to your Great-Uncle Roman."

"Hello," she says shyly.

"Hello," Roman says back.

"I like your name. I know a lot about the Romans. They invented calendars and laws."

Roman raises an eyebrow. "You know about all that? You must be pretty smart."

Eva nods, her shyness fading.

"Do you like lemon drops?" He holds out the candy, and she takes it.

Adri gently pokes her. "What do you say?"

"Thank you, sir, but I like cherry candy more."

Adri fights back a smile. "No. You just say thank you."

Roman laughs. "Well, we just met. I'll get it right next time." He turns to Rocky. "And who's this lug?"

Rocky's tail wags, and Adri's heart sinks as she realizes she didn't mention him on the phone. "Oh, shoot. This is Rocky. Sorry, I meant to ask you."

Roman bends to pet Rocky, whose tail wags faster. "Hey, Rock-O," he says, rubbing the dog's ears. "I don't sweat you." He looks up at Adri again. "The more the merrier."

Roman leads them all to his car, with Eva gripping Adri's hand in the cold. As Adri carefully buckles her into the back seat, she realizes she'll have to buy a booster seat at some point. In her rush to escape, she only grabbed what she could carry.

"I've got coffee," Roman says, turning on the car. "Figured you might need some."

Adri clasps the thermos gratefully. "Thanks." A heavy crucifix hangs from his rearview mirror—the same one that's been there since she was eight. "You're still driving the Charger?"

"What else? His birthday is coming up. Twenty-one."

"Mine too."

"Twenty-five for you?"

She nods slowly. She hasn't celebrated her birthday in years.

Roman whistles. "That means I must be ancient."

She laughs. As he drives through Sparta, she sips his too-strong coffee and worries about Owen. Has he realized they left yet? What will he do? Will he figure out where she is? She took every step to hide their trail, but fear still claws at her. She can feel her uncle looking at her again, so she turns to the window, wondering what he must think about her sudden appearance. Luckily, Eva chatters happily in the back seat, temporarily distracting them both.

"Is this where you were a kid, Mama?"

"Yep," she says, watching familiar scenes pass by her window. She lets Roman answer most of Eva's questions about the small steel-and-oil town. They pass the famous German bakery and the aging redbrick high school, where banners emblazoned with Adri's name used to hang in every hallway. In the distance, the mountains pierce the cloud-covered sky. She never imagined she could feel like a stranger in a place where she had so many memories, but she did.

Roman turns a corner, and Adri squints at an unfamiliar sign in front of the old community center. The sign is new—all spiked metal and blue glass—and looks unlike anything else in Sparta. *Lyons Training Center* glows in bold red letters. She stares at it. She reads it again, more slowly this time.

"Max has a gym now," Roman says, noting her gaze.

Adri turns toward her uncle. "Max Lyons?"

Roman nods. "He bought the community center and renovated it a few years ago."

Her eyes widen.

"You didn't know that?"

"Why would I know that?" she snaps, her heart picking up its pace. Last she'd heard—secondhand from Owen, since she would shut off the television whenever Max's name was mentioned—was that he'd retired after a long winning streak and moved on to coaching at some of the high-profile training camps.

Her uncle raises his brows.

"Sorry," she says, regretting the outburst. "It's just . . ." She fumbles for an explanation. "Max and I . . . don't talk."

"Who's Max, Mama?"

"He's . . . someone who used to be my friend." Adri frowns. It's been six years, but it feels like sixty.

"You don't like him anymore?"

Her cheeks flush. "No, butterfly, I just . . . haven't seen him in a long time." She turns to Roman again. "I thought he was coaching?"

"He was. Big-time stuff. Fights in Vegas, New York, Atlanta, all those places. He quit when Danny died."

Adri's skin turns cold, and for a brief, hopeful moment, she wonders if she misheard him. "What?" Her last memory of Danny Lyons flashes before her eyes—he'd brought a basket of her favorite junk foods, all arranged beautifully in a basket, to her graduation party. "Danny died?"

Roman sighs heavily, realizing he blundered again. "Sorry, kiddo. I figured Max would've called you about that, at least, but I guess not."

Her chest tightens. "When?"

"Coming up on three years ago now. That's when Max bought the community center."

Adri falls silent, staggered by the news. She knows her uncle never lies, but Danny Lyons can't be dead. She can't think of anyone more alive.

"I know you loved him, Adri. Everyone did. He was a good man."

"I just . . . didn't know."

"Why would you? My mistake."

She winces. She knows her uncle doesn't mean anything by it, but his words sting. They remind her that she's the one who abandoned everyone—not the other way around.

"Anyway, I think Max is doing good. The gym is always busy."

She stares out the window, not wanting to talk about Max and his success, but her uncle doesn't seem to notice.

"They do a little bit of everything. Judo and self-defense for the kids, boxing and mixed stuff for amateur fighters. One of their girls won a tournament in New Jersey." Roman smiles. "I always said Max would make a good coach, didn't I?"

They pass a small salon with a bright pink door and suddenly Adri remembers Yvonne. "Why did Yvonne answer your phone?" She's been curious ever since her conversation with her aunt's old friend.

Roman's cheeks redden slightly, surprising her. "She's been helping me go through some of your aunt's things. I put it off for too long."

She nods, though she suspects there's more to it. "That's nice of her," she says, leaving it at that for now. "I'd like to see her sometime."

"You want a haircut?"

Adri smiles. She hasn't cut her hair, aside from the occasional trim, since she was a child. Her aunt Dalila, Sparta's most in-demand hairdresser, never let her. Adri frowns at the memory as regret fills her. Dalila died shortly after Adri moved to Miami—another funeral she didn't attend.

A few minutes later, Roman pulls into a winding cul-de-sac of small Craftsman-style houses. He parks in front of the one with the tidiest yard, and they file out of the car. A neighbor stops and stares as Adri grabs their bags out of the trunk.

Roman waves cheerfully. "I hope you're ready to be the talk of the town, kiddo," he says, chuckling. "Adriana Rivera back in Sparta. People aren't going to let that one go for a while."

Adri sighs. She definitely wasn't ready for that.

Inside the house, they're greeted by soft growls. Rocky tilts his head.

"Shut up, Ivan," Roman snaps.

She stares down at the little dog in disbelief. "He's still alive?"

Roman bends to pat the tiny growling menace on the head. "We just celebrated his sweet sixteen." He grins. "Ol' Ivan is immortal."

"Apparently." She bends to pet him, but Rocky quickly moves to block her.

"Uh-oh," Roman says, still smiling. "Looks like someone is jealous."

She rubs Rocky's ears as she looks around her uncle's house. The furnishings are still immaculately clean and overwhelmingly Cuban. A heavy floral-patterned couch sits beside a glass coffee table piled high with Spanish tabloids and a well-worn Bible. Framed paint-by-number landscapes and countless family pho-tos, all freshly dusted, gleam in the sunlight. The tinsel-covered Christmas tree stands in the corner, but her aunt's beloved plants—draping ivies, African violets, orchids—are missing.

The shelf that displayed them is gone now, and nothing takes its place.

"They all started dying," Roman says quietly, aware of Adri's discovery. He clears his throat. "And I don't have a green thumb like she did."

Adri frowns. She wants to comfort him, but she can't talk about her aunt yet. That would mean talking about her own absence too. "You've kept the place up though," she says, trying to change the subject.

Roman shakes his head. "Nah, that's all Yvonne. She checks on me." His eyes are dry again when he beckons Adri and Eva toward the hallway. "Come see your room."

They follow him to Adri's old room, the dogs trailing. The small bedroom is untouched by time, except for a new crocheted blanket and a few pictures pinned to the wall. Adri's numerous trophies and belts fill up a bookcase in the corner.

"That's your mom when she was little, Eva," Roman says, pointing at one of the photographs.

Eva is delighted by them, but Adri's heart sinks as she looks at her younger, unfamiliar self. Her eyes are bright in every picture.

"Hey, E, you want to take the dogs outside?" Roman asks. "You can throw a tennis ball for 'em."

Eva looks torn. "But Ivan's not nice."

Roman laughs as he picks up Ivan, who bares his tiny fangs. "He won't hurt you, I promise. If he does, Rocky can eat him." Roman walks her to the backyard while Adri watches through the window. Rocky immediately runs wild, racing to the fence, while Ivan stays in the shade. Eva sits down beside him and gives him a cautious pat on the head. When Roman returns, Adri knows what's coming next.

"Ready to talk?"

She closes her eyes, aware that there's no more stalling. Her uncle doesn't wait for her to answer.

"Does Owen know you're here?"

She lets her breath out slowly, aware that Roman already knows more than she wants him to. She shakes her head. "No. I left without telling him."

"Okay. . . . What happens when he realizes you're gone?"

She stares at the carpet.

"I'm not trying to scare you, Adri, but it's going to happen eventually. I'd just like to know what we're up against."

"He won't come here," she says quickly, knowing that Sparta is the last place Owen will expect her to go, since she was always so eager to escape it. She's about to say more, but her voice catches in her throat. Part of her is stunned that her uncle is willing to help her after she spent the last six years avoiding him, but mostly she's just grateful that someone in the world cares.

"He'll be angry. He . . ." Her voice trails off as she realizes she has no idea what Owen will do. Until now, she never managed to leave him for more than a few hours. She searches for words until Roman gives her hand a reassuring squeeze.

"Okay, kiddo. I got it from here. You're safe, Eva's safe. That's all that matters."

A tear falls before Adri can stop it. She wonders how many times he said something like that to his sister—her mother—before she finally took off. Probably too many to count.

"And when you want to talk about it, I'll be ready to listen." His eyes fall to her bruises again, and he sighs heavily. "You've been fighting all this time, haven't you? I saw it when you stepped off the train—that same look I saw when you were eight."

He waits for her to say something, but she doesn't. She can't.

"Let's do something good with that fire, Adri."

2

ENZO PEERS THROUGH THE GLASS and waves at Max. "Hey, man." He fights back a yawn and opens the door for him. "Why'd you bail last night?"

Max doesn't make up an excuse. He doesn't have a good one. Enzo wanted him to stick around and go after one of Trisha's friends—a petite brunette with a pretty smile who'd stared at him all night—but Max bought her one drink and left an hour later, too bored to pursue anything else. He looks at the empty ring in the middle of the gym and scowls. "Where's Trisha?"

"Late," Enzo says, flipping on the rest of the lights. He looks unbothered, as usual.

"Again?"

"She's only been late one other time."

Max gives him a withering look. Trisha is Enzo's latest hire, and she's as bad as the one before her. "She's supposed to train with us. That was part of the deal."

Enzo waves away his concerns. "She'll be in soon. Let's just warm up."

Max agrees, even though his annoyance lingers. Early morning light casts shadows over the equipment as the men stretch in the ring. It's quiet until Enzo flips on hip-hop music and turns up the volume until the windows rattle. His head bobs as he stretches, making his curly hair bounce. Max frowns. Enzo has never appreciated silence.

"That guy from Williamsburg called yesterday," Enzo says, reaching for his wraps. "He wanted to know if you changed your mind about coaching him."

"The hipster guy?"

"Yeah." Enzo smirks. "I told him your answer was the same."

Max grabs a jump rope and starts jumping. "It is." New fighters are always calling the gym, asking if he wants to be on their teams, painting pictures of all the fame and money and glory that could be his, but Max's answer is a mantra at this point.

"I'm done with that part of my life."

Enzo pauses mid-stretch. "I heard back from my buddy at Combat House too. He said he'd be down with us hosting a fight here, if we want to."

Max doesn't stop jumping. "Aren't we busy enough?"

"It's just one fight. All we have to do is help them find a few fighters and promote it. They'd do most of the work."

Max doesn't respond. Instead, he increases his speed until the rope is a blur beneath his feet and his heart rate increases. Finally, he drops the rope. "I'll think about it," he lies breathlessly. Enzo's been asking about hosting a fight for months, but Max isn't enthused about filling the gym with Spartans who just want to talk about the past. He sees Enzo steal a quick glance at the clock.

"I'm firing Trisha."

"*What?*" Enzo stares at him. "Why? Because she's late one time?"

"By 'one time,' do you mean every time?"

"She's not even that late."

Max groans. He knows why Enzo is covering for Trisha, and it has nothing to do with her punctuality. "Dude, two parents already complained to me about her. Apparently, the kids asked Trisha when they were going to practice with real people, and she told them never. I get that she's hot, but—"

"She just doesn't understand what you want, Max. She—"

"She doesn't understand that a basic self-defense class includes practicing what you learn on *actual* people? Maybe she'd know that if she ever showed up for training."

Enzo scowls. "You don't like anyone I hire."

"I don't like mediocre people."

"Well, I quit then."

Max stares at him in disbelief. "Over Trisha? Dude. She's not *that* hot."

"No, I mean I'm done searching for an instructor. We're down to zero applications, and now you want to fire Trisha. You're on your own."

Max raises an eyebrow. "Maybe I should fire you too."

"Try it." Enzo grins. "No one else would put up with you."

"Oh yeah?"

"Sorry, buddy. You're not exactly easy to work with."

Max's temper flares, but he keeps it under control. "If you hired anyone decent, maybe I wouldn't have to be so difficult."

"It's not just this teacher thing, dude. It's everything. If it wasn't Trisha, you'd find something else to be mad about." Enzo shrugs. "That's the way it goes with you. You're too demanding."

Max's eyes narrow.

"And Skye agrees with me," Enzo adds quickly, throwing her under the bus with him. "She thinks you're working too much, and she's right. Whether it's here or at your dad's house, you're always working, but you never stop and enjoy anything. Skye says—"

"What are you guys, my therapists?" Max snaps, annoyed to learn his employees are talking about him behind his back.

"Dude, since your dad died, you've been—"

"Enough, Enzo." Max's eyes flash dangerously, and Enzo falls silent. "This conversation is over. As is Trisha's employment," he adds. "Make sure she fills out the paperwork whenever she decides to show up." Max drops his gear and leaves, slamming the door behind him.

He walks quickly to his truck, but he slows his pace when a car pulls into the parking lot. He smirks. Trisha has arrived—and she's Enzo's problem now, not his. He watches as she stumbles out of the car.

"Oh, hey, Max," Trisha says, noticing him. Her glazed-over eyes are smudged with last night's makeup. "Sorry. My alarm didn't go off."

Max nods absently, but he doesn't respond as he climbs into his truck.

He drives to the mountains, deciding to train there instead, despite the cold. Thunder rumbles in the distance and a few clouds swirl overhead, but bad weather has never deterred him. He finds his usual spot near the abandoned railroad tracks and sits on his hood, letting a few cold rain droplets splash on his arms and face. The wide-open sky and fresh air used to make him feel free, and he wants to feel that way again, but he doesn't. Instead, he feels just alone.

Why? he wonders, exasperated with everyone, but mostly himself. The gym is growing fast—something nobody ever really expected in a small, declining town like Sparta. Not only that, but he has more money than he knows what to do with, thanks to his fights. To top it all off, he can have just about any woman he wants. But Enzo's words still irk him.

Max grits his teeth. What a joke, he tells himself. Enzo loves that sort of thing, though—looking for a problem where there isn't one. Skye too. They'd be perfect for each other if either of them ever figured that out.

He decides to run. He follows the railroad tracks for a long time, until his body is slick with sweat, then slows to a jog. He finds himself back here often, by this old track, looking down at Sparta, breathing in the cold, clean air. From here, he can see his gym and his father's house—now his house. He can also see the train station in the distance, and he remembers the day he packed up his gear and left for his fight in Dallas after a quick stop in Miami.

That unexpected trip marked the beginning of his professional career, and sometimes he can't decide whether or not he misses those days. He loved fighting, but the rest of it—the constant pain, the parties, the pointlessness—wore on him until he barely felt like himself anymore.

He exhales. His father's death is what jolted him back to life. Max was living on the fumes of his success, but returning to Sparta and staring at the bloated corpse of his father—a perfectly healthy man until his heart stopped beating one morning after a workout—reminded him that life eventually comes to an end. That's when he decided he should probably do something better with his.

What now, Dad? Max opened the gym two years ago because that's what his dad always wanted to do—open a family-friendly place and teach kids to fight, whether for protection or discipline or just the pure, primal satisfaction of winning. *What's missing?*

He waits for an answer, but there's only silence, and he feels his anger rising as he stares up at the sky. He doesn't pray anymore. He decided a long time ago that if there was a God, he wasn't worth talking to. He called God every terrible name he could think of and dared him to say something back.

"What kind of God doesn't fight back?" he'd demanded six years ago, standing in the pouring rain, secretly hoping he was wrong. Deep down, he wanted there to be a God who stood up for the good guys and punished the bad ones.

His anger eventually gives way to tired resignation as he glances up one more time at the endless gray-blue sky. Silence then, and silence now.

The phone drops against Adri's bed with a soft thud. Her fingers are shaking, and Owen's voicemail is still ringing in her ears.

"I'm being patient, Adri. I'm waiting for you to come to your senses. Six days, and I haven't seen my daughter. Six days, and not a single word from you. I never . . ." There was a short, muffled sound before something shattered. "I *never* actually thought you'd do something like this. I love you, and you do this? Is this what you do to someone you love? You just leave?" Another crash. "If you don't come home, I promise I will find you, and . . ." He hung up with a sharp click before he finished that sentence.

Adri exhales. It was what she expected, but that doesn't make her any less terrified.

Yvonne appears in the doorway. Her face is perfectly made up with dramatic eyeliner and red lipstick, but her thin brows are creased with worry.

"Bad news?" she asks.

Adri nods slowly, gathering her racing thoughts. "Owen called." Her stomach twists with fear. "He's . . . upset."

Without hesitation, Yvonne glides past her and picks the phone up off the bed and leaves. Surprised, Adri follows after her.

"Roman," Yvonne yells, her heels clicking on the kitchen tile as she opens the cabinet that conceals the trash can. "Adri's going to need a new phone. She—" She halts midsentence when she realizes that Eva is in the living room. She and Roman were in the middle of a heated game of Battleship, but now they're both watching her curiously.

"Why?" Roman asks, frowning.

"A telemarketer," Yvonne says smoothly, dropping the phone in the trash. Shocked, Adri starts to protest, but Yvonne gives her a look she recognizes from her childhood. Resistance is futile. "He's harassing her," Yvonne adds pointedly, to Roman. "So she'll need a new number."

"Ah, okay," he says, suddenly understanding. "We'll get that sorted out." He gives Adri a reassuring look before turning his attention back to his battered ships. "Your move, E."

"I can keep my phone, though," Adri says hopefully, taking a few steps toward her. "We can just go get the number cha—"

"No," Yvonne says, firmly shutting the cabinet again before Adri can get to it. "Consider it a symbolic gesture. You're done with that telemarketer."

Panic pricks Adri. Without Owen, she barely has any money to her name. "I can't afford a new phone."

"I can."

"No, Yvonne." Adri would rather die than let her do that. Yvonne is nearing sixty years old, and she still works hard six days a week. Her salon does well enough, but she has her own children and grandchildren to worry about.

"Come with me for a second, honey." Yvonne glances uneasily at Eva again and beckons Adri toward the sunroom—a screened-in porch still stacked high with her aunt's half-finished mosaic tiles and painted garden stones. Adri reluctantly follows, her frustration growing.

Once Adri is inside, Yvonne shuts the door behind them. "Please don't be mad at me about the phone, Adri." She sits down in Dalila's favorite rocking chair and motions for Adri to sit as well.

"I'm not mad, I just—"

"You can pick out whatever brand you like."

"You don't need to do that," Adri says, softening her tone and taking a seat. Her annoyance lingers, but Yvonne's eyes are full of motherly concern. "I'll just change my nu—"

"But will you delete all the pictures too?" Yvonne interjects. "Of you two together? Of him and Eva?"

Adri is caught off guard by the question. "I . . ."

"And the texts? Even the nice ones?"

"Um . . ." Adri fumbles for an answer as memories resurface, like the random song lyrics Owen texted her whenever he was trying to make up, or pictures of pint-sized Eva burying him under a mountain of pillows and stuffed animals.

"What about his friends? Will you block their numbers too? Because you know eventually they'll be calling."

Adri forces herself to nod, but Yvonne shakes her head, clearly not buying it.

"I've done this a few times now, honey, and there's only one way to do it." She glances down at her bare, manicured ring finger and smiles sadly, and Adri knows why. Dalila helped Yvonne through two fast marriages and two subsequent divorces, all when Adri was still in high school. After the second, Yvonne got much more serious about her faith. "If you're really serious about staying away from him, then leave your phone with the banana peels."

Adri scowls. She wants to deny it, but she knows Yvonne is probably right. Even just the familiar sound of Owen's voice, as harsh as it was, made her momentarily question her decision.

"Do you still love him?"

Adri bites her lip. She has been dreading that question, but she knows that if anyone could understand the answer, it would be Yvonne. "Most of the time, I hate him. Other times . . . I miss him." Saying it out loud makes her feel so stupid and weak, but Yvonne's eyes are full of sympathy. "What's wrong with me?"

"The more distance you keep, the sooner those feelings will fade. You pick—a little pain now, or a lot of pain later."

Adri nods, willing the words to sink in and dissolve some of her doubts.

"Stay the course, honey," Yvonne continues. "You started a chain reaction when you left Owen, and now you just have to see it through." She doesn't say the rest, but she doesn't have to. Adri hears the words in her head.

"I've been through this before."

"Maybe you should get out of this house for a little while. You've been cooped up in here with us old folks for the last week." Yvonne thinks for a moment, drumming her tangerine-painted nails against the wicker coffee table. "What about that terrible fighting event they do on Friday nights at Teddy Bowser's club? You used to love that."

Adri is surprised by the suggestion. "He still hosts Fight Night?"

Yvonne nods uneasily. Adri and Roman used to be regulars a decade ago, but Yvonne and her Aunt Dalila preferred to watch *Rebelde Way* or play dominoes until midnight. They didn't appreciate mixed martial arts as much as she and Roman did.

"That could be a good little distraction for you."

Adri considers it for a moment, but then she shakes her head. She'd love to watch a few fights, but she'll almost certainly run into people she used to know, and she's not ready to answer their inevitable questions. "I can't go. Too many familiar faces."

"You can do whatever you like, Adri," Yvonne says firmly. "People are going to talk regardless, so you might as well enjoy yourself while they gossip." She smiles reassuringly. "I'll watch Eva for you and make sure Roman puts her to bed at a decent hour."

Adri is tempted. It would be nice to do something other than worry about Owen's next move. "Maybe . . ."

"I could do something with your hair, too, if you want," Yvonne says, apparently trying to sweeten the deal. "No reason you shouldn't look fabulous while you watch those poor people get their teeth knocked out."

Adri laughs at the pained look on Yvonne's face. "It's more fun than you think."

"That's what Roman always tells me. Maybe you can help me understand the appeal."

Adri's smile fades. Yvonne's tone is lighthearted, but her words remind Adri of how different things are now. Does she still love fighting as much as she used to? Six years ago, she never imagined that she'd be able to give it up for anything, but that's exactly what she did.

"Just take one night to yourself, Adri." Yvonne says, breaking through her dark thoughts. "Lord knows you need one."

Shade is already crowded when Max walks through the door later that evening. Madison, a woman he's been seeing for the last few weeks, hangs on his arm. She isn't the most interesting person he's ever met, but she is undeniably nice to look at. Most Sparta girls wore jeans and boots to Fight Night, but tonight she's dressed in a short dress and towering heels.

Max scans the growing crowd. Townies swarm the bar and clog the dance floor, and hypnotic music pulses through the speakers. Enzo and Skye arrive a few minutes later, and the four of them find a few empty seats near the cage.

Max is familiar with the appeal of Fight Night, having fought more than a handful of fights here when he was a kid. Every third Friday, Teddy, the owner, set up a cheap octagon in the middle of the dance floor, and people paid ten dollars each to watch Sparta's amateurs duke it out. Women dance around the cage while men cheer, and the night ends with blood and beer getting mopped off the dance floor.

"No way?" Madison shrieks beside him, laughing about something. "No way!"

Max grits his teeth as Madison and Skye giggle endlessly at Enzo's jokes. He already feels a headache coming on as blue lights flash in his face. When Madison reaches for his arm, he takes a step toward the bar. "I'll get us some drinks," he says, leaving her with the others.

He weaves through the crowd and recognizes many faces. A few people stare or whisper, but he barely notices anymore. When he finally reaches the bar, he intends to stay there until the first fight starts.

"Hey, Lyons. What can I get you?"

He nods at Blaine, the tall, tattooed bartender.

"Just a beer." Max glances back at Madison through the crowd. "Actually, make it two. And a shot. And a vodka cranberry."

When Blaine passes him his drinks, Max takes the shot and drinks the beers, thinking a buzz will make the night a little more bearable. He buys a third.

"And then she just left, and no one ever heard from her ag—"

Max hears whispering to his left. When he feels a pair of eyes on his back, he turns. A woman blushes. She jabs her friend in the shoulder, who also turns.

"Oh," she says, surprised. "Hey, Max."

He frowns. She's an acquaintance from high school, but he can't remember her name.

"See you later," she says, grabbing her friend.

Max watches as they disappear, perplexed, but then he spots Teddy making his way toward the cage, microphone in hand, which means the first fight is about to begin.

"Spartans!" Teddy roars into the mic as Max walks back to the table. He hands Madison her drink, and she leans in, pressing her body against his.

"What took you so long?" she whines.

"I ran into some people."

Terry introduces the fighters, two boys who look no older than sixteen. Max recognizes one from the gym, one of Enzo's students, but he gets distracted when Madison moves closer.

Her lips brush his ear. "Want to get out of here?"

"Let's hear it for our first fighters!" Teddy yells, competing for his attention.

Max stares at her as a chorus of cheers and whistles break out around them. "You want to leave *now*?"

She giggles at the look on his face. "What? I'm impatient to-night." She presses closer, and Max breathes in the scent of her perfume, torn. He wants to watch the fight, but he wants other things too. In the cage, the fighters tap gloves.

"Let's watch the first round at least."

Surprised, Madison sulks, but Max pretends not to notice. He watches the fighters grapple on the dance floor as neon squares light up around them. Later, when Enzo and Skye leave for the bar, Madison gives him a hopeful look.

"Ready to go yet?"

He shakes his head, but she leans closer and whispers something in his ear. He raises an eyebrow. "Wow. You really are impatient, aren't you?"

Giggling, she takes his hand and leads him toward the bathroom.

"Do you do this often?" he asks jokingly, as they wait in line.

She flashes him a coy smile. "Only for guys I really like."

Max's own smile fades.

"Wait a minute so it's not totally obvious," Madison says, slipping through the door first.

Max's uneasiness grows. Behind him, a line starts to form, filling the narrow hallway. Someone gasps.

"Was that her?" a female voice asks.

He turns, curious.

"Was it? I didn't see her face," someone replies.

Max looks around. For a split second, he sees the back of a woman walking in the opposite direction. He squints. A whip of black hair disappears as she turns the corner.

"I swear that was Adri Rivera," a woman says to the others in line.

Max freezes for a moment, stunned by the mention of that name.

"I haven't seen her since graduation!" someone exclaims.

Max's body moves faster than his mind as he walks past them. His feet feel heavy as he follows the woman, his clouded thoughts racing. He can barely see her in the crowd, but what he can see makes his heart pound—she's small, and her stride is quick.

It's not Adri, he tells himself, but his heart thuds anyway.

When she reaches the exit, he's only a few feet behind her, and he glimpses her profile. Softly curled black hair falls around her heart-shaped face, tucked under a red ballcap. Suddenly, she turns, and her eyes meet his. Shock hits him like a punch to the gut.

Instinctively, Max reaches out to catch her arm, but she makes it through the door just as a group of drunk college kids block his path. Max pushes through them, but by the time he steps outside, she's already gone. He stares at the sea of cars coming and going, surprised by the speed of his heart. For a second, he wonders if he imagined her.

"Max?"

He turns. Madison had followed him out.

"So you're ready to go now?" she asks, her annoyance obvious.

He ignores her and hurries to his truck, too stunned to think of a good excuse. Heart still pounding, he leaves her there and peels out of the parking lot, heading toward Roman's house as questions overwhelm him. Adri is in Sparta? Why now, after six years of silence?

His mind races with possibilities, and none of them are good.

His mind drifts to the few, fragmented pieces of her life that he can still remember after she moved to Miami—a few failed fights, a marriage to some big-shot fighter who fizzled out. That's all he let himself know before he forced himself to stop paying attention.

When the icy wind starts whistling outside his window, Max realizes he's speeding, so he forces himself to slow down and think things through. Even if Adri is staying with Roman, what exactly is Max going to say to her? Years ago, there was so much he wanted to say, but she didn't give him the chance. Now, no words come to mind—just a heavy wave of feelings he thought he'd lost along the way.

He turns sharply in a different direction. He can't show up at Roman's unannounced. He hasn't talked to Roman since his father's funeral, and besides that, does he even *want* to know why Adri's back? He remembers their last conversation in Miami, and the wound reopens.

No, he reminds himself firmly. He *doesn't* want to know, or he shouldn't want to know, at least. He learned that lesson a long time ago, the hard way.

When it comes to Adri Rivera, he's better off not knowing.

Adri grips the steering wheel as she drives the Charger though Sparta's empty streets. She wasn't at all prepared for the flood of feelings that hit her when she saw Max inside Shade.

When she left Sparta for Miami, they were barely eighteen. Max was tall and athletic, with his dark hair cut short by her aunt. Boys envied him and girls adored him, but he still had a slight shyness about him, except when he was fighting. Tonight, though, there was no trace of that shyness when he looked at her. He was a man now—more powerfully built than Adri had ever seen him, with wild hair curling near his dark eyes.

She inhales as she parks in Roman's driveway, cursing herself for going to Shade. She never should've let Yvonne talk her into it. She closes her eyes and tries to relax, but she sees Max's face again and groans. She's certainly *distracted* now, though not in the way she'd wanted. She enters the house quietly but finds Roman and Eva still awake, watching cartoons and sharing a bowl of popcorn. Rocky gives her a lazy greeting while Ivan snores beside him, both sprawled out on a nearby cushion.

"Mama!" Eva grins, while Roman looks guilty. "Uncle Roman is letting me stay up late."

"I see that," Adri says tiredly, kissing her forehead. "I'm here to ruin the fun." She sends Eva to the bathroom to get ready for bed and sinks into a chair.

Roman turns off the television. "You're home early."

"Was Eva good?"

Roman frowns at Adri's deflection. "She was an angel, just like you."

"I don't remember you ever calling me an angel."

"Not to your face."

Adri smiles weakly, but Roman frowns.

"Everything okay, kiddo? You look a little tense." His face scrunches with sudden concern. "Did something happen with Owen?"

"No, nothing like that." Adri sighs. She doesn't want to talk about her encounter with Max, but she forgot how well her uncle can read her. She toys with the key ring in her hand. "I just . . . bumped into Max."

"Ah." Roman's face searches hers, but she tries to keep her emotions in check. "Well, that was bound to happen eventually, I suppose. He likes Fight Night, and Sparta's not big enough to hide from anyone."

She nods slowly, feigning indifference. "Yeah, you're right. I just . . . didn't expect to see him so soon." She also hadn't expected to feel that jolt of electricity when he looked at her.

"Did you talk to him?"

"No. I was leaving."

Roman waits for her to tell him more, but her eyes settle on the blank television.

"Did you two have some kind of falling-out? I never got the full story from him. Or you."

"It doesn't really matter now, does it?" She feels cornered.

"Maybe not," Roman says, with the tiniest hint of amusement. "But going off the look on your face, it seems like it might."

She scowls. "It doesn't."

"Have you thought about patching things up?"

"No," she says flatly, though her answer isn't at all true. She's imagined that conversation for years—the one where she and Max could talk the way they used to, and somehow she could make him understand why she did what she did. "Talking to him won't change anything, Uncle Roman."

Roman scoffs. "You two used to be best friends."

"I used to be a lot of things that I'm not anymore."

Roman's brows furrow thoughtfully. He rises and heads for the kitchen, motioning for her to follow him. She briefly looks in on Eva, then joins him at the kitchen island. A rich, sweet smell fills the room—one that she instantly recognizes. He pushes the drink toward her, and Adri takes a sip of her Aunt Dalila's famous cinnamon tea. Her regrets linger, but the taste of something so familiar comforts her.

"I don't make it as good as she did."

Adri takes another grateful sip. "You make it just fine." For a moment, they're both quiet—lost in different memories, mourning different things—until Roman breaks the silence.

"Did you pay attention to what the pastor said last Sunday, Adri?"

She tries to recall the sermon she heard when Roman and Yvonne took her and Eva to the Presbyterian church on Sailor Street. Part of her was still in shock over the fact that her uncle was an actual God-fearing Protestant now, after years of dutifully but begrudgingly attending St. Anthony's with her devout aunt. At the new church, a silver-haired man talked about forgiveness and reconciliation. Suddenly, Adri realizes what her uncle is getting at.

"The sermon was about God," she says flatly. "Not people."

Not Max, she adds silently. The pastor said reconciliation involves an exchange in a relationship—exchanging brokenness and war for harmony and peace.

"Sure, but reconciliation with God can lead to reconciliation with people too," Roman suggests. "God doesn't want you to love him and just forget about your neighbor."

Adri thinks, then scowls, having no good retort.

"Listen, I'll say one more thing, and then I'll leave you alone about it," Roman says, pouring her more tea. "I have hardly any memories of you that don't include Max Lyons too." He smiles to himself. "You two were always competing, or helping each other, or laughing about something. Not everyone is fortunate enough to have a friend like that."

Adri is silent, but Roman's words hit their mark.

"I understand that it's a lot to think about, though, and you already have plenty on your mind." He gives her shoulder a light squeeze. "Sleep on it, kiddo."

She nods, and Ivan follows her uncle to his bedroom, leaving her alone in the dark kitchen with her thoughts.

"Reconciliation with God can lead to reconciliation with people too."

Adri sighs as she carries her mug to the empty sink, remembering the look in Max's eyes when he saw her. She has no idea what reconciliation could even look like.

It's been six years, but he looked at her like she left Sparta yesterday.

3

YVONNE TOYS WITH THE BLUE GINGHAM TABLECLOTH. "Anything new with Owen?" she asks, keeping her voice just above a whisper. "Adri hasn't called me in a few days."

Roman looks around warily, aware of curious ears in Bluebird's Café. It's always busy, but especially on Sundays. He and Yvonne are drinking coffee and sharing a slice of lemon meringue pie, their usual after-church routine, while Eva plays a short distance away, feeding quarters into an old claw machine.

He lowers his voice so she can't overhear them. "Nothing new other than he just won't leave Adri alone," he says, scowling darkly. "Had to get a lawyer involved the other day. And—"

He falls silent as Nina, his favorite waitress, appears with a carafe. She's worked at Bluebird's for at least twenty years.

"Adri was in here yesterday," she says with a big smile, pouring hot coffee in his cup. Her fake lashes are so long they touch her brows. "She and that little cutie ordered pancakes." She nods at Eva, then looks at Roman again. "I still can't believe she's back. Feels like a dream or something."

Roman nods. Sometimes he can't believe it either. Some mornings, when he wakes up to Eva's laughter in the kitchen or Adri's voice as she leashes Rocky for a walk, it really does feel like he's dreaming. They've been in Sparta for almost a month now.

"Is she still looking for work?" Nina asks.

"Yep." Roman frowns. "She's still at it." Adri's been looking since she arrived, but decent-paying jobs are sparse in Sparta. That, and she doesn't have a college degree.

Nina clucks her tongue sadly. "I'll let you know if anything opens up around here. We got high school students quitting all the time."

"Thanks, hon."

She leaves for the next table, and Yvonne leans in again. Her pretty face is tense. "Is Adri still staying strong? Not giving in?"

Roman smiles, happy to report at least one bit of good news. "She's doing pretty darn good, considering the circumstances." So far, her resolve impressed him. She ignored Owen's attempts to communicate on social media and focused her attention on Eva instead. Roman overheard one of their recent conversations.

"Is Daddy too mean to you, Mama?"

The way Eva said it—like it was a secret she'd been keeping—made Roman's heart feel tight and small, so he could only imagine how it made Adri feel.

Adri had cleared her throat carefully. "Butterfly . . . remember when we talked about bullies?"

Roman couldn't see from his seat on the porch, but Eva must've nodded.

"Well . . ." Adri had let the word linger. "Daddy's a bully to me. That's why you and I are going to live here for a while, and he's going to live in Miami."

That's when Roman finally glanced through the window and saw tears clustered on Eva's lashes.

"Then I don't love him anymore," she sobbed.

Adri pulled Eva close, and the little girl buried her face against her neck. "It's okay to love him, Eva. I don't want to take that away from you." Adri's voice broke, but she quickly steadied it. "I just want you to understand why we can't live with him anymore."

Yvonne's heavy sigh brings Roman back to the present moment. He watches as she spoons more sugar into her coffee.

"I just really want things to work out for her this time," she says, her bracelet clinking gently against her cup as she stirs. The late-morning sunlight picks up the silver strands in her hair. "I've been praying hard for that."

"Me too." Roman smiles gratefully. Yvonne has always been a remarkably good friend. He met her when he took a coaching job at the local high school where she taught Spanish. She was also the first person to welcome him and Dalila after they moved from Key West in the eighties. Over the years, she proved to be a faithful business partner to Dalila when they decided to open their own salon together in downtown Sparta.

Most notably, she was a woman of ceaseless prayer. It annoyed him at first, but he was thankful that she kept pestering him about church. He quit attending Mass after Dalila died, but Yvonne kept her promise to his wife and dragged him to her church instead, and somewhere along the way, it clicked. Yvonne saved his life and didn't even realize it.

The café door opens sharply and a bell jingles as someone steps inside. The familiar face pulls him out of his thoughts.

"Well, look who it is," Yvonne says, also spotting Max Lyons. He's dressed in his usual uniform of gym clothes and a Lyons Training Center sweatshirt.

Yvonne's eyes settle on his untamed hair. "He's overdue for a trim."

As Max waits for his coffee, he notices a little girl standing nearby. Her face is cute and sullen as she stares through the cloudy glass of Bluebird's ancient claw machine. He frowns. She looks oddly familiar. One of Skye's students, maybe?

"Hi," he says when another minute passes and no adult materializes.

She looks up at him with startlingly blue eyes. "Sorry, I can't talk to strangers," she says, even though her tone is friendly.

Max smiles. "That's good. You shouldn't talk to strangers." He surveys the café. "Where are your parents?"

"They're not here."

His eyes widen. "You're by yourself?"

"No." She grins, pleased by his concern. "I'm with my Great-Uncle Roman and Miss Yvonne." She points to a corner booth, and Max looks up. His stomach sinks as Roman Rivera smiles back at him.

"Ah," Max says, his mood darkening. He glances at the girl again and realizes why she looks so familiar. The dark hair, the little heart-shaped face, the confidence. Her eyes are blue, not brown, but they're unmistakable. She's Adri's daughter.

Roman approaches them. "Max," he says, smiling and gripping his hand like he used to when Max was still a teenager. "I see you met Eva, Adri's little girl."

"Yeah." Max forces a smile. "I just figured that out."

"Eva, this is Mr. Max Lyons."

He forces a smile when Eva stares up at him with newfound curiosity, but then he turns to Roman again. "Good to see you. It's been a while, hasn't it?" His hair is whiter than Max remembers, and he knows Dalila's death had something to do with that. Besides that, he looks pretty sharp for a man getting close to seventy.

"How's your gym?" Roman asks.

"Always busy. Can't complain, though." A waitress finally appears with his to-go coffee, and Max grabs it, eager to escape before Roman brings up Adri. "Well, I'm off—"

"Adri said she saw you a couple weeks ago."

Max halts, his back stiffening.

"At Fight Night," Roman adds.

Max curses silently, aware that he lost his chance at a quick exit. "Yeah, I saw her. Briefly."

"She and Eva are living with me now."

Max nods slowly, although his mind races with unanswered questions. He'd already heard that from Sparta's gossip mill—that Adri showed up with nothing but her daughter and her dog. He heard a lot of other things, too, but so far he's made good on his promise not to seek out more information.

"She's training a lot and looking for some work. . . ." Roman's voice trails off awkwardly, but when Max doesn't fill the silence, Roman takes the hint. "Anyway, always nice to see you. I hear good things about your gym all the time. Wish I was still young enough to enjoy it."

"You should come by sometime," Max says, relieved by the change of subject as he moves toward the door again. "I'll give you a tour."

"Great. I'll bring Adri too."

Max halts a second time. Roman's tone held a hint of challenge, so Max turns and looks at him with narrowed eyes.

"Unless you prefer I don't?" Roman asks innocently.

"I don't know, Roman," Max says coolly, wondering what the old man is playing at. "Maybe you should ask Adri what she prefers. She didn't seem too happy to see me at Shade." He hadn't been able to forget the stunned look on her face.

"Oh really?" Roman feigns ignorance. "You two should talk, then. Catch up, you know?"

"Pardon?"

"I said you should talk to Adri. You've probably got lots to catch up on."

Max stares at him in disbelief. Surely Adri hadn't put him up to this? "Does she want to talk to me?"

"Do you want to talk to her?" Roman asks, expertly sidestepping the question.

Max glances down at Eva, unsurprised to see that her curious eyes are fixed on him, waiting for his answer. "Roman . . ." Max carefully weighs his words and chooses the gentlest ones he can. "Adri and I haven't talked in a long time. I don't know why we need to start now."

Roman's face falls, but he lifts his hands in surrender. "Fair enough. You're busy, she's busy. She's been training like crazy, and—"

"You keep saying that," Max snaps, unable to ignore his curiosity. "What's she training for? I thought she quit fighting years ago."

Roman shrugs. "You'd have to ask her about all that. All I know is that she's out by the train tracks every other day, conditioning and such. She's out there now, in fact. She likes to go after church."

Max frowns. Roman's tone is casual, but his words sound like bait. "Where's her husband?" he asks, against his better judgment. It's the last thing he wants to talk about, but it's also the obvious elephant in the room. He watches as Roman's face turns tense.

"He . . ."

"Hey, Uncle Roman?" Eva says, interrupting them.

"What, honey?"

She points to the claw machine. "I can't win the lion."

He chuckles. "Sorry, sweetheart. You win some, you lose some." Roman glances at the machine, then winks at Max. "And with that thing, you lose more than you win."

Pouting, she turns to Max, and his scowl softens. He desperately wants to get out of Bluebird's, but Eva's face tugs at his heart.

Sighing, he looks through the glass. "That lion?" He points.

She nods eagerly. "The one with the blue bowtie."

"Okay." Max borrows a quarter from Roman. When the claw springs to life, he moves it above the toy as Eva watches with wide, happy eyes. The claw drops and clasps the lion's head, successfully lifting it from the pit. She fishes it from the dispenser and hugs it to her chest.

"What do you say, Eva?"

"Thank you, Mr. Max."

Max smiles weakly. "Sure."

"You've always been good at that thing. Used to blow through all your quarters winning stuff for Adri," Roman reminisces, but he frowns when Max doesn't respond. "Anyway, have a good rest of your Sunday, kiddo. He releases him with a fatherly pat on the shoulder. "Don't be a stranger anymore."

Unsettled, Max watches as he guides Eva to a booth where

Yvonne Turner waits for them. She starts to wave, but Max slips out of the café without responding.

Adri runs along the tracks, careful not to slip on the occasional patch of ice. Rocky follows closely behind, his tongue flopping happily. He loves Adri's trips to the railroad, where he can run freely and chase the occasional fox. Adri loves them too. Near the mountains, miles above Sparta, she breathes more easily, and her thoughts slow down as she listens to her own heartbeat. She feels less alone, with a presence quiet but powerful the longer she runs.

The woods are a far better alternative to the gym in the armory where people whisper in the locker rooms.

"I hear she's living with Roman again."

"Isn't she a little old for that?"

"Well, she's got a daughter now. Where's her husband at, any-way?"

"I heard she and the Lyons boy aren't friendly anymore. They used to be inseparable."

Secretly, she longs to spar with someone, just to see what she's still capable of, but she settles for long runs and shadowboxing, and embraces the solitude.

Sunlight streams through the trees as she winds between them, thankful for the short break from her worries, which are mostly about Owen. Roman set her up with Yvonne's attorney friend in New Jersey, who drafted some divorce papers, but Adri hasn't signed them yet. Mainly because she needs a job first, just in case Owen decides to go after custody of Eva, but there are other reasons too—like the fact that her stomach plummets every time she thinks about signing them, and her resolve wavers. But she doesn't say those reasons out loud.

She slows down and stops to stretch her legs in a patch of grass while Rocky circles her, tail still wagging. Her thoughts are stuck on Owen until she hears a twig snap somewhere close. Rocky's ears perk up, and she turns sharply.

"Are you going to run away again?"

Adri's heart skips. She recognizes the voice and meets Max's eyes. He's leaning against a nearby tree.

Rocky barks loudly, making her jump as heat fills her face. "Did you follow me out here?"

"No," Max says coolly.

Rocky growls.

"Then how did you know I was here?"

"Your uncle told me. He said you wanted to talk."

"He *what*?"

Max smirks. "That's what I thought." For a moment, it almost looks like he's a little disappointed, but he quickly makes his expression smooth again. "Talking wasn't your idea, was it?"

"Talking? With you?" Adri fumbles for words, filled with conflicting feelings—annoyance with Roman, shock at the sight of Max, and a tiny flicker of hope. Did *he* want to talk to her? The fact that he drove all the way out here makes her think there's a chance. "I—"

"Your dog is mad at me."

She looks down and realizes Rocky is still growling. "Hush, Rocky," she says, placing her hand on his head. When he begrudgingly quiets down, Max takes a step closer and lets his eyes move over her. When he looks up again, more color pours into her cheeks.

"So . . . should we talk?" he asks.

Her heart races. What on Earth should she say to him? She remembers a few of her practiced explanations and excuses, but they all fall flat now that he's actually standing in front of her.

"Adri?" He frowns as he waits for her answer. "Do you want me to leave?"

"No," she says quickly, overwhelmed by his closeness but unwilling to let her nerves get the best of her again. She knows she needs to face him. "We can talk."

He raises an eyebrow. "I'm honestly kind of surprised. You seemed in quite the hurry to get away at Shade." He takes another cautious step forward. "But I guess that's nothing new, is it?"

His words sting—like they're supposed to. "I'm sorry," she says quietly.

"How nice."

She ignores his sarcasm. "I mean it. I'm sorry about Shade, and I'm sorry about Miami. I shouldn't ha—"

"You want to talk about *Miami*? Six years later?"

"You deserve an expla—"

He makes a scoffing sound. "I don't need an explanation *now*, Adri."

Her heart sinks. That last time they talked on Mount Minsi, his voice was gentle. Not anymore. "You came all the way to Miami, and I—"

"We were young and stupid back then," he interjects. "What else is there to talk about?"

Stunned, she falls silent. For a moment, regret flickers across his face, but it hardens again.

"What are you doing here?" His dark eyes search hers, even as she looks away. "You're gone for years and now you're back, just like that? Where's your husband?"

She stiffens. No doubt gossip had made its way to his gym's locker rooms too. "I came back because . . ." The truth gets stuck in her throat. *God, I can't tell him. Not him.* "I want Eva to grow up around Roman," she says, a quick lie. "And Owen . . . travels. He promotes fights, and he travels a lot."

Max studies her with a skeptical expression. "Are you in some kind of trouble?"

"No," she says, too quickly. She's never been a good liar, but it doesn't matter. Max is the last person she wants to talk to about Owen.

"Roman said you're looking for work."

Adri curses silently. She's annoyed with Roman all over again, but her heart races with unexpected hope. She knows Max has been looking for an instructor—a job she's well-qualified for, unlike most of her other options. "I am."

"Any prospects?"

She shakes her head. "Not yet."

He's quiet for a moment, then rubs the back of his neck. "Well . . . I'm looking for a self-defense teacher."

"I heard."

He frowns at her noncommittal tone. "Are you interested in the job? I figured that was what Roman was getting at when he sent me out here."

The question stuns her. "I . . ." She hesitates as reality sinks in. That job could solve a lot of her current problems—but it could create problems too. "I don't know if we should work together."

"Why not?"

"Because we're not friends anymore."

"Oh, that's the reason?" He smirks. "I thought it was because you quit fighting."

Her eyes flash. He'd poked at her pride. "I still know how to fight," she says defiantly.

"Do you?"

Her eyes widen as he takes another step closer. When he leans down, Adri thinks he might kiss her, and her mind races back to a day years earlier—a day she's never forgotten and never will. It was snowing, but the sun shone brightly through the trees, making everything glow when he kissed her for the first time in the back of his dad's old Tacoma.

She'd been teasing him about something as they watched the snow fall, and midsentence he'd turned and pressed his lips to hers. At age seventeen, after so many years of friendship, that kiss was something she'd dreamed about but never thought he'd actually do. He kissed her gently at first, then more impatiently as her gloved hands slid under his coat and ended up somewhere near his thudding heart. It felt like magic—his lips, his tongue, his smell, his hands on her hands as he tugged her gloves off, his heaviness, the lightness she felt as he kissed her until she pulled away, breathless.

Now, she's stunned and still as she looks up at him, her body electrified by the memory when Max leans even closer. His eyes probe hers, searching for the answers to his questions, but she does her best to keep them hidden.

Somewhere near her legs, Rocky starts barking again, and Max steps back. Rocky continues barking, each booming bark grating on her raw nerves.

"Shut up, Rocky!" she snaps. His ears droop.

Max smirks. "Maybe *that's* why we shouldn't work together."

"I said I wanted to *talk* to you, not—"

He reaches for her, but she slaps his hand away. He finally notices her embarrassment and gives her an apologetic look. "Look, that was stupid, okay? I'm sorry." He takes a small step backward, giving her more space. "Do you want the job or not?"

Adri exhales, torn. "It's not about the job, Max. I just want . . ."

"What?"

She turns away from him, embarrassed by how much she responded to his touch, and now his gentler tone. "I thought if I apologized, you might . . ."

"I might what? Spit it out."

"Forgive me," she snaps, her voice wavering. The words barely slip out of her mouth, but, like she expected, they create a long, terrible silence between them. She watches as his face hardens again.

"I thought you wanted me to forget you."

She recognizes her own words thrown back at her, and tears form in her eyes before she can stop him from seeing them. He looks stunned, and Adri realizes why. Max has never seen her cry—not even after a bloodied, almost-broken nose or fractured fingers. Adri always made sure to keep her tears to herself, but she can't anymore.

He curses softly. "This was a mistake, wasn't it?"

She turns and leaves, heading for Roman's car, hiding the rest of her emotions. The look in Max's eyes briefly made her think that there was a chance he might let go of the past, but those hopes were already dashed to pieces again.

He was right—it was just another mistake.

4

MAX SLAMS A HAMMER against what's left of a wall in his father's kitchen and knocks it down in a dusty heap. He kicks the debris aside and wipes sweat from his forehead. The house is nearly done. He'd already remodeled the living room, tearing down the walls that closed it off and ripping out decades-old carpet to reveal pine floors underneath. He'd also re-tiled both bathrooms and updated everything—the tubs, the sinks, the lights. Only the kitchen remained, a project his father always talked about but never completed. Max's goal is to make everything new and unfamiliar.

He checks his watch. The gym doesn't open for another two hours, but he's impatient. Picking up the hammer again, he chips away at the grease-stained backsplash, splintering the blue ceramic tiles. Thankfully, his dad loved the quiet of the country, so the old house sits on four forested acres, which means Max's closest neighbor might as well be miles away. Max can hammer away to his heart's content, though at the moment he feels far from content.

His father's last bit of advice comes to his mind. Max found it written in an unfinished letter when he came home for the funeral: *Find a bigger purpose, Max. Don't lose yourself in this mixed-up world. There's more to life than the next fight. There's a lot more. You know that.*

His father knew what life was like as a fighter—endless training, endless escape—a far cry from the quiet, happy life Max lived in Sparta as a kid, where he spent his mornings taking the long way to school, afternoons working out, and evenings on his dad's porch, talking until stars crept into the sky.

Max frowns. Adri is in all those memories, laughing or teasing him or teaching him something. They were different fighters—she was fiery and unpredictable, while he was steady and strategic—but they were best friends nonetheless.

"You fill each other's gaps," his father once said, paraphrasing Rocky Balboa. Rocky was his favorite movie—Adri's too.

Aggravated, Max tosses the hammer aside, letting it clang against the broken tile. He wants to focus on the day ahead, but his mind wanders back to the conversation he had with Adri two days ago on Mount Minsi.

"I thought if I apologized, you might forgive me."

Roman duped him, and he was stupid enough to fall for it.

". . . she's out by the tracks every other day, conditioning and such. She's out there now, in fact. She likes to go after church. . . ."

Max lets out his breath slowly, annoyed that he'd let his curiosity get the best of him. Now his guilt frustrates him. Isn't *Adri* the one who ended their friendship? He remembers the day Roman returned to Sparta from Miami six years ago, looking so deflated. Roman was supposed to train Adri for her first semi-professional fight, but she'd shocked everyone by sending him home. When Max asked when she was coming back, Roman shrugged sadly.

"I don't know, kiddo. She met some big-name fighter and . . . she's not being smart. She's letting her training slip." He frowned. "And she's not talking to me like she used to."

At the time, Max brushed it off. Before Adri left to train for that fight in Miami, she'd promised Max that when she came back, they'd talk about the one thing they never talked about. He curses again, remembering his own foolish confidence. He thought Adri was the one, and no one could've convinced him otherwise—except Adri herself.

Finished, he leaves the house and walks to his father's old motorhome parked nearby, his temporary home while the house is under construction. He bangs the door open and turns on the shower. Six years ago, he knocked on the door of a swanky condo in downtown Miami—a place Adri would've never been able to afford on her own—and waited, his confusion growing. He heard nothing on the other side until the door finally opened and Adri stared at him like he was a ghost.

"You shouldn't have come here," she'd said, so stunned to see him that her voice shook. She was only gone for a few months, but she already looked much older than eighteen.

"Adri, what's going on? Roman said you fired him?" For a split second, Max saw it—the guilt—flash in her eyes before she narrowed them.

"Roman doesn't know what it takes to be a professional," she said with a strange new defiance. "I need someone with real experience."

Max stared at her in disbelief, shocked that she could say such a thing about Roman, the man who taught her almost everything she knew about fighting. She moved as if to shut the door, but he stopped her. "Can I come in, please? We need to talk."

"Max, why are you doing this?" Her voice was uncharacteristically shrill. "I thought—"

"You thought what?" He truly had no idea what she was thinking. The woman in front of him seemed more like a stranger than his best friend. Even her posture was different. It was as if she was shielding herself from something, but Max didn't know what. Surely not him?

"I thought you would just forget about me."

Those words landed like a sharp, unexpected kick to his chest. "Is that what you want?"

She hesitated for a moment, briefly torn, but then she'd nodded and turned from him slightly, hiding her eyes. "I didn't know what I wanted when I left, but now I do."

Max stood still and shocked, still not understanding until she reached for the door.

"I'm sorry," she said again. "I just want to be free."

"*I just want to be free.*"

Max sighs, refusing to remember anymore. He showers and gets dressed instead, deciding to get to the gym early and work on something, anything, even though his body drags. Since seeing Adri, he's barely slept, so he's been shifting his energies between the gym and the house, between the punching bag and the hammer, trying to break the memories.

Even as he drives, he imagines her face. He doesn't want to admit it, but the first thing he thought when he saw her by the train tracks was that she looked the way he remembered, before she left and changed. Before they *both* changed.

After arriving at the gym, his mind still races with the questions he still can't answer. Why is she back in Sparta? What happens if she doesn't find a job? Will she pack up and leave again? Where's her husband? Owen something, the guy who was supposed to be a big deal before he fell off the map.

Max knows she lied about not being in trouble—it was written all over her face—and that nags at him more than anything else. That, and the way she didn't resist his closeness. His skin goes hot remembering the torn look in her eyes.

He's surprised to see a light on in Enzo's office inside the gym. He walks toward it but keeps his footsteps quiet until he reaches the doorway. "What are you two doing in here?"

Both Enzo and Skye jump.

"Dude!" Enzo yells.

Skye clutches her chest. "Max!"

Max raises an eyebrow. They're sitting close to each other, leaning over Enzo's desk, a laptop and mango-flavored energy drinks between them.

Max frowns. "Why are you here so early?"

"We're working on the instructor search," Skye says, hand still on her chest. She eyes him curiously. "What are *you* doing here so early? Didn't you work late?"

"I . . ."

"Dude, guess what?" Enzo interjects and saves him from answering. "We found someone in River Falls who taught self-defense for four years at one of the big gyms. She'll probably want a pay bump for the commute, but we can swing it."

Skye starts listing off the woman's qualifications as Max looks between their tired faces, surprised and impressed by the extra effort they've obviously put into this. But he's barely listening.

"So, what do you think?" Enzo's hopeful voice breaks through his thoughts. "Do you want me to call her?"

Max sighs. He knows he should say yes, but he doesn't. "No."

"Seriously?" Enzo scowls at him. "What's wrong with this one?"

"Nothing's wrong with her. She sounds good, but . . ." Max frowns. "I already found someone."

"You did?" Skye sits up straighter. "Who? Do we know her?"

"Yeah, who?" Enzo demands.

"She's . . . uh . . ." Max doesn't even know what to call Adri. "An old friend? No, you don't know her, but she's got experience, and she'll be good with the kids." He remembers Eva. "She has one, actually."

Enzo crumples up a piece of paper and throws it at him. Max blocks it at the last second.

"Dude, why didn't you tell us? I'd rather be sleeping."

"I just decided."

Enzo frowns at his cryptic answer, but Max shrugs. It was true enough. He'd been going back and forth ever since he saw Adri, but he knows what he needs to do. Part of him wonders how much he might regret his decision later, although he knows it really doesn't matter.

Adri has always been his weakness.

When a car door slams, Roman glances out the window. His brows raise in surprise. "It's Max," he says, warning Adri.

"What?" Adri stands quickly and joins her uncle by the living room window, stunned by what she sees. Sure enough, Max Lyons is walking toward the door with a leafy plant in his arms.

"Want me to handle him for you?" Roman asks, standing a little taller. She'd told Roman that her conversation with Max by the railroad hadn't gone well, and she knows he feels guilty. She shakes her head. "No, it's okay. I'll talk to him." She tries to make her voice sound steadier than her feelings.

"You sure, kiddo?"

"Yes, but take Eva outside for a few minutes."

Eva pouts. "I want to talk to Max."

"No, Eva. Go with Uncle—"

The doorbell rings just as Roman takes Eva's hand and pulls her toward the backyard. Ivan follows them, but Rocky sticks close to Adri. Her heart skips as she turns the knob and opens the door. Max peers at her through the plant in his arms.

"Hi," he says quietly.

"Hi, Max!" Eva yells before Roman can close the back door behind them.

Max smiles faintly. "Can I come in for a minute?"

Adri narrows her eyes, but she steps aside to let him pass. "Sure."

"Thanks." He pauses to let her German Shepherd sniff his sneakers. "What's his name again?"

"Rocky."

Rocky dutifully looks up at the sound of his name.

Max bends to pet him. "Seems like a good name for him." Rocky lets Max scratch the brown spot between his eyes. "You can tell he's one of the good guys."

Adri nods. "He is. Go lie down, Rocky."

The old dog reluctantly obeys, flopping down on a nearby cushion, though he keeps a close eye on them. Adri glances down at the springy plant in Max's arms.

"Oh, right. Sorry. This"—he holds it out to her—"is for you."

Adri takes the potted houseplant and raises an eyebrow. "Thanks?"

"It's some kind of rose."

Perplexed, she places it near the kitchen windowsill and studies the tightly furled blooms. It doesn't have one of those little cards. "It's a desert rose, I think," she says. Her aunt had one for years. "What color are the blooms?"

"Uh . . ." Max frowns, shifting on his feet. "I forgot to ask."

Adri fights back an amused smile. "I guess I'll find out eventually. If I don't kill it first."

He laughs. "Yeah, sorry. I'm bad at apologies."

"Giving them or receiving them?" Adri's tone is light, but her words are pointed.

He sighs. "Both, I guess."

"Is that why you're here? You're apologizing?"

"I'm trying."

Adri's guard comes down slightly as she studies him. "Well . . ." She clears her throat. "Do you want to sit down?" She motions to the kitchen table. "Or would you rather apologize standing up?"

"Sitting is good."

He pulls out a pair of chairs as she clears the table of plates and Eva's latest pile of library books. As he slips off his jacket, she realizes he must've come straight from the gym. His red Lyons T-shirt is cut down both sides, barely covering his chiseled chest. When he notices her attention, she blushes.

He clears his throat. "Yeah, so . . . I wanted to come by because I probably gave you the wrong idea the other day." There's another long, loaded pause. "And I'm sorry about that."

She glances down at her hands. Truthfully, she's been thinking about their close encounter for the last forty-eight hours, even though she desperately wants it out of her mind. She has too many other things to think about—like Owen's strange new silence. "It's fine. It was just a . . . misunderstanding."

He raises his eyebrows. "Really?"

She nods.

He laughs. "Well, that was easier than I thought it would be."

She smiles weakly. "I like easy."

"Me too. There's one other thing, though."

She frowns, not sure what it could be. He'd already made it pretty clear he didn't want to talk about the past. "What?"

"I want you to take that instructor job."

She narrows her eyes.

"I know, I know . . ." He sighs. "I screwed everything up, but I think we can fix it."

"How?" she asks skeptically.

"By keeping things simple. I need someone who knows how to fight and teach. You need a job." He shrugs as if that's all there is to it. "Hiring you is the obvious solution. For both of us."

"Max . . ." Adri's heart picks up its pace. She *wants* it to be that simple, but they both know it's not. "I can't work for you."

His brows furrow. "Why?"

"Because I'm married."

He scowls. "So? What does he have to do with anything? I'm not proposing, am I? I'm just offering you a job—that you need, right?"

"I'm not worried about you *proposing*."

Max tries to look innocently confused, but Adri gives him a pointed look.

"Okay." He chews on his bottom lip, his expression lightly amused. "This is about the past, then? Our history?"

Of course it is! she wants to yell, but she keeps her face smooth. Forty-eight hours ago he was one moment away from kissing her, and she doubts she would've stopped him. "Our history is a factor, yes."

He gives her an exasperated look. "I thought you accepted my apology, though?"

"I do," she says quickly, not wanting to lose the little progress they made. "But I still don't think we should work together."

"Adri, if I hired you, it'd be strictly professional."

She frowns. He sounds convincing.

"And the job would include free classes for Eva, if she wants to try something, and we can talk about your pay. You have a lot of experience, but you'll need some certifications. . . ."

Adri's eyes drift to his mouth as she listens, increasingly torn. Everything sounds perfect—except for the close proximity to Max.

"Obviously, whatever you decide is fine," he says, interrupting her thoughts. "I just want you to think about it."

She nods, her mind already racing. She needs to earn an income for her and Eva, but another unpredictable man in her life is the last thing she wants.

Suddenly, she doubts her own hesitation. Is Max really the unpredictable one, or is it her own feelings?

When he stands to leave, she follows him to the door. "Thanks for the apology," she says, glancing at the windowsill. "And for the random plant."

He laughs freely, and Adri's stomach flutters. It's been a long time since she heard him laugh like that.

"Sure. Thanks for letting me in." He opens the door but pauses. "Oh, and after I leave, will you do me a favor and tell Roman I'm not a total jerk?"

She smiles weakly. "You know he'd never think that about you."

"As long as you don't either."

His voice is genuine, and her heart races as his eyes met hers. As Max lingers in her doorway, it sinks in that he isn't the shy young man she left behind—just like she's not the cold, closed-off woman he found in Miami six years ago. They're different now. Almost strangers, but not quite.

"Well . . ." He gives her one last smile that makes her stomach flip. "Let me know what you decide."

5

"SERIOUSLY, YOU'RE GOING TO BE SO GREAT."

Adri smiles at Skye, thankful for her steady stream of encouragement. Adri's first class starts soon, and she feels surprisingly nervous.

"The girls will love you," Skye adds, as she pulls her blond hair back into a short ponytail, revealing light freckles on her forehead and cheeks. She's only twenty-one, but she has a sisterly maturity about her that makes Adri feel more at ease.

Skye and Enzo spent the last month training her, and they both seem impressed by her progress. Adri, too, was surprised by how quickly her muscle memory returned, helped by the fact she put in the hours, arriving early and leaving late, determined to prove she's worthy of the position and not just some charity case.

For days, she debated whether or not to take the job after her years-long hiatus from training, but Yvonne had reminded her that starting over meant starting somewhere, even if it was far from where she used to be.

"But what about Max?" she asked, still unsure. "Won't it be weird?"

Yvonne looked amused. "Adri, if anyone can handle Max Lyons, it's got to be you, right? You've got years of experience."

Enzo appears in her classroom, drawing Adri's thoughts back

to the present. Like Max, he's broad-shouldered and muscular, but his face is more boyish and framed by a mop of sun-streaked curls. He grins at her. "You all set?"

"I think so."

"She is," Skye says confidently. "Do you have her roster?"

Adri watches Enzo hand Skye a clipboard, aware that he has a crush on her, even though Skye clearly has no idea.

"Woah, wait a second. Who is Max talking to?" Skye asks, distracted. She peers through one of the glass walls into the main gym and gasps.

Adri glances that way, too, where Max is speaking to a young woman. Adri squints. She looks familiar.

"That's Gemma Stone and her manager," Enzo says matter-of-factly. A short, stocky man with a glistening bald head stands behind Gemma. He laughs loudly at something Max says.

Skye's mouth falls open. "*That's* really Gemma Stone? In real life?"

"Yep. In real life."

"Who's Gemma Stone?" Adri asks, embarrassed that she's the only one who doesn't recognize the name.

"She's an up-and-coming strawweight," Enzo explains. "She's still new, but she's a big deal."

Adri realizes then why Gemma looks so familiar. She's seen her on television. Some of the details are fuzzy, but she remembers something about Gemma having a rough childhood in California before becoming a sought-after model, then a fighter. With startling clarity, Adri recalls her and Owen watching one of her first big fights. It ended with both of Gemma's elbows covered in her opponent's blood.

Skye turns to Enzo with starstruck eyes. "Did you get to talk to her?"

He shakes his head sadly. "She wanted Max, and Max only. They know each other, I guess."

Adri watches as Gemma's manager says something that makes her smirk, but Gemma keeps her eyes fixed on Max as she tosses her long braid of platinum-blond hair over her shoulder. She is strikingly beautiful, with delicate features and dark eyebrows, and she wears a sheer top over a sports bra cut to show off her curves. Adri glances at Max and frowns. Obviously, he noticed too.

"What does she want?" Adri asks.

"She wants what everyone wants." Enzo yawns. "For Max to coach her."

"He's going to, right?" Skye watches her through the glass. "I mean, I know he always says no, but she's amazing."

"I didn't hear that part of the conversation. Max told me to go check on Adri."

Adri scowls, not liking the idea of being checked on. Even after spending the last month working in the gym, she still has no idea what he thinks of her performance. And, truthfully, she's a little bit intimidated by him. As part of her training, she's observed a few of his classes, and he's an undeniably great teacher. With the smaller kids, he's still his usual stern self, but he's also quick to give out high fives and hugs as needed. He's especially good with the teenagers. Like Danny, he's always prepared and effortlessly motivating.

He mostly keeps his distance, though, leaving her to work with Enzo and Skye. Adri doesn't mind the space, but it does make her wonder if he regrets his decision to hire her.

She doesn't have time to wonder for long, though. Her students begin filing in, some chattering excitedly, others silent as they form uneven rows. They're only a few years older than Eva. Enzo gives Adri a thumbs-up before leaving, and Skye finds a spot in the corner of the room. She watches as Adri welcomes the girls.

"This class is all about protecting yourself," Adri says, trying to channel her favorite teacher, Uncle Roman, as she speaks. "Unfortunately, there are people in the world who want to hurt other people, so we need to know how to fight back." Adri slowly glances around the room, remembering her own volatile childhood before Roman and Dalila took her in. "Some of you might already know what it feels like to be in scary situations."

The girls listen, but one in particular named Kyla—the smallest in the class—watches Adri with wide, focused eyes.

"We'll start with something simple but important," Adri continues, "and then each week we'll build on what we learn."

They nod, eager to begin.

Adri gathers them into a circle. "What should you do if someone grabs your arm?"

Hannah, a girl with thick glasses and purple wristbands, raises her hand. "Run away?"

"Sure, if you can, but what if they're holding on tight?"

"Um . . . hit them?" someone else suggests to a chorus of giggles.

Adri smiles. "Maybe, but you need to make them let go of your arm first." She motions for Kyla to join her up front. She looks surprised, but she sprints to Adri and listens as Adri instructs her to grab her arm. Kyla obeys, gently grasping Adri's forearm with her small hand. With two simple movements—one inward, then up, Adri breaks the girl's hold.

"See?" Adri says, showing them again. "But Kyla's being pretty nice. She's not holding on tight. Do you think it'll work if someone holds on tighter?"

When Adri calls Skye over, the girls watch as she grips Adri's wrist.

"I'm going to do the same thing I did with Kyla," Adri says, moving her arm in the same, swift motion until she feels Skye's fingers loosen.

The girls look around excitedly and a few whisper.

"Now, Miss Skye is very strong, but will this work with someone even stronger? What if someone much bigger than you grabs your arm?"

The girls whisper as Adri walks to the door. She intends to find Enzo for a final demonstration, but she doesn't see him.

"Do you need something, Adri?"

Adri turns sharply, surprised by Max's voice. He and Gemma are standing in the hallway, a few feet from her classroom.

"Oh . . ." Flustered, Adri watches as Gemma gives her a withering glance before returning her attention to Max again. She's even more beautiful up close.

"Um . . ." Adri fumbles for words. "Can you help me with a demo? It won't take long."

"Sure." He glances at Gemma. "I'll meet you in my office."

Her eyes narrow as he follows after Adri.

"Sorry," Adri says, walking fast. "I was looking for Enzo, but—"

"It's fine," he says shortly, in step with her. "What are you doing with them?"

"Wrist releases," Adri says, irked by his brusqueness but not sure why. "I want them to see a realistic scenario before they practice on one another."

The room hushes when Max enters, and the girls watch as he stands beside Adri.

"Mr. Max is going to grab my arm and hold on *very* tight. He's going to pretend to be a bad guy."

Max waits until Adri nods, then grabs her, his callused fingers digging into the smooth skin of her wrist. The girls gasp, but Adri repeats the same maneuver and breaks his grip.

"This time, he'll use both hands."

At her command, Max takes a step closer, grabbing both of her wrists and yanking her toward him. "Come here," he says, making his voice low and threatening for added effect, taking her by surprise.

For a split second, Adri is reminded of Owen and freezes. Her pulse quickens, and Max loosens his grip.

"Adri?" He frowns down at her.

Mortified, she quickly repeats the motion, breaking free from him. He lifts his hands in surrender as the girls cheer.

"Thank you," Adri says quietly, trying but failing to hide her embarrassment.

"Sure. You need anything else?"

"No."

He hesitates for a moment, still looking concerned, but she turns her attention back to her class, so he leaves. Adri can feel Skye's curious eyes on her as she talks.

"You practice with each other now," Adri says, putting them in pairs. "Just remember, when you're being the bad guy, don't be too gentle."

As the girls practice, Adri walks around the room, correcting techniques and smiling when little Kyla shows off her strong grip on her partner's wrist. Minutes later, when the class ends and the girls scatter, Skye gives her a high five.

"Amazing, as I expected." She hands Adri a bottle of water. "I heard one of the girls talking to her mom," she says with a grin. "It sounds like she likes Miss Adri."

Relieved, Adri moves to the main gym and watches as her bright-faced students mill around the gym with their parents. A small crowd is forming by the ring, but she can't see what they're watching, so she gets closer—and instantly regrets it.

Max is training with Gemma, to the delight of their small audience. He calls out complicated combinations, and Gemma strikes his mitts, reacting with perfect precision. Gemma's body glistens as they practice, moving in a hypnotic rhythm, her gorgeous eyes fixed on Max. Adri's students watch her move, clearly in awe, and Adri feels a sharp pang of envy.

"Hey, Adri," Enzo says, giving her a reason to tear her eyes off Max and Gemma. "Skye and I want to celebrate your first class tonight. You down?"

Adri frowns. "What kind of celebration?"

"Ever been to Coralou's? Skye loves that place."

Adri nods, familiar with the small, popular speakeasy just south of Sparta, known for loud music and the strength of its drinks. Partying was always Owen's activity of choice. It used to be hers, too, but he'd sucked most of the fun out of it.

"I don't know . . ." She glances at the ring again, and this time finds Max and Gemma tangled together on the mat. She scowls.

"Come on," Enzo says, nudging her. "Work hard, play hard, right?"

Her eyes narrow as Gemma straddles Max for some groundwork. A strong drink suddenly does sound pretty appealing.

"Sure." She shrugs, too distracted to come up with a good excuse. "Why not?"

Enzo grins. "It's a date."

Linc Wilds leans back, stretching his tattooed arms behind him in the seat across from Max's desk. He's surveying his office with an amused smirk on his face, and Max can guess why. It's a small room, cluttered but clean, and like the rest of the gym, it's simple. Linc probably expected something much flashier. That was his style.

Max watches as Linc's eyes move to one of the framed photographs on the wall. Zane Furi on the ground, his face bloodied, and Max's gloves rest beside him. Max's arms are raised in victory, but his face is in shadow.

"That was quite a fight," Linc says, nodding at the photo. "Thirty-seven seconds, right?"

Max nods.

Linc whistles. "I lost some money on that one."

"You bet against me?" It doesn't surprise him. Linc always preferred fighters like Furi—more street, less technique.

"I bet Furi would last two rounds, at least. Poor shmuck."

Max smirks. "Anyway," he says dryly, ready to get this over with, "you wanted to talk about Gemma's next fight?"

Linc frowns. "You sound awfully bored, Lyons, and I can't imagine why. There's nothing boring about Gemma Stone."

Max shakes his head absently. "No, not bored. Just busy." He forces himself to sit up straighter. He's never liked Linc, but he also doesn't want to be on his bad side. "What have you got planned for her?"

"This year is going to be the big one, Max. She's fighting Jenny Lin next month, then Chloe Valentine if she wins. I think she could get Lanie Ryan if she keeps her record."

Max drums his fingers against his desk, imagining each fight. After spending the afternoon working with her, he suspects

Gemma has a good chance of winning all three. "If she beats Ryan, she can fight whoever she wants."

"Bingo," Linc says, eyes glinting. "That's why she needs the right coach."

"Tommy's a good coach."

"Yeah, he's great, but Gemma's outgrown him."

Max frowns. "How so?" He worked with Tommy Erling years ago, and there was hardly anyone better, especially for an up-and-comer.

"He's not you." Linc grins knowingly. "Apparently, Gemma's a real big fan of yours. I wouldn't be willing to make a change if she wasn't dead set on it."

Max frowns, unsure of how much Linc knows about their history. "That's flattering, but—"

"You should see the sponsors we have lined up, Lyons. . . ."

Max tries to focus as Linc speaks, but he feels vaguely unsettled the longer he listens. He knows Linc is studying his body language and searching for some kind of advantage. Back when Max was still a new fighter, Linc Wilds always had a way of making him feel like he was just an animal in a cage—a sort of sophisticated savage. To him, Gemma is probably just a particularly beautiful savage, and roping in Max could add even more spectacle to the circus.

"Surely life out here in the boonies is wearing a little thin." Linc prods. "You're content teaching little kids karate in the middle of nowhere? Sorry, but I don't buy it, Lyons. I just don't. Aren't you hungry for more?"

Max shrugs dismissively, but he doesn't answer the question. Partly because he wants to get Linc out of his office as quickly as possible, and partly because he truly doesn't know the answer.

"What'd you think of Gemma? Honestly?" Linc asks, trying a different angle. "Maybe fame and money don't get you going anymore, but every man is tempted by something." He winks. "She's got great form, doesn't she?"

Max smiles wearily. "She's beautiful. She'll draw crowds just by her looks." Sex appeal always sells, no matter the profession, and Gemma had clearly embraced that particular advantage.

Linc's eyes light up.

"And she's a very good fighter," Max adds, and he means it. In fact, she's the best female fighter he's seen in a very long time.

"You should've seen what she did to the last girl she fought."

Max guesses it was a bloodbath, as usual. "She's the whole package, but I'm still not interested in coaching her."

Linc falls uncharacteristically silent for a moment. "Can you give me a good reason?"

"Not one you'll like."

Linc crosses his thick arms. "Try me."

"Because I'm done with that part of my life."

Linc's dark eyes flicker back to the photograph on the wall. "You're telling me you don't miss that? Not even a little?"

Max is silent, but feelings war within him.

"The glory? The money?" Linc grins. "The women?"

"All fun while it lasted, but it didn't last."

"You were a hero to those people, Max. They miss you. You don't miss them?"

"I gave you my answer, Linc." Max lets his voice have an edge of annoyance, but Linc presses on.

"Can I tell you something, buddy? Don't get mad, though, it's just an observation." He throws Max a small, knowing smile. "You remind me of a lion pacing around in his cage."

Max's eyes narrow. Linc's assessment gets under his skin. Max's father embraced fighting as a vital discipline, something that made a person better, more able to protect others, and Max always wanted to be like his father—which is why he opened the gym. But the more Linc talks, the more Max wonders if there isn't some truth in what he's saying. The truth is, whether he's in the cage or not, he still feels trapped.

"King of the jungle, all cooped up, instincts denied." Linc's mouth curves. "You should be wild and free."

Max doesn't say anything. He doesn't want Linc to see he's rattled him.

"Oh, sorry—"

They both look up at the sound of a woman's voice.

"Sorry," Adri says again. "I didn't mean to interrupt." She stands in the doorway, her face flushed. Max's own heart races. They've barely talked since that day at Roman's.

"What is it, Adri?" He sounds more impatient than he means to, and he regrets it. He's just eager to be rid of Linc.

Her eyes dart between them. "I just . . ."

Linc's scrutiny makes her blush harder, and Max's irritation grows.

"It's nothing," she mutters, glancing at him again with an apologetic expression. "I'll talk to you later." Max wants to stop her, but she disappears as quickly as she came.

Linc wiggles his eyebrows. "Who was that?"

"One of my instructors," he says flatly.

"What'd you say her name was?"

"Adri."

"What's her last name?"

Max frowns, surprised and annoyed by his interest. "Rivera."

"Huh." As Linc strokes his chin thoughtfully, Max fights the urge to punch him. Almost everything about Linc grates on his nerves, but nothing more than his calculated smugness. "Could've sworn I've seen her before." He grins at Max. "She's memorable."

Max fights back a scowl as Linc leans in with renewed interest. "Do you remember Owen Anders?"

Max shakes his head, although the name sounds vaguely familiar. But he isn't in the mood to reminisce.

"He peaked before you came on the scene. Before he fizzled out, though, he was fun to watch. I saw him break a guy's clavicle once." Linc laughs darkly, clearly fond of the memory. "But then he started drinking too much. Had a scandal. Lost his sponsors. You know how it goes. . . ."

Max's agitation grows the longer Linc talks, impatient to end the conversation. "Is there anything else I can do for you, Linc? Or are we done here?" He would much rather talk to Adri about her class, anyway. She seemed unusually tense during the demo.

"Actually, there is something you can do for me."

"What's that?"

Linc grins. "Take Gemma out tonight and let her down easy."

Max frowns, surprised by the request. "I don't know if that's a good idea." On the one hand, it wasn't unreasonable. On the other, Max is aware of his own temptation—temptation that isn't helped by Adri's new, near-constant presence in the gym.

"Do it for me, buddy," Linc says as he stands. "Tell Gemma I tried everything to convince you. She could have any coach she wants, but we came all the way to Nowhere-ville because she wanted you. The least you can do is buy her a drink and tell her your lame reasons."

"Fine," Max says. He still has his reservations about a night out with Gemma, but he's willing to get over them if it means getting Linc out of his office and away from Sparta.

"Thanks, Lyons. You've always been a class act." Linc grips Max's hand and throws him another one of those awful, knowing winks. "And who knows? Maybe Gemma will find a way to change your mind."

———

Adri sits at the kitchen counter as Yvonne finishes her makeup. A punchy Adele song plays from her phone while Eva and Roman watch Yvonne's careful movements. She'd come straight over after her shift at Hot Rollers.

"Maybe you should use purple lipstick," Eva suggests, looking longingly at Yvonne's rainbow-colored palette. "Or the orange one."

Adri laughs. "I'm not that adventurous. How about red?"

Roman glances down at her feet and frowns. "You sure about the shoes?"

Adri looks down at her black high-tops. She's paired them with a simple short black dress she found at a thrift store.

"Hush," Yvonne says to Roman. "Adri's got her own style. She always has."

Adri smiles, thankful for the compliment from someone as stylish as Yvonne. Makeup and fashion never came very easily to Adri, the way it did for some girls. The more obvious choice would be heels, but Adri left the only pair she owned behind when she left Owen, and she didn't miss them one bit. She did miss Owen, though. Sometimes more than a bit.

"Who are you meeting again?" Roman asks.

"The other instructors," she says, trying to hold still for Yvonne. "Enzo and Skye."

"Enzo who?"

Adri doesn't like her uncle's investigative tone. "Does it really matter?" Even though she's almost twenty-five years old, sometimes Roman still acts like she's a teenager.

He's about to retort when Yvonne blocks Adri from his view. "Shoo, you two," she says to him and Eva. "I can't concentrate with all your jabbering. I'll call you when I'm done."

Roman frowns, but he and Eva head to the living room and dig out their beloved Battleship pieces. Alone now, Yvonne smiles down at Adri as she applies a mix of brown and bronze shadows to her eyes. "So . . . are you looking forward to a night out?"

"Uh-huh," Adri mumbles. Her feelings are still mixed about it.

Yvonne chortles. "You don't sound terribly convincing, honey."

Adri smiles weakly. "I am. It's just been a while since I did something like this." She can't even remember the last time she went out with "friends" without Owen.

"Is the job going well?" Yvonne asks, expertly switching to a smaller brush for Adri's brows.

"Well enough," Adri says, and means it this time. She glances down at her newly scraped knuckles and the small blue bruises on her wrists. She and Skye have sparred a little between workouts. "It's fun to train again."

"You missed fighting?"

She starts to nod, but Yvonne gently holds her face in place.

"Hold still, hon. We're almost done." She pulls out a thick tube of mascara and starts coating Adri's lashes, her expression thoughtful. "What exactly did you miss about it, Adri, if you don't mind my asking?"

The question surprises her, and it takes a moment for her to decide on an answer. "All of it," she says. It's true—the repetition, the experimentation, the thrill of getting something just right— every part of the process. She searches for a way to explain it, aware that Yvonne, like most people, doesn't understand the allure of the sport. "You know how much you like reading your mystery novels? Fighting is like that for me. I can just get lost in it." For Adri, mixed marital arts isn't just blood and sweat and hurting someone. It actually lives up to its name as an art—the art of using one's mind and body in unison in an unparalleled test of the will. "I also just missed being good at something," Adri says lamely, unable to articulate her feelings just right. Roman is the only one who seems to understand.

She frowns, remembering Max. He understands too.

Yvonne smiles. She still looks skeptical, but there's a little more understanding in her eyes now. "I'm glad to hear that, honey. I just wondered if it brought up any regrets. . . ."

Adri knows what Yvonne is saying as her voice trails off. *Because of Owen.* "The only regret I have is not fighting when I should've," Adri says with a sigh. Owen, too, understood the power of being a skilled fighter, but he used it in the worst possible ways. A quick rush of anger fills her—directed at him, but at herself too. There was more than one occasion where she could've put an end to his abuse, but she never took it.

"There," Yvonne says, stepping back. "*Terminado.*" She holds up a small mirror, and Adri raises her eyebrows at the unfamiliar woman staring back at her.

"Wow." Her skin glows, and her eyes are bold and bright. Yvonne had added tiny, perfect eyeliner wings to the corners of her eyes that Adri will never be able to replicate.

"You look so pretty, Mama," Eva says, rushing to the kitchen to see the final product. She grins up at Adri before her eyes dart to Yvonne's bag. "Maybe Miss Yvonne can do my make-up too."

"Thanks, butterfly." Unexpected tears form in Adri's eyes as Yvonne leans down to dab some pink gloss on a beaming Eva's lips. Adri pulls Eva into a tight hug. "Have fun with Uncle Roman and Yvonne tonight, okay? And take a bath, please. But not with Ivan." Adri glances down at the little dog by Eva's feet, who looks back up at her with his usual scowl. He and Eva recently became inseparable.

Roman hands Adri his keys.

"Thanks for letting me borrow the car again," she says, carefully tucking them into her purse. The first thing she wants to buy with her new income is a used car—something cheap but reliable. "I won't be out too late."

"Just have some fun tonight, kiddo," Roman says, changing his earlier tune. He smiles as he waves her out the door. "You've been working hard."

It's dark and loud inside Coralou's when Adri steps inside, her nerves resurfacing. Moody pop music pulses against the walls, and a few people sing along with the song. Adri weaves through the crowd, looking for Skye or Enzo, but she halts when a man beckons her toward the dance floor, lightly grabbing her hand. He's tall and blond, and for a moment, she's briefly reminded of Owen—back when he was younger and still danced.

Thankfully, Skye intercepts her and shoos the man away, pulling Adri away from the dance floor. "It's crazy in here tonight!" She shouts over the music, her green eyes glittering under the flashing lights. "I love your dress, by the way."

"Thanks." Skye, too, dressed up for the occasion and looks stunning in a denim jumpsuit. It shows off the intricate tattoo on her collarbone—stars and swirling clouds.

Skye grins. "Amazing what not wearing sweaty gym clothes can do for a girl's confidence, isn't it?"

"Hey!"

They both turn and find Enzo heading toward them, his curly hair slicked back and away from his face. His eyes light up when he sees Skye, and Adri smiles as Skye fixes her hair. Enzo motions for them to follow him to a darker, quieter corner of the bar where they slide into a cracked leather booth.

"What do you want to drink, ladies? I'll get the first round."

Skye wants a gin and tonic, but Adri hesitates, realizing it's been years since she drank with anyone besides Owen. His drink of choice was whiskey, and she usually went along with him, even though she hated the taste. "Maybe . . . something with rum?"

When Enzo leaves for the bar, Skye leans in so Adri can hear her over the music. "How does it feel to have your first day under your belt?"

Adri relaxes slightly for the first time since she's arrived and smiles. "It feels pretty good." Her classes went better than she expected, and the long, challenging day reminded her how much she loves fighting—and how much she'd missed it, though she tries not to think about that too much.

Enzo returns a few minutes later, balancing three drinks in his hands. He slides one to Adri. "It's a dark and stormy."

She takes a sip of the amber-colored cocktail and winces.

He frowns. "Not good? I can get you something else—"

"No, no, it's good," Adri reassures him. "Just strong." She takes another small sip. It's definitely better than whiskey. "Thanks."

Skye gives her a curious glance. "Not much of a drinker?"

Adri plays with the tiny black straw in her glass. "Not as much I used to be." Owen's almost daily drinking made it less and less appealing over the years.

"Same here. I just drink every once in a while. Enzo, though . . . he knocks them back."

He pretends to be offended. "Excuse me?"

She smiles coyly. "I'm just saying that you enjoy your fair share of alcoholic beverages."

"Yeah, well, it's not my fault." He winks at Adri. "Max drives me to drink."

The next hour passes quickly as they talk, all three of them laughing more easily as the night goes on. When they finish their first round, Enzo buys another. Adri learns that Enzo, a judoist, met Max near the end of Max's fighting career, and they became fast friends, despite their different personalities. Enzo tried fighting professionally, but he quit after three fights.

"I just don't like people punching me all the time, you know? I mean, look at this face." He presses Skye's hand to his cheek as she laughs. "This face needs to be preserved, right?"

Adri also learns that Skye joined the gym when it first opened, and she quickly impressed Max. She started boxing when she was eleven, earning wins up and down the East Coast throughout her teens, until her mom's health brought them back to Sparta, where they had family. Now, she splits her time between the gym and helping taking care of her mother and younger sister.

"I do really want to fight again, though," Skye says, with a look of longing. "I bug Max all the time about setting up a fight for me, but you know how he is." She sighs. "I think he thinks I'm too young or something."

"Nah, he just doesn't want to lose you at the gym," Enzo quips. "Then we'd have to find *another* coach, and you know how well that goes."

Skye smiles weakly before turning her attention to Adri. "How'd you get into mixed martial arts?"

Adri frowns. She finds both of their stories fascinating, but now they're curious about hers—and she doesn't know if she's ready to share it. "Um . . ." She picks out the most basic details. "My uncle is the one who got me into it. He taught me how to box. Then I started wrestling. Then judo."

"I still can't believe your uncle is Roman Rivera," Enzo says, shaking his head in amazement. "What a freaking legend."

It didn't take long after her mother left her with Roman for Adri to realize that she was in the presence of a local celebrity. Spartans stopped them everywhere, wanting to shake the hand of the man who knocked the world champion off his feet in 1973, despite being a poor Cuban immigrant with zero odds of winning. Adri frowns, remembering the rest of the story—the end of Roman's short career—which isn't hers to tell. But Skye and Enzo wait expectantly.

"He started training me when I was eight," she adds.

"*Eight?*" Skye's mouth falls open. "So you must've been crazy good, right?"

Adri shrugs. "Yeah, I was pretty good." If Roman was there, he would've scolded her for saying such a thing, but she doesn't want to get into the details. The truth is, she was on track to be one of the best. Before she screwed it up.

Enzo frowns. "Why didn't you go pro?"

"I tried, actually."

"Oh." His brows crease. "Didn't work out, then?"

"Not exactly. . . ." Adri takes a long drink until the ice presses against her lips. "I got pregnant," she says.

He and Skye fall silent.

"Then I got married," Adri adds, filled with a rush of regrets. Not about Eva—Eva was the best gift God ever gave her—but about everything else. "And then it just never happened. . . ." she trails off as Enzo and Skye exchange glances, unsure of what to say, until Adri changes the subject. "Anyway, did you guys hear anything else about Gemma Stone? Is Max going to coach her?" Adri recalls watching them fight earlier, how they seemed perfectly in sync. Her jealousy returns. Max talked to her manager for a long time.

"I seriously doubt it," Enzo says, with a shrug. "Max doesn't like being used."

Adri frowns. "She using him?" *For what?*

"Probably. He's got a whole mystique thing going on ever since he moved out here. People know that if they can get him on their team, they'll be on everyone's radar." Enzo sighs. "Gemma's not the first, and she won't be the last."

Adri wants to ask more questions about Gemma, but their conversation comes to a screeching halt as she follows Skye's eyes and looks up. Her stomach drops.

Max—and Gemma—are walking toward them.

Enzo whistles in disbelief. "Dang. That's a first."

The three of them watch as Max leads her through the crowded bar. People quickly move out of their way and glance admiringly at the impressive pair. Gemma stuns in tall black boots and a short leather skirt.

"I told him we were going out tonight," Enzo explains. "But I never thought he'd show up."

"Why?" Adri asks, dismayed.

"I don't know. . . . He's just kind of a loner these days." Enzo lowers his voice. "He's been that way ever since his dad died, but it's getting wor—" He falls silent when Max reaches their table.

Adri's heart races as Max glances at each of them, starting with Enzo and Skye first, then her. When his eyes linger for just a second too long, heat fills her cheeks. "Hey," he mumbles, and Adri nods in acknowledgment.

"Where's Gemma?" Skye asks, looking past him, her disappointment obvious. "I really want to meet her."

"She wanted to dance," he says flatly.

Skye looks heartbroken, but Max doesn't seem to notice. His eyes fall to the only empty seat in the booth, the one next to Adri. "Can I sit?"

She moves to make room for him as he slides in.

"Thanks."

Adri nods, ignoring her heart's picked-up pace. Unsurprisingly, he looks just as good in a black polo and jeans as he does in workout clothes. Seated so close to him, she can see a scar near his left eye—one that he didn't have when she left Sparta. The shape of it reminds her of those leafy crowns that ancient Olympians wore, but the scar disappears into his eye before the circle is complete.

Max turns and catches her looking at him. When he smirks, more heat fills her face. Even worse, for the first time in the entire evening, both Enzo and Skye are uncharacteristically quiet as their eyes shift between her and Max—until he breaks the silence and taps Adri's empty glass with his finger.

"What are you drinking?"

She looks to Enzo, forgetting the name. She'd just finished her third.

"A dark and stormy. She said she likes rum."

Max frowns. "I thought you liked the adios amigo."

When Adri realizes what he's talking about, she bursts out laughing, surprising everyone.

"I forgot about that drink," she says, still laughing.

"What's in it?" Skye asks.

"I honestly don't remember." Adri turns to Max and finds him smiling. "It was blue, right?"

He nods. "Yep, with a tiny sombrero. It was also disgusting."

Adri laughs again, remembering their many failed attempts to sneak into bars when they were teenagers. Max never wanted to, but Adri could always convince him to go with her. Coralou's was one of the few places that let them in. "Remember when—"

Max turns from her abruptly, and she realizes why. She can't help but stare as Gemma strides toward them like a queen, her posture effortlessly intimidating. Her hair is long and wildly curled, framing her face. Everything about her is seductive—especially the way she looks at Max. Adri's stomach twists. As he makes introductions, Gemma barely glances at the rest of them.

"I'm thirsty," she says instead.

Her voice reminds Adri of cold metal. Gemma holds out her hand, and Max takes it, following her to the bar without a second look at Adri or the others. Adri watches them until they're swallowed up by the growing crowd and tries to ignore the hot spark of jealousy growing inside her chest.

"Oh my gosh . . . did you guys see her arms?" Skye asks, awestruck.

Enzo grins sheepishly. "I wasn't looking at her arms."

Skye slaps his shoulder. "You creep. Seriously, you really don't think Max will train her? I know he always says no, but will he really say no to *her*? I mean, she used to model for *Vogue* or something, right? And she has a camp for foster kids. They're totally perfect for each other."

Enzo shrugs. "I don't know. . . . Maybe she'll be the one who finally breaks him."

"I'm going to go get more drinks," Adri interjects, unable to listen any longer. She slides out of the booth as quickly as she can, ignoring her dizziness as she weaves through dancing people. When she has to slow down to avoid stumbling, she's thankful that she doesn't own that pair of heels anymore. When she finds an empty seat at the bar, she catches the bartender's eye.

"Can I get a gin and tonic, a dark and stormy, and a . . ." She bites her lip, forgetting Enzo's drink.

"Sixpoint."

She looks up and finds Max looking back at her from across the bar. He looks annoyingly amused. "Enzo likes Sixpoint," he repeats.

Adri ignores him and turns back to bartender. "A Sixpoint, please." Someone sitting to her left leaves, and she scowls when Max takes his place. When he leans in, she smells his cologne. Citrus and pine and something else.

He frowns. "You doing okay?"

"I'm fine."

"You just seem a little . . . unsteady."

"I said I'm fine," she snaps, surprising him. It dawns on her that Gemma is missing again, but he doesn't seem to mind. His eyes are fixed on her, and that gives her a jolt of confidence. She glances at him over her shoulder. "I wasn't expecting you to be here."

"Change of plans," he says, with a shrug, but his brows briefly furrow. He doesn't seem terribly happy about it. "What did you want earlier?" he asks, changing the subject. "When I was talking to Linc?"

Adri frowns. Her thoughts are cloudier than they should be, thanks to the rum. Finally, she remembers. "Oh, that. I was just going to run some ideas by you for my next class." Skye and Enzo were great, but she still wanted Max's approval too—even if she'd never admit it out loud.

"I heard today went pretty well."

She smiles, thankful for the good report. "Yeah, it did, I think."

"But wrist releases are kind of basic, aren't they?"

Her smile quickly fades. "They're useful."

Max shrugs. "Sure, but they're a little boring. You could try some ground defense next time to get them moving. Or some basic punches."

Adri's temper flares. She know he's just thinking out loud, but she feels strangely defensive. "Not every conflict requires a knockout, does it?" His brows raise at her challenging tone, but Adri can't stop herself. "Where's Gemma, anyway?" she asks. "You lost her again already?"

For a moment, his mouth parts in surprise, and Adri wishes she could take her words back. Her cheeks flush as she realizes she gave herself away.

His mouth curves into a small smirk. "Yeah. . . I should probably go find her, shouldn't I?"

She shrugs, feigning disinterest. "Have fun. I heard she modeled for *Vogue* and loves foster kids." She turns from him and smiles flirtatiously at the bartender instead.

Max laughs but doesn't leave. Instead, he drums his fingers against the bar. "I figured something out earlier." His face darkens slightly. "When I was talking to Linc."

Adri throws him a bored expression, even though her interest is piqued. "Who's Linc?"

"Gemma's manager."

She frowns. "Oh." The sleazy guy with the practiced smile. She takes her drink as the bartender slides it over. "What did he say?"

"He knows Owen."

His name sends a shiver down her spine.

"Which reminds me . . ." Max glances down at her bare fingers, then back up again with questioning eyes. "Where's your ring? I've never seen you wear one."

Adri's head swims with excuses as he waits for an answer. "I take it off to train," she says, avoiding his gaze. "And I forget to put it back on."

"You're still not a very good liar, Adri."

"And you're still not good at leaving things alone," she snaps, flustered.

"You mean leaving *you* alone?"

When she doesn't respond, he turns from her, but she instinctively grabs his arm. He slowly turns back to her, and his eyes fall to her hand on his arm before they take in the rest of her. When he looks her in the eye again, heat fills her face.

He leans in until his lips brush against her ear. "You have no idea what you want, do you?"

Face burning, Adri pulls away. "Funny question, coming from you." She remembers what Skye and Enzo have told her about his restlessness. She sensed it too, ever since that day at the tracks.

He smiles roguishly. "I know exactly what I want."

"Max." Her heart beats faster as he looks at her. "We agreed that—"

"I also know what we agreed to, Adri," he says, cutting her off with a sigh. He scowls down at the innocent look on her face, and she feels a prick of shame. She's being reckless with his feelings—and her own.

Embarrassed, she grabs the drinks and slides off her barstool, but her steps are unsteady. He reaches out to help her, but she moves away from his touch.

"Go. I'm fine. Gemma's probably waiting for you."

He shakes his head in exasperation. "Fine. Be that way. At least get a ride home, please? Can you call Roman?"

"I'll ask Enzo," she mutters. "Happy now?" She leaves before he can answer, but she catches a glimpse of his scowl.

Back at the booth, she dodges Skye and Enzo's questions and keeps her eyes away from the bar and on the dance floor, watching as people rush to it when a new song blasts through the speakers. Her mind is racing with competing feelings—fresh anxieties about

Gemma's mysterious manager's connection with Owen, plus a small glowing ember of jealousy at the thought of Max searching for Gemma in the sea of people. But those temporarily fade when someone approaches the table and asks Skye to dance. Enzo watches them leave with a look of disappointment.

Adri frowns. She's not used to seeing him look so deflated, and it tugs on her heart. "Want to dance?" she asks.

He looks surprised. "You want to?"

She smiles knowingly. "Maybe you can make Skye jealous."

His eyes widen. "Am I that obvious?"

"Not to her, apparently. Come on." Adri takes his hand and pulls him to the dance floor, surprised by her own bravado, which probably has something to do with too many strong drinks. She guides him toward the middle of the floor, until they're surrounded on all sides.

"Wow," Enzo says, watching her dance. "You've loosened up a little bit, haven't you?"

Adri laughs as she looks over his shoulder. She wants to take her mind off Max for a while, but he's only a few feet away, with Gemma winding around his body like she's in a music video. His arms are wrapped around her slender waist, but more than once, his eyes drift to Adri. Aware, Adri continues to dance, her hips grazing Enzo's until he takes the hint and pulls her closer. Gemma competes for Max's attention, her short skirt lifting slowly as she dances, but Max doesn't seem to notice. He watches as Adri pulls Enzo even closer, pressing her body against his as she dances, slower and more sensual as the song continues. Max's jaw tightens.

"No church tomorrow, then?" Enzo asks, slightly breathless when the song ends and Adri releases him. He grins, clearly meaning it as a joke, but Adri feels another rush of embarrassment. She turns from him.

"Adri!" Enzo catches up to her. "Woah, I'm sorry. I didn't mean anything by that, I just—"

She waves his apology away. "I know you didn't. It's fine. I just . . ." It dawns on her in bits and pieces how much she's been drinking and what she's been doing. Snippets of her conversation with Max replay in her mind, but parts are missing now. Her embarrassment grows. "I should go home."

"Are you good to drive?"

She bites her lip. She wants to be alone, so she's tempted to say yes, but she knows she shouldn't. "Could you give me a ride?"

From the dance floor, Max watches with narrowed eyes as Enzo leads her out of the bar. He tries to focus on the music and Gemma—anything besides where Adri and Enzo are going or what they might be doing—but he can't. It never crossed his mind that Enzo might be interested in her, but after seeing them dance together, Max isn't so sure. Jealousy claws at him.

When he finally convinces Gemma to call it a night, she follows him out into the cool evening air with a slight smile playing on her lips. Max frowns, remembering that smile. His thoughts race as they get into his truck. He'd forgotten how easy it was to get caught up in her charms, like he did a few years ago. Their brief, fiery fling came to an end when his dad died, but he doubted that would stop her from trying to rekindle something tonight—and he isn't sure if he'll stop her. His thoughts drift back to Adri and her movements on the dance floor.

"Is this the part when you tell me why you don't want to coach me?" Gemma asks.

Max turns to face her and finds her smirking at the tense look on his face. He sighs inwardly. She's more beautiful than he remembered—more mature, less desperate for his attention than she used to be. He doesn't want to upset her, but he forges ahead, doing his best to explain his decision with a long list of practiced excuses. She keeps her gaze impassive for most of it until, suddenly, she bursts out laughing.

"Wow. You're trying *so* hard to let me down easy. It's really cute, actually," she says, inching closer. "But the thing is . . . I'm not going to *let* you." Before Max can react, she leans over and kisses him hard, her lips moving expertly over his.

His head is still swimming from the kiss when both of her hands start moving dangerously fast for his belt. Before he can think straight, he's kissing her back, partly fueled by lust, but partly by jealousy—Adri's dancing still burned into his mind. Gemma almost loosens his belt before he catches her hands.

She stares at him in disbelief. "Are you serious right now?"

Max silently curses. Like her, he's surprised—and annoyed—by his own willpower. "Unfortunately, yes."

"*Why?*" She sounds as if she genuinely fears for his sanity.

Max searches for an excuse, aware that none of them will make any sense to her. They barely make sense to him. "I'm just . . . tired."

She throws him a skeptical look and reaches for him again, but he places his own hands firmly on the steering wheel.

"I'm sorry, Gemma." He turns the key quickly, thankful when the engine springs to life. "I'll take you to your hotel."

"But you're not coming in, are you?"

For the first time in the evening, her cool voice holds the hint of a whine. As Max drives, he's careful to keep his eyes off her and on the road. "Look, it's nothing against you. Honestly. I just . . ." He's not even entirely sure of his reasons for turning her down, other than a nagging feeling in his stomach. "It's just not a good time right now," he says, deciding that was probably the best way to put it. Gemma couldn't care less about his issues with Adri.

When she scoffs from the passenger seat, Max remembers that that was the same thing he said to her the last time he broke things off with her. He frowns. Apparently, it was never a good time for them.

"Well, I guess that's *two* decisions you'll regret then," she snaps when he parks in front of her hotel. She slams the door behind her, rattling the truck, and his mood darkens.

As he watches her walk away, he suspects that she's probably right. Coaching her would've been the perfect excuse to pack up and leave Sparta for a while, and a few nights with her might've burned up some of his pent-up passion.

Instead, he chose to torture himself. He'll spend the rest of the night awake, replaying his conversation with Adri and wondering if Enzo dropped her off at Roman's or took her back to his apartment.

6

ADRI SITS BESIDE ROMAN, her hands in her lap, trying to listen to the sermon despite her throbbing headache. Light shines through stained-glass windows and casts brightly colored shadows on the pews as the minister speaks. He says something about the Holy Spirit being like wind—mysterious but constant, imperceptible but powerful. Adri wants to listen, but her head pounds.

"Very often, we look to rules, or a lack of rules, or people, or our own will, to transform us into who we wish we were and make us feel worthwhile. . . ."

Adri groans inwardly as flashbacks from last night hit her. Enzo walked her to Roman's porch and helped her unlock the door, then waited until she locked it again before he left. She closes her eyes, trying to remember more. Enzo just laughed it off.

"Don't sweat it, Adri. Happens to the best of us."

She frowns, remembering dancing with him. Using him. Against Max. Max, she thinks miserably, as their heated conversation comes back to her in a rush. Max, her former best friend, her current boss. She sighs, overwhelmed by the mess she's made.

God, why do I feel this way about him?

From the moment she saw him at Shade, she'd been drawn to him, despite burying those feelings so many years ago. Last night, those same feelings overpowered her. Again. She closes her eyes, trying to shut the past out, but her thoughts won't let her.

She realized too late after marrying Owen what she'd done, despite her mother having done the exact same thing. When Adri met Owen in Miami, she ignored every warning sign. He was thrilling and unpredictable, older and wiser, experienced and fascinating. Most important, he offered her the chance to escape the small, safe, suffocating world of Sparta—and she took it.

Shame gnaws at her as she remembers the part of the story she'd tried to erase. Max wanted to talk to her before she left for Miami. She knew what he wanted to talk about, but her eighteen-year-old self balked, afraid that if he told her he loved her, she might never leave his side. Because Max had that effect on her—when they were together, she easily could get lost in him, and that scared her more than the unknown.

She forces her wayward thoughts back to the present. *What on earth am I doing?* she wonders, sighing inwardly. She hasn't even sent Owen the divorce papers yet. Doesn't she have enough problems without adding Max to the mix? For her sake and his? Her heart sinks as it dawns on her that she was as flippant with his feelings last night as she was with them six years ago.

"Transformation is not our work, friends. It's the work of the Holy Spirit."

The minister's words capture her attention again. She watches as he looks down at a leather-bound Bible on the altar in front of him.

"If anyone is in Christ, they are a new creation. The old has passed away; behold, the new has come."

Adri frowns, still not understanding *how*. She's been in Sparta for three months and attends the weekly Bible study with Roman when she can, but she still feels hopelessly behind. Especially in a room full of people whose lives seem so neat and put together.

She lets her eyes drift to one of the windows. In vibrant hues, Jesus stands in a rocky pasture. A lamb rests on his shoulders. She finally gets that part—Jesus died for every kind of sinner, and the ones who believe in him will be saved from hell. But what does that mean for her *now*?

When the service ends minutes later, people start filing out of the sanctuary, and Roman turns his attention to Adri. "Something wrong, kiddo?"

She sighs miserably. "I don't think I'm a very good Christian."

He laughs. "Well, that means you're better than some."

"I don't think so."

He frowns. "Adri . . ." They're alone now, besides a few children playing tag between the pews. "You know, it's not really about being good, per se. It's more . . ." He chews on his bottom lip for a moment. "Shoot. I wish I was better at this sort of thing, like Yvonne." He sighs. "Of course, being a Christian means you want to be good and do the right thing and all that, but it's more about progress. Learning. Growth. Getting back up when you get knocked down and knowing *why* you can get back up again." He smiles lightly at her disheartened expression. "You're going to mess up along the way, my dear. That's why you need Jesus."

Adri closes her eyes. That's what she's most afraid of—more mess-ups, more mistakes. She's already made enough. She looks up at the stained-glass window again, drawn by the serene look on the shepherd's face. Roman looks too.

"Why does he carry the sheep like that?" she asks, remembering Eva's question from just a few months ago, when she first stepped into a church. That already feels like a lifetime ago.

Roman thinks for a moment. "If I had to guess, I imagine it's because she's tired of wandering around in the wilderness." He puts a hand on her shoulder. "He's carrying her so she can rest."

———

"You're seriously not going to coach Gemma?"

Max bites the inside of his cheek. He's tired of Skye's endless questions. "Like I've already said a hundred times, I'm not coaching *anyone*."

It's Monday afternoon, and he and Skye are alone in the gym, waiting for Enzo and Adri before their evening classes begin.

"Not even her, though?" Skye nags. "Enzo said she wants you and Jair Jimenez on her team. That would be amaz—"

His eyes narrow at the mention of Enzo's name. Since Coralou's, the mere thought of him puts Max in a bad mood.

"Couldn't you just train her short-term or something? Enzo could take over your class—"

Max ignores her and walks to the weights, trying to keep his temper in check. He grabs a set and starts lifting, but his frustrations mount. He honestly can't explain why he rejected Gemma's offer—just like he's rejected every offer, no matter how good. He also can't explain why he keeps glancing at the door and hoping that Adri will walk through it.

"I wonder who Gemma will work with since—"

"Drop it, Skye," he snaps.

The door swings open before she can respond, and Max drops his weights as Enzo strides in. Enzo grins, but his smile quickly fades. "What?" he asks, his eyes moving between Skye and Max. "Who died?"

"You're late," Max snaps, his irritation rising all over again.

Enzo glances at the clock and frowns. "Barely." He looks at Skye next, who also looks unhappy all of a sudden. "Where's Adri?" he asks.

"We thought maybe you would know," Skye says, with a hint of resentment.

Enzo's brows scrunch. "Why would *I* know?" He looks between them, clearly puzzled. "I haven't seen her since I dropped her off at her uncle's house on Saturday."

As his words sink in, Max relaxes slightly. Skye, too, looks relieved.

Enzo stares at them. "What, weirdos? She drank too much, so I gave her a ride. That's *it*." He scowls. "Get your minds out of the gutter."

"Whatever," Max says, downplaying his relief. "Let's just get started." He can't help but glance at the door one more time, but there's still no sign of Adri. Enzo and Skye follow him to the ring.

"Hey, before we get into class stuff, can we talk about my brilliant idea?" Enzo asks.

"Which one?" Max throws him a tired look. Enzo always has something up his sleeve.

"Hosting a fight in the gym."

"Oh. That one."

"What's wrong with it? All we have to do is find some fighters and promote it."

"It sounds fun to me," Skye interjects, looking hopefully at Max. She makes her face angelic. "And maybe . . . I could fight?"

Max scowls, realizing he's outnumbered. He can already imagine the breathless phone calls from promoters begging for a spot and hordes of Spartans anxious to relive the past. But after too many sleepless nights, Max is too tired to argue with them.

"Come on, dude." Enzo grins, sensing his indecision. "Can't we have some fun for once?"

"If you two want to organize it, fine," he says wearily. "Just keep it small."

Enzo and Skye cheer as the door opens again, and when Adri hurries inside, Max understands why she's late. Eva is with her, taking two quick steps for each of Adri's. She waves when she sees him.

"I'm so sorry I'm late," Adri says, meeting them in the ring. She looks down at Eva by her side, then up at Max with apologetic eyes. "Eva woke up with a stomachache, and Roman had to help someone at the church. And Yvonne's working." Breathless, she turns to Skye. "I thought maybe Eva could watch one of your classes? She's been saying she wants to box for a while now."

Skye smiles down at Eva, who smiles back shyly.

"Sure! Have you ever boxed before?"

Eva nods, suddenly more confident. "I know uppercut, haymaker, weaves and bobs," she says, demonstrating a few moves.

Skye raises an impressed eyebrow and whisks Eva away to find hand wraps and gloves, and the mood turns more tense as Adri and Max face each other in the ring—the first time since Coralou's. She listens as he runs through his list of weekly announcements and opportunities for the kids, but neither of them meets the other's eyes.

"Well, I'm going to go set up," Enzo mutters, throwing a final curious glance between them. "Catch you two later." When he leaves, Adri finally meets Max's eyes.

"Sorry again about being late," she says, with a downcast expression.

"It's fine." Her presence reminds him of the roller coaster of emotions she put him through on Saturday, but he also knows his jealousy is partly his own fault. He could've stepped up and taken her to Roman's himself—something he's still kicking himself over. But he forces himself to focus on the present moment. "For future reference, if you can't find a sitter, Eva is always welcome here. She can play in the gym as long as she doesn't bother anyone."

Adri looks surprised but grateful. "Thanks." For a second, she looks like she's going to say something else, but then she changes her mind.

For the rest of the day, Adri's classes pass in a blur as she teaches the girls palm-heel strikes. She has them practice on standing bags first, then carefully with each other. Later, when she goes to retrieve Eva from Skye's classroom, she finds her jumping rope and laughing at a song they've made up.

"Thanks for letting her hang out with you," Adri says to Skye, who's stacking gloves in a corner of the room.

Skye nods, but her expression is oddly cold. Adri frowns. Skye is usually all smiles.

"Is something wrong?" she asks.

"No," Skye says, too quickly.

"Are you sure?"

Skye scowls. "I wish I had one of those faces that could hide emotions."

"Why?" Adri asks, confused. "What are you trying to hide?"

Skye sighs miserably. "Fine. I'll just say it. . . . Do you like Enzo?"

Adri's mouth falls open. "What?"

"Don't act like that's such a stupid question!" Skye's eyes narrow defensively. "The way you were dancing with him on Saturday was pretty . . . intense."

"Skye, no. Absolutely not. I like Enzo as a friend. That's it."

"And you're married, right?"

Adri blushes furiously. And she feels even worse about Saturday. Apparently, her grand plan to make Skye notice Enzo totally backfired. "Yes," she says. "That's . . . complicated, but yes."

When Skye notices her discomfort, her face softens again. "Sorry. It's none of my business. I just . . ."

"Have a crush on Enzo?"

When Skye's freckled cheeks turn pink, Adri's own embarrassment subsides. "Why don't you just tell him, Skye?"

Skye stares at her like she's an alien. "Um . . . because we *work* together? He's technically my boss. He'll think it's totally weird and unprofessional."

Adri smirks. "I don't think he will."

"Why not?"

"Because he *obviously* likes you too." Adri laughs at the stunned look on her face. "You're the only one who hasn't noticed."

Skye falls silent. Her mouth slowly stretches into a smile. "Wait, what? He does? Seriously? Don't lie to me."

Later, Enzo finds them huddled together, still talking and laughing in the back room. They break apart quickly when they see him.

"What's up?" Adri asks, frowning. His cheerful face is uncharacteristically tense.

"Oh, nothing new." He sighs heavily. "Max just stormed out. The usual. I guess I'm taking over his last class tonight."

"Why?"

Enzo shrugs. "I asked him about Gemma, and he just blew up. I guess that whole thing with her didn't end well—"

"Mama?" When a quiet voice interrupts their conversation, the three of them look down and find Eva poking Adri's leg in a steady rhythm. "I wanted to give Mr. Max the picture I made him." She points to Adri's gym bag, where she tucked a drawing she'd made earlier that day.

An idea strikes Adri. It's a terrible idea, but a persistent one. She tries to resist it, but the gentle nudge grows stronger. She sighs. "Why don't we go check on him?"

Eva looks delighted, but Enzo raises an eyebrow. "You sure? He's not very fun when he's in one of his moods."

Adri nods, aware of that, but she's already made up her mind. "I should talk to him."

The drive to Danny Lyon's house is a long one. Eva cheerfully bops her head to a Creedence Clearwater song, but Adri doesn't sing along with her. Her hands lightly grip the steering wheel as they take in the beautiful views on all sides—picturesque fields dotted with horses, rolling farmland, and jagged mountains, all under one stunningly big sky. Eva stares in wonder. She's used to city life, but it's obvious that Sparta is growing on her. Adri smiles, surprised by her own growing fondness for a place she used to scorn.

When they reach Max's house, the windows are dark, but his truck is parked on the gravel driveway. In the distance, a creek gurgles and geese honk—it's an unusually warm day for late February. Ignoring her nerves, Adri knocks on the front door. As they wait, she studies the property, puzzled by the piles of debris in the front yard.

Eva frowns. "He's not home."

Adri is partly disappointed, having mustered her resolve to talk to him about their conversation at Coralou's, but she's also undeniably relieved.

"What about that thing?" Eva points to a large weather-beaten Winnebago parked a short distance from the house. *Zeus*—its nickname—is printed in peeling blue paint. Adri is shocked to see it's still around. Danny and Max used to take summer trips in it, traveling up and down the coasts between his tournaments. "Is he in there? What is it?"

Adri smiles, realizing that Eva's never seen a motor home before. "It's like a little house, except you can drive it places."

Eva looks at it again, even more in awe. "Maybe we can get one? How much do they cost?"

They approach the motorhome and knock, but again, Adri hears nothing on the other side. Disappointment fills her. Maybe Max is avoiding her, and she can't blame him. She turns to Eva, who's face is crestfallen. "I'll give him your picture tomorr—"

"Adri?"

Adri turns quickly at the sound of her name, and her eyes widen. Max is walking toward them from the back of the house, carrying a sledgehammer in his left hand. She swallows. He's wearing dusty jeans, work boots, and nothing else. He looks as shocked as Adri does as Eva rushes to meet him halfway.

"Max!"

"Hey, Eva."

"I made you this," she says proudly.

He drops the hammer to take the picture from her. He smiles faintly. The lion's mane is black, and it wears a blue bowtie. She added dark slanted eyebrows. "Thanks. I like it." He looks up at Adri again, puzzled. "What are you doing here?"

"Do you have a river?" Eva asks before Adri can answer. Eva eagerly looks past Max at the creek that runs behind his house.

"Yep," he says, amused by the misnomer. "It's a tiny river, also known as a creek."

"Can I see it?" she asks.

He glances at Adri. "If your mom says it's okay."

Eva starts walking in that direction.

"Eva!" Adri calls after her. "Stop—"

"I'll stay where you can see me!" Eva hurries to the creek but stops a safe distance away, still in Adri's line of sight. "See?"

Adri starts to protest, but Max waves her concerns away. "She'll be fine," he says dismissively. "You know how shallow it is." They had spent countless afternoons as kids dipping their toes in the cold, muddy water.

Adri falls silent, but her heart pounds as he walks the rest of the way. His hair is damp, and his chest is slick with sweat.

"Did something happen at the gym?" he asks.

Suddenly, Adri forgets her practiced speech. "No, um, everything's fine. . . ." She trails off as he looks over her, annoyingly flustered. "Enzo just said that you were upset about something."

His eyes narrow. "And he sent you?"

"No," she says quickly, wishing she hadn't brought up Enzo. "No, he didn't send me. I . . . volunteered."

Max stares at her in bewilderment as heat fills her cheeks. "Okay . . ." he says, frowning. "Well, I don't know what Enzo told you, but I'm fine." He smiles wearily. "As you've probably noticed by now, he likes to be dramatic."

As he walks past her, he's careful to leave some space between them, though not much. He pushes the door to the motor home and holds it open for a moment. "I'd invite you into the actual house, but it's a mess." He motions for her to follow him, but she stays put.

"I'm good here." Adri wants to keep her eyes on Eva. And off of him.

"Should I put a shirt on, then?"

Her face blooms with color. "Do whatever you want," she snaps.

She waits as he drops Eva's picture on the dining table and pulls on a T-shirt before meeting her outside again. "I can always count on Enzo to blow things out of proportion." His annoyed expression gives way to exasperation. "I honestly just got tired of talking about Gemma Stone."

Adri frowns. "Skye said you decided not to train her."

He nods. "I'm not interested in coaching anyone. Even her. Skye and Enzo can't seem to comprehend that."

Adri keeps her face smooth as he talks, but, truthfully, she's relieved. Gemma's interest in Max bothers her more than she wants to admit.

"So . . . you came all the way out here just to check on me?" He throws her a lightly skeptical look, and her nerves resurface again.

"No," she says, sighing. "I wanted to talk about Saturday too." Of course, she didn't *want* to, but she knows she needs to.

Max raises an eyebrow. "Really? I figured that was one of those things we'd just pretend never happened and ignore forever."

She laughs bleakly. "I actually considered that, but I'm trying to be more mature."

He makes a sound somewhere between a scoff and a laugh. "Yeah? Well, you were acting very *mature* at Coralou's. Especially on the dance floor."

She blushes again at his teasing tone. She wants to be defensive as he scowls down at her, but she catches a glimpse of something underneath his cool exterior—the gentler part of him, the part that she could still hurt—and her annoyance fades. "I'm sorry for sending mixed signals on Saturday," she says, forcing the words out. "Obviously, you were right when you said that I don't know what I want all the time." She bites her lip, still embarrassed to admit it. "And that made me mad."

"Mad enough to go home with Enzo?"

She narrows her eyes. She can tell from his tone that he knows she didn't, but he wants to get a rise out of her—a small payback, probably. "You're the one who didn't want me to drive, remember? If you would've offered to take me home, I would've gone with *you*." Her heart beats faster as she says it, realizing that she might've done much more.

Max realizes it, too, because his eyes drop to her mouth before she turns away. "What *do* you want, Adri?" he asks exasperatedly. "You say one thing, but your eyes say the exact opposite."

"If you would stop looking at me like that, I could tell you!"

Her outburst surprises him, but Adri can't help it. His magnetism frustrates her, but she's even more frustrated with herself. Even now, she's sending mixed messages.

He raises his hands in surrender. "Just tell me. I'm listening."

She exhales, recalling the questions she's been asking herself ever since she left the church with Roman. What *does* she want now that she has to start over? "I just want my life to be simple. I want to teach classes and save money. I want to take care of Eva." She almost leaves it at that, not wanting to be teased further, but she knows she can't. "And I want to get closer to God." She ignores the surprised look on his face. "As you've probably guessed, I'm going through some stuff, so those are my priorities right now, and I don't need any distractions."

He waits for her to tell him more, but she looks back at him with guarded eyes.

"What kind of *stuff* are you going through?" he asks pointedly.

For one brief, fleeting moment, she considers telling him. There was a time when almost nothing was hidden between them, including their worst mistakes—but, of all people, Max's reaction is the one she dreads the most. "It's just . . . private stuff."

He scowls but doesn't press her. Adri watches as his eyes drift away from hers to Eva, who's still throwing rocks in his creek.

"Anyway . . ." Adri tucks a windblown strand of hair behind her ear. "I just wanted to let you know where I'm at. It seemed like the mature thing to do. I just don't want any—"

"Distractions," he says flatly, with a slight sigh. "Got it." He ticks her list off with his fingers. "Teach, save money, take care of Eva, and be more religious."

Adri nods, surprised by his gentler tone.

"Well, I can really only help you with one of those things. Do you like working at the gym?"

She nods again. "I do."

"Good. Everyone likes you."

She smiles at the unexpected compliment, but his face is strangely serious. Without another word, he turns and disappears into the motor home again, leaving Adri standing in the warm evening air. She wonders if she upset him, but then he reappears with a few slices of bread. He motions for her to walk with him toward the creek. "It's stale," he says matter-of-factly, walking in step with her. "Eva can feed it to the geese before you go."

She watches from a distance as he shares the slices with Eva. The two of them toss pieces into the water, and white-necked snow geese fight over the bread, honking indignantly and flapping their dark-tipped wings. Adri smiles at the sound of Eva's laugher when Max honks back, though the sight and sound of them laughing together makes her heart feel strangely tight; Danny used to do the same thing.

Max leaves Eva to finish throwing the bread and stands beside her again. "You're not going to run away again, right?"

The question surprises her, and it hurts coming from Max—but it's fair. She ran away when her life was easy, so why wouldn't she run away now that it's hard?

She shakes her head. "No. I think I'm done running."

7

"ONE HUNDRED AND NINETY-SEVEN SINGLES," Skye says, clicking her stopwatch. "In a minute."

Adri drops her jump rope and catches her breath.

Skye grins. "You beat Enzo's record."

Adri cheers. It's already April, which means she's been training at the gym for almost three months now, and with Skye's help, she's only five pounds below her old fighting weight. Enzo says she's giving him a run for his money, and Roman can't hide his delight. All three of them want her to fight in the upcoming Combat House event at the gym. It's only a month away.

"You should do it, kiddo," Roman said, when they passed a flyer in Bluebird's. Skye had posted them all over Sparta.

Adri balked. "I don't know. . . . I don't really feel like embarrassing myself just yet."

"Why not?" Roman said. "I do it all the time."

She'd laughed but still shrugged the idea away. Combat House was a decent-size promotion, which meant she might get matched up with a real professional.

"You know what I think," Roman said, still trying to convince her. "Always better to go down swinging than give up while you're on your feet."

"Hey, can you guys help me with something?"

Enzo's voice brings Adri back to the present as he beckons her and Skye to the ring.

"I want to try something with my beginners," he explains, positioning them in the center. "Adri, you know judo. Kouchi Gari?"

She frowns. She hasn't practiced judo in years. "Is that . . . pulling someone in to take out their ankle?"

Enzo snaps his fingers. "Exactly. I want to show the boys how to do it, but with a soft landing." He places one hand near Adri's neck, then the other on her opposite arm. "I'll go slow. Roll back, okay?"

Adri nods, vaguely understanding, while Skye steps back to watch. Enzo pulls Adri toward him, then presses his foot against her ankle, breaking her balance. As she falls, she curls her body slightly and hits the mat with a loud but painless thud. Enzo lands with her, though he expertly stops his body from slamming into hers.

"Good, right? Didn't hurt?"

Adri nods.

Enzo motions to Skye. "You two try it. You probably weigh around the same."

Her face wary, Skye stands in front of Adri. She tenses up when Adri grabs her and repeats Enzo's movements, and she goes down harder, despite Adri's efforts to be careful. She looks up from the ground, slightly winded.

"See, that's why I prefer boxing," she says when Adri helps her up. "If you hit the mat, it's because you're already unconscious."

She and Adri continue practicing, tweaking things at Enzo's instruction, until they're moving seamlessly and laughing as they take turns. Soon, they add in light punches, both of them easily dodging what the other throws.

Enzo watches with an amused expression. "Maybe you two should should fight each other at the match."

"Is that your fantasy?" Skye asks teasingly.

Enzo laughs, though his cheeks redden. "Hey, a man could have worse fantasies."

Adri and Skye eventually move on from judo to boxing at Skye's request, while Enzo referees. Adri doesn't realize people are watching them until someone cheers for her. She turns and sees a few students have gathered near the ring. Max is watching too.

"Look out, Adri!" Enzo yells, as Adri barely blocks a good hook from Skye.

"Why'd you tell her?" Skye complains. "I was finally going to land one!"

"She got distracted," Enzo says, glancing at Max.

Adri scowls.

"Oh," Skye says, noticing the curious onlookers too. She smiles sheepishly, then shrugs, before turning back to Adri. "I don't mind if you don't. Finish the round?"

Adri's self-consciousness grows, especially since boxing is Skye's forte. But her uncle's words come to mind again: *Better to go down swinging than give up while you're on your feet.*

She exhales. "Sure. Finish the round."

They tap gloves and resume, this time with Skye fighting harder, throwing faster punches. Adri matches her pace but slips up, and Skye's glove makes contact with her chin. She lands a good strike to Adri's torso, no longer holding back, and Adri winces at the small burst of pain. A few people gasp while others cheer.

Skye throws a quick hook, but this time Adri ducks and lands her own hook into Skye's side, surprising Skye—and everyone else—when Skye stumbles backward. More gasps and excited murmurings come from the small audience, but Max steps toward the ring and says something to Enzo, who moves between Adri and Skye before Skye can retaliate.

"Let's call it a tie, shall we?" He glances at the wide-eyed elementary schoolers staring at Skye and Adri. "Miss Skye and Miss Adri both did great, didn't they?"

They clap, but Skye continues to scowl, still caught up in the moment.

Adri lightly punches her arm. "Don't worry. You won that round."

Her face softens. "Well, we can have a rematch sometime."

"Skye," Max says, getting her attention. "I think your students are ready for you."

Skye's cheeks redden. "Sorry." She gathers the children, and the gym grows quiet as she and Enzo lead them away. Adri pulls off her gloves and starts to unwrap her hands, but she stops when she feels Max's eyes on her. When she looks up, he's leaning against the ropes.

"Did you decide if you're fighting in Combat House?"

She frowns, surprised. Enzo must've told him that she was considering it. "I'm still thinking about it."

He watches with narrowed eyes as she drops her hand wraps into two tangled piles. "Here," he says, extending his hand. "Give me those."

She laughs as she hands them over. "Sorry. I forgot that drives you crazy."

He doesn't respond, too engrossed in undoing her work and properly rerolling them into neat little bundles. "They'll last longer if you do it the right way. And they take up less space."

Adri laughs at his teacherly tone. "I know, I know. You and Roman never let me get away with it."

He smiles faintly. "There," he says, finishing.

"Thanks." Adri tries but fails to ignore the brush of his fingertips as he hands them back to her.

"Anyway . . ." He clears his throat and leans against the ropes again. "You've been training a lot."

The comment surprises her. They haven't talked much since she and Eva went to his house, aside from hellos and small talk, but she's been sparring with Skye more often lately, and apparently he'd noticed. She watches as his eyes fall to the boxing gloves by her feet—the same worn-out pair she wore in high school. He used to tease her about the cracked, flaking leather, but Adri insisted on keeping them. Roman would've bought her brand-new ones, but she liked the familiar way they hugged her hands.

"You never told me why you quit fighting."

She stiffens. Another surprising question. "You never told me why you quit fighting either," she says, deflecting.

He shrugs. "Three years was long enough."

She nods, although she knows Danny's death had something to do with it too—but she doesn't want to be pressed about her own unexpected departure from the fighting world, so she drops it. She takes a small step, intending to leave the ring, but Max stops her.

"No, see, now you tell me why you quit." He smiles. "That's how a conversation works."

Her heart races as she tries to think of an answer that doesn't include Owen. "I quit when I got pregnant with Eva," she says, glancing at the ground.

He nods, but his eyes are skeptical for obvious reasons. Plenty of fighters become mothers. It's an uphill battle, but it can be done, and Adri loved fighting enough that she could've done it—if Owen hadn't stopped her. If she hadn't let him.

"Do you miss it?" Max asks.

She crosses her arms, hugging her gloves against her chest like a shield. His tone is light, but she can tell that he's trying to dig beneath the surface. Ever since she mentioned her "private stuff" at his house, she's noticed a deeper look of concern in his eyes whenever they meet hers.

"Sometimes," she says, lying. The truth is, she misses it all the time—but it doesn't matter. "I'm going to go set up now," she says quietly.

He takes the hint and moves out of her way.

Adri tries to focus as she teaches, but Max's questions nag at her for the rest of the afternoon. She thought she buried her passion for fighting a long time ago, but lately it has been harder to ignore. She told herself over and over again that it was futile, that she threw away ten years of training for six years of failure, but that doesn't make any difference. She still feels the fire.

Later, as she's packing up to leave, she notices a light on in Max's office. She steps inside, intending to turn it off and leave, but she pauses to look at one of his photos for a moment. Danny Lyons looks around the age he was when Adri first met him as he smiles for the camera, showing all of his teeth. Like Max, he has dark hair and strong, handsome features, and young Max stands beside him, smiling more shyly than his father.

Adri stares at their faces with a sinking feeling in her stomach. Max grew up without a mother too—a commonality that cemented their unusual friendship. His mom died shortly after he was born, unlike Adri's, who'd abandoned her, but they'd been fortunate. Adri had Dalila, who was better than any mother she ever met, and Dalila loved Max like he was her own son.

"Adri?"

She jumps. Whipping around, she finds Max standing in the doorway. She realizes how odd she must look, standing in his office, gawking at the photos on his desk. "I thought you left after your class," she says lamely, as if that would explain her presence.

"I was working out."

Her eyes fall to the damp shirt molded to his body. Her cheeks burn.

He frowns. "What are you doing in here?"

"I was just turning off the light, but then . . ." She tears her eyes off of him and motions to the photo. "I hadn't noticed this one before. Of Danny."

He relaxes slightly, although his voice still holds an edge of uncertainty. "Yeah, Skye has been bugging me to clean my desk for a while." He throws her a questioning look, but Adri glances at another photo on the wall, the one of his final fight. Owen left the apartment to watch it with his drinking buddies, but she stayed behind with Eva and kept the television turned off. She heard later that it was one of the fastest finishes in MMA history, and that made her happy and jealous at the same time. It was the kind of fight that made someone a legend.

"Do you ever miss fighting?" she asks, her own curiosity taking over.

"Sometimes," he says, repeating her own cryptic answer from

earlier that afternoon. He smiles wearily. "But I've got some scars I can look at if I need to reminisce."

A long, loaded silence follows, and they both know why. Adri was always the one who wanted to fight professionally. Max wanted to coach; fighting was never his dream the way it was Adri's. The irony of the conversation isn't lost on either of them.

"Did Danny get to see it?" she asks.

"See what?"

"Your last fight." Her heart plummets when Max shakes his head.

"No," he says sadly. "He died two weeks before it."

"I'm . . . sorry." She wants to say something better, but that's all that comes out. She's sorry for Max's pain, but she's even more sorry for herself—that she didn't get to say good-bye. "I'm sorry I wasn't at the funeral."

Max's eyes darken, and, for a moment, he looks like he wants to be angry with her, but he doesn't say anything harsh. He just shrugs. "You had your own life, right?"

Her breath catches in her throat. Something about the way he says it pierces her heart, and she wants to apologize again—for more—but he moves out of the doorway, giving her space to pass. She blinks at the abrupt dismissal.

"I'll get the lights when I leave," he says quietly.

"Okay." She slips by him, embarrassed but thankful for the escape. "Good night." She almost makes it down the hallway when she hears him curse softly.

"Adri, hold on. Wait a second."

She turns around slowly, bracing herself for something, though she doesn't know what. "Yeah?"

"You do miss fighting, don't you?"

She exhales. Max, like Roman, knows her too well. "Yeah." She shrugs. "I do. But it doesn't matter."

"Fight in Combat House."

She shakes her head. "Do you actually think I can win?"

"It depends on who you end up fighting."

106

She laughs cheerlessly. It stings, but she appreciates his honesty.

"Winning doesn't really matter that much, though, does it? Just fight. Even if you lose." He shrugs again. "If you love it, it's worth the risk."

Adri thinks for a long moment as her heart and mind war against each other. Finally, she nods. "I'll let you know what I decide."

8

S KYE CHATS WITH MAX as kids file into the classroom, most of them already wearing their gloves and mouth guards. Eva, dropped off by Yvonne, enters the room and waves at both of them. Max waves back before focusing on Skye again, listening as she fills him in on all the last-minute details surrounding the fight—now only two days away.

"Enzo just confirmed that Louie Garza is bringing his food truck, so that's all set. And the fighters have their entrance times . . ."

Skye's face is slightly downcast as she speaks, and Max feels a twinge of guilt. Hosting the fight turned out to be more work than Enzo initially thought, so Skye had to forfeit her place in the lineup to help him. But she'd taken the disappointment like a champ.

"Oh, and the after party will be at Roman Rivera's house," she adds, perking up a bit. "He said he'll take care of everything for that."

Max raises a surprised eyebrow. Since Dalila's death, Roman hasn't been nearly as social as he used to be, but he suspects Adri's decision has something to do with breaking him out of his shell. Ever since she announced that she would fight again, Max could feel a buzz in Sparta. He knows Adri must feel it too, because he's never seen her train harder. He gave her the afternoon off, hoping she might rest, but instead she went to the track to run.

"Max!"

He turns just as Enzo is closing the classroom door with a loud click. His face is tense. "Woah, dude." Max frowns. "Why do you look so freaked out right now?"

Enzo doesn't reply. He's too busy scanning the room until his eyes fall on Eva.

"What, Enzo?" Max says, his concern growing. "Use words."

"Someone's here," Enzo says, finally addressing him again. "I've never seen him before." He lowers his voice to a whisper. "He says he's Adri's husband."

For a second, Max wonders if he misheard him. "Sorry, what?"

"I don't know. He says he's her husband," Enzo repeats. "And he wants to pick up Eva. I don't like his vibe. Owen something."

Max feels like he's been dunked in cold water. "He . . . what? He wants Eva?" A fierce protectiveness fills him as he glances at her. Thankfully, she's too busy playing with friends to notice.

"What should I tell him?" Enzo asks, looking at the door again. They both knew there was a good chance that Owen might burst through it at any moment.

"I'll talk to him. Wait here and keep them busy. Especially Eva." Max leaves quickly, locking the door behind him, and searches the gym until he spots an unfamiliar tall man dressed in black jeans and a black sweatshirt. The man meets Max's gaze with cold, challenging eyes, confirming his suspicion. Max walks toward him, ignoring the curious glances of parents lingering in the gym.

"Where's my daughter?" the man demands as Max gets closer.

"Sorry, who are you?"

"I already told the other guy," he snaps, already irate. "Owen Anders. Eva Anders is my daughter."

Max forces himself to speak calmly, even though the sight of Owen makes him want to smash something. He never thought they'd actually stand face to face. "Sorry. We don't have an Eva Anders here."

Owen narrows his eyes. "Rivera, then, or whatever you call her. She's my daughter, and I want her."

Max frowns. Owen's eyes are dull, and he looks ready to throw a punch. He recalls the man Linc described—the disgraced fighter, always hungry for blood. "You're Adri's husband?"

"That's right," he says mockingly. "And you're her boss, right?"

Max stiffens. Why would he know that? Did Adri tell him? Based on the way Owen's eyes dart around the gym, he seriously doubts it. Max never bought Adri's story about him "traveling" for work. He crosses his arms but keeps them poised for action. "Adri didn't list you as an emergency contact, so I can't let Eva go with you."

"Cut the crap, Lyons. She's my kid."

"I believe you," Max says flatly, noting the blue eyes. Unlike Owen's, Eva's are warm and innocent, but they're unmistakably related. "But Eva still can't go with you."

Owen takes a menacing step toward him. "You're not really going to try to keep my kid away from me, are you?"

"I'm not going to *try* anything." Max gives Owen a look of warning while noting the short distance between them now. "Because you're not going anywhere near Eva until Adri tells me otherwise." He nods toward the door and prays that Owen picks that option. He doubts Adri would appreciate him brawling with her husband in front of their students. "Thanks for stopping by, though."

Owen glares at him, his expression a mix of surprise and red-hot hatred as he reaches for Max, but Max shoves him, sending him backward. Somewhere behind them, a woman gasps.

"You've got about ten seconds to get out of here before I call the cops," Max says, closing the distance between them, ready to do more if necessary. Now that Owen stands before him, Max remembers more stories of "The Hammer," known for his explosive punches. Owen Anders was the type of fighter who actually wanted to hurt his opponents—or worse. Max rejected that approach to fighting, but with Owen, he was more than willing to embrace it. "Don't make me do that in front of Eva."

Owen looks like he's going to throw another punch, and Max almost wants him to, but the onlookers deter Owen. One woman is already pressing buttons on her cellphone. Begrudgingly, he gives Max one last long, hate-filled look. "You're lucky, Lyons."

Max raises his eyebrows. "Am I?"

"Yeah, but you won't be forever." Owen takes a step toward the door but pauses. "Next time you see Adri, tell her I'm not signing her papers."

Max is silent, but his heart races at the look in Owen's eyes. It's a look he recognizes—a kind of deadly determination.

Owen smirks confidently. "Tell her she's not going to win this one."

A sprinkling of May rain on the railroad tracks makes everything glisten in the midafternoon sun as Adri runs deeper into the trees. Her body relaxes despite her fatigue. Max let her off early, and a few hours in the woods were just what she needed. She's been on edge ever since she made the decision to fight again, especially after she learned she'd be matched up with Raquel "Hacksaw" Reid—a young, hungry fighter known for speedy finishes. Also weighing heavily on her mind were the divorce papers that she'd mustered up the courage to send a few days earlier.

She exhales. Her thoughts drift to Owen less often now, and that feels like progress, but her heart is still a tangled mess of the past and present. Sometimes she misses him, sometimes she hates him, and other times she feels nothing whatsoever. She suspects Max's presence has something to do with that—the more she's around him, the more Owen's grasp on her seems to loosen—but that frustrates her too. As tempting as it is to give in to those feelings, she knows that running from one man into the arms of another won't miraculously solve all her problems. She needs to learn to stand on her two feet.

She continues her run, but she slows down when she almost trips on something in the soft ground. Curious, she bends down to take a closer look at the small twisted piece of metal. When she realizes what it is, her mouth parts. She starts digging around the damp earth with her fingers until she loosens the railroad spike, then she uses it to dig deeper until she finds what she's looking for. Finally, her fingertips brush against something cold and smooth.

Stunned, Adri stares at the dirt-smudged coffee canister that she and Max buried almost ten years earlier, marked only by the twisted spike she holds in her hand. Inside the canister, a plastic bag protects two pieces of notebook paper. She carefully opens the bag and retrieves the notes. She recognizes Max's neat, all-caps handwriting on one. She looks at the other and sees her own. She sits down, careful to protect the papers from the drizzling rain, and reads Max's note first. *Learn from Grandmaster Yaggi. Teach MMA. Buy a Ford F350. Get Married, Have 2 Kids. Be Mayor of Sparta.*

Adri smiles at the goals he wrote down when they were sixteen, unsurprised by their practicality. She laughs at the last one, which is written in her handwriting instead of his. When they were teens, she teased him constantly about his popularity.

She turns to her own list next. *Earn a National Strawweight Championship Title. Live in California (or Hawaii). Travel the world. Finally beat Max at Scrabble. (Good luck with this one, loser).*

Adri laughs again at the last part, written by Max, but tears fill her eyes as she rereads the rest of her discarded dreams. She knew no limits back then, and she expected to do everything on that list and much more. As she stares at the note, regret fills her. But, just as quickly, a Bible verse she memorized comes to mind: *Therefore, if anyone is in Christ, he is a new creation. The old has passed away; behold, the new has come.*

More and more, she can remember what she's read in the Bible, and the words have a calming effect on her thoughts. She reads the notes one more time, amazed at how perfectly preserved they are despite spending ten years underground. Unsure of what else to do with them, she puts them back in the coffee can and takes the capsule with her.

Later, she finishes her run and slides into an old weather-beaten Honda Civic—a recent purchase, thanks to her first batch of savings and a small loan from Roman. She finds her phone in the glove compartment and glances at it. Her eyes widen. Eight calls from Roman and eleven from Max. She looks at her text messages, all from Max, telling her to call him immediately. She calls him, but Enzo answers.

"Adri! Thank God. Max was just about to go find you."

"What? Why?" Her mind races with possibilities as she turns the key in the ignition. "Is Eva okay?"

"No, yeah, Eva's fine." Enzo sounds breathless. "Roman just picked her up."

She frowns. "Why? What's—"

"Max wants you to come back now. Are you alone?"

"*Why?*" Adri asks again, her frustration rising. "Yes, I'm alone. I'm still at the tracks. What's happening?"

He falls silent.

"Tell me what's going on, Enzo," she asks again, annoyed and increasingly concerned at the same time.

"Your husband came to the gym."

This time Adri is the silent one. The thought of him in Sparta makes her feel lightheaded.

"He wanted Eva."

"*What?*" Her skin turns cold despite the sweat dampening her hair and clothes. "I . . . how? How did he know she was there?"

"We don't know. You didn't tell him?"

"No! He . . ." She struggles to catch her breath as her panic sinks in. "No. . . ."

"Max didn't let him take Eva, Adri," Enzo says, trying but failing to calm her down. "She's safe, I promise. Come to the gym, and we'll figure it all out. You shouldn't be out there by yourself right now."

When they hang up, Adri punches the gas. She flies down the

winding roads, undeterred by the rain slapping her windshield. Her body is moving instinctively despite her mind's temporary paralysis. The same thought repeats over and again, chilling her.

Owen found us.

When she rushes into the gym, Skye meets her with tear-filled eyes. Adri's about to ask where Max is, but she doesn't need to. His hand closes lightly around her wrist.

"Come with me."

Adri inhales sharply. She's not used to hearing so much uneasiness in his voice. She follows him, and Max shuts the door behind them. When they're alone, he drags a hand through his hair. "As soon as I let him leave the gym, I kicked myself," he says, cursing softly. His expression is a mix of anger and concern, but his face softens with relief the longer he looks at her. "Thank God you're okay."

Adri nods, but she feels unsteady on her feet. Obviously, Max feared for her safety, but she isn't thinking about that. She's thinking about Eva and just how close she'd come to losing her. Max was the only person who stood between Owen and his plan.

He frowns as she draws a shaky breath. "Do you want to sit down?" When she nods again, he guides her to his chair and waits until she's sitting before he tells her the full story. "Roman said to tell you not to worry about Eva," he adds, noting the fearful look in her eyes. "Sheriff Shepson is at the house."

She sinks farther into his chair, still reeling. "Did Eva see Owen?"

"No. None of the kids did."

"Did any parents see him?"

Max frowns. "Yeah. A few. When I was . . . talking to him."

Adri lets out a dismal sigh. Even though Eva didn't see Owen, Spartans will undoubtedly gossip about Max's heated encounter with him, so Eva will likely still hear about his appearance from the other girls at the gym. Adri is already dreading her inevitable questions.

"And there's something else. . . ."

Adri looks up sharply. "What? What else?"

"Before Owen left, he . . ."

She can see that Max doesn't want to add to her worries, but she doesn't let him off the hook. "What, Max? What did he say?"

He sighs. "He told me to tell you that he's not signing your papers."

Her heart sinks heavily inside her chest. Of course—she should've known Owen wouldn't make any part of this easy. The papers are probably what pushed him over the edge and made him decide to show up in Sparta. Her eyes fall to her hands, which are clasped in her lap. She hears Max clear his throat somewhere above her.

"Divorce papers?"

She nods but quickly covers her face with her hands. He kneels in front of her, and when their faces are level, he gently pulls her hands down. The knowing look in his eyes brings tears to the surface.

"Adri, it's time to tell me what's really going on." One of her tears falls and hits his knuckle. "Because I already have a pretty good idea."

She turns her face away from his, filled with shame. "I left him."

"That's why you came back to Sparta?"

She nods, fighting back a heavy wave of regret. "He's an alcoholic," she says quickly, hoping that will be enough, but Max waits for more. She looks at him through her tears, and he looks back, straight into her eyes.

"Did he hurt you?"

Her heart breaks all over again. It's clear from the look on his face that he wants her to say no, but she can't. "Yes." She says the word so softly that she barely hears it.

Max's eyes darken like thunderclouds as more tears roll down her cheeks. "How long?" he asks.

She stifles a sob.

"How long, Adri?"

"Since the beginning," she chokes, remembering the exact moment she'd realized her mistakes—a few months into her hasty marriage. She and Owen were bickering all the time, so she tried to "fix" it with him by hiring a babysitter, making an elaborate meal, and forcing herself into some expensive lingerie. Despite her efforts, the evening ended with a dark blue-black bruise around her right eye.

She already knows what Max's next question will be, and she already hates her answer.

"*Why?* Why did you stay with him?"

"I . . ." She sighs, knowing he can't understand no matter how much he wants to. She barely understands it herself. "It's hard to explain," she says, her voice coming out in broken pieces. "I thought I loved him." At some point, he might've loved her too. Or he thought he did, at least. But it sounds so stupid when she considers how much it cost.

"I don't understand why you stayed with him for so long," Max says, trying but failing to keep the frustration out of his voice. "You could've left—"

"I was *going* to leave him," she snaps, fresh waves of regret crashing over her. "But we have a child. I thought I could fix him. I thought I was helping her."

Max opens his mouth to say something, then closes it. She knows what he's thinking—that she of all people should've known she couldn't fix Owen. She watched her own mother try and fail to fix someone for years.

"It wasn't *always* bad," she says, trying to justify it. The wounded look in his eyes makes her want to make it make sense, even though she knows she can't. "It was okay until he started drinking more and losing more fights and losing more money and . . ."

She exhales, remembering the darkest years of her life—when Owen fell apart and took her down with him. "He promised he would change, and he made it seem like he could, but he didn't. It was a mistake, okay? One mistake, then another, and then a million more. And *yes*, I fought back." She gives him a fierce look, aware that he probably wondered about that. "I fought him so many times, but I couldn't make him stop, and then . . ." She trails off, unable to find the words he wants to hear. "I just thought it was too late to leave. I thought I'd made too many mistakes."

"I would've helped you, Adri. You know that."

"You really don't understand why I didn't call *you*?" She's filled with more regret as she remembers the last words she said to him in Miami. Max was her last chance to get away, the answer to prayers she hadn't even prayed yet—and she'd sent him away.

He frowns. "Why? Because of that day in Miami?" He shakes his head. "Adri, you really think that would've stopped me from driving back there and killing him if I—"

"It doesn't matter now!" she yells, cutting him off, unwilling to think about how much that one decision cost her. "That was another mistake, okay? Sending you away was a mistake. And I live with it, like all the rest." She rises and starts to turn from him, but he gently catches her arm and pulls her back. She half-heartedly tries to break free. "Let go, Max. Please."

He loosens his fingers but doesn't let go of her completely. "Why are you still running from me?"

Adri's heart breaks. He sounds hurt, which is the last thing Adri wants. No doubt he thinks she's comparing him to Owen, which is the last thing she would ever do. There's no comparison between the two. But she can't spend another moment in his arms. "Please. I need to go see Eva."

Sighing, he releases her, and her footsteps echo in the empty hallway, matching the wild beat of her heart. She can't believe that just a few hours ago she was running in the woods, dreaming about her upcoming fight. Now, thanks to Owen, that short-lived dream turned into a nightmare.

Now, instead of fighting, she wants to flee.

9

ARLY MORNING MIST SETTLES OVER THE CITY, blurring
the mountain peaks from the few Spartans who woke up
early enough on a Saturday to catch the sunrise. Max stands
on his dad's back deck, listening to the distant sound of a rumbling train.

He scowls at the trees. In a few hours, people will pour into
his gym, wanting to socialize and be entertained, and he's in no
mood for either. He'd cancelled classes so Enzo and Skye could
spend the day preparing for the big fight tonight, so he has nothing to distract himself with. His mind wanders to Adri and the
conversation they had after Owen's surprise drop-in.

*"Sending you away was a mistake. I live with it, just like the
rest."*

He wonders what he should've said to that, or if it even matters
now that silence has filled the gap.

Owen disappeared as quickly as he came. As soon as he left the
gym, Max finally gave in and searched for *Owen Anders* on the
internet, and what he found filled him with an even deeper hatred.
Story after story and picture after picture of him partying were
intermixed with brutal, bloody fights and scandals. Adri was in
a few, either tightly holding onto Owen's arm in a sea of people

or standing far-off with a tense expression while he weighed in or squared up. One headline punched him in the gut.

Rivera Promises a Comeback after Anders's Second Relapse. Critics Are Doubtful.

He grits his teeth as Owen's face flashes before his eyes, wishing he hadn't let him go. If he ever gets a second chance, Max won't make that mistake again.

As the low roar of the train fills his ears, he closes his eyes, annoyed that everything reminds him of Adri—even his dad's creaky old deck. He can't help but remember the times he and Adri sat out here, talking and laughing and kissing until her curfew. His own dad was never much a of rule-maker, but Roman was, which was good because they needed them.

Once, after one of Max's tournaments, he and Adri had sat together on a pile of pillows, looking up at the stars. His father was supposed to be supervising, but he was off with buddies, leaving him and Adri to their own devices. Roman would have been furious.

Adri had gently touched his bandaged shoulder. "Does it hurt really bad?"

"Of course it hurts, Adri," he'd said indignantly, making her laugh. "How could a dislocated shoulder not hurt?"

"Yeah, it must, because you're extra snappy tonight," she said, giggling harder.

He smiled weakly. At least one of them was having a good time. "Sorry. I'm just tired." He winced. "And in pain."

"And you hate losing."

He sighed.

"I wish there was something I could do to make you feel better."

His pulse quickened. Her voice sounded so strange—bold and unsure at the same time—but for once Max didn't overthink it. Adri had a way of making him do that. She would say something flirtatious enough to make his blood go hot, but then she'd look up at him with a maddeningly innocent expression, as if he'd just imagined it.

She'd told him after their first kiss by the tracks that she was worried romance would mess up their friendship, but that night, Max stopped worrying. He kissed her again and again and again, until they lost count. Kissing was the one thing that Max was better at than she was, and he loved—and hated—hearing the small breathless sigh she made right before she pulled her lips away from his.

"I have to go," she'd say, her face still buried against his chest. "I don't want to, but I have to."

Max sighs. He should've gotten used to her leaving, but he never did.

Suddenly, he hears gravel crunching under tires, and his head turns sharply in that direction. A car door slams in his driveway. He frowns. "Enzo?"

Enzo grins back at him. He looks like he just rolled out of bed, with half of his hair matted on one side while the other springs up wildly. He's carrying a paper bag and two coffees. "I thought you might be up."

Max stares at him. "What are you doing here?"

He holds up the coffees. "It's a special occasion."

"It is?"

"Yep." Enzo joins him on the deck and settles into an old lawn chair. "It's almost time for Combat House. Ready for the festivities?"

Max sits down in the opposite chair as Enzo hands him a coffee. "You tell me."

"You're going to love it. Lots of hype and pumped-up Spartans and randos from other cities gawking at you. Your favorite."

Max laughs bleakly at the accurate description and watches as Enzo pulls a bagel out of the bag and slathers both halves with cream cheese. He slides one to Max.

"Seriously, though, I'm proud of you," Enzo says, taking a bite. "For once, you weren't a total control freak. That must've been really hard for you."

Max eyes the bagel warily. "You shouldn't eat that crap."

"Why?" Enzo demands, taking another defiant bite. "I work out three times a day." He nods to the untouched half. "What's your excuse? You work out more than I do. Live a little."

"Nah, I'm good."

"Good, because I didn't really want to share it with you anyway."

Max laughs again, and his mood lightens slightly. Enzo's endless cheerfulness usually grates on his nerves, but sometimes he's grateful for a break from his own dark thoughts. He would never say it out loud, but he needs a friend like Enzo. Still, though, he knows that his early-morning visit means something is wrong. "So . . . what's up?"

"I was just doing some last-minute stuff for tonight." Enzo shrugs casually. "Thought I'd stop by."

Max smirks.

"What, a guy can't visit his buddy?"

"You wouldn't drive all the way out here for nothing. You like your beauty sleep too much."

"See, that's your problem. You're too suspicious."

"Just tell me, dude. It is about Adri?" Max braces himself, knowing it must be. With him, she keeps her distance, but he knows she's different with Skye and Enzo. He ignores a twinge of envy.

"Fine. No small talk, then." Enzo sighs. "We'll do it your way. Have you talked to her since . . . the *thing*?"

"No, not since Thursday." She didn't come to the gym on Friday to teach or to train. Max took over her classes. He watches as Enzo chews thoughtfully, clearly weighing out his words.

"Well, I guess Skye talked to her last night at Bluebird's. It sounds like she's fine, but you know Adri." He frowns. "She keeps her cards kind of close."

Max nods, waiting for more information. He frowns as Enzo's eyes fall to the ground.

"I guess . . . she's thinking about taking Eva and leaving town."

Max doesn't respond, but frustration bubbles beneath the surface.

"That's the impression she gave Skye, at least."

Max exhales. His first impulse is to drive to Roman's house and change her mind. His second is to break something. He remembers the words she said only a few months ago.

"I'm done running."

His feelings war within him—anger at Owen, frustration with Adri, and something else, something he doesn't want to feel again. He'd told himself he wouldn't let her break his heart a second time.

"Anyway, I thought I should tell you since you guys have a—how should I say?—*unique* relationship."

Max narrows his eyes. Enzo looks at him like he's a bomb about to go off, but Max feigns indifference. "I'll have to find another instructor, then. But we managed before Adri, didn't we?"

Enzo looks unconvinced. "You never told me the story between you and her."

Max shrugs, hoping to drop it. "It's not much of a story. She hasn't told Skye?"

"Nope. She's a closed book." He smiles tiredly. "You have that in common."

Max crushes the lid to his coffee cup. "We were friends for a long time. Then we got older, and we . . . felt more." He frowns, remembering Adri's uncertainties. "I did, at least."

"I don't blame you, man. She's beautiful."

Max sighs. "We were young, so I was just going to wait and let her figure out what she wanted."

"And then she left?"

He nods, ignoring the tight feeling in his chest. "Yep. She left for her first semi-pro fight in Miami. A couple months later, I found her, and she was already living with Owen. Then she married him." He laughs bitterly, remembering the day that Roman told him. Of all his many injuries, that was the one that hurt the most. "Not exactly a great love story, is it?"

"Yeah, dude." Enzo grimaces. "That story sucks."

"Told you."

"But what's the story now?"

Max glances at him. "Huh? What do you mean?"

"Now that she's back in Sparta and getting a divorce." Enzo wiggles his eyebrows knowingly. "That sounds like it could be a pretty good story."

Max shakes his head. "It's not that simple." He'd be lying if he said he wasn't happy that Adri was divorcing Owen, but he won't let himself think beyond that. There's no point.

"What's so complicated?"

Frustration mounting, Max tosses his mangled lid in a nearby trash can. He's been asking himself the same question for months, and the answer still eludes him. "I don't know, Enzo. Neither of us knows what we want, I guess. At least not with each other."

"You don't care about her anymore?"

"Of course I care about her," Max says sharply, annoyed that Enzo has him talking about feelings he spends most of his time ignoring. "I'm just saying, she and I can't just pick up where we left off. There's too much baggage. And besides, if she's leaving again, there's no reas—"

"What if she doesn't leave, though? What if she stays?"

"So? That's another big question mark, isn't it?" Max shakes his head, wishing he could read her mind. "I don't know what she wants. I don't think she even knows, honestly." He remembers her list from a few months ago and frowns. She'd made it pretty clear that a new relationship wasn't on it.

"Dude, I've never seen you hung up on any girl. Not a single one." Enzo smiles faintly. "Except her."

Max is silent. He wants to deny it, but he can't.

"Maybe you both want the same thing."

Max snorts. His patience with Enzo is wearing thin. "Listen to yourself. You sound like one of those talk-show hosts who gives dumb people relationship advice."

Enzo drums his fingers against the metal table. "Well, maybe you're being dumb, and you need some advice."

Max rolls his eyes.

"Think about it, Max. Adri came back to Sparta to start over.

So did you, back when you started the gym. Now you're both here. Maybe you're looking for the same thing."

"We aren't, though," Max says flatly. "She told me what she wanted three months ago." He rattles off Adri's list. "Teach. Save money. Take care of Eva. Get closer to God . . . whatever that means. Aside from giving her a job, there's nothing else I can help her with."

"She told Skye she wants to fight again. Professionally."

Enzo's statement stuns him. "She said that?"

"Yep. When she said she was thinking about leaving, Skye asked her what she would do, and Adri said she wants to fight again. She doesn't think she can do it, but we think she can." He gives Max a pointed look. "With some help."

Max chews his lip, his thoughts racing at Enzo's strange revelation. "And . . . what? You think *I* should coach her or something?" He waits for Enzo to say that's not what he's saying, but he doesn't. Max stares at him. "Seriously? That's kind of a stretch, even for you."

Enzo shrugs innocently. "Like I said, I think you want the same thing that she does. A fresh start."

Max rakes a hand through his hair in frustration. Enzo is talking in circles. "First you tell me Adri's leaving town, and now you're telling me to coach her. Which is it?" Truthfully, he hates the first idea, but the second one strikes him as ridiculous. Does Adri even want his help, or is this just another one of Enzo's crazy ideas?

Enzo laughs at the mystified look on his face. "Look, I have no idea what Adri's going to do, okay? I'm guessing. Maybe she'll leave Sparta and you'll never see her again, or maybe she won't." He sighs and looks past Max for a moment, at the dense, dark trees behind him. "I'm just telling you what I think—which is, if you get the chance to start over with her, I think you should probably take it. For everyone's sake."

Max scowls, but he doesn't argue with him. He wants to shrug off what Enzo's saying, but the words settle under his skin. "Is she still fighting tonight?"

"As far as I know. I heard the girl she's up against is good. She's bringing in a bunch of coaches with her."

"Who's coaching Adri, then? You?"

"No, Skye and I will be too busy." Enzo shakes his head solemnly. "So I guess she'll just have to go it alone. Poor girl."

Max smirks. "Nice. Very subtle."

Enzo grins. "You know subtlety is my specialty."

Roman rests his hand on Eva's shoulder, keeping her close in the thick crowd.

"Wow," Yvonne says, looking at the almost-full gym. Behind them, a line snakes out the door. "Are all these people coming to your house later?"

Roman chuckles. "No, thank goodness. Just the fighters and their coaches. The gal who asked me to host the party said they want it to be an exclusive event."

"Well, aren't you special?"

Roman smiles. "Oh, there she is." He waves at Skye Nolan, who waves back. She looks a little overwhelmed as she talks with officials. A curly-haired young man stands beside her. Roman recognizes him too—Enzo Something. A top-notch judoist with a bit of a reputation.

Eva tugs on Roman's sleeve. "Uncle Roman, where's Mama?"

Roman peers through the crowd, looking toward the hexagonal cage set up in the middle of the room, but he doesn't see Adri. "She's probably warming up," he guesses. She left the house hours earlier, unable to sit still any longer.

They find a small table reserved for them near the cage, and Roman helps Yvonne and Eva into their chairs before settling into his own. All around him, Spartans talk excitedly, their voices trapped by the cinderblock walls. Roman smiles, feeling the familiar thrill of waiting for a fight to start. He stopped going to fights when Adri left.

"Uncle Roman?"

He glances at Eva again, who fidgets in her seat.

"Can I go look for Mama?"

"Sweetie, remember what I told you when we left the house? You have to be patient. She's not fighting until the very end. And fights take a little while." He knows that sitting through three five-minute rounds is a lot to ask of a four year old.

Yvonne's brows crease with concern. "Do you think these fights will be very violent, Roman?"

Roman smiles faintly. A fight by definition is violent, but Yvonne is gentle-hearted, just like Dalila was. He knows she doesn't care for the bloody sport that he and Adri love so much. "I expect they'll be pretty standard, but you never know."

Yvonne glances at Eva again and frowns.

"She'll be fine, Yvonne. Adri was little when I took her to a fight, and she loved it."

"That's because Adri loved everything that you loved." Yvonne smiles as she says it, and Roman smiles back.

Even though Adri isn't really his daughter, they both know she might as well be. Like his father, and his father's father, she was born with a God-given ability to fight. Some fighters, like Max Lyons, learned how to be great with discipline and dedication, but others just had the fire. Roman saw it burning in Adri the moment he met her, which is one of the reasons why he's so proud that she decided to fight again.

Still, he knows Owen's appearance in Sparta rattled her, and the timing couldn't have been worse after she'd made so much progress over the last five months since she arrived. Roman scowls. Another reason to despise the man—as if he didn't have enough already.

"There's Mr. Max! And Mr. Enzo!"

Roman looks up as Eva points toward the cage. When Max glances in their direction, Roman catches his eye. Max nods in acknowledgment.

"He's as popular as ever, isn't he?" Yvonne says, noting the gaggle of young women admiring Max from their front-row seats.

Roman laughs. "And he still couldn't care less." In fact, Max looks like he'd rather be anywhere else than in his own gym. "He's never liked being the center of attention."

"Did he and Adri work things out?" she asks.

"Sometimes I think so. Other times, I'm not so sure." There's obviously something going on between them, but when it comes to Max Lyons, Adri has always been a mystery. Roman could talk with her about fighting for hours, but boys were a totally different subject. He sighs, missing Dalila. She'd know how to help.

The lights dim, and a shaky spotlight lands on the cage, illuminating Max and Enzo. Roman watches as Enzo holds out a microphone to Max, which he takes begrudgingly as Spartans erupt with applause.

"Is it starting?" Eva asks, excited. She stands up in her chair to get a better look.

Roman wonders how Adri must feel. Soon, she'll be in the cage again—for the first time in almost six years—and that thought thrills and worries him at the same time.

Downstairs, in an ancient locker room, Adri pauses from warming up when she hears the distant sound of Max's voice. She listens as his voice fades, replaced by Enzo's, then thumping music, signaling that the first of the night's five fights has begun. More applause shakes the old lockers, and she exhales. She feels a new rush of nerves as reality sets in.

She's going to fight again.

She approaches a cracked, speckled mirror. There are several fights before hers, but she knows from experience that the time passes quickly. She braids her hair before winding it into a tight bun, leaving little for her opponent to grab, then studies her unfamiliar reflection. Owen always preferred her hair down—it was an easy way to hide the bruises on her neck and shoulders. Now, though, up and braided, every angle of her face is revealed. She looks younger and fiercer, which gives her a jolt of confidence.

She changes into a simple black sports bra and matching shorts, paired with her worn combat gloves. She practices—jab, cross, hook, uppercut—finding her rhythm, until she feels her body easing into each movement as memories resurface.

Her last fight was in Orlando. She was only eighteen, and she'd been matched up with a popular but overrated fighter. It was a fight she should've won easily, but after she met Owen, she let her training regime slip.

That, and she and Owen had a fight—one of their first big ones—right before Adri was supposed to walk through the tunnel. Owen was angry because he was on probation for assaulting another fighter's coach, and he didn't think Adri cared enough. He said it was unfair that she was still fighting when he couldn't.

Adri laughs bitterly at the memory. It took years for her to realize how immature he was, despite him being seven years older than her. When she turned to leave her locker room that night, Owen yanked her back and wrapped his hands tightly around her neck. When he let her go, she entered the cage shaking and traumatized, and her opponent pounced.

It was the most humiliating loss of her life.

She tries to push aside the painful memory. She knows there's a real possibility that a younger, fresher fighter might embarrass her tonight, but she keeps her mind on the conversation she had with Yvonne the night before. She met her at Bluebird's and sat patiently while Adri spilled her guts.

Thanks to Owen, she wanted to give up and disappear and save Eva from rumors—something her own mother never did for her. Yvonne sat beside her and stroked her hair as she talked, and then she asked her a surprising question.

"Is that who you are, though, honey?"

"What?"

"Is that who you are?" Yvonne asked again, her voice gentle but firm. "Do you just give up now? Do you let Owen win again? Or do you fight for what you want?"

Adri's heart raced as she considered her answer. For the last six years, she'd been ruled by manipulation and fear, but was that who she had to be? Owen had already taken so much from her—was she really going to let him take more?

Skye knocks on the door to let her know her fight is next. Adri exhales. One last time, she touches the sign taped to her door.

Female Fighter, Strawweight, RIVERA

Adri stares at it, thankful it's not a dream. Moments later, she enters the main gym to incredible applause. She didn't choose a walkout song, letting Skye choose instead, but she can't hear anything over the thundering cheers. She knows Spartans are excited to see her fight again, but she had no idea they cared so much, not until she saw a hundred of them standing on their feet.

The applause continues as an official checks Adri's mouthguard and dabs Vaseline on her nose and cheeks to help prevent potential scrapes and cuts. Adri finally hears the song Skye chose. "Barracuda" plays through the speakers.

Skye grins. "Max said you're a Heart fan."

The song ends when her opponent appears, and Adri swallows.

Raquel "Hacksaw" Reid is barely twenty-two, but she's a head taller than Adri, and her impressive body is clad in royal blue. Spartans boo her entrance, but she dances to thumping electro music, clearly confident. Two bulky coaches trail behind her.

A few tables away, Eva watches anxiously. When she tries to call out to Adri, Roman shushes her.

"No, sweetheart, none of that. Your mom needs to focus now."

Eva looks between him and the cage with wide eyes. "Is she going to win, Uncle Roman?"

"I hope so." Roman hides his worries from Eva, though he senses from the tense look on Adri's face that she's overwhelmed. He doesn't blame her. Her opponent looks tough. "Do you want to pray for her, Eva?"

"I already did."

Roman laughs at her matter-of-fact tone. "Well, what are you worried about, then?"

"Ladies and gentlemen, Spartans and non-Spartans, it's time

for our final fight of the night," Enzo says, speaking smoothly into the microphone, earning another round of cheers. "Your very own Adri 'La Tormenta' Rivera—"

The crowd goes crazy.

"—faces off with Raquel 'Hacksaw' Reid, joining us from Newark, New Jersey. Fighters, please join me in the center of the cage."

Adri meets Raquel in the middle and extends her gloved fist. Raquel quickly thumps it with her own and throws her a smirk, and the fight begins. Spartans cheer as they move around one another, Adri moving much more cautiously. When Raquel throws the first punch, she narrowly misses Adri's nose.

Eva watches with increasing concern as Adri barely blocks another punch. She pokes Roman's arm. "Actually, we can pray again. It's okay to pray more than once." She clasps her hands together, waiting for Roman and Yvonne to follow suit.

"Dear God and Jesus, please help Mama win her fight an—" Eva opens her eyes when someone taps her shoulder. "Max!"

Max looks from her to Roman and Yvonne with a confused expression. When he arrived at their table, he found all three of them with their heads down and eyes closed.

"We were praying for Adri," Roman explains.

"Oh." Max smirks. "Hopefully God answers those kinds of prayers."

"He does," Eva says firmly.

"Yep. Sometimes he just says no." Roman winks and motions to an empty chair near their table. "Join us, Max."

Max hesitates, but when Eva looks at him with her hopeful eyes, he sits. After going back and forth in his mind for hours, he finally made the decision not to coach Adri. It also helped that she barely looked at him when she arrived at the gym earlier that day. He took that to mean she wasn't as interested in his help as Enzo had suggested.

They watch as Adri throws her first punch, late in the first round. Raquel easily dodges it before throwing a hook of her own that hits Adri squarely in the face. Shaken by it, Adri struggles to protect herself from more powerful strikes. When she lands a solid punch, Raquel counters it, and the crowd gasps as blood pours from Adri's nose. Max winces. Thankfully, the buzzer sounds, signaling the end of the first round.

Roman watches Adri retreat to her corner. "I figured it might come down to speed," he says, with a heavy sigh. "That Hacksaw girl is fast. And Adri is still getting back into it."

The next round isn't much better. Max watches with gritted teeth as Raquel slams Adri to the ground and manages to hold her down for almost a full minute, twisting Adri's arm back. Spartans watch with deflating enthusiasm as Adri struggles to break free. "Come on, Adri," he mutters.

She manages to hang on until the second buzzer, but she looks defeated when Raquel releases her. Gloating, Raquel rises and bangs on the cage, grinning at Adri's disgruntled fans.

Roman curses softly under his breath. "Adri's in her head."

Max watches as Adri gets up and rubs her injured arm. Beside him, Eva starts to cry. She turns to Roman.

"I want to see Mama now, Uncle Roman."

Roman sighs again. "I know, Eva, but we have to wait." He pats her head. "Do you want to go outside?"

Eva shakes her head, but she continues to cry. Yvonne puts her arm around her and whispers something in her ear.

Max looks at Adri again, torn. Her right arm is red and her face is smudged with blood. The crowd, too, looks miserable. Like Max, most of them have rarely seen Adri lose. On the other side of the cage, one of Hacksaw's coaches laughs loudly, and that's the last straw. Without thinking, he stands up and moves quickly. In another minute, the buzzer will go off.

Adri turns, stunned to see him in her corner. "What are you—"

"Let me see your arm."

She starts to protest, but then she extends it. Max opens her palm, then massages her bicep. He presses hard, watching as she winces. "Helping or hurting?"

"I can't tell."

He presses more gently. "You need to ice it, but we don't have time." Her eyes dart to the clock behind him. Sensing her panic, he moves closer, purposefully blocking all else from her view. "You're in your head, Adri."

"I know, but—"

"Get out of your head and fight."

"I'm try—"

"You're a better fighter than she is." He looks over his shoulder at Hacksaw, who glares back at him. He turns to Adri again. "When she throws one of those little jabs, get her with a real hook. If she blocks that, throw a knee. She won't see it coming." The buzzer sounds again, and Max puts his hands on her shoulders. "Don't think about winning or losing. Just fight."

Adri nods slowly. She's surprised by how much his presence calms her. Her arm, too, feels better. The pressure he applied numbed some of the pain. His dark eyes are reassuring.

"Fight because you love it, remember?"

She meets Hacksaw in the center for the final round, slightly more relaxed now. As the round goes on, Hacksaw fights more recklessly than before, impatient for her win. When she throws another wild combination, Adri takes advantage and slams her with a hook. As the crowd cheers, Adri feels something shift. For a moment, it feels as if she steps out of her body and takes everything in—Hacksaw's look of shock, the Spartans' roar, Max's eyes on her as she fights. Minutes ago, before he showed up, she was telling herself she couldn't win. But she can.

It's time to fight again.

Adri's body is poised and ready when Hacksaw approaches again with only a few seconds left on the clock. She blocks Adri's hook, but Adri steps in and grabs her shoulder. In one swift motion, Adri draws her knee back, then forward, and hears a crack as it slams against Hacksaw's forehead. Suddenly, she feels heavy in Adri's arms. Adri releases her and watches as she falls. The crowd cheers wildly as they wait for Hacksaw to stand up again. Adri waits, too, her mind ablaze with adrenaline. She looks at Max, and his smile makes her heart skip as Spartans cheer.

"La Tormenta! La Tormenta!"

In the cage, the referee lifts her hand, signaling her victory.

"Mama!"

Adri looks up and sees Eva struggling to get to her. Her small body is barely visible in the tumultuous crowd.

"Eva!" Adri pulls away from the referee, but she stops when she sees Max scoop Eva up and lift her out of harm's way. Adri waits as he opens the cage door and lets her in. She runs to Adri.

"Mama! I prayed for you!"

Adri bends to embrace her, savoring the hug. She looks past Eva, at Max. He watches them for a moment, before he's pulled away by Enzo.

"Thanks, butterfly. I think God heard you."

———

"Hungry, huh?"

Adri looks up from loading her plate with food and grins sheepishly at Enzo. "This is my third."

"No judgment here. I always ate like that after a fight. Everyone does, right?"

Adri nods. For years, after her tournaments, she and Roman would eat like kings in whatever city they were in. Roman had a knack for finding the best buffets. Or, if there was a Cuban place, he got them the best table. There was always at least one waiter who knew who he was.

"Your aunt really outdid herself tonight," Enzo says, eyeing the spread.

Adri agrees, though she doesn't correct him about Yvonne. Both she and Roman went above and beyond for the after party, traveling an extra hour to buy ingredients at Sedavo's Supermarket. When they returned, Roman dug out lace tablecloths while Yvonne did her best to replicate Dalila's *croquetas de jamon*, fried plantains, and rice pudding—three of Adri's childhood favorites.

She and Enzo join the others in the backyard, where Roman arranged every chair he could find in a circle around the bonfire. Enzo sits beside Skye, and Adri finds a seat near Yvonne, who holds Eva in her arms. The circle listens as Roman tells his stories. The summer sky is dark, but the fire casts a cheerful glow on their faces. A few others play dominos in the grass, joined by Rocky and Ivan.

Adri settles into her camp chair and relaxes. She's still feeling the high of her win, but her body aches all over. Max sits a few seats away, but he seems intent on avoiding her eyes, instead preferring to watch the fire. She frowns. She wants to thank him for his help at the fight, but not in the company of so many strangers. On the other side of the fire, a young coach asks Roman about his boxing career.

"What was Willy La Cruz really like?" he asks, between sips of sangria from a Solo cup. "I've watched that fight a million times, and it just never gets old."

Roman chuckles. "Willy was a good guy. He was cocky, but I think that was for show." He smiles wistfully. "He congratulated me after the fight, and I could tell he meant it, even though he was as shocked as I was."

"You didn't think you'd win?"

Roman shakes his head. "Nope. I was twenty years old and stupid, and it was a once-in-lifetime chance. Anyone with half a brain would've said no, but I guess I didn't have half a brain back then." He smiles. "But, by the grace of God, I knocked him down. Otherwise, I would've left in a stretcher."

Adri smiles. It's the one millionth time she's heard the story, but the coach was right—it never gets old.

"It's cool that you were brave enough to do it," he says, the fire reflected in his eyes when he looks up at Roman. "Now you'll always be a legend."

Adri nods for her uncle, knowing that he's too humble to agree.

"My great-grandfather Leon is the real legend," Roman says,

waving off the praise. "He boxed in Cuba even when it was banned—risked his freedom for it. If it wasn't for him, I would've never learned to fight."

"It runs in the family, then?" the coach asks, glancing between Roman and Adri with a grin. "Like father, like daughter?"

"Adri's my niece, actually," Roman says, correcting him before she can. "But she's better than any daughter I could've dreamed up."

His words bring Adri surprisingly close to tears. She glances at him, unsure of what to say, but he gives her a reassuring smile. He knows she feels the same way about him and Dalila, even though she didn't say it nearly enough.

"Oh, and speaking of Adri's fights . . ." Roman stands and gives Adri a mischievous wink. "I've got some great pictures inside. Hold on."

"No!" Adri groans as her uncle strides away. "No pictures!" When she hears Max laugh, she turns sharply. "What are you laughing about? If he's getting pictures of me, that means he's getting pictures of you too."

His laughter ceases. Sure enough, when Roman returns, he carries a leather album full of pictures of Adri and Max at wrestling matches, boxing tournaments, and judo competitions, all intermixed with birthday parties and school dances.

Enzo whistles. "Look at Max in a tux. James Bond."

Skye gasps. "And Adri in her dress! You look stunning."

Enzo bursts out laughing so hard he wheezes. "Dude! You were Prom King?"

Max hides his face in his hands while Adri laughs.

"And Adri should've been Prom Queen," Roman interjects, turning surly. "But some airhead won instead. Her father worked for the school. I think he rigged it."

Enzo grins. "Well, I think we all know where Adri got her competitive spirit."

Yvonne snorts. "You have no idea."

"You have to tell us what teenage Max and Adri were like,"

Enzo says, still flipping pages. "All the most embarrassing stories, please."

"Well, Max was pretty shy . . . unless he had a problem with you. In that case, he'd let you know." Roman glances at Max, who quickly looks at the grass beneath his feet. "He and Adri met at wrestling tryouts. Danny Lyons was the first coach in Sparta history to let girls join the wrestling team."

Adri sees a small smile playing on Max's lips. His father was never one to shy away from a little scandal.

"Those boys gave Adri such a hard time for being the only girl," Roman continues. "Until Max told them to lay off."

Adri still vividly remembers that day. Max told them to shut up and then volunteered to be her partner. Over time, he and Danny helped her become one of the best on the team.

"Max was also kind of a perfectionist, always wanting to get better at everything. Teachers and coaches loved him. Adri . . ." Roman glances at her with a pained expression. "Not so much."

Adri laughs at the true statement. For a moment, she catches Max's eye—and his smile.

Suddenly, Enzo stops turning pages and holds up a loose picture of a baby. "Who's this? Adri?"

Adri squints through the firelight, but her stomach drops when she recognizes it. She looks to Roman, who takes the picture from Enzo and glances at it.

"Ah. My son Tomas." He tucks the photo into his shirt pocket. "He died a long time ago."

There's an audible gasp as the mood changes. Yvonne, who'd been stroking Eva's hair, stops and looks up at Roman with concern. She's one of the few people who knew Tomas Rivera.

Enzo tries to stammer out an apology. "I'm sorry, Roman. I didn't mean—"

"It's alright, kiddo." Roman gently pats his shirt pocket. "It was in the wrong album." His hand lingers over the picture for a moment, covering his heart.

As the night grows cooler, the tired guests say their good-byes until only a few remain. Adri watches as Enzo wraps his arm around Skye and she leans into him. They both look exhausted but elated with the night's success. When Eva finally falls asleep in Yvonne's arms, Adri gently lifts her, intending to head straight to bed, but she passes by Max on her way inside. He looks at her, then down at Eva, who's nestled against Adri's chest with her arms draped over her shoulders.

"She lasted longer than I thought."

Adri nods. "She's my social butterfly." She lingers for a moment, wanting to thank him, but more people are approaching. Adri bites her lip. "Well . . . have a good night."

He frowns. "You too."

Skye and Enzo leave together, and Max intends to follow them out, but he stops in the living room when he sees the album Roman brought out on the coffee table. Curious, he starts in the middle, turning each page slowly.

"Great event tonight, Mr. Lyons. Outstanding, really."

He looks up. Roman stands in the kitchen with a pile of paper plates. "Thanks, but I can't take any credit. It was all Skye and Enzo."

"Well, you definitely helped Adri."

Max doesn't say anything. He turns to the album again.

"I hope I didn't embarrass you too much earlier with those."

Max smirks. "I'll survive."

"There's a couple good ones of your dad in there."

Max nods as he finally finds the one he was searching for. Adri and his father sit on the steps of the Philadelphia Museum of Art, both mid-laugh. Adri's hair whips around her face, and his father's eyes are crinkled with happiness. The bronze Rocky statue stands behind them, gleaming in the sunlight. Max remembers taking the picture on one of their last days together before she left for Miami.

"You going to church anywhere these days, Max?"

Max frowns at the odd question. "Nope."

"It helps."

"With what?"

"All kinds of things." Roman glances around the kitchen, Dalila's old domain. "I know from experience."

Max's jaw tightens. He shuts the album harder than he means to. "Thanks for hosting tonight, Roman."

"Sure thing." Roman's voice has a touch of sad resignation to it as he finishes tossing the plates in the trash. "Take care of yourself, kiddo."

Max stands. He nearly reaches the front door, but he pauses when he hears footsteps. Turning, he watches as Adri steps into the hallway, her movements purposefully quiet and careful. She's wearing a red Lyon's T-shirt and shorts, and her hair, now unbraided, curls wildly around her face. Clearly, she expected everyone to be gone. When she sees him, her cheeks flush.

"Where's Roman?"

Max glances toward the kitchen, where Roman stood just moments before with his little tyrant of a dog. Now, he's nowhere to be found. "I don't know. Maybe he went back outside?"

"Mama!"

Adri groans at the sound of Eva's voice on the other side of her bedroom door. "She doesn't want to sleep," she explains wearily. She waits, clearly bracing herself.

"Mama!" Eva yells again, louder this time. "Come back!"

He frowns at the exhausted look on her face. "Want some help?"

She looks surprised by the offer—and a little skeptical. She shrugs. "You can try, but she's pretty stubborn."

Eva sits up excitedly when Max and Adri enter the darkened room, but as soon as she starts chattering, Max holds a finger to his lips. Adri watches, amused.

"Max—"

"Shhh," Max says again, keeping his voice quiet but firm. He grabs a nearby stuffed animal—the lion he won at Bluebird's—and hands it to her. Eva quiets down and snuggles it. He drags a chair over and sits while Adri leans against the door. "We're going to play a game," he explains. "I'll tell you part of a story, and then you tell me the next part."

Eva nods eagerly, but her eyelids are already heavy.

"Once, there was a little girl and her pet lion," he begins. "They lived—"

"What were their names?' Eva interrupts.

"Huh?"

"The girl and her lion." She frowns. "Don't they have names?"

"Oh." He shrugs. "Yeah, sure. You decide."

"Yvonne and Samson."

He hears Adri laugh behind him and smiles. "Sounds good. So, Yvonne and Samson have to rescue their friend from an evil prince named Enzo . . ."

As they take turns telling the story, Max studies the room that Adri's been living in for the past six months. It's the room she grew up in. A small, overstuffed duffel bag, a Bible on the nightstand, and Rocky, asleep near Eva's feet, are the only clues that she ever left.

After a few minutes of storytelling, Eva turns away and hugs her pillow, although she claims she's still listening. When he hears soft snores, he signals to Adri, and they slip out quietly.

Back in the living room, Adri smiles up at him. "I'll have to remember that one."

"My dad used to do that when I was wired," he says, following her to the kitchen. "Our stories were usually about soldiers and monsters, though. Not princesses and their pet lions."

Adri smiles and flips on the light. "Do you want something to drink?" She glances in the fridge. "It looks like we have water and wine." She laughs. "Sorry. Not a lot of options."

He's surprised by the invitation to stay but takes it. "Water is fine." He sits on a barstool as she pours them both glasses of water from a yellow pitcher. Truthfully, wine sounds better, but he knows water is safer. Especially after their disastrous night at Coralou's.

An old plaque near the coffeemaker, emblazoned with a Bible verse catches his eye. *Remember not the former things, nor consider the things of old. Behold, I am doing a new thing; now it springs forth, do you not perceive it? I will make a way in the wilderness and rivers in the desert.*

He's reminded of his earlier conversation with Roman. "I think your uncle is trying to convert me."

Adri laughs softly as she slides him his glass. "Any success?"

"Not yet. Still a heathen."

She smiles but quickly changes the subject. "Anyway, I guess now I need to say thank you twice."

"For what?"

"First, for getting my child to sleep." She exhales deeply. "She was driving me nuts."

He laughs. "You're welcome." He glances at the clock and realizes how late it is. Adri has to be exhausted from her fight. That, and she probably hasn't slept much since Owen's impromptu visit. "What else?"

Her face turns more serious as she tucks a loose strand of her hair away. "And for earlier, at the fight. Thanks for being in my corner."

He shrugs. "You could've turned it around without me."

She smiles skeptically. "And thanks for being gentle with my ego too."

He smiles back. He said what he said partly because he doesn't want to steal her thunder, but also because it's true. It was clear from the way she fought tonight that she was still a great fighter. She just needed to rediscover her confidence.

"Hang on a second."

He watches, surprised, as she rises from her stool and quietly disappears into her bedroom again. When she returns a minute later and sits beside him, she holds out a yellow coffee canister. "Remember this?"

His brows furrow as she hands it to him. He lifts the lid and sees two unfurled pieces of paper. Suddenly, he remembers the cold spring day from years and years ago. The snow had just melted, and Adri had the idea to bury a time capsule somewhere by the tracks. Max thought it was a weird idea but went along with it. As he reads the notes, his eyes widen. "How'd you find this?"

"I almost tripped on the twisted spoke when I was running."

"Wow. That's crazy, after all this time." He reads their lists again and laughs, surprising himself. "I guess this means we're underachievers."

She giggles. "Hey, at least you got two of your goals—your gym and your truck," she says, pointing to his list. "I'm still at zero."

"Well, to be fair, you aimed pretty high." He turns to her list. "You wanted a championship title and to travel the world. I wanted a truck and a family." He laughs again at his list, remembering his naïve teenage self and his many plans for the future "Oh, and I wanted to learn from the greatest mixed martial artist of all time. You know, typical stuff."

As she laughs harder, it hits him just how much he missed this—sitting with her and laughing after a fight. It also hits him how much their letters seem to have drawn them back into the past. He feels strangely young and free again, sitting beside the girl he used to love in Roman's darkened kitchen. He glances at the last goal on her list. "If it'll make you feel better, we can play Scrabble sometime." He smiles playfully. "I'll finally let you win."

Her laughter fades as she looks up at him with a torn expression, still feeling high from her win but also aware of the electricity flowing between them. He sees the tempted look in her eyes as she downs the rest of her water. He fights the urge to pull her mouth to his.

"Do you want to hear something crazy?" she asks, breaking the thick silence.

He nods slowly, conflicted over the subject change.

"I think I want to fight again."

He raises a surprised eyebrow, although he remembers his conversation with Enzo.

"I know how it sounds, but . . . I think it's what I'm supposed to do. Maybe."

He frowns. Her voice is full of self-doubt, so he keeps his tone as neutral as possible. "Would you try to get a sponsorship or something?"

Her eyes drift from his as she traces the rim of her glass with her finger. "Hmm, well, that's a good, practical question, isn't it?" She sighs. "Honestly, I don't know. It's been so long since I was part of that world. I'd need a sponsor, wouldn't I? And a coach. Oh, and some fights." She laughs bleakly. "I am totally crazy, aren't I?"

He shakes his head as he weighs his words, searching for the ones she needs to hear the most. "I mean, I don't think it's crazy, Adri. It definitely won't be *easy*, but you can do hard things. You're the only one who knows if it's worth it or not."

She looks surprised by his answer. When she doesn't respond, he wonders if he said the wrong thing, but when she looks at him again, her eyes are grateful. "I should've known you'd get it." She exhales. "I just feel like I have to try. One more time."

He nods, understanding. Fresh blue bruises blossom down her neck and disappear into her shirt, but her eyes are bright and determined, the way they used to be when she still dreamed of being a champion. Apparently, those dreams never died. He never doubted she could do it—which is part of the reason why his hatred for Owen burns so hot.

"I think you should go for it," he says, lightly nudging her shoulder with his own. As their bodies brush, she looks up at him, and his heart races. Her eyes tell him that if he kisses her, she won't stop him, but he realizes what he needs to do. If he does what he *wants* to do, there will just be more regret between them.

"I better go," he says, standing. "Thanks for the water." He catches the flicker of disappointment in her eyes but moves quickly, wanting to minimize her embarrassment and his own temptation. Another minute alone with her in Roman's dark, quiet house, and what's left of his resolve might disappear. "If you want to talk about fighting sometime, when all the dust settles, you know where to find me," he adds, reaching the door.

When he faces her again, she looks hopeful, and that hopeful expression scares him more than anything else. It takes all his willpower to leave her without an answer, but it's the right thing to do. He knows she should make her decision when her mind is clearer—not when other feelings might be clouding her judgment. After all, they both know those feelings could come back to bite them both.

10

ADRI WIPES A DROP OF SWEAT FROM HER FOREHEAD as she parks outside the gym. It's a blistering day in August—all sunshine, no clouds—and the air conditioner in her Honda is less than reliable. She's been rushing around all morning, and there's no time to stop now. She's still got plenty to pack, Yvonne needs her to help pick up a topper for Eva's cake, and she's twenty minutes late for her meeting with Max. Not to mention, she's just days away from fighting Sabine Renux—a realization that makes her stomach twist with nerves and excitement every time she thinks about it.

As she hurries through the door to the gym, she finds Skye and Enzo huddled on one of the mats, shoulder to shoulder, moments away from a kiss before Skye leaps up to greet her. She smiles casually, but her cheeks are bright red—either from the heat or Enzo or probably both. Her smile fades as she studies Adri's face.

"What's wrong?" she asks. "Is it something with Owen?"

Adri opens her mouth, then closes it again as her conflicting thoughts tumble. Truthfully, she hasn't thought very much about Owen in weeks, which probably isn't wise, but she's been consumed with nonstop training. It's been almost eight months since she left Miami and nearly three months since his drop-in at the gym, but she knows him too well to believe he's given up. Especially since he still hasn't signed the papers.

"Adri?"

She and Skye turn at the sound of a familiar, impatient voice. Max stands in the hallway, his eyebrows raised as he waits for her to follow him. She shoots Skye an apologetic look before heading to his office. She inhales softly as she settles in across from him. She's been crying on and off since early that morning, but she did her best to hide it with makeup and prays he won't notice. When she meets his eyes, he's staring at her hands.

"What?" she says, glancing down.

"You're . . . glittering."

"Oh." It's true. Her fingertips are coated in gold glitter, and they sparkle under the lights. "Whoops. I was finishing decorations for Eva's party this morning."

"Right. That's this weekend, isn't it?" He frowns. "I forgot about that."

She nods as uninvited tears threaten to rise again. She wishes she could forget too. She thought she'd taken care of everything, but that morning Eva woke up with her usual questions—how many days until her party, who RSVP'd, would Yvonne paint her nails—but apparently she'd forgotten one very important detail. Her party, planned months ago, is on the same day as Adri's fight.

As soon as Adri realized the conflict, she promised Eva that they'd have their own celebration when she returned to Sparta from New York, and Eva seemed okay with that—until just a few hours ago. Her breathless sobs made Adri feel like the worst mother in the world, and that wasn't even the worst part. The worst part was when she begged Adri to call Owen.

"We need to call him in case he wants to send me something," Eva insisted, more tears rolling down her cheeks. "Please, Mama! He might have a present for me."

"Everything okay, Adri?"

Her head snaps up as Max's eyes move over her curiously. "Yes," she lies, forcing herself to smile. The last thing she needs is for him to think she's getting cold feet. "I'm fine, just a little stressed. Want to talk about the trip?"

"Sure." He slides an itinerary across the desk, and she takes it, impressed as usual by his organization. "I think we should try to drive halfway tonight, and then finish the rest tomorrow. I booked time at a gym on Wednesday night and all day Thursday. After that, we can just train at the venue. . . ."

Adri nods, though she's barely listening. Too many thoughts compete for her attention. Eva's disappointment weighs on her, plus the stress of packing and preparing. Not only is she about to fight in a new, growing MMA promotion—a rare chance made possible by one of Max's many connections—but she's also about to spend the next six and a half days in his near-constant company.

"Don't forget to pack something nice for the press event. And you'll need different clothes for the weigh-in." He pauses. "Are you sure you're okay, Adri? I know we haven't had a lot of time to train, but—"

"What?" She refocuses on the present and finds him frowning again. She curses silently. "Sorry. No, I'm good. Really. I'm just . . . thinking about a lot."

He nods, but he looks unconvinced, which only makes her feel worse. She knows he's already gone out on a limb for her. When she approached him about fighting again, after that strange night in Roman's kitchen, she knew she was asking for a lot. If he agreed to help her and she crashed and burned, his reputation would suffer too. Still, he'd taken the risk and agreed to set up a fight, though he was very clear that their arrangement was only temporary until she found a permanent coach.

"I'm ready," she says, feigning confidence. She's never felt less ready for anything in her life, but there is no turning back now. "Really."

He nods again, but his eyes probe hers. "Any updates on Owen?"

She shakes her head. She also ignores how strange it feels to discuss Owen with Max. Usually, they just avoid the subject. "Nothing new. Roman's not going to let Eva out of his sight, and her

teachers know what's going on. Oh, and I finally got a hearing."
She lets her voice trail off, unsure why she mentioned that detail.

He frowns. "You mean for the divorce?"

She nods as heat creeps into her cheeks. After nearly six months
of Owen refusing to respond to the divorce papers, a judge is going
to review her case. But obviously that doesn't concern Max. She
clears her throat. "Anyway . . ."

He coughs. "Yeah, well, that's good." His eyes drift to her hands
again. "I think that's everything, then. I'll pick you up around seven."

As she stands, his eyes wander to her torso, then down to the
ground. Confused, she glances down just in time to see a thick
cloud of glitter fall from her clothes before floating to cover his
desk and the floor. She sighs. "Sorry." She starts to sweep some
up with her palms, but he stops her.

"It's fine." He smiles faintly as she straightens again. "It adds
a nice touch."

She returns the smile with a tired one of her own. Ever since
she won her fight at the gym, Spartans have been talking about
it—especially Max's involvement. Between his dramatic scuffle
with Owen, and then him stepping in to coach her against Sabine,
there's been no shortage of rumors about their relationship, even
though they've both kept things strictly professional. "Thanks, by
the way," she says, shoving her hands in her pockets to keep some
of the glitter at bay. Three months probably wasn't long enough to
prepare for a fight, but she's improved faster than she ever thought
she could—and that has a lot to do with Max.

"Don't thank me just yet." His eyes meet hers. "You still have
to make it through this week."

After Max picks up a rental car, he stops at home to finish
packing and lock up. His thoughts race from one subject to the
next as he fills a duffel bag—the trip, the fight, the gym. Skye and
Enzo assured him they had everything under control for the next
few days.

"Trust me, no one will miss you," Enzo said before blocking Max's answering slap.

Max wondered if his students' parents might be annoyed by his and Adri's absence, but to his surprise, most of them were excited. The students were especially thrilled to learn that one of their teachers would be in a "real" fight in New York, and they'd been talking about it for weeks.

He briefly pauses from packing when something glittery catches his eye in the fast-falling sunlight. It's Eva's birthday invitation—a postcard covered in stickers and sparkles that he stuck to the fridge weeks ago. He frowns, remembering his conversation with Adri earlier that morning.

She seemed distracted, but he assumed it was probably just fatigue or nerves, and he can't blame her. Between teaching, they squeezed in two daily training sessions, switching between cardio, weight-training, boxing, judo, and wrestling for three hours at a time. It was a grueling schedule after years without regular training, but Adri surprised him with her endurance. They both know she's going to need it if she's going to last five rounds with Renux.

As he finishes and zips up his bag, a question comes to his mind—one that he realizes he's been ignoring until now.

What are you doing, Max?

He scowls. *I'm just helping someone*, he tells himself. When Adri asked for his help, he made a few calls, not expecting much to materialize, until an old acquaintance mentioned a new promotion getting off the ground. The promoters were willing to give her a spot in the lineup—if Max would be her coach.

"Max Lyons back in the cage with an underdog?" The promoter had sounded ready to faint. *"That's* exactly *what we want."*

He exhales, aware that he's doing the exact thing he said he'd never do again, which is exposing his quiet, simple life to the demanding fight world, but he tells himself that everything will go back to normal soon enough. If she wins, it'll be easy to find a good coach to take over. And if she loses . . . well, it'll be over before it ever started.

His phone buzzes against the table, breaking through his thoughts. He glances at the number but doesn't recognize it. He almost ignores it until it occurs to him that it could be another promoter. Sighing, he answers. "Hello?"

"Lyons. How are you, buddy?"

Max's eyes narrow at the sound of the oily voice on the other line.

"It's Linc," he says, although he needs no introduction. "New number. Did I catch you at a good time?"

"No. You didn't."

Linc chuckles at Max's icy tone. "I'll keep it short, then. I heard you have a fight coming up. Imagine my surprise."

"It's not my fight. I'm helping—"

"I heard that too. Owen Anders's wife, huh? She's the one who finally got your attention? Interesting move, my friend. Not smart, but definitely interesting."

Max grits his teeth. Linc's smugness confirms what he already suspected—that Linc was the one who told Owen about Adri working at the gym. He wishes he and Linc were face to face so he could repay him for sending Owen to Sparta. "Is that why you called, Linc? You're still mad that I didn't pick Gemma?"

Linc snorts loudly. "You're the one who should be mad about that, Max. You screwed yourself. But since you've decided to coach someone after all, maybe we should revisit Gemma's offer."

"I'm not—"

"Why don't I set up a fight between your girl and Gemma? That's fair, isn't it? They can fight, and then you can choose based on merit instead of whatever else might be motivating you."

Max's grip tightens around the phone.

"Besides, it'll be a great opportunity for your little nobody instructor. We can make it a big thing, if you want." Linc's voice drips with condescension. "It'll be a downgrade for Gemma, obviously, but she'll be a good sport about it. What do you say?"

Max forces himself not to take the bait. "My answer is the same."

There's a long cold pause before Linc sighs heavily. "You know, Lyons, I don't think you're as smart as everyone says. That, or maybe you are, and you know your girl doesn't have a chance in—"

"Thanks for the call, Linc." Max cuts him off but keeps his voice even, not wanting to give him any kind of satisfaction. "Feel free to lose my number." He hangs up just as Linc starts to laugh.

Cursing, Max throws his phone in his backpack and grabs the rest of his belongings. As he drives to Roman's house, he barely notices the stunning summer sunset melting into the horizon. Instead, his mind races until it fixates on one troubling question.

If Linc knows about Adri's fight, does Owen know too?

When he arrives at Roman's, Adri is sitting on the porch watching Eva catch lightning bugs. Eva runs to Max's window as he pulls in.

"Max! Did you get a new car?"

"Just for a few days," he says shortly, still distracted by Linc's unsettling phone call. He walks quickly past Eva to Adri, greeted by Ivan's growls and Rocky's barking. He ignores them both and grabs Adri's bag.

Surprised, she reaches for it. "I can carry—"

"It's fine," he says, walking back to the car and tossing it in with his. "Ready to go?"

Adri scowls, but he's distracted by Eva tapping on his leg. He looks down in exasperation. "What, Eva?"

"Look." She shows him a lightning bug trapped in her cupped hands.

"Cool," he says, glancing impatiently at Adri. He didn't realize until now what a bad mood Linc put him in, but Eva still smiles up at him.

"It's okay with me that Mama won't be at my party," she says matter-of-factly. "We're going to the zoo when she comes back. You can come, too, if you want."

Max frowns. As her words sink in, he snaps out of it. Linc's schemes still loom in the back of his mind, but the hopeful look on

Eva's face temporarily eclipses them. "Thanks," he says, softening his tone. "That sounds fun."

He waits as Adri bends down to hug her good-bye. She holds Eva for a long time and whispers something into her ear. As he looks down at the glitter still sticking to Adri's hands, he realizes what she was so upset about earlier and feels a pang of guilt.

"It's okay, Mama," Eva reassures her. "I promise I won't miss you."

Adri laughs through tears that she quickly tries to hide. Just then, Roman appears in the doorway.

"You all good here?" Max asks him, glancing between Adri and Eva. He wants to mention the phone call and his concerns about Owen, but he doesn't want to bring it up in front of Adri. If nothing comes of it, he'll have worried her for no reason.

Roman nods reassuringly. "Yep, all good. I'll take care of Eva. You just take care of Adri." He gives Max a pointed look. "Keep her mind on the fight."

Max nods, understanding. When Adri looks at him again, she looks more confident. "Are we ready now?" he asks.

She exhales. "I think so."

11

ADRI STARES AT THE CEILING OF HER HOTEL ROOM, tracing the dusty paint swirls with her eyes. Her stomach flutters, then growls, thanks to her strict training diet. She's fighting in four days, and it still feels like it might not be real. Ignoring her sore muscles, she rolls out of bed and does a quick workout, only stopping when she feels a bead of sweat break out on her forehead. As she showers, her mind drifts to Owen, against her will.

She dreamt about him again last night, but now she can't remember the details. She can only remember the mood—happy at first, then uneasy, then dark. The dream was about Miami. That first year was fun and games—workouts in luxury gyms, designer shoes and dresses, parties, Owen's rough hands all over her body in bathrooms and bars—but soon afterward dissolved into screaming matches and emotional torture until he finally hit her. She shivers despite the hot water. He always had a way of convincing her that she was weak even when she felt strong.

One of her recent conversations with Yvonne comes to mind. Over the past few months, they've been meeting at Bluebird's for a casual sort of Bible study, and she's been learning a lot from the wise older woman.

"Do you want to know what the scariest Bible verse I ever read was?" Yvonne asked at their last meeting. Her hair was piled on top of her head in an elaborate style, showing off pretty pearl earrings.

Adri nodded, although the question surprised her. Yvonne clearly loved the Bible, so it was hard to imagine her thinking any part of it was scary.

"The one that says, if you don't forgive other people for their sins, God won't forgive you for yours. It's in Matthew somewhere."

Adri frowned. That *was* scary. "I thought God forgives us because of Jesus, though?"

Yvonne smiled. "That's right, he does. It's just getting at that in a different way." She glanced down at her Bible for a moment and gathered her thoughts. "See, we're saved because of Jesus, like you said. He died on the cross for us, despite our sins. But if we really understand what that means, then we won't think of ourselves as better than anyone else."

Adri nodded, although she didn't quite understand. She knew she had plenty of flaws, but surely Yvonne wasn't suggesting that she and Owen were the same?

"That was a hard thing for me to realize," Yvonne went on, apparently sensing her confusion. "Lots of people have treated me *much* worse than I treated them, so I spent a long time either feeling like a victim or like I was superior or something, but neither of those approaches make you very happy in the long run." She sighed lightly. "Because the truth is, I needed God's forgiveness as much as anybody else does. And when I figured that out, it set me free." As her eyes met Adri's, Adri was briefly reminded of her aunt. "If you can stay humble enough to keep hate out of your heart, you'll be a much happier woman than I was, honey."

Adri finally understood what she was saying—that the next step in her journey was forgiving Owen—but she also knew that would be much easier said than done.

She pushes those thoughts out of her mind and tries to focus on the day ahead. She hopes Max will be in a better mood today.

He seemed anxious and distant yesterday. After a long, uneventful drive, they arrived at their hotel just after midnight, and he disappeared into his room with a quick "good night." She frowns, annoyed that his silence bothered her in the first place. Why should it matter, anyway? He's her coach, she reminds herself as she finishes getting dressed. Sometimes it felt like they were close again, but those were just rare moments in the midst of training. He knocks just as she's pulling on her jeans.

"Hey," he says tiredly when she opens the door.

She frowns, noticing the dark circles under his eyes. He looks like he barely slept. "Good morning."

"You sleep okay?"

She shrugs and grabs her bag, unwilling to let him carry it this time. "Decent. No chocolate on the pillow, though." In fact, the room barely had anything in it besides a bed and a closet-size bathroom.

He smirks. "Are you hungry?"

She thought he'd never ask. "Yes." Her stomach growls before she can get the word out.

"Let's feed you."

She follows him to the car, and he hands her the GPS. "Find someplace close."

Half an hour later, they're back on the highway, two black coffees between them and a bag of beignets on Adri's lap. The café she found didn't have any healthy options, aside from a basket of overly bruised bananas.

"That's your last cheat meal," he says as she takes a bite of one of the pastries.

She nods and savors it, knowing from now until Saturday night, she'll be eating lean protein and vegetables. "You're really not going to eat *one*?" she asks, extending the bag to him. "I have to eat all three?"

He laughs. "Oh, you have to, huh?"

"Unless you take one for the team."

"Fine. For the team." He opens his mouth and waits as it occurs to Adri that his hands are occupied. Reluctantly, she lifts the pastry to his lips, and he takes a bite.

"Crap!" she says as they hit a bump and powdered sugar sprinkles his shirt and lap. She reaches for a napkin but makes a bigger mess as more sugar spills from the bag. "Sorry. Hold on."

He laughs as she grows more flustered. "You kind of missed my mouth a little." He wipes the sugar from his lips with the back of his palm and finishes chewing. "Gross."

"*What*? Gross? They're so good!"

He shakes his head in disgust. "They're way too sweet. Like, straight-up sugar. Can I get a napkin, please?"

She drops a stack of napkins on his leg, unwilling to go anywhere near his lap. "Here."

As he brushes the remaining sugar away, she digs through her backpack and finds her Bible. Since they started training together, she's fallen way behind in her reading.

"Heard anything from Roman today?" Max asks, giving her and the book a sideways glance.

She nods, though she's surprised by the hint of concern in his voice. "Not this morning, but he texted last night. Apparently, he let Eva stay up and watch *The Hunchback of Notre Dame* again. She's really milking her birthday."

"Smart girl." He seems to relax slightly as he flips through radio stations. He stops when he finds a familiar Nine Inch Nails song and turns the volume up, momentarily distracting her. He quickly turns it down again.

When she feels his eyes on her profile, she looks up from her reading. "What?"

"You made a face."

She frowns. "No I didn't."

"Yeah you did. About the song."

She shrugs but feels color fill her cheeks. She watches as he searches stations again, his expression amused, until he finds a sappy Christian song.

"Better?"

She scowls.

He smirks as he listens to the lyrics. "Sorry, but there's no way this is better than Nine Inch Nails."

"I didn't say you had to change it."

"What, are you not allowed to listen to songs about sex or something?"

Her scowl deepens. "Listen to whatever you want, Max." She pretends to be engrossed in the Psalms. "I don't care."

"That's something I never understood. Why are religious people so against sex? What's the big deal?"

"I'm not against sex," she says crossly, annoyed to be lumped in with all the other "religious" people in the world, but more annoyed that she's having this conversation with him, of all people. "I just think you should have it with the person you're married to."

"Well, what if the person you're married to is a jerk?"

Her face goes hot, but she keeps her voice cool. "Believe it or not, I don't really want to talk about my sex life with you."

He keeps his gaze on the road in front of them, but his face softens slightly. "Sorry. That was stupid. I shouldn't have brought up Owen."

She doesn't respond.

"I just think he's scum," Max adds, scowling. "Actually, no, scum isn't bad enough." His face darkens. "There's no word that describes how much I hate that guy."

Adri sighs. "You're not wrong, but . . . I want to forgive him."

There's a long, loaded silence. "What?" Max finally asks.

"I need to forgive him," she repeats simply. It's something she and Roman talked about too—how to forgive without forgetting. She hasn't mastered the skill yet, but she's determined to.

Max shakes his head slowly, as if he has water in his ears. "Sorry, what? Say that again? You're going to *forgive* him? For beating you?"

His tone annoys her, but she nods.

"That's the stupidest thing I've ever heard, Adri."

She sighs again and shuts her Bible. Apparently, he isn't going to let it go. "Okay, then. What other options do I have?"

"Oh, I don't know . . . how about *hating* him?" He looks away from the road for a moment to meet her eyes. "You know, what normal people do?"

"I've already spent a long time hating him." She shrugs. "I don't want to anymore."

"Because of *that*?" He nods at her Bible.

She ignores his acrid tone. "That's part of it."

"That's so stupid," he mutters.

Her temper flares. "I didn't ask you, did I?"

"No, you didn't, but you saying crap like that makes me think you're going to run back to him." She watches as his hands tighten on the steering wheel. "If you can forgive him for what he did, then you're easy prey."

It dawns on her what's really bothering him, and some of her annoyance fades. Still, she makes her voice as firm as she can. "I know what I'm doing."

He throws her a skeptical look. "Why are you forgiving him, then? Isn't that what your mom did a million times? 'Forgave' your dad, then let him beat her all over again?"

"My mom didn't forgive my dad. She worshipped him. There's a big difference." She draws in a sharp, shaky breath. The mention of her parents brings up a wave of unwelcome emotions. "I don't want to worship any man, okay? And I don't want to carry hate around for the rest of my life. That won't fix anything."

For a moment, he looks stunned by her declaration, but then he shrugs it away.

"I'm not going back to him, Max," she says firmly, wanting him to believe her—for his sake, and her own. She wants to believe it too.

His eyes stay fixed on the road in front of them, and her heart sinks. She can tell from his distant look that he's not convinced.

Adri finishes braiding her hair and ties it back. She's been dreading meeting Max for their first training session, but she forces herself to leave her quiet room and make the long trek down the narrow hallway. His text said to meet him in the hotel gym as soon as she could. That was an hour ago.

As she walks, she steels herself for another unpleasant interaction. When they arrived in Albany earlier, they went their separate ways as soon as possible, both of them still frustrated with the other. Sighing, she finds her key card and swipes it. Inside the gym, she finds Max, already working out near the weights.

She swallows. He's stripped down to his undershirt and shorts, and a heavy barbell rests on his shoulders as he lunges, flexing his tanned, muscular legs. He's obviously aware of her presence, but he doesn't stop his workout. When she approaches, he drops the weight and faces her with a smile that makes her skin go hot. He wipes the sweat from his neck with a towel. "Why don't we just train here? Since we have the place to ourselves?"

She nods, though her heart drums uneasily as he reaches for his gym bag and pulls out two pairs of combat gloves. He motions to a nearby mat.

"Let's do some sparring."

She stretches, then positions herself on one side of the mat. He stands on the other. She frowns, noticing an odd, determined look in his eyes.

"Sabine is going to rely on her Muay Thai on Saturday, so let's focus on that."

She agrees, and they start moving. Years of familiarity make it easy to work around each other despite their disparate sizes. Max throws fast combinations and kicks, but he's careful, mindful of their unequal strength. She matches his pace and blocks his movements, until he pushes her against the wall in a clinch. She curses against his chest.

"She's a head taller than you, Adri," he says, not loosening his grip. "How are you going to get out of this?"

She writhes against him, but he keeps her in place.

"You need to step in and grab my shoulder," he reminds her. He lowers himself slightly to make it easier for her to reach around him, and she immediately makes her escape.

They continue, and she does well on her feet, but Max purposefully wrestles her to the ground. He presses his lower body against her hips, effectively locking her in place as she struggles underneath him. "Stop panicking," he says, easily holding her down. "She's bigger than you, so you're not going to muscle your way out."

She continues trying to wrench free, annoyed that he's right and also angry at herself for letting him put her in such a vulnerable position. She glares up at him. "You're not being fair."

"No, you're just not being smart."

His satisfied smirk pushes her over the edge. Finally, she remembers what to do and thrusts her hips upward, taking advantage of his relaxed position. Surprised, he falls forward, and his hands land near her face. Adri quickly captures one and hooks his ankle with her foot, then uses his lopsided weight to roll over, reversing their positions. Now, she sits on top of him, in control. She tries to stand up, but he pulls her back down.

"If Sabine gets her way, she's not going to fight you standing up."

Furious, she wraps her legs around his torso and moves to strike him, but he catches both of her hands, immobilizing her. When he doesn't let go, she scowls down at him.

"Don't look at me like that," he says, hardly concealing his amusement. "I'm testing your strength."

She narrows her eyes and ignores her hammering heart. "I know what you're doing."

His mouth curves as he pulls her closer, so their faces are only inches apart. "Yeah? What am I doing?"

Her heart races. His dark eyes are as tempting as they are intimidating, and his fingers lightly bite into her wrist, feeling her pulse. She's about to lower her mouth to his when he abruptly lets go of her arms. Stunned, Adri falls forward, and her body lands against his before she quickly rolls off, her heart pounding harder than ever. He sits up, too, but he doesn't look at her.

Tears burn the corners of her eyes. "You just think I'm a flight risk, don't you? You think I'm going to run off to Owen again." She hears him sigh heavily beside her and knows she's right.

"What do you want me to say, Adri? Do you want me to lie?"

"Just say what you're thinking for once," she snaps. "Say that you think I'm weak. *Easy prey*, right?"

He curses softly and rakes a hand through his hair. "Fine, if that's what you really want. Yeah, it's crossed my mind that you might quit and run off again if you get a reason to." He still won't look at her. "Given our history, I think that's pretty reasonable."

"Why do you care so much?" Her emotions surface before she can stop them. "This is just temporary, isn't it? Until I find someone who actually *wants* to coach me?" The words surprise her as they tumble out of her mouth. Until that moment, she hadn't realized how much his uncertainty bothered her.

Max looks surprised, too, but his face darkens again. "Good point," he says coldly. "I guess I don't care. Run away if you want to."

She throws her gloves on the mat and rises to leave, unwilling to let him see her cry. After all, she thinks bitterly, he already thinks she's weak. She enters her room and locks the swing bolt, as if that'll protect her from the wave of conflicted emotions Max Lyons stirs within her.

She leans against the door and lets herself sink to the floor, tired of constantly fighting her feelings. She wonders silently if Max will ever forgive her, but God doesn't give her an answer.

12

ADRI STARES AT THE EARRINGS ON THE DRESSER, two dangly gemstones. Yvonne let her borrow them. She slips them on and studies her reflection. She did her makeup too. She wants to make a good impression on a new potential coach, especially after a night of restless sleep.

After their terrible training session, Adri expected Max would cool off and then she'd get a text about their evening session, but she didn't. Disappointed but determined, she trained alone, going over every Muay Thai maneuver she could remember, though it was hard without a partner. She fell asleep hours later, frustrated by her slow progress.

Her nerves resurface as she thinks about her upcoming fight. Sabine Renux is still a fierce mixed martial artist despite being older, and Adri knows she can't afford to miss any more training. In two days, they'll face each other, and there's too much at stake to enter unprepared.

When there's a knock on her door, she looks through the eyehole and takes a deep breath before opening the door for Max. He glances down at her outfit, then up at her face, with a confused expression.

"Are you going somewhere?"

She blushes under his scrutiny. "Yeah, actually." She toys with an earring but stops when she realizes it. "I'm meeting someone for coffee."

His face scrunches. "Who?"

"Levi Savitsky." She shrugs. "Roman knows him."

Max's eyes flicker to her outfit again and his brows knit. She's wearing jeans and a drapey top that shows off her shoulders. He frowns. "Why are you meeting him?"

"Because he might want to coach me."

For a moment, he looks surprised—and annoyed—but he quickly makes his face smooth again. "I told you I already have interviews lined up after your fight."

"I know," she says quickly, surprised by his disapproval. She thought he'd be relieved to know she was looking for a new coach. "I still want to meet them, but I think I should meet with this guy too. Roman says he's good." Apparently, her uncle met Savitsky at some kind of MMA church charity event, and they hit it off.

Max still doesn't look enthused. "What's his background?"

"Cage Rage, mostly. Plus a few UFC fights." Adri tries to recall what else she was able to learn about Levi from a hasty internet search. There wasn't much, aside from his stats and a few highlight reels, which were impressive. He was in his late twenties, and he retired after two knee injuries.

"Why didn't you say anything about him?"

"I didn't know I needed to," she says, with an edge of defiance. He scowls.

"What, Max? What's the big deal? We're meeting for coffee. You can come, but I just figured you wouldn't want to."

He makes a sound between a scoff and a laugh. "I don't."

She stares after him, baffled, as he turns to leave. "Um . . . did you want something?"

He barely slows his pace. "No."

She sighs in exasperation. Apparently, distance hadn't improved his mood. "Are we training today?"

He shrugs. "It depends on when you get back from your coffee date."

"It's not a date!" she yells after him, but he ignores her, disappearing around the corner. She curses under her breath.

"Adri?"

At first, she doesn't hear the low, hesitant voice. She's staring out the café window, deep in thought over her strange encounter with Max.

"Adri Rivera?" the voice repeats.

She turns sharply and sees a man walking toward her table. She raises an eyebrow as he gets closer.

"Hi," he says, extending his hand. "I'm Boom."

"Oh." She's confused, but she still shakes it. "You're not Levi?"

He sits down across from her and smiles. "Well, that's my name, but no one calls me that."

She nods until it dawns on her what he just said. "So, wait . . . Boom?"

He laughs, revealing a wide smile and nice teeth. "Yeah, I know. It's a stupid fight nickname, but it stuck."

She smiles weakly. She didn't expect him to be so good-looking. She saw a few pictures online—the typical stony, serious-faced photographs that most fighters take—but in real life his smile is easy and charming. He sports a thick beard, and his dark, coarse hair is tied into a small knot on top of his head.

"Do you have one?" he asks.

She blinks as his voice pulls her out of her thoughts again. "Have what?"

"A nickname."

She gives him an apologetic look, aware that she probably isn't making the greatest impression. "Yeah. I do."

"What is it?" he asks, glancing at the drink menu posted behind her head.

"La Tormenta."

He stops looking at the menu and gives her his full attention again. "Spanish?"

She nods. "It means 'The Storm.'"

He studies her for a moment with a strangely serious expression. Finally, he cracks his knuckles against the table. "Seems like a good fit. Beautiful but fierce." He springs up again. "Hang on, I'll be right back."

Adri's mouth parts at the unusual compliment as well as his abrupt exit. She watches as he approaches the drink counter and says something she can't hear that makes the barista laugh. Like Max, he's tall and well-built, but he isn't nearly as intimidating in his loose flannel shirt and skinny jeans. When he returns, he carries a teacup and saucer.

"I always forget to ask for a to-go cup," he says, carefully setting it on the table.

She can't help but laugh at the sight of him holding the dainty stenciled cup. "That one is cuter, though."

He sticks his pinky out for emphasis as he takes a drink, making her laugh harder.

"You have a daughter, right?" he asks, as he stirs honey into his tea.

She nods. "Eva. She's almost five."

"Cool. I have a son. He's nine."

"Really?" She glances at his left hand before she can stop herself.

"I'm not married." He smiles faintly, noticing where her eyes went. "I had Rocco when I was young."

She's embarrassed he caught her scrutinizing his fingers, but he doesn't seem to mind. "I was young, too, when I had Eva."

"You're not married either, right?"

"I'm going through a divorce." As the words slip out, her own candidness surprises her. Usually, she avoids mentioning Owen at all costs, but something about Boom made her slip. "It's . . . complicated."

His smile fades. "Oh, crap. That's right. I'm sorry." He shakes his head, the one who's embarrassed this time. "Roman mentioned a little bit about your situation." His eyes fill with genuine concern. "How's all that going?"

She frowns, wondering how much Roman told him about Owen. She really doesn't want her potential coach to pity her or to wonder if she'll go crawling back to Owen, like Max accused her of secretly wanting to do. "Um, it's going good, I think." She reaches for a nearby napkin. "I have a hearing when we get back to Sparta, so hopefully that will be the end of it. . . ." She trails off when she realizes she's torn the napkin into jagged pieces. "Anyway, do you want to talk about fighting?"

He nods, and she's grateful for the change of subject. Over the next hour, she learns that he's a relatively new coach—he just started training fighters in the last two years—but he used to teach Brazilian jujitsu training camps before he started fighting for Cage Rage. The longer they talk, the more she relaxes. Boom Savitsky seems perfectly at ease sitting across from her, drinking green tea from his comical cup.

"Roman also mentioned that you just became a Christian," he says, when their conversation hits a lull.

Her eyes widen. "He did?" Apparently, nothing is private information with Roman. Heat fills her face. "He's trying to make me sound like a weirdo or something."

Boom laughs. "I don't think that's weird." He leans in slightly. "I'm a Christian too."

Suddenly, she remembers—Roman met him at a church thing. "Oh. Right." Still, she's not quite sure what to make of his admission.

"Yeah, been one for about four years now. Lots of fighters are, actually. It's a strange phenomenon—people praying for one another, then beating the crap out of each other in the cage." He grins, but then his face turns more thoughtful. "I guess it makes sense, though. Most people who choose to fight for a living understand something special about the human condition—our real capacity for good and evil. That brings a lot of us closer to God." His eyes meet hers with genuine curiosity. "How's it going for you?"

Adri hesitates. Nobody besides Roman or Yvonne has ever asked her about her faith, so she's not sure how to answer him. "Um, good, I think? Mostly. I'm learning a lot. . . ."

"But?"

She struggles, still piecing her thoughts together. "I guess . . . it's still just kind of hard to believe it sometimes."

He frowns. "To believe that you're a Christian now? Or to believe in God?"

She bites her lip, surprised by his probing questions. "Both, I think. . . . But mostly it's hard to believe that I'm *new* now. You know? The Bible says a lot about that. That we're new creations and stuff like that."

He nods slowly. "Yeah, I feel that. I used to think being a Christian changed you into some kind of super-good person, but then I became one, and I'm still . . . *me*." He smiles slightly. "But I'm a better me, so that's something.

"What makes you better now?"

He strokes his beard thoughtfully. "Well, now I know that God is doing something, and that gives me hope." His hazel eyes meet hers. "That's why we have to witness to people. Everyone needs more hope."

She frowns. Apparently, "witnessing" is another Christian thing she doesn't understand. Sometimes she feels so hopelessly behind. "What does that mean?"

"To witness? That just means telling people about your faith."

She grimaces as she takes a sip of her cold coffee. "Yeah . . . I'm not very good at that."

He laughs at the pained look on her face. "Have you ever tried it?"

She frowns as Max comes to mind. "Sort of."

"Hold that thought."

Surprised, she watches as he takes her cup to the counter and asks the barista to refill it. She smiles when he returns and slides it to her. "Thank you."

"Sure. Cold coffee is so gross." He settles in again. "Anyway, have you ever tried talking to people about why you became a Christian?"

She takes a long, thoughtful sip. "Not really, I guess. I've sort of tried talking to my coach a little, but—" She halts, instantly regretting bringing him up. So far, she'd managed to avoid it.

Boom frowns. "He's not interested?"

She laughs bleakly, recalling Max's dismissive attitude. "Definitely not."

He gives her a sympathetic smile. "Well . . . not everybody is ready. But he might come around. You're in his life for a reason."

As his words sink in, Adri secretly wonders if Max wishes she wasn't in his life, but she wants to drop the subject. She's already told Boom much more than she intended. "How'd you become a Christian?" she asks, deciding to flip the spotlight back on to him. "Did someone witness to you?"

He passes her the sugar when she reaches for it, and his fingers lightly brush hers. "Yep."

She raises an eyebrow. "Who was it?"

"It was a pretty girl, actually."

She looks up from stirring and finds him smiling. A hint of heat fills her face.

"So don't rule yourself out just yet."

Adri ignores her nerves and knocks on Max's door. An hour earlier, she'd said good-bye to Boom and called an Uber, and she's been mulling over their conversation ever since.

She understands now why Roman suggested she meet with Boom. He was certainly qualified. And nice. And charming. She frowns. Maybe too charming. She exhales, aware that her decision just got more than a little complicated. Thankfully, Max opens the door.

"Oh. Hey."

"Hi," she says, forcing herself to smile despite his own unreadable expression. "Can I come in?"

He looks surprised but opens the door wider. She slips past him and glances around the room. The sheets on the bed are tangled, his laptop is open, and one of the chairs is covered in clothes.

The voice of a fight commentator blares on the television until he turns it down.

"How was your date?" he asks.

She ignores his teasing tone. "Not a date. But it was good."

He waits for her to tell him more, but she doesn't. He glances at the clock. "You were gone for a while."

"He invited us to train at his gym today and tomorrow."

"I already booked—"

"I know," she says, cutting him off gently. "I told him that. We can do whatever you want. He just made the offer, so I wanted to let you know."

His face softens at the unexpected capitulation. "Well . . . did you like him?"

"Yeah. He's nice."

"Do you want him to coach you?"

She shrugs, though the question weighs heavily on her mind. "Maybe? I'm not really in a position to be picky, am I? If he wants to work with me, I'll consider it."

It's clear by the look on his face that her answer irks him, but she doesn't understand why. Max is the one who made their arrangement temporary in the first place.

"Well . . ." He clears his throat. "Let's just go train. We need to make up for yesterday."

As he says it, his words strike her. *We need to make up.* Her heart races as she remembers their argument. He seems to pick up on it, too, because he looks like he wants to say more, but she turns to leave before he can.

As she gathers up her gear, she tries to push the regretful look on his face out of her mind, but she can't. She sighs, realizing that the biggest fight of her life is in two days, and she's exactly what she doesn't want to be—distracted.

Later, in the car, Max forces himself to put their exchange behind him. He's annoyed by his own annoyance. Once again,

Adri's beauty had struck him, as did his jealousy at the thought of her meeting with another man.

He'd knocked on her door earlier to apologize after a night of tortured sleep, having spent most of it figuring out what he was going to say—*I'm sorry, I care about you, you're not weak*. There's so much more, but he can't say the rest out loud.

Begrudgingly, he asks for the name of Boom's gym. He watches as her eyes widen.

"You really want to train there?"

He shrugs coolly and plugs it into the GPS. "I'm just curious."

Half an hour later, they arrive at a small brick building on the corner of a busy street. Inside, they're hit with the strong smell of sweat and incense. He frowns as he looks around. "Pretty weird place for a gym."

Adri looks as surprised as he does. They're inside some kind of historic building with polished wood floors and two arched windows. Vined plants crowd the ledges and drape down the brick walls. A few items are scattered around the room—weights, grappling dummies, headgear—but the focal point is a battered hexagonal cage that someone spray-painted gold. Folk music warbles through a hidden speaker.

"Adri?"

Max turns swiftly and sees a bearded, hippie-type approaching them, dressed in shorts and a faded T-shirt, with numerous tattoos snaking around both his arms and one of his legs. He also looks vaguely familiar—and definitely not like Adri's type. He relaxes slightly. "That's him?"

She nods, and Max watches her out of the corner of his eye as the man pulls her into a quick shoulder hug. She hugs him back, but her shoulders are rigid. Max can't tell if it's because of the hug or because it happened in his presence.

The hippie uses his watch to turn down the music, then grins at both of them. "I didn't know you guys were coming." He extends his hand to Max. "Hey, brother. It's been a while."

Max stares at his hand for a moment, then frowns. "What's your name again?"

Adri glares at him, but the man looks amused. "Levi Savitsky, but I go by Boom. You seriously don't remember me?"

Max's eyes narrow. "Should I?"

"Dang, dude." He laughs. "That's rough. I fought you in Nebraska five years ago. You won, remember?"

Max's eyes widen as he remembers. "Holy crap. You're right." He shakes Boom's hand. "Sorry. I've fought a lot of people since then."

Boom smirks. "And we all start to look the same after a while, huh?"

Max laughs even though he doesn't want to. "No, I just . . ." He thinks for a moment, letting the memory resurface. "Yeah, that was a pretty good fight, wasn't it?" It was one of Max's first. Boom was a few years ahead of him in the fight circuit. "You did that crazy kick thing that almost got me in the first round."

Boom snorts. "Yeah, that was an accident. I slipped."

As they laugh, Adri's eyes move between them with growing uneasiness. "So . . . you know each other?"

"I guess we do," Max says, nodding. "If you count fighting each other for fifteen minutes as knowing each other."

Boom smiles. "Adri mentioned your name at coffee, but I didn't put it together until now."

Some of Max's joviality fades as he's reminded of the fact that Adri just spent hours talking with Boom—his potential replacement. And, apparently, they'd talked about him. He feels a prick of annoyance and more than a little bit of jealousy. The realization that Boom is likable makes it even worse.

"You guys want a tour of the place?" Boom offers, interrupting his thoughts.

He and Adri follow him around the gym, but he barely listens as Boom talks, too busy wondering what Adri thinks of him and his weird gym, but her face is unreadable. A few fighters stop training and glance in their direction.

"Hey, Adri, do you want to work with Lizzy for a bit? She can help you get ready for Saturday." Boom motions to a young woman stretching nearby. "She's a Muay Thai beast."

Adri glances at the woman, but Lizzy's eyes are fixed on Max as she pulls her long silky hair into a ponytail. He raises an eyebrow when she flashes him a bold smile.

"Sure," Adri says tersely, moving past him to meet her on the mat.

"Adri's got a fight coming up with Sabine Renux," Boom explains.

Lizzy raises one of her perfectly arched eyebrows and clucks her tongue. "You know Muay Thai, right?"

"Yeah. Some."

She gives Adri a pitying look. "Well . . . I'll do my best."

Max watches them work through a few moves on a mat until he feels a light tap on his shoulder.

"Can we talk for a minute?" Boom asks.

Reluctant but curious, he rises and follows Boom to a small office crammed full of secondhand furniture. Sketches of bicycles—clearly drawn by a child—cover an entire brick wall. Boom gestures to a chair, and Max sits stiffly. No matter what, he's determined not to like Boom. He hopes Adri feels the same.

"Do you own this place?" he asks, glancing around again. There's no computer or phone, but a worn-out Bible rests on the desk. He scowls.

Boom shakes his head. "No, unfortunately. I'd like my own place, but I don't have the funds." He looks around the cluttered room with a faint smile. "It's sort of a co-op. People use it for all kinds of stuff. Mostly yoga."

Max grimaces.

"Hey, don't knock yoga until you try it."

"I've tried it. It's called stretching."

Boom laughs, but then his expression turns more serious again. "So . . ."

"You want to talk about Adri, right?"

He nods. "Mostly, I just want to know why you don't want to coach her. She didn't tell me a whole lot about your situation, other than it was temporary." He leans back in his chair. "So, I'm curious. . . . Why do you want to drop her?"

Max scowls at his choice of words. "I'm not *dropping* her. I can't coach her full-time because I have a gym back home, and that's my main priority."

"Makes sense. And that's the only reason?"

Max's eyes narrow at the hint of skepticism in his voice. "Adri works harder than anyone I know, if that's what you're asking me. I don't have any issues with her." Aside from their personal ones, he thinks, which are none of Boom's business.

"Well, then—"

"Albany is your home base?" Max asks, cutting him off with a question of his own. Through an open window, he hears cars honk and zoom by. He wonders if Adri's thought about that. She and Eva are pretty settled in Sparta.

"Yep," Boom says, motioning toward the drawings. "My son lives here. And we have a church family."

Max's displeasure grows. Of course Boom has a son. And goes to church. "Adri and her daughter are happy in Sparta," he says flatly.

"Right, but I think we can work something out. She might have to travel—"

"Did you mention that to her?"

Boom raises an eyebrow at Max's increasingly sharp tone. "Yeah, of course. We talked about her traveling or her moving here if we end up working together." He shrugs dismissively. "She seemed open to both ideas."

He frowns.

"You good, brother?"

He looks up and finds Boom looking puzzled. "Huh?"

"You kind of look like you want to punch something." Boom smiles faintly. "You want a Nebraska rematch or something?"

For a moment, Max is too surprised to respond. Is his annoyance that obvious? He curses silently. His feelings for Adri are making him feel like a fool, which is another reason why he knows he should put more distance between them. But he definitely doesn't want to give his place to easygoing, Bible-reading Boom. "No," he lies. "Not at the moment, anyway."

Boom laughs. "Well, that's good. Give me a five-minute warning if you change your mind."

Max forces himself to smile, although he's struck by a memory—the time when Boom's foot nearly collided with his face and put an early end to his career. His smile fades. He's beaten Boom before. Surely, he can beat him again.

"Anyway, I'll let you get back out there, but I'm glad you and Adri came in." Boom stands, releasing him with a small brotherly smirk. "Come back tomorrow, too, so you can get used to me."

Max knows he's being way too quiet as he drives Adri back to the hotel. He's still bothered by his conversation with Boom, but thankfully she makes up for his silence.

"You missed it, dude. I got Lizzy *so* good. She had me in a guillotine, but then I got her with a Von Flue Choke."

Max smiles at the elated look on her face. "I wish I'd seen it."

"She asked about you."

He frowns. "Who?"

"Lizzy. She wanted to know if you were single."

"Yeah?" He catches the hint of annoyance in Adri's voice. "What'd you tell her?"

"I told her to ask you yourself."

He laughs at her snappy tone. "Well, she didn't, so that must mean it wasn't true love."

"Didn't you see her staring at you the entire time?"

He laughs again. Truthfully, he noticed Lizzy's attention, but he didn't return it. "Most women like the *idea* of me more than the actual me, Adri. She probably would've been disappointed after our third conversation."

She frowns. "Why?"

"Oh, you know . . . the whole famous fighter thing." He sighs. "Once she got to know me, she'd realize I'm not as exciting as she thinks. I'm just a guy who knows how to fight."

"The real you is exciting," she says defensively before making a small surprised sound—like the words slipped out before she could stop them.

He gives her a sideways glance and finds her cheeks blooming with color. "Thanks," he says quietly.

"Would you date her?" she asks, quickly changing the subject.

"Who?" he teases.

She glares at him. "*Lizzy*."

"Maybe?" He laughs, then shrugs. "I don't know. She's not really my type." He's lying, of course—she was exactly his type—but that doesn't matter when Adri is inches away from him. In fact, he can barely remember what Lizzy looks like, aside from her hair and height. Adri must sense his reluctance to talk about Lizzy because she drops the subject.

"Hang on a sec." He slows the car when he spots a gas station. "I'm going to grab some stuff."

When he returns minutes later, plastic bag in hand, Adri looks more relaxed in the passenger seat. She also looks exhausted, but that was to be expected after training all afternoon. Most dauntingly, her fight with Sabine Renux is looming closer than ever, and no doubt that's weighing heavily on her mind. Thankfully, Owen hasn't made any surprise appearances—in New York or Sparta—but Max is still on guard so Adri doesn't have to be.

He watches as she presses her fingertips to a small bruise blooming near her eye. "A little gift from Lizzy?" he asks.

She nods. "Yep."

"You looked better than she did, though, by the end. She's going to feel some of those jabs tomorrow."

She's silent for a moment, but she smiles at the compliment. "What did you think of Boom?" she asks.

"He seems fine," he says flatly. He knows she wants him to say more, but he doesn't elaborate. He wants to know what *she* thinks.

She lets her breath out slowly, like she's still working out her feelings. "I think he'd probably be a good coach." She waits again, as if she expects him to challenge her, but he doesn't. "I mean, obviously you beat him, so that means he's not better than you," she continues, and Max feels a small twinge of pride. "But he's still a good option, I think. Maybe . . ." As her voice trails off, he notes her growing uncertainty. She throws him another questioning look.

"It's your decision, Adri." It kills him to say it, but it's true. And, deep down, he knows that Boom probably *would* be a good coach, and there's no reason why she shouldn't work with him. He frowns as she falls silent.

It's late when they arrive at the hotel. Adri takes slow, tired steps down the hallway and Max matches her pace. Occasionally, she lets out a small huff of pain.

"Doing okay?"

"Yeah." She covers a long, lingering yawn with her hand. "Just tired. And sore."

He is familiar with the feeling—the kind of soreness you feel from the top of your head to the tips of your toes. "Get in the tub for a little bit," he suggests.

She nods again. "Good idea."

"How's your weight?"

"One-sixteen."

"Nice. You're on track." He reaches into the plastic bag and pulls out a mini-Snickers. "You can have this after you weigh in tomorrow."

Her eyes widen in surprise before she laughs. He offers her the candy bar, but she shakes her head. "Thanks, but that's too much temptation right now," she says, gently pushing it back to him. "You'll have to keep it safe."

"I appreciate your honesty, ma'am." He drops it back in the bag. "I'll put it on your pillow tomorrow."

She laughs again, more freely this time as her exhaustion takes over. "Sounds good. I'll pretend like I'm a big-time fighter sleeping somewhere fancy."

"Hey, depending on how Saturday goes, that might happen sooner than you think." He says it to be encouraging, but her eyes darken, and he can see that she's deep in her thoughts again, weighing the stakes. He doesn't blame her. If she can pull off a win against Sabine Renux, something they both know is incredibly unlikely, she'll make big waves in the fighting world. Max wonders if she's prepared for that. God knows he wasn't when he knocked out Bradley Unger in Dallas at age nineteen.

He waits as she searches for her key card, his eyes moving from her cuts and bruises to the small dark circles under her eyes. "You've been working really hard, Adri."

"Let's just pray it pays off. For both of us." She smiles wearily. "See you in the morning."

When she disappears behind the door, he almost heads to his own room, but he hesitates as his abandoned apology comes to mind, along with a tight knot in his stomach. He knocks on her door, despite the voice in his head that warns him not to, and ignores his racing heart. When she finally opens it, she frowns up at him, and for a split second he's reminded of Miami.

"What's wrong, Max?"

Her hair is loose around her shoulders, and he can hear the sound of water running behind her. "Nothing. . . . I just . . ." He fumbles for the right words, which seem to slip and slide out of his grasp, but he knows he needs to tell her the truth before she fights again. "I just wanted to say something about the other day . . . when we were training."

Her eyes widen. "We don't have to talk about—"

He holds up a hand. "I know we don't have to, and we won't talk about it ever again, okay? But I just wanted to say . . ." He hesitates, frustrated that she can still make him feel so unsure of himself. And that he can do the same to her. "I don't think you're weak."

Her mouth parts, but he continues, ignoring her surprise.

"You're one of the strongest people I know. I just wanted you to know that, okay?" He considers saying something else as she looks at him with those eyes, something that always lingers in the back of his heart, but he shakes his head, aware that it isn't the right time—and it might never be.

"Anyway, that's all." He turns before she can stop him. "Good night, Adri."

13

A DRI PEERS THROUGH TWO THICK BLACK CURTAINS. Max stands behind her, his eyes also fixed on the stage where fighters weigh in. The walls rumble as rap music fills the convention center, and a man with a slick voice officiates.

"Let's hear it for the challenger, Tamie 'Tornado' Ross!"

Adri's nerves surge. The packed crowd cheers as Tamie, a young, tan blonde with impossibly long legs, walks onto a crowded stage plastered with sponsor posters. There, she teasingly strips off her Daisy Dukes to reveal her perfectly muscled body, which is barely covered by a pink bikini. When an official announces her weight, she blows a kiss to more wild applause.

Max nudges her. "You and Renux are next."

She exhales. Between hunger pains, soreness, and anticipation, her nerves are raw. When the song changes, signaling her entrance, she looks up at him uneasily, but he gives her a reassuring smile.

"Relax. This is the fun part." He flashes her his most serious face and makes her laugh. "You just go out there and look mean."

"Ladies and gentlemen, it's time for our co-main event of the evening—the Women's Strawweight Bout between Adri Rivera and former Coronet Flyweight Champion Sabine Renux!"

Max's grip tightens on her shoulder as the crowd cheers. The man with the microphone glances in her direction.

"Introducing the challenger, Adri 'La Tormenta' Rivera!"

Applause mingles with boos as Adri walks through the curtain, but they sound strangely muffled, thanks to her nerves. Max follows closely behind, and she's never been more thankful for his steadying presence. All eyes are fixed on them as she peels off her jacket and steps on the scale in a black sports bra and leggings. On the scale, she has a clear view of the vast room. At least two hundred faces stare back at her, interspersed with camera operators and officials.

"One hundred and fifteen pounds!"

More applause, followed by more boos as music vibrates beneath their feet. She breathes a sigh of relief and takes her place beside Max as the official takes the microphone again.

"And now, the champion, Sabine 'Medusa' Renux!"

The applause is louder as Renux approaches the stage, followed by her team of coaches, all clad in matching athletic apparel.

"She's big," Max says, almost too quietly for her to hear. His voice holds a hint of concern.

Adri keeps her face expressionless as Renux walks to the scale, but her heart thuds so hard it hurts. Renux is a much older fighter at age thirty-eight, but her body is as impressive as ever as she strips off a designer track suit. She's built more thickly than Adri, and her short hair is slicked back, revealing a sharp chin and dark, confident eyes. She grins at the enthusiastic crowd.

"Face off, ladies!"

Adri meets Sabine in the middle of the stage where they face each other. Adri makes her face as smooth as stone—something Roman taught her to do a long time ago—but Sabine stares back at her with a confident smirk that has its intended effect. They break away, and Sabine turns to her coaches, while Adri turns to Max. She's intimidated by Sabine's size and confidence but refuses to show it as a horde of reporters storm the stage.

"Max Lyons!"

"Max, can we get a comment from you?"

"A lot of people have been wondering when you'd come back—"

Adri stands frozen, stunned by the barrage of people and cameras pointed in her direction. She's also surprised to see that Tamie Ross, still wearing her bikini top, is glaring at her in the midst of the crowd.

"Max, what's the plan if your fighter wins tomorrow night?" a reporter demands, shoving his way closer to Max. "Anyone you want to call out?"

Trapped on all sides now, Max looks annoyed and defeated at the same time. "No," he answers flatly. "We're taking it one fight at a time."

"Is it true that you were tapped to coach Gemma Stone?" another reporter asks. "What made you choose Rivera instead?"

Cameras flash in her direction, and Adri blinks in the blinding light.

"I'm working with Adri because I believe in her," Max replies.

The words are barely out of his mouth before someone else jumps in with another question, something about Adri's lack of professional experience, but she pushes her way out of the fray.

As she pulls on her shirt and shoes, unexpected feelings war inside her. She wants to believe Max, especially after what he said last night, but a part of her doubts him. If he believed in her so much, wouldn't he want to coach her, instead of handing her off to someone else?

"Hey, La Tormenta! Over here."

She looks into the crowd and is surprised to see a familiar face. Boom sits near the front with a young boy. Smiling, she hops off the stage to meet them. The boy is obviously his son. His freckled face is lightly sunburned, and his dark hair curls around his collarbone. Boom's hand is on his shoulder.

"Rocco and I like weigh-ins," Boom explains.

Adri extends her hand, and Rocco shakes it. "Nice to meet you."

He mumbles shyly in agreement.

Boom raises his eyebrows at the lingering crowd. "Pretty good turnout."

"Yeah . . ." Her nerves return, along with her doubts. "I thought it was going to be smaller for some reason. But between Sabine and Max, I should've guessed people would show up."

He looks past her, at the stage, where Max is still trapped by reporters and fans. He grins. "Popular guy, huh?"

Adri sighs. "Always."

He frowns at her deflated tone but changes the subject. "What's your strategy going to be with Sabine? She's bigger than I remember."

She repeats the mantra she and Max created. "Stand and bang. Stay off the ground. Knock her out."

Boom grins. "Sounds perfect."

She shrugs, but his smile is comforting. With Max so preoccupied, she needs all the reassurance she can get. "That's how I like to fight."

"Me too. That's how I got my nickname, actually. Making people go *boom*."

She laughs as the crowd around them dwindles, until finally their voices are the only ones she can hear, aside from the distant sound of Max and the reporters.

Boom clears his throat. "Hey, I also wanted to ask you something else."

She frowns. For the first time since she met Boom, he looks mildly uncomfortable.

"My house church meets at my apartment this Sunday," he says, toying absently with his beard. "So, depending on how you're feeling in the morning, you're welcome to join us. And Max, too, if he wants."

"Thanks." She's touched by the offer, but she already knows she won't be able to drag Max to any kind of church service, let alone one in Boom's apartment. "I'll try to make it." She remembers Sabine and frowns. "If I'm not dead."

Later, when Boom and Rocco say their good-byes, she looks at the stage again, hopeful that Max is ready to go. Most of the reporters have dispersed, but now Max is talking to Tamie, who still hasn't put her shirt back on. Adri scowls. A few reporters snap pictures of them laughing.

Annoyed and tired of waiting, Adri finds the nearest exit and climbs the stairs. When she reaches the top flight, she opens the door to a small terrace. Thankful for an escape, she breathes in the cool air and looks down at the twinkling lights of cars and buildings, relaxing slightly now that she's so high above the chaos. Still, she feels a twinge of jealousy when she thinks about Max taking his sweet time with Tamie.

"It's true, then. Great minds really do think alike."

Adri turns sharply and finds Sabine Renux smirking at her. Her eyes widen as Sabine joins her by the balcony.

Sabine chuckles. "I thought I was supposed to be the headliner tonight, but then you showed up with Max Lyons."

Closer, Adri can see a few faint lines around her eyes and mouth, almost hidden by makeup. "Yeah, sorry about that. Max has that effect on people."

"No need to apologize." Sabine winks. "Men like him always make things more interesting."

Adri gives her a curious look. She has a light, charming sort of accent that makes everything she says sound more sophisticated. Most fighters avoid interacting with their opponents before a fight, just to keep their headspace as clear as possible, but Sabine doesn't seem to mind their unexpected rendezvous. She pulls a sleek black package from one of her pockets.

"Don't worry," she says quickly. "They're totally herbal. Mint and bergamot. No harm done." A strange, sweet smell fills the air as she lights one. "I get them in Morocco." She offers Adri one, but she declines. "You must have better vices, then."

Adri laughs. "No, not really."

She flashes Adri a knowing smile. "I doubt that."

For some reason, Adri can't help but think she's still talking about Max. Color fills her cheeks as she quickly changes the subject. "It really is an honor to fight you. I didn't get to say it back there, but I watched all your fights growing up." Her teenage self spent countless afternoons sitting in her aunt and uncle's living room, Max beside her, watching the famed Medusa claim another victim.

Sabine smiles, but there's a touch of smugness. "Are you ready, then?"

Adri nods, but Sabine shakes her head somberly.

"I'm sorry, my dear, but I don't think you are. I just have a feeling that it's not your time yet."

Her assessment unsettles Adri, but she doesn't show it. Instead, Adri lets her eyes drift to the cars below and ignores her racing heart. "Well, I guess we'll both find out tomorrow." She gives Sabine a cordial nod and starts to leave, but she pauses when she hears a sigh. When Adri turns back curiously, Sabine meets her gaze.

"Watch out for Owen."

Adri stares at her, momentarily frozen. That was the *last* thing she expected her to say. "You know Owen?"

Sabine shakes her head. "No, but I know of him." Her expression darkens. "And I know what he's been saying about you. He has friends with big mouths."

Adri scowls. She hasn't even fought yet, and Owen's already trying to ruin it for her? "What are they saying about me?" she demands.

"Nothing very nice."

"Well, he—"

"No, don't." Sabine cuts her off with a sharp wave of her fingers. "Don't tell me the sad love story. That is your business. I'm just warning you. Be smart."

Her sudden coldness puzzles Adri until she realizes the reason for it—Sabine doesn't want to feel sympathy for someone she has to pummel in twenty-four hours. It's hard enough to fight people you don't like. It's even harder to fight the ones you do.

"Apparently, you broke his heart," Sabine continues, blowing a final plume of scented smoke in Adri's direction. "So he wants to break yours too. Don't let him."

⁂

"Wow."

Adri punches Max's mitts with impressive power as he moves

around her, then she throws an unexpected knee that he barely blocks. She's been on fire all morning, moving seamlessly from one combination to the next.

"I think you're ready," he says.

She nods and pauses to catch her breath. Her fight with Sabine is only hours away. Her face darkens as she recalls their conversation on the terrace and Sabine's cryptic warning about Owen. Last night, in a moment of frustration, she messaged him on Instagram to tell him to stop being so stubborn and to just sign the papers, but she instantly regretted it. He never responded, but she spent the entire night tossing and turning and checking her phone.

She hides a yawn from Max as she gathers up her gear. She hasn't told him about Owen yet and hasn't decided if she even should. It'll only stress him out too.

"Hey, Adri, before we go, I have something to show you real quick."

Surprised, she follows him down a hotel hallway, unsure of what to expect. She waits for an explanation as they walk, but he doesn't offer one. "Where are we going?" she asks, wondering if he scheduled a last-minute photo shoot or something. Their trip to Albany was busier than she expected, with meetings and interviews crammed between her training sessions. She'd forgotten about that side of the fighting world.

Max doesn't answer her question as he opens the door to a small conference room. She waits for him to go in first, but he steps aside. Confused, she reaches to turn on the lights, but he gently pushes her hand away. When she glances up at him questioningly, he nods to a projector on the wall facing them. It clicks on, and she gasps.

"Hi, Mama!"

Adri's eyes widen as Eva waves at her from the screen. She wears a ruffled gold dress and an impressive cardboard crown, no doubt cut by Roman and decorated by Yvonne. "Hi, butterfly," she says, getting closer to the screen as tears spring into her eyes. "Happy birthday."

"My party is soon! Miss Skye is coming."

Adri's heart aches terribly. She's only been gone a few days, but Eva already looks older. Her party still doesn't start for a few hours, but her eyes are bright with excitement. "You're going to have so much fun today."

Roman appears and sits beside Eva on the couch. He fiddles with the screen for a minute, then grins at Adri. "Hey, kiddo. It's the big day. How are you feeling?"

The time passes quickly as they talk about Eva's party guests, the weather in New York, and a few of Roman's last-minute tips until the screen eventually freezes, capturing him giving her a thumbs-up while Eva is frozen in a twirl.

"Yvonne and I will be watching tonight," Roman says, his voice warbling slightly before cutting out. "Eva and I are going to pray about it before bed."

Adri smiles. The fight won't start until much later that night, and they'd all agreed that it was probably best if Eva didn't watch it this time—just in case things didn't go her way.

Max does his best to fix the connection, but they disappear with a quiet click right after Eva shouts out her final bit of advice to Adri.

"Knock her out, Mama!"

Laughing and crying at the same time, Adri turns to Max and wraps her arms around him before she even realizes what she's doing. He stiffens, surprised, but then he hugs her back.

"Thank you," she says, her voice muffled against his shirt.

"You're welcome." He looks down at her and frowns at her tears. "You're happy, right?"

She nods.

"I thought so, but it's hard to tell with all the crying."

She smiles and breaks away from him, her heart racing. Somehow he knew exactly what she needed. Seeing Eva's face fills her with fresh motivation, despite her fatigue.

The next hour passes in a flurry of activity as she and Max pack up and leave for the venue. Their footsteps echo softly as they make their way to her locker room, and each small step reminds her of how close she is to the biggest fight of her life.

She's momentarily distracted when they pass by a full-size poster of Tamie 'Tornado' Ross on one of the walls. "Do you know her?" she asks, recalling how familiar they seemed the night before.

He glances at the poster. "Tamie? Yeah, we used to hang out. A long time ago."

"Like, you dated her?"

He nods, but his eyes narrow. "Did Boom tell you that?"

"No, no one told me anything," she says tersely, following him into her locker room. "It just looked like you knew each other pretty well. Maybe that's why she didn't bother to put her shirt back on."

"Oh, you mean when you were talking to Boom for half an hour?" He gives her a pointed look, which she ignores. "She and I dated for like a month, Adri. I don't even remember when. Years ago."

Thankfully, someone suddenly bangs on the door, and he stops mid-explanation to open it while she seizes the opportunity to slip into one of the stalls. While he talks to an official, she changes clothes and curses herself for bringing up Tamie. What reason does she have to be annoyed with him? She was the one who married someone else, not him, but she still feels hurt.

Exhaling, she steps out in her red sports bra and shorts, her heart drumming uneasily inside her chest. The official is gone, but Max is leaning against one of the lockers, waiting for her. Adri's pulse jumps. His eyes move over her slowly and carefully, as if he's studying someone in a photograph and can't figure out who it is.

"Does it bother you?" he asks.

"What?"

"That I dated Tamie?"

His voice isn't smug or teasing, but her face still fills with heat.

"I . . ." She almost denies it, but there's no point. Once again, her frustrating feelings for him got the better of her, and she spoke without thinking. "I was just curious," she says quietly, sidestepping his question. She focuses her attention on taping up her hands. "Shouldn't we warm up?"

His eyes briefly lock on hers with a questioning expression, but he agrees. Once she finishes, they fly through her warm-up, with Adri moving even faster than before. The feelings surging through her—fear, regret, hope—are overwhelming, but she knows from experience that fighting will overpower them. At least temporarily.

As she walks through the tunnel, she remembers God is with her now. More than any moment in her life, she's aware of her newfound need for his power as she gets closer to the cage.

"Hit her first," Max reminds her as she unzips her jacket and hands it to him. "You always hit her first. And if she hits you once, you hit her twice."

Adri stands still, unblinking, as an official smears Vaseline on her cheekbones and the bridge of her nose, then checks her mouthguard. She enters the cage and cracks her neck, then her wrists, easing some of the tension that's steadily building in her body. Roman's voice mingles with Max's mantras, creating a rhythm in her head that slowly merges with the pulsating beat of her song. *You're free.*

Adri exhales slowly, electrified by those words as they cut through all the noise. They remind her that despite all of it—the abuse, the doubts, the disappointment, the mistakes—she's free. And in that moment, she really *believes* it, and that fills her with a strange, soaring feeling as she realizes she's free to fight for herself again, for the simple joy of it—not just to survive.

On the other side of the cage, Sabine enters to a slow, haunting Slayer song as her fans scream. Adri holds her gaze as Sabine paces the cage, dressed in purple, her eyes fixed on Adri like a predator watching its prey. There's no hint of the warmth she showed Adri last night—just hard, practiced coldness. Adri's fear resurfaces for a moment, but it rises and falls like a wave when she and Sabine meet in the middle.

"Be first, Adri!" Max yells, behind her. As she and Sabine circle each other, Adri and Max both know that all of Adri's work culminates to this—twenty-five minutes or less in a cage. Seizing her first opportunity, she shoots in and lands two hard jabs to Sabine's face. Sabine instinctively punches back, and Adri barely slips them as the crowd goes crazy.

"Watch her reach!" Max yells as Sabine swings wildly and nearly hits Adri with a nasty hook. Adri tries to listen to him, but her ears are ringing now as pain and adrenaline flood her.

Sabine's arms are inches longer than hers, but Adri manages to close the distance and land another powerful jab. Sabine's face contorts in pain, but in one expert motion, she drops down and grabs Adri's legs, pushing her against the cage.

"Sprawl!" Max yells, as Adri struggles to stay standing.

She bears down to stop Sabine from swiping her left leg and knocking her to the ground, but it's a struggle against Sabine's size. Adri's back is pushed against the cage, while Sabine's head and shoulders press against her torso, pinning her in place. Desperate, Adri throws the only thing she can, her elbow, slamming it repeatedly against the side of Sabine's head. The crowd collectively groans with each hit that makes its mark.

"Don't let up, Adri!" Max yells. He sounds as desperate as Adri feels.

Adri keeps at it, only stopping when Sabine rams her in the ribs with a sharp knee. Adri quickly adjusts, ignoring the searing pain, and keeps throwing elbows until Sabine finally releases her.

"Get after her, Adri!"

Max sounds more hopeful now, but Adri's not fast enough. Sabine swings first and hits Adri with a powerful punch, and warm blood gushes from somewhere near her right eye just as Sabine goes for another takedown. Adri's vision blurs as she struggles to break free, pinned down by Sabine's legs.

"Thirty seconds left!" Max shouts. "Get out of there!"

Blood still pours from her face, but Adri barely notices as she fights off Sabine's grip, which is slowly inching toward a choke. She feels Sabine's arm slide, damp with sweat and blood, so she uses it to slip out of her grasp. The audience roars.

"Ten seconds, Adri!"

Sabine dodges two strikes from Adri but fails to block a heavy hook just as the buzzer sounds. She staggers backward but recovers quickly enough to flash Adri a cocky grin before retreating to her corner.

Breathing hard, Adri ignores the lingering pain and meets Max in her corner and sits down. A camera circles them as he works fast, pressing ice against Adri's torso and pouring water into her mouth. When he wipes the blood from her face, Adri winces.

"I think she got my eye."

A hint of panic flickers across his face. "Can you see out of it?"

She blinks a few times. Slowly, the angles of Max's face become sharper and more vivid. "Yeah. I think so."

He signals for a medic, who examines her quickly. He flashes a light in her eye, temporarily blinding her again.

"Her eye is fine," he says, after some more light prodding. "The cut is right underneath it."

Max breathes a sigh of relief, although he and Adri both know it's a significant disadvantage. When the medic leaves, Max lowers his face to Adri's so their foreheads almost touch.

"Adri, listen. You scared her." He looks over his shoulder at Renux, who's being tended to by her coaches. "Look at her."

Adri glances in that direction and sees he's right. Sabine looks rattled. Her chest is rising and falling fast, and she can't keep her hands still as her coaches motion wildly toward Adri.

"New plan," Max says, pouring more water into her mouth. "If she gets you on the ground this time, just finish it there. I wasn't sure before, but you can do it." As he helps her to her feet, his hands close firmly around hers. "Knock her out standing up or on the ground. Just finish it. This round."

Surprised but out of time, Adri meets Sabine in the middle of the cage a second time. They lock eyes, and Adri sees a hint of fear again, which dissolves some of her own as the second round begins. Her uncle's voice fills her head.

"Everybody's the same in a fight, Adri. No matter who you're

fighting, there's always some kind of unknown. The smallest person can throw the hardest punch. The tough guy can stall out in the first round. The only thing that's not unknown is you—your weaknesses, your strengths, what you can do. So, focus on that."

She exhales.

"Ask yourself—what can I do to win this fight? What's it gonna take?"

Sabine seems more willing to stand and throw punches this round, so they exchange blows for a while, both of them growing more fatigued but also more determined. After what feels like an eternity, Adri lands the one she really wants—a heavy uppercut that cracks against Sabine's jaw. The audience cheers wildly as Sabine staggers back, her eyes slightly crossed, but she waves off the ref when he approaches.

"I'm fine," she says, fixing her cold gaze on Adri again. Her eyes still have a slightly dazed look to them, but she manages to throw two fast punches that knock Adri off balance before going for another takedown. She curses as Sabine pulls her to the ground a second time.

"Finish it on the ground, Adri!" Max roars. They both know this is the moment that will determine Adri's future in the fight world.

Adri and Sabine's limbs slide with sweat as Sabine struggles to mount her, but neither of them lets up, not wanting to give the other an inch of momentum. Sabine tries to throw a few punches as she works on the mount, but every time she raises her arm to strike, Adri inches upward, erasing her advantage.

Fatigued, Sabine stops punching long enough for Adri to throw her own barrage of hammer fists. Sabine's body presses painfully against her, but Adri fights through it. She knows she only has mere seconds before Sabine takes the winning position.

"Don't stop punching, Adri!"

Adri punches with as much power as she can, one strike after another, hitting the sides of Sabine's head. She can hear Sabine's labored breathing and the occasional sharp gasp of pain. When

Sabine groans in frustration and moves to avoid another punch, Adri knows that's her opening. In one swift motion, she rolls, taking Sabine with her and reversing their positions. Sabine, slowed from so many blows to the head, can't react fast enough to stop Adri's mount, nor does she protect herself from Adri's elbow as she slams it against her face.

"You have her now, Adri! Finish it!"

Sabine wrestles to break free and manages to shift Adri's weight some, but it's too late. Adri is poised to strike, and that's exactly what she does, throwing relentless elbows and fists. Blood pours from Sabine's nose, but she doesn't give up, and neither does Adri. She feels a storm brewing within her as she punches—black clouds and pouring rain, lightning and whistling wind, heaviness and lightness mixing together as time seems to stand still.

Suddenly, she feels rough hands pull her away from Sabine.

"She's done, fighter," the referee says sharply, bending to protect Sabine from Adri's strikes. "You're done. She's done. It's over."

Adri blinks, momentarily stunned by his words and the sight of Sabine motionless on the mat. As Adri stands up again, the audience erupts, and it hits her—the sounds, the people storming the cage, the colors and cameras, Sabine still on the ground, struggling to stand. Adri turns and finds Max standing amazingly still in all the uproar. His eyes meet hers, and for a second, it's like the veil between their past and present splits, like light pouring through heavy clouds. It was the kind of moment she used to dream about before she gave up on dreaming.

The referee takes her hand and lifts it high in the air. "The winner, by technical knockout, Adri Rivera!"

She hears people talking somewhere behind her.

"Wow. I can't believe Sabine Renux got knocked out by a nobody."

Someone else laughs. "Well, she's not a nobody anymore."

An official approaches, holding out a microphone. "Adri, how does it feel—"

Strong arms wrap around her waist as Sabine, recovered now,

easily lifts her up before she can answer the question. Adri laughs, surprised and touched, as Sabine carries her around the cage to more wild applause until she sets her down again and takes the mic. "Come on, let's hear it for this underdog," she yells, before leading the crowd in chanting Adri's nickname.

"La Tormenta! La Tormenta!"

When Sabine sets her down again, Adri's eyes are filled with tears.

"I guess I was wrong for once," Sabine says with a wink. Her face is still tinged with blood, but her smile is genuine. "It was your time."

When Max takes Adri's hand and raises it a final time, she feels that soaring feeling again and gives God a silent thank-you, aware that it's much more than just a win or her name filling the arena.

It's the sound of a broken dream being put back together.

14

"DO YOU WANT COMMUNION, ADRI?"

Adri looks up and finds Boom looking at her. Five other pairs of eyes stare too.

"Oh. Sorry," she whispers. She was lost in her thoughts, reliving her fight with Renux from the night before. She glances at the plate of bread in Boom's hand and frowns.

"You tear off a piece and then dip it in the wine," he explains, with a slight smile. "Then I'll say a prayer, and we'll eat."

"Okay." She tears off a small piece of bread and dips it in the wine glass in Boom's other hand. The others already have theirs, aside from a young woman strumming a guitar.

Boom dips his bread in the wine and closes his eyes. "God, thank you for giving us all of you. As we eat this bread and drink this wine, remind us of your love and what it costs."

"Amen," Adri says in unison with the others before eating the wine-soaked bread. She feels oddly moved by Boom's simple prayer. "Communion" at Roman's church involved small flavorless crackers, grape juice, and a lot of words she doesn't understand yet.

The woman with the guitar ends the service with a classic hymn, filling Boom's living room with her beautiful voice. Her hair is ink-black and streaked with blue, and when she finishes singing,

Adri feels at peace for the first time since her fight with Sabine, which left her with plenty of euphoric feelings, but conflicted ones as well. She catches Boom's eye and returns his smile, but she turns away when Rocco nudges her.

"Does your eye hurt?" he asks. He sits nearby on a floor cushion. His hair is in a small bun today, like Boom's.

"Honestly?" She touches the bandage beneath her eye. "Everything hurts right now."

Rocco looks sympathetic. "I do jujitsu with my dad sometimes. I hurt my wrist really bad once. I had to use a brace for a while."

Adri smiles at the hint of pride in his voice. "That's cool. Have you ever tried judo?" As they talk, she discreetly studies Boom's apartment. It's small but sun-filled, and secondhand furnishings give it a cozy feeling. Interesting art—mostly of faces and places—covers the walls. Her eyes linger over a photo of Boom and a woman covered in intricate tattoos. A much younger Rocco sits between them, smiling wide enough to show off a few missing teeth.

"Hanging in there?"

She turns as Boom takes the empty seat beside her. He's dressed up in a denim shirt and suspenders. She smiles. It suits him. "If I don't move at all, I'm fine."

He laughs. "Yeah, the morning after sucks. But it's worse if you lose, right?"

She nods, acutely aware of the sharp pain in her ribs where Sabine kneed her, but she turns her attention to Boom's interesting guests again. The guitarist laughs with a young man named Vinny, while Charlotte washes coffee mugs with her granddaughter, Ruth. Charlotte flashes Adri and Boom a motherly smile as she takes their cups. Vinny is a former fighter turned street preacher, but none of the others are fight fans, which meant Adri didn't have to spend the morning answering any questions about Sabine or Max or her fight. Instead, she just talked about God—easily and openly—with strangers. She smiles faintly, remembering the time in Miami when she stepped into an old, quiet church with Eva.

That feels like a lifetime ago. "This was really nice, Boom. Thanks for inviting me."

"Of course. Are you and Max headed back to Sparta after this?"

She nods. She can't wait to see Eva, but she's less enthused about spending so many hours alone with Max. Things between them are complicated as ever. Their last conversation ended abruptly in her hotel room late last night. Max ordered room service to celebrate her win, but when she mentioned going to Boom's church in the morning, he fell silent and left before the food arrived.

"I think we could make a good team, Adri." Boom's voice breaks through her thoughts.

He grins sheepishly. "If you want to work with me, that is. I think we have a lot in common."

She blinks, processing what he said. "I . . ." Just then, her phone buzzes, and she glances at it without thinking. To her relief— and dismay—it's a text from Max letting her know he's waiting outside. When she looks up again, Boom smiles knowingly at her apologetic expression.

He extends his hand. "Anyway, congrats again on your big win. I'm sure there will be many more in your future."

She frowns at the subtle hint of resignation in his voice. "Boom . . . let's talk again, okay? When things settle down." She knows she's not thinking clearly now, not with her lingering exhaustion and the unspoken words between her and Max. "You should come to Sparta sometime. You too, Rocco." She finds her purse and hurriedly drapes it over her shoulder. "There's not a lot to do, but the mountains are beautiful."

"I'm sure it has other draws."

Color fills her cheeks as her eyes meet his. Of course he knows there's something going on between her and Max, even though she desperately wishes there wasn't. Flustered, she says hasty good-byes to the others, makes her way down a long flight of stairs, and finds Max waiting in the rental car, his music blaring. He turns it down when she opens the door.

She glances at him as she slides inside. His hair is unkempt, his face covered in dark stubble, but he still looks annoyingly handsome.

"Hey," he mumbles.

"Hey."

He waits for her to buckle her seat belt, then starts driving. He seems to be in a hurry to get out of Albany because he drives faster than he needs to and occasionally hits the brakes too hard. Adri grips the edge of her seat.

"How was it?" he asks.

"I liked it."

He throws her a skeptical look. "How do you have a church service in someone's apartment?"

"It's small. There were only seven of us."

He frowns. "Did you sing and stuff?"

She nods.

"Weird. Sounds like a cult or something."

"No, not really. Boom said they do it that way because it keeps the church small. That way, everyone can know each other."

He makes a soft scoffing sound. "I bet he did."

Adri glares at him, tired of his ever-changing attitude. "What does that even mean, Max?"

He looks at her out of the corner of his eyes and smirks. "It means that it's pretty obvious that Boom is interested in more than your soul."

Her mouth parts as her face fills with heat.

"That's why he invited you to his weird little church."

"He isn't interest—"

Max ignores her, swiftly turns the car around, and parks it in front of an outdoor market. She watches, confused, as he unbuckles his seat belt and almost gets out, but then he hesitates. He ducks his head back inside with a small sigh. "Come on. I need your help with something."

For a moment, she doesn't move, irked that he can switch so easily between teasing her about Boom to making pit stops at random street markets, but she gets out and follows him, although she refuses to match his impatient pace and trails behind. He eventually steps inside a tent filled with paintings and studies them.

Adri frowns. "You decided you need some art all of a sudden?"

He shakes his head but keeps his eyes on the art. "I'm getting something for Eva. For her birthday."

"Oh." Her annoyance fades slightly as his focused gaze moves around the cluttered tent. They peruse different sides, both of which are lined with paintings of all sizes, mostly of whimsical flowers and animals. When she glances at him again, his hands are shoved in his pockets, and his eyes are fixed on one painting in particular. She joins him. "She'll love that one," she says with a faint smile. "It's perfect."

He nods and lifts the painting—a cloud of jewel-toned butterflies dancing around a neon orange tiger—and signals the artist. "Can you put this in a frame, please?"

They wait as an elderly man with an orange scarf slips the picture into a simple white frame, then drops it in a bag with tissue paper. Max pays, and they make their way back to the car.

"Thanks," he says quietly.

"You didn't really need my help after all."

He smiles but doesn't respond. The car is parked near a gated playground, where a young mother pushes a babbling toddler in a swing while an older child complains about his broken shoelace. Beyond them, trees sway in the morning breeze. Adri lingers near the entrance, trying to sort out her muddled thoughts and racing heart. Max stops walking when he realizes she isn't following him.

He frowns. "You good?"

She looks up at him and gives in to the feelings she's been fighting. "Can we . . . take a walk?" She nods to a shaded path that disappears into the trees. "Before we lock ourselves in the car for eight hours?"

He looks surprised by the request, but he nods. He drops the painting in the trunk and joins her again as she opens the gate.

This time he matches her slow pace. "How's your side?" he asks. "Any less red?"

She nods. "It's more purple now, but it feels better. I have been getting some weird looks about my face, though."

He laughs, familiar with the way people stare at a fighter's bruises, but then they both fall silent again. The wind picks up a few strands of her hair as they walk in a long winding loop. Finally, she stops beside a thick patch of trees and faces him.

"I want to talk to you about something, Max."

"Okay?"

She toys with a loose bandage on one of her fingers. "I've been thinking about who I want to coach me."

He frowns. "So . . . you want to talk about Boom?"

She nods, although at the disappointed look on his face, she wonders what he thought she was going to say.

"Apparently, he wants to coach me, and . . ." She hesitates, still unsure of what she wants.

"Well? Did you tell him you want to work with him too?"

She shakes her head.

"Oh." He looks confused, but his face softens. "I thought you liked him."

She sighs. "I do like him." In fact, she likes Boom a lot, and she doesn't doubt he'll be a good coach. And he would certainly understand her more than Max does—at least certain parts of her. She lightly wrings her hands. "I don't know what I want to do yet. I just don't want to make another mistake." There's too much at stake to let her feelings mess everything up again.

"Adri, after last night, you can have your pick of good coaches. You don't have to choose Boom if you're not sure about—"

"I know that, but . . ." She crosses her arms, then uncrosses them and lowers her hands, like she's surrendering. "It's just . . . I don't know if I want to work with *anyone* else." She bites her lip as she looks up at him. "Not just Boom."

She hears Max exhale slowly as her words sink in and settle between them. A strange, slow moment passes, and she doesn't know if he's the one who kisses her, or if she kisses him, but it doesn't matter because, for the first time since she returned to Sparta, neither of them resists it.

His hands tangle in her hair, and her fingertips scrape the back of his neck as he picks her up easily, mindful of her injuries, and carries her off the walking path until they're hidden in the shade. She kisses him harder, her tongue meeting his as his hands slide down her body, moving gently over her bruises until she gasps and reluctantly pulls her lips away from his.

He slows down. "What's wrong?"

"We . . . can't."

"Why?"

Her heart races. She doesn't speak, but when he looks into her eyes, she knows he sees the reason.

He curses softly. "What are you so afraid of, Adri? I feel the exact same thing you do."

Her fingers shake as she gently pushes his hands away. Even as she does it, she wants to pull them back. "This . . . it's . . . just not going to work. Us. Together." Tears temporarily blur her vision. "As much as I want it to."

"Why?"

She nods but then shakes her head. Her mind is clouded by his closeness. "It's too complicated, Max."

He groans. "You love saying that, don't you? It doesn't have to be complicated, okay?" His eyes flash with exasperation. "What's so complicated about this?" Before she can stop him, he kisses her again, more gently than before.

When he lets go, she's breathless. She looks up at him with tear-filled eyes. "It's not enough."

"What isn't enough?"

"Love is more than this."

"*Love?*"

She winces at the way he says it—like it's ridiculous or a long-forgotten fairy tale.

"Look, Adri, I care about you, okay? I think about you all the time. I haven't stopped thinking about you for six years, and I've tried my best. That means something, doesn't it?"

She sighs. His words fill her with hope, but it's fleeting. There's too much distance between them—not physically, but in other ways. "It's still not going to work."

"*Why?*"

"Because God is important to me and not to you." She can barely force the words out of her mouth, but she does. It feels strange, like she's exposing the most vulnerable part of herself, but for once in her life she just wants to be honest, regardless of the consequences. Especially with Max.

His face darkens like a storm cloud. "So now *God* is the reason we can't be together?"

"Max . . ." She searches for the right words to explain it to him, but she doubts anything will break through. "I'm a Christian now, okay? I want to be with someone who cares about that, or at least doesn't hate it, and—"

"Enough." He pulls away from her, and more tears fall from her eyes as she sees how much her words hurt him—much more than she expected they would.

"If that's really what you want, then you're right. It's not going to work. Maybe you *should* train with Boom. He's into your dumb religion."

She glares up at him. "You're so cold sometimes. And clueless." His eyes flash, but she continues. "I wanted *you* to go to church with me this morning. Have you figured that out yet? That's why I brought it up last night. So you could learn more before you decide that you hate everything about it—"

Suddenly, he cups the back of her head and pulls her close again. "Adri, I would do just about anything for you, but I'm not walking into a church."

"Why not?"

"Well, for starters . . ." He gives her a wicked smirk. "I can think of better ways for us to spend our mornings."

She rears her head back, but he gently pulls her close again.

"Where was God when Owen was hurting you?" he asks. "Where was God when my dad was dying alone at the gym? Where was God when Dalila got sick?"

"Let go of me." Her heart breaks as she says the words softly. She doesn't know the answers to his questions, but she does know that as much as she loves him, he's still too far away. They'll pull each other in different directions until one of them breaks. "Just let me go."

He gives her one last lingering look of frustration, then releases her.

———

"Mama!"

Adri's heart swells as Eva runs to her. Eva and Roman were sitting on the porch, waiting for them, when she and Max pulled into the driveway. Rocky appears in the window, barking wildly, while Yvonne carries Ivan in her arms.

Adri lifts Eva and embraces her. She feels heavier, and her soft hair tickles Adri's chin. She smells like lemonade and peanut butter.

"Is your face okay, Mama?"

Adri kisses her forehead. "Yes."

"Are you a champion now?"

Adri laughs and puts her down. "Not quite." She turns to hug Roman, who inspects her bruises.

"Here, Adri, come into the light for a minute. Let me see that eye." He gently lifts the bandage. "Oh good. It's shallow, like I thought." A wide smile breaks across his face. "What a finish, kiddo. When you reversed her . . ." He whistles and turns to Max with raised eyebrows. "I almost jumped out of my skin."

Max forces a smile.

"You both put a lot of work into that fight. What a team—"

"I'll take your bag inside, Adri," Max interjects.

She briefly glances at him before he steps past her and Roman to enter the house, causing another round of barks.

Roman frowns at their stiff exchange. "How was the trip?"

"Fine."

He looks unconvinced, but Adri sends a silent message with her eyes. *You're not getting any more information, old man. Drop it.* Roman scowls and changes course. "What'd you think of Boom?"

"He's nice."

"Do you think you could work with him?"

"I—"

Just then, Max steps outside again, this time followed by Yvonne, who lets Rocky and Ivan loose. Rocky bounds for Adri and puts his paws on her shoulders for a hug. She rubs his ears and lets him get one quick lick on her nose. In all the commotion, Max takes a quiet step, intending to leave without making a fuss, but Roman stops him.

"Hey, Adri, Eva. Why don't you go inside with Yvonne? Aren't you hungry, Adri? You gotta be. Yvonne made chicken parmigiana."

Adri looks between her uncle and Max, suspicious.

"I'll join you in there shortly," Roman says, waving her away. "Just want to visit with Max for a few minutes."

Adri scowls. Max looks as unhappy as she does, but Yvonne beckons her before Adri can stop Roman from pulling him aside. Begrudgingly, Adri follows her to the living room.

"Forgive the mess, honey. Roman and I haven't gotten around to cleaning up yet."

Adri looks around and sees the remains of Eva's party—a few gift boxes and bags, glitter on the coffee table, and a tattered piñata leaning against the fireplace. "I'll do it." It's the least she can do for them for salvaging Eva's birthday. Adri starts to reach for one of the boxes, but Yvonne stops her.

"No, no, you just sit down and rest a bit." She skips asking if Adri's hungry and starts arranging pasta and chicken on a plate while Adri obeys and sits on a barstool. The air smells faintly of garlic and Yvonne's Chanel perfume. Eva joins them with new toys in her arms.

"Look, Mama. Skye got me this." She holds up a stuffed llama draped with a colorful saddle.

Adri smiles and pets its fluffy head. "Nice."

"And Uncle Roman got me this."

Adri raises an eyebrow at the foam *daito* in her daughter's hand—a type of Japanese sword. "Oh boy."

"That's what I said," Yvonne says wryly. "Thankfully, she's only been using it on the dogs." She sets a plate in front of Adri. "Here you go, hon."

Adri's stomach grumbles loudly. She and Max didn't stop for food—neither of them had much of an appetite—but now her hunger hits full force. She savors every bite.

A few minutes later, Yvonne finishes washing dishes and sits beside her. "Did you and Max have a—"

"Mama!" Eva appears again, this time wearing one of Adri's old sweatshirts over a pair of unicorn leggings. The shirt almost touches her knees. "I'm going to go see Uncle Roman and Mr. Max. Just for a minute."

Adri shakes her head. "No, Eva—"

"You should let her go," Yvonne says, surprising Adri. She smirks knowingly. "She'll help keep Roman in check."

Adri considers her point. Eva doesn't understand what Yvonne means, but she grins hopefully. "Please?"

"Fine," Adri says, giving in. "But put some shoes on first."

Eva zooms to their bedroom and pulls on shoes in record time before racing out again. Adri briefly hears Max's voice before the door slams behind her. She frowns, wondering what he's telling Roman.

"Did something happen between you and Max, Adri?"

Adri looks up mid-bite. "No." She swallows her pasta, but it sticks in her throat. "Why?"

A small smile plays on Yvonne's lips. "Well, when he came in here, he just looked a little . . . bothered. You do too."

Adri's cheeks redden. She and Max almost reached a truce in the car, with both of them agreeing to drop what happened at the park in the past, along with everything else, but then Adri announced her decision when they were a few miles away from Sparta.

"I'll work with Boom," she said softly, more to herself than to Max.

He didn't say anything else after that. Clearly, the walls were up again and higher than ever—and maybe that was for the best.

"Hon, if you don't want to talk about it, we don't have to." Yvonne taps her graceful fingers against the countertop. "I just want to help if I can."

As Adri ponders Yvonne's offer, she feels a sudden, terrible ache for her aunt. Who does she have to talk to about love anymore? She lost the few friends she had when she moved to Miami and married Owen. And she loves Skye, but she can't talk to her about Max. He's their boss. She groans. "Yes," she says, tired of bottling it up. "He and I fought."

"About what?"

Adri hesitates, unsure how to answer that. Was their fight about love? God? Both? "About . . . our relationship."

"Are you attracted to him?"

The straightforward question surprises her. Adri fumbles for an answer. "I mean . . . it's Max."

Yvonne laughs at her deflection. "Yes, Adri. It *is* Max." She smiles. "And he's grown up a bit since you left, hasn't he?"

Adri blushes harder. She pushes her plate aside and rests her elbows on the counter. "Fine. Yes, I'm attracted to him. But it doesn't matter becau—"

"And he's attracted to you?"

She pauses. Yvonne's question sends her mind back to that morning, when Max kissed her. The memory of his hands moving down her body makes her skin go hot. "Yes. But . . ."

"But what?"

"It's just not going to work. We're too different." She shrugs, unsure of almost everything, but especially herself. After Owen, she wonders if she has any reason to trust her feelings anymore.

"That's what you fought about?"

Adri nods. "I told him I don't want to be with someone who isn't a Christian." She sighs heavily and lets her gaze fall to the tile. "And, as you can imagine, that didn't go very well."

Yvonne's eyes widen in surprise. "Well, honey, I'm sure that wasn't easy to say to him, but I'm proud of you for saying it."

Adri lets her breath out slowly. It *wasn't* easy, but she's learned too much to make the same mistake again. She remembers falling in love with Owen when she was eighteen—it was all passion, no real substance. He hated talking about God, too, on the rare occasions that it came up. She shakes her head. "I just can't lose all my progress. Not over a man. Not again."

Yvonne frowns slightly. "That's wise, Adri, but to be fair, Max isn't like Owen. He's not perfect, but you know he'd never hit a woman. Ever. Danny Lyons raised him right."

"Oh, I know that," Adri says quickly, and she means it. "Max is a million times the man Owen will ever be in every way, but . . . I need someone who will keep me steady. Not someone I'll get lost in."

Yvonne nods, but then she pauses, deep in thought. "Actually, hon, I think you want a little bit of both. That's the best kind of love. Someone who makes you feel off the charts in love but also someone who helps keep your feet on the ground." A touch of sadness flickers across her face. "Max is a fine young man, but he's closed himself off to God. You did, too, but you got out of that, thank goodness."

"I know," Adri says, reminded of how much freer she's felt ever since she found her faith. "That's why I want him to be more open. I think it would help him, but . . ." She sighs miserably. "He's just so against it."

Yvonne lightly pats her hand. "You're doing the right thing, even though I know it's hard. And who knows? Sometimes people change, and sometimes they don't. Max might *never* change, but that's something you have to recognize. You can't really change anyone but yourself."

Adri nods. She remembers Owen's many promises to change. And her father's. And her mother's.

"Just keep the Lord in front of you, honey. Ask God what he wants you to do, then do that, one thing at a time. Try not to worry about Max, as hard as that is. Let God sort him out. And when you feel weak, pray something like, 'God, win or lose, with or without Max, just stay close to me. Amen.' Something simple but true."

Adri frowns. Yvonne's prayer doesn't comfort her very much, but she tries it anyway. *God, what* do *you want me to do with Max?* she wonders silently. Part of her hopes for some kind of miraculous transformation, but her doubts take over.

She glances at the closed door. Just beyond it, she knows Max is standing on her uncle's porch, like he used to when they were kids.

15

"Miss Rivera?"

Adri looks up at the sound of her name. A gruff elderly man—the bailiff—waves her over.

"The judge is ready for you now."

She stands quickly and feels a rush of nerves. She reminds herself that it'll just be her and a judge. At first, she was furious with Owen for ignoring her divorce papers, but now, as she stands alone in the old courthouse, she realizes it's a blessing in disguise because she doesn't have to face him. Her heels—borrowed from Yvonne—click noisily on the floor as she follows the bailiff inside. It's early October, almost two months since her fight with Sabine.

"You stand there," he says, pointing to a podium.

Adri briefly makes eye contact with the judge and does a double take until she realizes she's mistaken. It's not the same judge who she stood before years and years ago. That judge—a tall woman with shiny, tightly-pinned hair—was the one who made Roman and Dalila her legal guardians after her mother disappeared.

The judge who sits before her now has the same pinned-up hairstyle, but she's too young. Adri squints at the name on her placard and recognizes it from the church bulletin. Judge Jane Piper. She teaches Sunday school.

Adri surveys the room, unsurprised that everything is the same.

Dark wooden furniture with bronze accents fills the space, along with worn powder-blue cushions on all the chairs. A Pennsylvania state flag hangs beside the American flag, both unmoving in the stuffy room. Another memory hits her. She and Owen were married in a courthouse.

"Miss Rivera?"

Adri faces Judge Piper, who looks down at her through stylish glasses.

"You are requesting a divorce and full custody of your daughter, correct?"

"Yes."

"And you're representing yourself?"

Adri nods. Despite her nerves, Yvonne's lawyer friend insisted Adri could handle it on her own. Judge Piper opens the folder of documents Adri submitted and thumbs through them.

"Was your husband informed of this motion?"

"Yes. Many times."

"But he's offered no response?"

"I haven't heard from him since I moved back to Sparta." She considers mentioning Owen's drop-in at the gym five months ago but decides against it since he's been silent ever since. That, and Yvonne's friend mentioned a pesky little legal trend in Pennsylvania—namely, that the courts were notorious for overturning default divorce rulings if a deadbeat father showed even the slightest bit of interest.

The judge gives her a lightly skeptical look. "Mr. Anders hasn't contacted you at all regarding custody of his daughter or visitation?"

"No," Adri says flatly, reminding herself that she's technically telling the truth. "He hasn't." She thought Owen would fight for Eva just to spite her, especially after her strange conversation with Sabine, but after spending an evening with Skye combing through his social media, she figured out what's been distracting him. Skye showed her picture after picture of Owen with his hands all over a new woman. The photos stung more than Adri expected them to— partly because they reminded her of her foolish, younger self—but she was also thankful he'd been so preoccupied.

"Your documents do certify that you attempted to reach Mr. Anders multiple times."

Adri does her best to listen to the judge, but her mind races with unwelcome memories. When she and Owen met, when they got married, when they had Eva. His laugh, which was surprisingly soft and didn't fit the rest of him. The most painful memories are the ones that involve Eva and how much she loved him. When she was a toddler, she used to press her lips against their sliding door and wait for Owen to kiss her through the glass. And no matter what kind of mood he was in, he'd always play the game.

Adri doesn't let any tears rise to the surface, though. Even during the good times with Owen, she couldn't shake the feeling that their "love" was always bound to self-destruct, no matter how hard she tried to keep it together.

". . . and you've satisfied the state's residency requirement . . ."

Her mind dives farther into the past, when she stood between Roman and Dalila while they listened to a judge say things Adri couldn't understand about "abandonment" and "adoption." They stood close behind her, but neither of them touched her, knowing she'd just shrug their hands away. Their love was unshakably patient.

". . . so the court grants your request for a decree of divorce and full custody of the child."

Judge Piper's voice jolts Adri back to the present. She blinks. "I'm sorry. What?"

Judge Piper frowns down at her from her throne. "Pardon?"

"Did you say . . . I'm divorced now? Like, officially?" Her heart skips wildly. She believed it would happen, but the announcement sinks in with surprising power. Yvonne's shoes bite into her ankles, and she wants to sit down. "It's really over?"

As the judge's face softens, Adri recalls seeing her at the church, surrounded by little children.

"Yes, dear," she says, giving Adri a small, sad smile. "This part is over."

Boom grins as Adri and Eva approach the entrance to the Sparta City Zoo. Eva hurries beside Adri, her hair bouncing in two black braids that dangle over her pink backpack straps.

Boom raises an eyebrow at Adri's pencil skirt and heels. "You're a little dressed up for the zoo."

Adri smiles as she digs a pair of flats out of her purse, slips them on, and puts the heels inside Eva's backpack. "I had my hearing today. That's why we're a little late. I didn't have time to change."

"Oh, right." Boom gives her a questioning look. "That's big news. Did it go well?"

She nods but doesn't offer any more details in front of Eva. She wants to talk about it later, when they're alone. Thankfully, Boom flashes her an understanding smile. He's as handsome as ever, dressed in tight jeans and an army jacket.

Adri turns to greet Rocco. "Rocco, this is my daughter, Eva. Eva, this is Rocco and his dad, Boom."

"Hi," Eva says. "I like your names."

Boom laughs, and Rocco's mouth turns up slightly.

"Ready to go in? Eva really wants to see the polar bears today."

Boom holds the door open for them. "I like those too."

They let Rocco and Eva walk a few steps ahead of them. Adri smiles as Eva does most of the talking, while Rocco listens with a thoughtful expression. As they walk down cobblestone paths, red leaves swirl by their feet.

"The church is growing," Boom says, making easy small talk. "We've got three new people coming. I think I'm going to hand it off to Vinny for a while."

Adri frowns. She's grateful that Boom agreed to train her in Sparta for her upcoming fight, but that means he has to split his time between Albany and Sparta for the next few months. He says he doesn't mind, but she knows how much he loves his church.

They stop to buy a soda for Rocco and a cherry popsicle for Eva. She shares it with Adri, but Adri immediately regrets taking a bite when she shivers in the cool weather. Boom notices and shrugs off his jacket.

Adri frowns. "It doesn't really go with my outfit, does it?"

"No, but it looks cool." He helps her slip it on. "Sort of like a combat secretary."

She laughs. "If you say so. You're obviously the more fashionable one."

Eva and Rocco race ahead of them, spotting the polar bears.

"So . . ." Boom clears his throat. "Still feeling good about Zoe Chase?"

Adri nods, remembering her upcoming fight. Her divorce hearing had distracted her for the last few weeks, but now she feels ready to focus. "Yeah, I'm excited."

"I know she's not as well-known as Renux, but she's a good fighter." Boom's eyes hold a hint of uncertainty as he glances at Adri. "You have similar styles."

She nods again, but the conversation halts as they enter a small underground cavern painted to look like the North Pole. Eva and Rocco stand with their faces pressed against thick glass, waiting for one of the bears to swim by. Adri and Boom join them.

She glances at him. "So, these are your favorite, huh?"

He smiles. "I think so." They watch in momentary silence as a huge snow-white bear glides through the water, graceful despite her size. Her black eyes twinkle. Boom nods more thoughtfully. "Yeah, they just seem the happiest. I feel bad for the lions and monkeys, you know? They're restless. But polar bears? They just go with it."

When the bear disappears again, Rocco and Eva move on to the penguins. Boom turns away from the glass. "So, are you officially divorced now?"

Adri sighs. "I am." The word *divorced* still sounds strange and unfamiliar, but she needs to get used to it.

"And?"

She raises an eyebrow. "And . . . what?"

"Are you happy about it?"

She smiles faintly. She'd forgotten about Boom's bluntness. For a moment, she's silent as she lets the rest of her feelings sink in. "Yeah, I'm happy. Happy and sad at the same time."

He waits.

"I mean, obviously, I'm happy it's over and done, but I loved Owen at some point. And he thought he loved me too. And Eva still loves him, even though she doesn't want to." She pulls Boom's jacket closer, fighting back another shiver in the cold, dark cave. "So, there's plenty to be sad about too."

Boom doesn't say anything. He just gives her an understanding smile. They meet Eva and Rocco by the penguins, who squawk noisily in every direction. Adri listens, amused, as Eva informs Rocco that little blue penguins are the smallest kind of penguins in the world. Not to be outdone, he tells her that gentoo penguins are the fastest.

"Want to step outside for a second?" Boom asks.

Surprised, Adri follows him out, blinking in the bright sunshine. He looks unusually nervous as he fidgets with one of his thumbnails. Adri's own nerves rise unexpectedly.

"So, listen. I know you've had a lot on your mind lately, but, uh . . ." He lightly runs a hand over his beard. "Have you thought any more about moving to Albany?"

Her heart races, but she keeps her face smooth and contemplative. "Yeah, I have." In fact, she's been thinking about it ever since she called Boom and told him she wanted him to coach her. "And I think, if it's possible, I'd like to stay in Sparta. At least, just for a few more months." Roman told her to go chase her dreams, but she's not ready to say good-bye to him again. Not yet.

Boom frowns, but he doesn't look surprised by her answer. "I get that." He strokes his beard again, still thinking. "If I can find a decent place for me and Rocco, then I can definitely split my time between here and home. I'm just worried there won't be a lot of options."

Adri chews her lip guiltily as she listens. She knows it would be easier for her to move to Albany than for him to travel back and forth for months at a time, and there are more opportunities to fight in New York than there are in Pennsylvania.

"But, hey . . . why don't we just see what happens?" Boom says, throwing up his hands. "I won't give up if you won't."

She forces herself to return his smile. If Boom can't find a place in Sparta, she'll revisit Albany. She has no reason not to, aside from the fact that Sparta has started to feel like home in a way that it never did when she was growing up. That, and her lingering questions about Max, even though he's turned as distant and mysterious as the mountains ever since that night on Roman's porch two months ago. She sighs and makes up her mind.

If she has to say good-bye to Sparta a second time, then she'll find a way to do it.

16

"SORRY!"

Boom laughs as one of Adri's kicks grazes his beard instead of the kick shield. "You don't have to apologize every time, Adri," he says, adjusting his position. "That was a good kick."

"Sorry," she repeats, not thinking. She blushes.

He laughs again, then drops the shield on the mat. "How about a little break?"

Flustered, she steps out of the ring as Boom shuts off the music blasting from his iPhone. It's almost six o'clock in the evening, so it's empty in the gym besides the two of them. Adri takes a long drink from her water bottle. She's felt strange all evening, and she knows it's showing. "Sorry," she says when Boom stands beside her. "I'm a little off tonight."

"Adri, seriously, stop apologizing. The word *sorry* is officially banned from your vocabulary." He smiles reassuringly. "You're doing fine."

"I can do better, though."

"Don't be so hard on yourself. It's going to take some time to get used to being coached by someone different." He lightly squeezes her shoulder. "We'll figure each other out."

Her eyes meet his and she smiles—just as the door swings open.

"Hey!" Enzo shouts, making them both turn sharply. "I heard Sparta's newest divorcée is training in here tonight." He strides toward them, followed by Skye. "Is that true?"

Adri, already warm from her workout, feels new heat flood her face. She's been divorced for less than forty-eight hours.

Skye slaps Enzo's arm. "What is wrong with you?"

"What?" He frowns. "Isn't it good news?"

Skye throws Adri an apologetic look. "You don't just bring up someone's divorce, you weir—"

"It's fine, Skye," Adri says, smiling. She's used to Enzo's brotherly teasing. "He's right. It's good news."

He grins. "Good, because . . ." He reveals a crinkled paper bag with a bottle inside. "We bought you some champagne. The fancy kind."

Adri laughs as he displays it with a flourish. "You would." He holds out the bottle to her, but she shakes her head. "Sadly, you three will have to enjoy it for me." She glances at Boom, who's been listening with an amused expression on his face. "I'm officially on my training diet. No alcohol for me."

Enzo finally notices Boom. "Oh, hey, man. Sorry." He extends his hand. "I'm Enzo, Adri's coworker. Former coworker, actually, since she's leaving us for the big time."

Adri scowls. "Stop saying that." It's Enzo's latest refrain.

"And this is Skye, my girlfriend." Enzo smiles as he says it, like he can't help it, and Skye's cheeks turn a light shade of pink. They made it official a few weeks ago.

"I work at the gym too," Skye adds, also shaking Boom's hand. "And I'm a fighter, like Adri. Boxing, mostly, but other stuff too." She studies Boom curiously before flashing Adri a mischievous smile. "We've heard good things about you."

"Yeah?" Boom looks surprised. "I'm glad—"

"Who are you fighting again?" Enzo interrupts, turning to Adri. "Max told me, but I already forgot her name."

"Zoe Chase," Boom says, answering for her. "She's from Team Belladonna. In Atlanta."

Enzo's face scrunches. "Yeah, never heard of her."

"She's new, but she's a beast," Skye interjects. "It'll be a good fight."

Adri frowns, aware that Skye's voice has a touch of envy to it.

Boom starts to tell them more about Chase, but the door swings open again, distracting them. Adri's stomach flips as Max walks through it. The last time she talked to him was the night they returned from Albany. Roman had come inside with a sad, solemn look on his face while Adri waited for him to say something. She knew it was bad when he made her a cup of tea.

"Max said to tell you good night and good luck."

That was the beginning of the end. A few days later, she called Boom, and he agreed to coach her. Then she called Max, and he changed her schedule at the gym to accommodate her training. That's when his classes stopped overlapping with hers, and their communication dwindled from necessary phone calls to short texts. He forwarded emails from promoters and reporters but never included notes of his own.

In a moment of weakness, she almost asked him about Eva's painting, but then, as if he sensed she was going to break their stretch of silence, the painting showed up next to her locker, still in the same paper bag.

"Hey, Max," Boom says, his voice cutting through her thoughts. "Been a while."

Max greets him with a curt nod. He's carrying a box of new combat gloves. "Boom." His eyes move to her next, with obvious reluctance. "Adri."

"Hey," she says quietly. He looks good with shorter hair and a darker tan, but neither of their eyes linger any longer than necessary.

He glances at the champagne in Enzo's hand and raises an eyebrow. "Celebrating something?"

"Yeah. Good timing. We're about to toast to Adri's divorce." Enzo seems oblivious to Max's stunned expression as Adri blushes all over again. "She can't drink, but we can. Here, hold this for a second." Enzo takes the box from Max and hands him the bottle before Max can protest, then heads toward the break room.

Max glances down at the bottle then up at Adri again. "Uh . . . Congratulations?"

Thankfully, Enzo returns before she has to respond. He expertly pops the bottle and offers Boom a coffee mug full of champagne, but Boom shakes his head.

"Thanks, but I'm not drinking either." He smiles at Adri. "Solidarity."

Adri catches Max's smirk.

"More for us, then." Enzo grins as he, Skye, and Max raise their mugs. Adri and Boom raise their water bottles.

"To Adri, our beautiful, fearless mama bear and friend who can kick anybody's butt, except mine. Or Skye's." Enzo winks as Adri laughs. To her surprise, Max smiles. "Here's to being single and all its joys, like not having to share your drinks with anyone and being able to watch decent television instead of *The Bachelorette*."

Skye rolls her eyes. "You love *The Bachelorette*."

"Not really, but I suffer for you. Anyway, Adri, we love you." Enzo gives her a genuine smile. "And we're happy for you." They lightly clink their cups together and drink.

Adri steals a quick glance at Max over her water bottle, but his face is unreadable. "Thanks, guys." She hugs Enzo, then Skye, who's standing next to Max, who looks as uncomfortable as she does as she takes her place beside Boom again. An awkward moment passes until Boom clears his throat, and Enzo takes the hint.

"Well, we'll let you crazy kids get back to training, then," he says abruptly. "Max, you need help with the rest of the boxes?"

"Sure."

He and Enzo start walking toward the door, but Boom stops them. "Hey, Max, I just wanted to say thanks for letting us train here. We'll stay out of your way."

Max looks surprised for a moment, but then he shrugs. "It's nothing," he says flatly.

"I'll help you guys with those boxes."

He follows Max and Enzo outside, leaving Adri alone with Skye. Adri relaxes slightly until she sees the look on Skye's face. "What?"

She grins. "So . . . Boom is hot."

Adri scowls. "Stop—"

"And I think he's into you."

"You saw him for like five minutes, Skye."

"Yeah, and his body was totally pointed toward you the whole time."

Adri scoffs. "No, it's not like that. He's just nice."

Skye wiggles her eyebrows. "Well, to be fair, it's probably hard to compete with Max. His body was pointed toward you, too, by the way."

Adri's cheeks bloom with color, but Boom reappears before she can give a retort. Skye skips off to find Enzo.

"Your friends seem nice."

Adri smiles weakly. "They're something."

Alone again, they resume their workout. As Adri trains, she tries to keep her mind off Max—what he's thinking, who he's seeing, what he's been doing—and focus on Zoe Chase, her skilled, fresh-faced opponent. But her thoughts wander back to him until Boom calls time. Exhausted, she falls back on the mat and catches her breath.

"Good work tonight. I think you just need—"

She barely hears Boom. Across the gym, Max is leaving his office, his footsteps making a steady rhythm against the concrete floor. She waits, but he doesn't give her a second look, and that hurts more than it should. She curses silently.

Boom extends his hand, surprising her. She takes it, and he helps her stand. "So . . ." He grins sheepishly, and Adri remembers what Skye said. "I have kind of a weird question for you."

She frowns. "What's up?"

"Can Rocco hang out with you and Eva tonight?"

"Oh." She exhales, relieved. "Sure, of course. Do you have plans or something?" He and Rocco are staying in Yvonne's spare room, and Roman has the whole evening planned out—Yvonne's famous chicken piccata and dominoes.

"Yeah . . . something just came up." Boom scratches the back of his neck indecisively. "Max invited me to get a drink with him and Enzo tonight."

Her stomach drops.

"And I figured I should hang out with them, you know? Since Max is letting us train here for free. Seems like the nice thing to do."

She waits too long to nod.

Boom frowns. "Is that okay with you?"

"Sure," she says, though the word comes out more shrilly than it should. "Why wouldn't it be?"

"If you don't want me to, I won't."

"No, Boom, it's fine," she lies, ignoring her racing heart. "Eva and I can entertain Rocco tonight. Go have a drink." *With Max*, she adds silently, fighting back a scowl. She wants to protest, but she doesn't want to reveal even more of her conflicted feelings.

"Okay, thanks. And I'll just have water tonight." He smiles. "I meant what I said about solidarity."

Adri sighs. It's an incredible smile, but it doesn't make her heart flip.

When Max pulls into the gym parking lot the next morning, he's shocked to find Adri sitting on the steps near the entrance, barely visible in the early-morning fog. He's even more surprised when she stands and makes a beeline for his truck. Before he can roll his window down, she's already tapping on the glass. When he finally gets the window down and sees her face, his heart races. She looks upset, and his mind immediately goes to Owen. "What? What's wrong?"

"What are you doing?" she demands.

"Excuse me?"

"What are you doing, Max?"

"Uh, opening the gym?" He scowls at her, but his pulse quickens. Her hair is damp and pulled away from her face. He hasn't been this close to her since Albany. "What are *you* doing?"

"Don't play stupid." Her eyes flash indignantly as they meet his. "Boom told me about your little *arrangement*."

Suddenly, he understands, but he still gives her a blank look. "So? He and his kid need a place to stay when they're in Sparta. I have a place. What's the issue?"

"And when did you decide to make such a generous offer?"

He shrugs. "We talked about it last night at the bar. I offered, he said yes." Adri gives him a skeptical look, but that truly was the gist of it. His conversation with Boom wasn't nearly as productive as he hoped it would be. If there were any red flags about Boom, he was good at hiding them. "Did you know he doesn't drink? Like, at all? Not just in solidarity with you or whatever he said."

She narrows her eyes. "So?"

"Was he an alcoholic or something?"

She throws her hands up. "Seriously, Max? I don't know. Maybe? Why does it matter if he doesn't drink now?"

"Why does it matter that I offered him a place to live?" he asks, copying her accusatory tone.

She makes an exasperated sound. "Whatever. He's probably just a responsible person. . . . Not everyone likes to party all the time."

His temper flares at her not-so-subtle comment. Since their fight in Albany, he's been keeping easy company in a failed effort to move on and forget about it. Adri probably heard rumors. "Yeah, maybe you're right. Maybe Boom's just a good little religious boy." He watches her eyes darken as his words hit their mark. For a moment, she looks hurt, and he feels a small twinge of guilt that he ignores.

"I thought you didn't want to be involved anymore." She sighs as she crosses her arms. "You made that pretty clear in New York."

"I *don't* want to be involved anymore," he says flatly.

"Then why are you helping Boom? And why are you sponsoring me?" She gives him a pointed look. "He mentioned that too."

Max scowls. It's a good question, but he doesn't have a good answer for her. He does his best to keep his tone even. "What, Adri? Boom said you need a sponsor. I can afford it."

"Oh, that's the reason? Not so you can see your name plastered all over my body?"

He smirks, aware of her rising temper. "Why can't it be both?"

Furious, she turns on her heel and walks toward her car, but he hurries out of the truck and catches up to her. "Adri, stop." She won't slow down. "Look, I'm just trying to stop Boom from wrecking your career before it even starts, okay? Why did you agree to fight Zoe Chase?"

He reaches out to her, but she yanks her hand away and glares up at him. "What's wrong with Zoe Chase?"

"Other than the fact that she's an absolute nobody?" He drags his hands through his hair. "You can fight Angel Sobo, Gigi Jacobs, or KC Reynolds—and Boom picks *Chase*? Don't let him screw everything up for you—"

"Boom isn't screwing anything up," she snaps, her voice shaking slightly. "None of those people want to fight me anymore."

Max scoffs. He has an inbox full of emails that prove otherwise. "What are you talking about?"

"They don't want to fight me anymore because of *you*. You're not on my team anymore, remember?" She tries but fails to hide the disappointment in her voice. "Apparently, they only wanted to fight me because of you."

He curses softly as her words sink slowly in. He hates the wounded look on her face—especially since she's trying so hard not to let him see it. He sighs. "Okay. . . . I didn't know that. But I can fix it. I can make some calls—"

"No!"

"Adri, let me—"

She covers her face with her hands. "Please stop, Max. Please."

"Stop what?" he asks, his exasperation growing. Despite their falling-out, he still wants to help her keep her dream alive. Why won't she let him? "I thought you wanted this. I thought you wanted to be a professional fighter." When her eyes meet his again, he can see that she does. She wants it way more than he ever did.

"I do. But I want other things too."

He frowns, not understanding. "You're so close now, Adri. Just let me—"

"No," she says firmly. She drops her hands, revealing her full face again. It's torn but determined. "I need to get over you and do this on my own. So let me. Please."

Her words stir up more conflicted feelings. "Adri . . ." Without thinking, he reaches out to touch her, but she turns from him.

"Please don't make it any harder than it already is."

His frustration rises to the surface. Apparently, she's so determined to keep her distance from him that she's willing to lose everything she's worked for to do it—and that realization stings.

"Fine," he mutters. "I guess you should go tell Boom to find somewhere else to live. And to find a new sponsor too. Fight Chase. Whatever." He shrugs dismissively. "It's your fight, not mine." His voice sounds harsher than he means it to, but he turns away before he has to see the look on her face.

The familiar smell of burning leaves wafts through the motorhome's open windows, along with the distant sound of laughter. The neighbor kids are having another bonfire in the stone pit Max's father dug years ago. He sighs. They're in better spirits than he is.

As he stretches out on his bed, he accidentally knocks over a couple of overdue library books, only narrowly dodging them before they land with a thud near his head. Ol' *Zeus* is starting to feel smaller and smaller, but his dad's house is worse. Max put the finishing touches on it after he and Adri returned from New York, but he can't bring himself to move into it. Even with new slate-gray paint and modern lighting, it still feels like a coffin.

He sighs. What's left to do? That's the burning question. He spent all day teaching advanced mixed martial arts—the thing he loves most in the world—and even that is losing its appeal. He struggled all afternoon to keep his mind on training and off his earlier conversation with Adri.

He grabs one of the books and flips through it, bored but determined to do something besides drink. The voice of his father is starting to scold him, and that's always a bad sign. First, he skims a Bible commentary—one that he haphazardly grabbed off the *Religion and Spirituality* shelf at the Sparta Public Library. He grew up going to the occasional Mass with Adri and Roman, but he never understood much. He expected the book to be gibberish, but to his surprise, he can follow along pretty easily. Some guy named Paul is writing to people in a place called Corinth, telling them how to be Christians. They're bad at it.

The second book he checked out was about Greek gods, and they make more sense to Max. War, money, sex, power—things that are easy to worship, even if they leave a bad taste in your mouth.

He hears a hard knock on the door.

He frowns, not expecting anyone. "Who is it?"

"Boom. I brought food."

Surprised, Max pushes the books away and sits up. When he opens the door, Boom holds out a plastic grocery bag like a peace offering. Max gives him a wary look. "You talked to Adri, I take it?"

He nods and glances past Max at the cluttered motorhome. "Yep. Sounds like you two had an eventful morning." He sounds amused and annoyed at the same time. "Can I come in?"

Max hesitates for a moment, then nods. He takes the bag and leads him to the small kitchen table. Boom slides into the opposite booth seat while Max inspects the food. It's some kind of pasta and salad. Both look delicious. "Yvonne?" he asks.

Boom nods again. "Enzo mentioned you're kind of a health freak, so I asked her to go light on the sauce."

Max narrows his eyes, still unsure what to make of Boom Savitsky. He's never met a man who seems so perfectly at ease wherever he is, even in hostile territory. He sets the food aside. "Is Adri still mad at me?"

Boom gives him a half smile. "Honestly, she doesn't want to talk about you very much. She just said that you decided it was best that I didn't rent from you and that you didn't want to sponsor her anymore." Boom crosses his arms on the table. "She wouldn't tell me why, so I figured I'd ask you."

Max shakes his head in exasperation. "Dude, that was all her idea, and I have no idea why. You'll have to pry that out of her."

Boom studies him for a long moment, then laughs wearily. "Is this what you guys do, then?"

"Sorry?"

"You and Adri. You just play ping-pong with each other's feelings until somebody gets tired of the game?"

Max scowls. "I'm not playing games. Adri knows how I feel about her, but it's not *Christian* enough."

"Interesting." Boom strokes his beard as Max fights the urge to punch him. "So, basically, she doesn't want the kind of relationship you want?"

"How do you know what kind of relationship I want?" Max snaps.

"I know because we have more in common than you think."

He scoffs. "I doubt it."

"No, we do. I messed up a good thing, too, a long time ago." Boom's smile temporarily fades. "I met someone I was crazy about. Then Rocco happened, and she decided to grow up and figure stuff out. I didn't." He sighs sadly. "Well, I did eventually, but it was too late by then. The damage was already done."

"I'm not you," Max says flatly, though he's unsettled by Boom's words.

Boom drums his fingers against the table in a quiet rhythm, thinking. After an annoying amount of time passes, he smirks skeptically. "Okay, then. Do you want to marry her? Do you want to be Eva's dad? Do you want to stay together until one of you dies? Are you willing to lay down your life for her? Put her first?" Boom looks him in the eye. "Or do you just want to sleep with her? Have some fun and see what happens?"

For a moment, Max is too stunned to respond to Boom's barrage of blunt questions. "I . . ." He fumbles, his mind racing with possible answers, though he's unwilling to commit to any of them. On the one hand, Adri makes him feel a way no other woman has ever made him feel in his life. One the other, the word *love* unsettles him. His father loved his mother, and he lost her. Adri's mother loved her father, and all she got was heartbreak. Max thought he loved Adri, and . . .

"The thing is, Max, she's moving forward," Boom says, interrupting his thoughts. When his face softens, Max is unexpectedly reminded of his father. "You're staying still."

"Why don't you go after her, then, if you're so mature?" Max retorts, before it dawns on him how immature he's being.

Boom laughs. "Well, maybe I would if there wasn't such an obvious boulder in the way."

"A boulder, huh?"

Boom grins at his irked tone. "Why don't you tell me what you are? Do you feel like you're moving?"

Max narrows his eyes. Boom's observation bothers him for multiple reasons, but mostly because it's true. He's been stuck in the same dark place for a long time. He changes the subject. "Look, I honestly wasn't trying to upset her earlier. I just think that she should fight someone more well-known than Chase. She's worked hard and—"

"I agree," Boom says, cutting him off, annoying Max even more. Between his exchange with Adri and Boom's surprise visit, he's tired and tense. "I'm sure Adri does too," Boom continues. "But she's been seen with you, so now that's what people expect. I'm a good coach, but, like you said, I'm not *you*."

He lets Boom's words fill the camper as a tight knot forms in his stomach. Max should've known something like this would happen. Truthfully, part of him did, but he'd waltzed back into the circus anyway, for Adri. The last thing he ever wanted to do was make her life any harder, but that's what happened.

He sighs, knowing there's only one obvious solution. "Let me fix it."

17

I'T'S GOING TO BE FINE, ADRI."

Adri stares out the passenger window of Boom's car, her fingers toying with the hem of her shirt. Eva's head swivels between them in the back seat, waiting for her response.

Boom laughs at her stony silence. "Your face is killing me right now. You look miserable, and we're not even at his house yet." He smiles reassuringly. "It's not going to be as bad as you think. I've been working on him."

She sighs. "I'm glad you're so confident."

"I'll be the mediator if we need one."

"What's a mediator?" Eva asks.

Adri glances at Boom. "I'll let you explain."

"It's a person who keeps everyone in check," Boom says, flashing Adri a wink. "Sort of like a peacemaker."

Adri listens as Eva asks Boom more questions, each one coming out faster than the next. Adri's never seen her so excited in her life. Not only is she going to watch Adri's upcoming fight, but she's also going to ride in Max's motorhome—two of her dreams coming true in one trip.

Adri, however, is far less enthused. It's been a little over three weeks since Boom convinced her to let Max coach her again, and as they approach his house, her uneasiness returns. She'd emphatically said no when Boom asked her about bringing Max on as a second coach, but he promised there'd be no issues. That, and he reminded her that her upcoming fight was the opportunity of a lifetime. Rivera versus Sobo on Thanksgiving in Miami, one of three headliners, the venue already sold out. The only condition? Max Lyons had to be in her corner.

"Mama, does Max's car have a microwave?"

Adri snaps back to the present. "What? Uh, yes, it does. And a stove. And a bed. And a little refrigerator, I think."

"And a toilet?"

"Yep."

Eva makes a face. "How does it flush?"

When they arrive a few minutes later, Max is waiting for them. He bends down when Eva runs to hug him and puts his arm around her while Adri watches with her heart in knots. So much has changed since that windy morning in Albany after her fight with Renux.

Max helped Boom move into his dad's house, and Boom spends his time in Sparta whenever Rocco is with his mother. To Adri's surprise, Boom and Max seem to have become friends—or, at the very least, Max doesn't respond to him with the same kind of competitiveness as he did before. She'd noticed the two of them laughing together on more than one occasion or talking for long stretches of time in Max's office.

When Boom's away, Max takes over coaching her, and she's noticed changes with that too. He keeps plenty of physical distance from her, but some of the emotional distance between them is gone. His posture, usually rigid and protective, is more relaxed, and when she looks into his eyes, he meets her gaze without his usual guardedness. She's not sure what inspired the changes— maybe just time, or Boom's influence, or both—but she still doesn't trust herself with him. Her feelings are too strong to believe that another trip together will be easy.

"Come on, Mama!" Eva bounds into the motorhome, her backpack slung over her shoulder.

"You're sure this thing can make it all the way to Miami?" Boom asks, arranging their luggage in the back.

Max thumps the side of the motorhome. "Guess we'll find out." He glances at Adri as she's about to step inside. "Hey."

"Hey."

His phone buzzes in his pocket. He pulls it out and frowns.

"Is something wrong?" she asks.

He quickly looks up again. "Not really." He starts to type something, then stops, slipping the phone back in his pocket again. "It's just Skye. She's mad at me."

"Why?"

"She wants me to set up a fight for her."

Adri feels a pang of guilt. Of course. Skye, like everyone else, has probably noticed that—twice now—Adri is the only person Max has been willing to help since his retirement.

He rubs the back of his neck. "I told her I will soon, but I need her and Enzo at the gym. Especially now."

She nods awkwardly and hurries past him. She knows Skye is happy for her, but she also knows it's probably hard to watch Adri's whirlwind success, especially after she spent the last few years faithfully working alongside Max.

Adri takes the seat next to Eva, who's already lined up a row of stuffed animals on Max's bed. Adri notices a few books tucked away in a built-in shelf and frowns. The titles—both about religion—surprise her, but she's distracted again when she hears Max and Boom talking outside.

"Skye will come around," Boom says. His voice is muffled by the wind.

Adri hears Max sigh. "Honestly, she's not the one I'm worried about," he says.

She frowns. Boom says something else, but she misses it. She hears Max's voice again, something about repeated calls from someone.

"Mama, can we listen to music while we drive? Can I choose the songs?"

"Sure, butterfly," Adri says quickly, trying to hear more, but both Max and Boom have fallen silent.

"Adri." Owen's voice is low and soft. "I need you."

Adri feels cold sweat break out on the back of her neck as Owen grips her shoulders. Stunned, she tries to shake her head, but she can't move. She's paralyzed. Owen, too, seems frozen in one place—impossibly far away but close enough to touch her. His hands roam.

Stop, she cries, but no sound comes out. Owen doesn't respond.

"Adri . . ."

No! Stop! She says it louder this time, but she still can't hear herself. Her heart hammers. Why isn't she stopping him?

He kisses her, and his mouth feels like a flame. Her body recoils and responds at the same time.

"Adri . . ."

As Owen kisses her, her thoughts move like cold water. Slow, slipping, sinking, but she's still not fighting it. She's sinking deeper and deeper into him, and it actually feels good.

"Stop!" she yells, trying to fight.

"Adri!"

She snaps awake and discovers someone kneeling in front of her, with their hands on her shoulders. His face looks unfamiliar until she blinks, and he slowly comes into focus.

Boom's grip loosens. "Sorry, I had to wake you up. You were yelling."

Her eyes widen. "I was?" She looks past him and sees Max looking back at her, concern etched into his face before he turns back to the road. Eva sits in her booster seat, watching Adri with round, worry-filled eyes. Embarrassment floods her. "Sorry." She wonders what she said, but she's too afraid to ask.

"It's okay." Boom straightens and takes his seat again. "Bad dreams are pretty typical before a fight. All kinds of nerves mixing togeth—"

"Hey, Boom," Max interjects, as the motorhome lurches around a corner. "This is it, right?"

Boom peers out the window. "Yeah, the house on the right. With the orange mailbox."

Eva presses her face against the glass. "Mama, look! The beach is in the backyard!"

They wait with anticipation as Max parks, carefully navigating the massive motorhome. Luckily, the street is wide and nearly deserted, aside from a few cars parked in front of aging beach bungalows.

"This is your sister's place?" Max asks, looking at one of the houses.

"Yep."

Vine-covered lattices lean against the porch, and the shutters are painted an electric shade of blue. Countless ceramic pots crowd around the door, all of them bursting with tropical flowers. They follow Boom out single file, and there's a collective sigh of relief as they stand and stretch in the evening breeze. A lingering halo of light rests above the horizon, signaling that they just missed a spectacular sunset, but they couldn't care less. After two long days on the road, they're finally free.

Adri's back cracks softly as she twists her body, letting her sore muscles relax. Eva runs to the fence and peers through one of the slats. Beyond it, dark waves break against white sand.

"Look, Mama!"

Adri feels a heavy drop of rain against her cheek. She turns to the house and notices its darkened windows. "It doesn't look like your sister's home."

Boom carries his bag and hers. "Hannah's in New York for work this week, but she'll be back in time for Thanksgiving. She's bringing Rocco with her."

"Mama, can we go to Rosita's?" Eva begs. "Please?"

Adri is silent.

"The little Cuban place?" Boom asks, as he searches for a key under the welcome mat. "With the umbrellas?"

Eva nods eagerly. Rosita's is known for serving diners seated under bright pink umbrellas that are lined up a few feet away from the water. It's Eva's favorite.

"Can we, Mama?"

Adri still hesitates. In the distance, lighting strikes, followed by a crack of thunder that temporarily splits the sky. More raindrops fall, and Boom signals for them to follow him to the small porch. Eva huddles beside Adri, still waiting for her answer.

"We don't have time, butterfly," Adri says. As she looks at Eva's bright eyes, she realizes how much her daughter misses the life Adri left behind. Eva's been asking questions the whole drive down, about her friends from school and their old neighbors in the apartment complex. That's something Adri's been thinking about more lately— all the memories Eva had to say good-bye to. They weren't all bad.

"You could squeeze it in," Boom says, no doubt trying to be helpful. He unlocks the front door. "You could take her after the fight, if you want. That'd be a good victory meal."

Adri nods uneasily, no longer having a good excuse as Eva beams up at her.

Boom goes inside with the bags, and Eva follows, but Max stays on the porch, watching the storm with Adri.

"Have you heard from Owen?" he asks, surprising her.

They haven't talked about him since her divorce was finalized last month, but she knows why he's asking now. Her fight with Angel Sobo has been all over the news, so Owen has definitely heard about it. She shivers in the evening breeze. She knows she should tell Max the truth, but she doesn't, knowing he won't understand. She's not even sure if she does.

"No," she lies, shaking her head. "I haven't."

The next morning, Adri wakes up before the sunrise and quietly slips out of the beach house. The night before, she'd set her swimsuit, shorts, and sandals by the bathroom so she could sneak out without waking Eva.

She changes quickly and makes her way to the back door, passing through the living room and a breakfast nook. Both are filled with tasteful furniture and art. Adri pauses to look at a few watercolor seascapes and an oversized photograph of women wearing brightly colored sunhats. She wonders what Boom's sister is like—probably a little quirky, like him.

Outside, she finds herself in a small fenced-in backyard filled with more ceramic pots and overgrown flowers, all shaded by a giant sweetbay magnolia. Beyond Hannah's fence, it's sand and water, and as soon as she reaches the shoreline, she slips off her shoes and digs her feet into cold sand.

She mostly hated living in Miami for obvious reasons, but the one thing she loved was the beach. Sometimes, when Owen was having a good day, they'd pack food and booze and head for the small, crowded public beach closest to their apartment. He would wade into the water with Eva in his arms and jump before the waves could break over them, making her scream and laugh, while Adri stretched out the sand, savoring the sunshine. Then they would order dinner at Rosita's, where they always let Eva pick their umbrella. Inevitably, the evening would end with some kind of argument, followed by a fight behind closed doors—but the days were sweet, while they lasted.

Adri runs along the shoreline, taking advantage of the sand's built-in resistance. Endurance will be especially important with Angel Sobo, who's ranked ninth in the strawweight division. Adri pictures Sobo as she runs—a hard but youthful face, neon-blue hair, tattoos of sugar skulls decorating her muscled neck. She'll be one of the toughest opponents Adri's ever faced.

After her run, she wades into the water until it reaches her chest. The cold stings her flushed skin, but she ignores it, instead focusing on Hannah's house, which is now just a little blue speck in the distance. With clear, calm water on all sides and no one in sight, she relaxes and prays out loud, letting the words come naturally as she floats. "God, thank you. Thank you for this." For sunshine and water. For Boom and his wisdom. For Eva and her joy. For another fight. Another chance. For Max."

She plunges her head underwater and lets the shocking cold eclipse her before emerging again. *Max.* She exhales. Apparently, he fought Sobo's coach "a lifetime ago." Those were Max's words, but Adri understood what they meant. She and Max have both lived different lives for so long, purposefully distancing themselves from one another, but that doesn't seem possible anymore. She remembers the message on her cell phone. The message she hasn't mentioned to anyone yet.

"Adri, it's Owen. Please don't hang up. Please. It's about Eva."

She shudders. She almost didn't listen to the rest. She almost deleted it, alarmed that he'd figured out her new number. But she didn't delete it, and that haunting decision left her with more questions than answers.

It's still early when she returns to the house, so she's quiet as she opens the back door. She leaves her sand-covered sandals outside and steps into the kitchen, still careful to be quiet.

"Oh." The word escapes her lips before she can stop it.

Max is sitting at the breakfast table, in shorts and a sweatshirt, his hair still tousled from sleep. Behind him, Hannah's fancy coffeemaker gurgles on the counter. He looks up, surprised to see her too. "I didn't know you were up."

"I went for a run."

His eyes move from her wet hair to her bare torso. "And a swim?"

She nods, ignoring the heat that fills her face. "Why are you up so early?"

A flicker of embarrassment flashes across his face. "I'm reading."

She glances down at the book in front of him and then back up again in disbelief. "*The Bible?*"

"Yeah." He smiles weakly at the stunned look on her face. "I started reading a book about the Paul guy, so I figured I should read the rest of the story and see what happens."

She's still too shocked to reply. "Well," she says. "That's . . . unexpected."

He smirks and reaches for a sheet of paper tucked into the book. "Boom gave me this reading plan thing. He's doing it too. Guess he figured out that I can't resist a competition."

She smiles. "He's perceptive like that."

He laughs, and for the first time in months, she feels relaxed in his presence. And dangerously hopeful.

"So . . ." She tucks a wet strand of hair behind her ear and keeps her voice as light as possible. "What do you think of it so far?" As much as his interest excites her, she doesn't want to push him. He has to make his own decision.

His face is serious as he glances back down at the book again, thinking. Finally, he flashes her a small, reluctant smile. "It's not as stupid as I thought."

"I'm just so fascinated by women who do mixed martial arts." Hannah Savitsky speaks over her shoulder as she rummages in a cabinet, looking for a particular pair of wineglasses. She's back early from her business trip and wasting no time trying to make Adri feel at home. "It's such a brutal sport, but I think it's amazing what you guys do." She starts to pour light pink wine to the top of the glass, then stops. "Oh, shoot. You can't even drink this, can you?"

Adri shakes her head sadly. Her fight is in three days.

"Dang it." Hannah takes a long sip. "It's my favorite Moscato ever." She corks the bottle again. "After your win, then."

Adri smiles. Like Boom, Hannah is funny and charming. They also share the same hazel eyes and fair skin, and she has her own set of interesting tattoos—sunflowers on each elbow. She pulls herself up so she's sitting on the counter, facing Adri.

"So, like, how do you mentally prepare for someone to punch you in the face? Boom says you just get used to it, but is that really true? I'd be a bawling mess if someone punched me once, let alone multiple times. How many rounds is it again?"

"It's three rounds in a standard fight, five rounds if it's a main event," Adri explains, still pondering the rest of her question. "I mean, yeah, it always sucks to get punched hard, but you do eventually get over the shock of it. Aside from training, though, there's not a lot you can do to prepare for it." She taps her fingernails against the quartz countertop. "Of course, your mindset matters. The whole, 'I'm not locked in here with *you*, you're locked in here with *me*' thing. I think that's from a movie or something, but that kind of attitude really does make a difference."

"Wow." Hannah takes another long drink. "That's weirdly profound." She frowns. "And kind of scary. Do you ever wish you had a different hobby? Like, a less bloody one?"

Adri laughs. "I mean . . . not really." She shrugs. "When I was younger, sometimes I wished that I liked cheerleading or something more traditionally girly, but fighting has a feminine element too. It's an art. And it makes you feel powerful. Obviously, that can be a bad thing, but it doesn't have to be."

"Right, that makes sense." Hannah nods along politely. "And I bet it feels super awesome to know that you can defend yourself if you need to."

Adri hides a frown. Of course, Owen comes to mind. Before she met him, she felt invincible, but their fights revealed the cold, hard truth about her limitations. She simply couldn't compete with his size or strength, no matter how much she tried. "Well . . . you can't stop everyone who wants to hurt you, but you can definitely slow them down and make them think twice."

Hannah frowns at her answer, but, thankfully, Boom rescues her. "Hey, Adri, can I borrow you for a second?"

"No!" Hannah yells. "We're having girl time."

He appears in the doorway. "I'll give her back."

Hannah scowls. "Fine. I'll go check on Max and the children. Boom, you should listen to Rocco. I haven't heard him talk so much in his entire life. Like, since his actual birth." She grins at Adri. "Eva is a miracle worker."

Boom smiles. "They're good for each other." When Hannah

leaves, he takes her place in the kitchen. His eyes flicker over Adri. "You look beautiful, by the way."

She blushes, still not completely used to his blunt way of saying things. "Thanks," she says, glancing down at her dress. Max said the press party would be a mix of fancy and casual people, so she picked something in between—a short, swingy red dress with a sweetheart neckline. It was one of her aunt's favorites. She kept everything else minimal, aside from bold red lipstick. She frowns when she realizes Boom's still in his workout clothes. "What's up?"

When he sighs, Adri can tell it's going to be bad news.

"I think I'm going to take a rain check tonight."

Her eyes widen. "*What?*"

He glances down at the countertop, avoiding her gaze. "I think you and Max should go without me."

She stares at him, unsure if he's trying to be funny. "Boom, you can't not go."

"Why not? You guys are getting along now, aren't you?"

She doesn't know what to say to that. It's true that since they arrived in Miami, she and Max seem to have reached a new understanding, but that doesn't ease her mind. "It doesn't matter. I need *you*."

"Parties aren't my scene anymore, Adri."

"You think they're mine?" Her frustration grows as she looks down at her dress and heels, both of which make her feel silly given her sore muscles and scraped knuckles. "I feel ridiculous right now. I need moral support."

He laughs at her desperate tone. "You don't look ridiculous. And you do *have* to make an appearance. You're the fighter, remember? Max too." He smiles wryly. "No one will care if I show up."

"I'll care."

He smiles but still looks unmoved. "I know, but I'm just going to hang out with Hannah and Rocco tonight. We're not together very often. You and Max can handle one press party together."

She covers her face with her hands. "I can't believe you're doing this to me, Boom."

"Stop, you'll be fine. Just go for a little bit, say hi, get your picture taken, then get out of there."

She's about to retort when they hear Hannah whistle in the living room, followed by Max's laughter.

"You look *good*, sir," Hannah says.

Max laughs harder.

"Sorry, was that awkward?" Hannah asks. She giggles as she and Max join Adri and Boom in the kitchen.

Max turns to Boom. "Dude, I think your sister just hit on me."

Hannah giggles again and accidently snorts. "Guilty."

Boom gives her a weary look. "Yeah, she has no filter, unfortunately."

Normally, Adri would point out the irony of Boom's words, given his own usual bluntness, but right now she's too distracted. Max is dressed for the party, and he looks particularly handsome in black chinos and a white button-down. "Boom's not coming," she says miserably, interrupting their laughter.

Surprised, Max glances at her, then at Boom. He frowns. "Why not?"

Adri throws Boom another pleading look, but she can see he's not going to change his mind.

"I want to hang out with Hannah and Rocco while I have the chance," he explains. "I figured you two could handle the party tonight."

Hannah's and Max's eyes drift to Adri, no doubt sensing her discomfort. There's a long silence as they wait for her to speak, which only flusters her more.

She grabs her purse. "Whatever. Let's just get it over with." She leaves to say good-bye to Eva before she can see the looks on their faces. Her daughter and Rocco are in the backyard, slathering paint on some of Hannah's old canvasses.

"Bye, butter—"

"Mama, look at Max's picture!" Eva says, pointing to another canvas drying under the sweetbay magnolia. "He painted you. And Uncle Roman is in it too."

Surprised, Adri walks over and examines it.

"It's kind of messy," Eva says, giggling.

"No, it's just a style," Rocco says firmly. "It's called abstract."

Adri smiles weakly at their disagreement, but her heart races the longer she studies the painting. The edges of the canvas are streaked with grays and blues and blacks, creating the shape of an octagon. In the center, a figure dressed in red—clearly Adri—stands with her arms raised while her opponent is sprawled out on the ground. Suddenly, Adri recognizes the inspiration behind it—the iconic aerial shot of Muhammad Ali versus Cleveland Williams. Some people say that was the greatest fight of Ali's whole career.

Her phone chimes inside her purse and she glances at it, momentarily distracted. She frowns, still not used to seeing Owen's number on her phone.

When she returns to the kitchen, Boom and Hannah are gone, but Max is waiting for her. "I got us an Uber," he says, putting his phone away. "It'll be here in five minutes."

She doesn't mention the painting as she follows him to the porch. It's almost dark, and the sky is a mixture of clouds and scattered stars. A light breeze ruffles Hannah's wind chimes and gently lifts Adri's dress before she quickly pushes it back down, though not before she hears a low whistle. She turns and finds Max grinning sheepishly as her cheeks fill with color.

"What?" he says, amused by the scandalized look on her face. "Hannah started it."

Their Uber arrives before she can respond. To her surprise, Max opens her door, then joins her in the back seat, though he sits a safe distance away. They ride for a few minutes, not speaking, just listening as the driver flips through stations. When she glances at Max out of the corner of her eye, she sees a smile playing on his lips.

"If it makes you feel any better, I don't think this will totally suck," he says. "Aaron isn't a jerk like a lot of fighters. And we can make it quick."

She exhales gratefully. "Okay."

"And I'll be on my best behavior."

She hides her own reluctant smile.

Max lightly cracks knuckles. "Did you see that Angel is still talking about you?"

She nods, aware that her opponent's been spewing all kinds of insults about her online. "That's kind of her thing, isn't it?"

"Yeah, she likes the drama. You're smart to stay above it."

Their driver pulls up in front of a pastel-painted mansion. Max gets out to open her door and offers her his hand. She surprises herself and takes it, letting him lead the way to the entrance, which is manned by two bouncers equipped with not discreetly hidden handguns. One of them extends his fist and Max bumps it.

"Did you know him?" she asks, as they enter the house.

"I don't think so. He knew me, I guess."

Adri smiles to herself. So many years have passed since Max's last fight, but not much has changed. He is still oblivious to his own popularity—even more so now—and she still feels like a fish out of water. They pass through a room with two spiral staircases and reach the pool, where most of the partygoers are. She expected lots of drinking and general mayhem, typical of the parties she used to go to with Owen, back before he ruined his career, but Max was right. This one is tamer.

Bright blue lights hang between a row of palm trees, illuminating a diamond-shaped pool. A few feet away, a DJ bops his head to thumping music while women dance near the pool. The handful of reporters are obvious, with heavy cameras slung over their shoulders, but the rest of the guests are other fighters with their entourages. Max draws lots of attention, but to Adri's surprise, she does too. Multiple people ask about her fight with Sabine. But she's most surprised when a stranger kisses her on the cheek before turning to give Max a wobbly high five.

"Hey, Aaron," Max says, with a bemused smile. "Having a good time?"

"Working on it," the man says in a thick Australian accent. He uses Max's hand to steady himself. Aaron's lankier than most fighters, but his body is obviously all muscle beneath his designer clothes. He turns to Adri and lifts his sunglasses. "Well, here you are, in the flesh. Everyone's been waiting for you."

Her eyes widen. "They have?"

"Of course, love. We all want you to beat the snot out of Angel." He finishes what's left in his champagne flute. "And don't worry, I staggered you two. She won't arrive until after you leave." He winks at Max, who looks relieved. "You're welcome."

"Thanks."

"Of course, mate." Aaron grins at Adri, revealing perfect teeth, aside from one that's missing. "He's not very much fun, is he? Oh, and by the way . . ." He nods toward a young, frazzled-looking reporter standing by the bar, who's typing something on her phone. "Watch out for that one. She hasn't let up since she got here. Rivera this, Max Lyons that, Angel Sobo, on and on and on. I told her to rack off, but she's relentless. Steer clear."

When Aaron stumbles off to find his date—who turns out to be a stunningly tall Brazilian woman in a green caftan—Adri and Max make their way over to two empty pool chairs. He leans back in his, but Adri stays upright with her legs crossed, partly to keep her dress in place and partly because she feels anything but relaxed surrounded by so many strangers. She watches, a little bit envious, as a couple swims to the edge of the pool and kisses passionately, oblivious to the party happening around them.

"Thanks for coming with me unchaperoned tonight," Max says, drawing her attention again. "I know it was a risk."

She raises an eyebrow. "Oh?"

"Well, you thought it was, at least."

She looks over her shoulder and finds him grinning. She throws a nearby pillow at him, which he catches and slips behind his head.

"But I've been a good boy, haven't I?"

She hides her own smirk. "So far." She relaxes slightly. "Are you still doing that reading plan with Boom?"

"Yep. I don't get all of the weird stuff, but I get the gist."

She nods. "Yeah, it takes a while. I feel like I'm always learning new things."

"What made you get into the whole God thing in the first place? Roman?"

"No, it started before I came back to Sparta." She pauses, realizing that was almost a year ago. "Things with Owen were getting worse. I'd cut myself off from pretty much everything, but then I went to a church—just some random one close to our apartment." She exhales, overwhelmed and grateful for everything that happened since. "I don't know how to explain it, really. I just knew it was true. God wanted to help me. I finally felt some peace."

Max frowns, but she can't tell if it's because of the Owen part or the God part. "I sort of know what you mean," he says. "When I read certain things, I feel . . . peace, I guess."

She almost jumps in with a question, but she makes herself wait.

After another moment, he sighs lightly. "After my dad died, I started thinking more about stuff. Like, what's the point of everything, you know? I spent so much of my life chasing a bunch of accomplishments . . . but then I wondered, why? Why do that when they can just go up in smoke—"

"Well, look who it is," a cool voice says, cutting him off.

Adri turns sharply, recognizing the low tones. Gemma Stone is standing a few feet away, dressed to kill in a short, sheer dress that reveals intricate black lingerie underneath. Her mass of curls is straightened into a silky mane that flows past her shoulders. Adri's heart races as Gemma's eyes slide past her and onto Max.

He clears his throat. "Gemma."

Adri frowns. He sounds oddly tense. Just then, a short, tattooed man—Linc, Adri remembers—sidles up to Gemma with two drinks in hand. He's wearing a suit made out of some kind of slippery-looking leather material, and a cigarette dangles from his lips. Unlike Gemma, his eyes linger over Adri for a long time, and she can't help but think of a snake. The poisonous kind.

He eventually turns to Max. "Hey, Lyons. You've been hard to reach lately." Linc smirks. "I figure that's on purpose."

Max doesn't respond with anything except an icy stare, so Linc sets his sights on Adri again.

"How are you, sweetie? Enjoying Miami? Nice to be back?"

Adri's skin crawls.

"You talked to Owen lately? I heard about the divorce and all. I bet he's in bad sh—"

"Hey, Linc," Max says, cutting him off sharply. "Screw off."

Linc lazily raises one of his eyebrows. "Touchy subject?"

"Does she ever talk?" Gemma snaps, interrupting them to glare at Adri. "Or do you have to do that for her, too, Max?"

Adri's temper flares. "I save my words for people who are worth my time."

Gemma laughs. "Oh, that's *hysterical* coming from you. You win one fight against an old lady, and I'm not worth your time? You're lucky I even offered you a fight. It would be over in ten sec—"

Adri frowns. "What fight?"

Max stands and grabs her hand, which makes Gemma's eyes flash. "Come on, Adri," he says, his fingers tightening around hers. "Let's go."

Linc moves in front of her, blocking their path. "Before you rush off, I wanted to let you know we found another fighter since Adri isn't available."

Adri looks between them, her confusion growing. "Available for what?"

Max ignores the question and pulls her to her feet.

"You know this girl, actually," Linc says, looking at Adri with a glint in his eyes. "She's pretty brave." He laughs. "And pretty stupid."

"Who is it?" Adri asks, still trying to piece it all together. Gemma offered to fight her? And Max didn't tell her?

Gemma grins. "Just some little girl named Nobody Nolan." She laughs at her own joke as Adri feels Max tense up beside her. He curses under his breath. Adri, too, feels a rush of panic.

"You're going to fight Skye?" Skye is a talented fighter, but she's got far less experience than Gemma.

Linc nods. "I called your gym the other day, and guess who picked up? Poor thing is so desperate for a fight that she's willing to get in the cage with a killer." He smiles at Gemma, who looks as smug as he does.

She turns to Adri. "I'm going to finish her in the first round." She winks. "You're next, if Max ever decides to let you off your leash."

Before Adri realizes it, her face is an inch away from Gemma's, and her hands are clenched into fists. It's been a long time since she's disliked someone as much as she dislikes Gemma Stone, and the hot burst of anger clouds her judgment. "Just name when and where."

A few feet away, the reporter Aaron mentioned glances in their direction as Gemma laughs.

"Why not right here, then? I'd love to embarrass you before Angel does." She takes a step forward, so their noses brush, but Adri feels Max's hand on her arm.

"Don't, Adri," he says. "She's trying to screw everything up."

Gemma throws him a quick, wounded glance before turning to Adri again, her expression even more scathing than before. As they stare each other down, Adri's emotions war within her. Max is right, of course. If she starts a fight now, she might get injured—but punching Gemma might be worth it. Linc, too, with his slimy grin.

But she doesn't have time to make her up her mind. Without warning, Max wraps his arms around her waist and picks her up, moving her out of Gemma's range.

"Put me down, Max!" Adri yells, but he doesn't listen.

As he carries her toward the exit, the reporter watches them with a focused expression, her camera poised. Adri hears a few rapid clicks as she fights against Max's grip. "Put me *down*," she repeats, struggling to break free.

"No. I'm not letting you blow everything on Gemma Stone. She's not worth it."

Adri curses as her hands tug at his. When they reach the driveway, a safe distance away from Gemma and the reporters now circling her and Linc, Max finally sets her down. Adri ignores the curious stares of people getting in and out of their Ubers and faces him head-on, her emotions raging.

"She wanted to fight me, and you didn't tell me?"

"Linc just wants to get back at me for not coaching her," he says tersely. She almost believes him, but then she sees a hint of shame in his eyes as he fumbles for an explanation. "I didn't think she was serious about it—"

"If you didn't think it was serious, then why didn't you tell me?"

He drags a hand through his hair in exasperation. "I don't know, okay? It didn't seem that important, I guess? You already have a fight coming up. That's all we need to worry about." He turns to flag a taxi, but Adri doesn't move.

"You don't think I can beat her, do you?" She watches, heart sinking, as his mouth opens, then closes.

"I . . ."

Her skin turns cold as another wave of disappointment crashes over her. The guilty look on his face reveals more than his doubts. "Did you sleep with her? Is that part of it?"

His face darkens, but he doesn't deny that either. He reaches for her, but she shrugs him away. "Let's go, Adri."

"No." She hails her own taxi, trying but failing to ignore the stabbing pain in her heart. "You go." She makes her decision before she can second-guess it anymore. "I've got something else to do tonight."

———

Rosita's is quiet when Adri arrives over an hour later. She'd taken three different taxis around Miami before she'd told the last one where she wanted to go. The awful encounter with Gemma, coupled with so many familiar sights and sounds in downtown Miami, overwhelms her. More than anything, though, the crushing swell of disappointment threatens to drown her.

She'd seen so many small, hopeful changes in Max over the last month. It really seemed like he was trying to understand her and meet her somewhere in the middle—but that came crashing down in a torrent of self-doubt when she saw the guilty look on his face tonight. Was it all an act? Does he really care? Does he actually believe in her? Truthfully, she knows she's not thinking clearly, but the betrayed feeling makes her feel momentarily justified in what she's about to do next.

"Señorita, are you ready to order?"

She looks up and sees the waiter again, who's growing impatient. "Um . . ." She glances at her phone. "I'm waiting—"

The door jingles and her heart—and time—stand still. The waiter follows her stunned gaze and turns. His dark brows raise at the intimidating figure standing in the doorway. The man's face is illuminated by string lights and the few melting candles flickering on the tabletops.

Owen Anders, showered and sober, swiftly searches the patio. His blue eyes are startlingly clear as he looks for her, and when he finds her, he smiles. It's the kind of smile she hasn't seen from him in years—one that appears to be without any hidden intentions. Her hands shake as he takes the seat across from her.

"Hi." He exhales slowly as his eyes meet hers. "Thanks for finally talking to me."

18

YOUR GROUNDWORK IS A LOT BETTER, but we should focus on takedown defense." Boom motions for Adri to join him on the mat.

She wipes away the sweat dripping from her forehead and tries to focus. They're alone in Anchor Gym—a small, sweltering training center owned by one of Max's many friends. The heat is heavy, but the views are spectacular, thanks to a wall of glass facing the ocean. Puerto Rican pop music blares from mounted speakers.

"Sobo's not afraid to charge in, and she's good at ankle picks," Boom adds.

Adri nods, familiar with Sobo's signature attack, which usually results in quick wins by submission. She and Boom spend the next hour going over footwork, escapes, and counters, and Adri channels all her energy into training. She has to. Otherwise, her mind will race with thoughts of Owen, and she'll be consumed by the suffocating feeling in her chest that she recognizes but refuses to acknowledge. Their conversation last night went much better than she could have ever imagined, but she still can't shake her doubts.

To her surprise, Owen seemed genuinely impressed by her comeback, but he kept most of his questions focused on Eva. He also mentioned that his new friend Erin, the woman in the pictures Adri saw online, was in rehab now. Apparently, her addiction had spurred him to seek help—well, that, and the divorce—and he was coming up on his first month of sobriety.

"I understand why you had to do it," he said, lowering his eyes. "You had no choice. I gave you no other choice." He'd sighed regretfully, and, for once, it seemed strangely real. "I just don't want to lose Eva too, Adri. I don't want to lose everything." She desperately wanted to believe him, for Eva's sake, but she went to bed with more questions than answers.

Now, in the gym, her mind drifts away from Owen to the note she found under her door that morning, from Max. It lifted her spirits, then sent them crashing down again.

Adri, I'm sorry. Last night had nothing to do with you. I'm the one who didn't want to face Gemma.

It was a rare, powerful moment of honesty from him. The last line made her heart race.

I'm not proud of who I used to be.

She left the house earlier than everyone else that morning, unable to face him. He and Eva were practicing a few punches in Hannah's backyard, and the sight of Eva's focused little face as he coached her filled Adri with too much guilt.

Thankfully, Boom hasn't asked about the press party last night. He'd probably already heard all about it from Max. Or maybe from the blog post—with more than fifty thousand views—about her altercation with Gemma.

Cat Fight! Gemma Stone Calls Out Rivera, Lyons Intervenes.

Adri scowls. The featured photograph is Max carrying her away, her mouth open mid-yell. She didn't bother to check, but she's sure Angel's having a field day with it on social media. *Perfect timing*, she thinks. Their fight is tomorrow night.

"Let's go over that knee counter again," Boom says, drawing her attention back to the present. "When she shoots in, you should—"

Suddenly, the door swings open with so much force that it slams against the wall. Adri jumps at the awful sound—metal banging against concrete—as Max steps into the gym. Her eyes widen. She's never seen him look so angry.

"Did you do it to spite me?"

She stares at him, heart racing, as he walks toward her.

"Max?" Boom looks between them, his mouth open. "Woah, calm down, brother—"

"Shut up, Boom." He keeps walking toward her. "Did you do it to spite me?" he repeats, only stopping when their faces are inches apart. "Did you meet with him because you were mad at me, or did you plan it before last night?"

Boom puts his hand firmly on Max's shoulder and tries to put some distance between them. "Dude . . . what are you talking about?"

Max shrugs his hand away, but he keeps his eyes firmly fixed on Adri. "She didn't tell you either? Well, at least I'm not the only one being lied to."

Boom frowns at her. "What he's talking about, Adri? What's going on?"

Adri keeps her eyes locked with Max's, despite the way her heart hammers against her chest. "He's talking about Owen. . . . I met with Owen."

Boom's face falls, and his disappointment is almost as painful as Max's anger. "You did?" he asks. "When?"

"I was going to tell you both, I just—"

"You want to know how I found out about it?" Max says, cutting her off. "From Eva. She asked Hannah if she could invite someone to Thanksgiving. I asked her who, and she said *Daddy*." He glares at her. "She said he's being *nicer* to you." He shakes his head in disgust. "I can't believe you got her hopes up like that, Adri. After everything she's been through—"

Adri's face fills with heat. His words make her angry—and ashamed. When she glances at Boom, he looks stunned. She exhales shakily. "I—"

"You planned it, didn't you?" Max demands, still not letting her get a word in. "You've been planning to meet him, and you weren't going to say a word to anyone because you know it's insane—"

"I didn't plan anything," she snaps back, defensive. "He called me about Eva a few weeks ago, but I didn't talk to him until last night, after the party." She crosses her arms defiantly. "And it's not like I owe *you* some kind of explanation. I'm Eva's parent, not you. And you lied to me too—"

She falls silent when he leans in.

"You know those are two different things. I didn't tell you about Linc's stupid fight. You met with Owen and put yourself in danger." His eyes flash like lightning. "Let me guess. He called and cried about Eva, and now he's clean and sober and ready to make up for all those times he beat you?"

She winces, partly from his harsh words and partly from their accuracy.

"I can't believe you would—"

"You don't have a child!" she yells, unable to listen any longer. "Just because I didn't have a dad doesn't mean she can't have one. He's not perfect, but—"

"No, enough," Max snaps. "I'm not going to listen to your excuses for him. I said this would happen when you started with all that forgiveness crap."

"Max, come on, man." Boom tries to keep his voice calm, but the tension in the room is too thick. "I get what you're saying, but it's hard when you have kids involved."

Max ignores him. His anger is still obvious, but there are more emotions in his eyes now. Frustration—and sadness. He looks wounded as he stares at her. "After all your talk about mistakes and distractions, after all your progress . . . you do this?" He curses as he takes a step away from her. "I'm done, Adri. I have to be done."

Boom stares at him. "Max. . . . You can't just walk out the day before her fight—"

"Let him go, Boom," Adri says, forcing down her rising tears. She knows there's nothing she can say that will appease Max, nor does she have the energy to try. Because, on some level, she knows he's right. Owen seems to be in a better place now, but she knew there was a risk when she agreed to meet with him—and she took it.

Max shakes his head. "You know better." She can feel his eyes searching hers, but she keeps her gaze on the floor. "If anyone knows better, it's *you*."

She and Boom watch in silence as he leaves the gym, not slamming any doors behind him this time, though his anger is still a palpable force in the room. As his footsteps fade, it dawns on Adri that there might be something even worse than making another mistake: the uncertain time in between—when she doesn't know if she did or not.

Boom's face is uncharacteristically tense as he finishes wrapping Adri's hands. Her fight with Angel is just minutes away, and the only sound in her locker room is the slow, sticky scraping of tape as Boom wraps the roll around her knuckles one last time, then rips it with his teeth.

"You feeling good?" he asks, trying but failing to keep the hesitation out of his voice.

She nods as she slips on her combat gloves, but it's a lie. Like him, her body is tense, and inwardly she feels deflated. She also feels alone, despite Boom's many efforts to keep her spirits up. Not only is she about to step up against one of the fiercest fighters of her career in front of tens of thousands of people, but she's been fighting with herself.

"Max will come around, Adri."

She looks up and meets Boom's eyes. Unlike Max's, they're sympathetic, but they still hold a hint of doubt. She looks away again.

He sighs. "I think he just wishes you would've told someone about it, just to be safe. . . ." Despite the minutes ticking away on the clock, he sits down beside her on the mat. "I get it, though. You wanted to give Owen a chance to do better for Eva. If Max was thinking more clearly, I think he'd get where you were coming from. He just cares about you." Boom smiles weakly. "A lot."

She exhales. Hot, unwelcome tears surface. They rise partly

out of anger—anger that Max would question her so harshly and demand so much honesty when he kept his own secrets too. But the tears also trickle down her cheeks because of her own uncertainty. Wasn't Max at least a little bit right? Ever since she left Miami, she swore to herself that she'd protect herself from Owen, and in one weak, impulsive moment, she let him back into their lives.

"You're trying to make the best out of a horrible situation," Boom says, his voice breaking through her thoughts. "That's not easy. For anyone."

Adri desperately wants to believe him—after all, isn't that what she told herself as she sat at Rosita's, waiting for Owen to arrive? Now, though, she's not so sure. What if she's just weak, like her mother? Owen swore he was a changed man at the restaurant, and he was convincing, but Adri knows his kind of anger isn't something a person can just switch off without a lot of help. Real change would take time.

Boom rises and helps her to her feet. "Just put it out of your mind for now, okay? Max, Owen, Eva . . . all of it. Just for a little while. Focus on you."

She nods but she doesn't take his advice. She wants to use *all* of her anger and frustration as she fights and channel it into her punches and kicks. She knows she'll need every little bit of help she can get if she's going to make it out of the cage alive.

Just as she and Boom are about to head for the tunnel, Max finally arrives. They both stop and stare at him, but his face is unreadable as he takes his place on Adri's other side.

"What are you doing here?" she asks, stunned but relieved to see him.

"I said I would coach you for this fight." Max keeps his eyes straight ahead of him, on the little speck of light at the end of the tunnel. "I'm keeping my word."

When she starts to protest, Boom desperately holds up his hands. "Adri, we don't have time to argue about it. You've got to go now."

Her heart races as Max's eyes meet hers. Truthfully, she wants him close, but it's clear from the look in his eyes that the distance between them is greater than it's ever been. Still, she swallows her conflicted feelings and steps into the arena to wild applause.

Boom stands on one side, Max on the other. Boom's hand rests on Adri's shoulder, and he offers a steady stream of encouragement as she walks toward the cage. Max is silent, but he stays close enough that Adri can hear him exhale when they reach the octagon. He's quick but careful as he unzips her jacket.

A knot tightens in her stomach as she realizes what he's doing. She thought he would bail on her, but he's way too loyal for that. Instead, he's fulfilling his promise to stay in her corner for this fight. *Then* he'll wash his hands of her.

She ignores the ache in her heart as she enters the cage and hears the door slam behind her, metal on metal. Angel "Candy Crush" Sobo enters on the other side and bounces up and down, her blue braids swinging around her shoulders. She's even more fearsome in person, and the crowd is clearly on her side. She shoots Adri a look of pure venom.

"Sobo! Sobo! Sobo!"

The referee stands in the middle. "Ready to fight, ladies?"

Adri has never felt less ready for a fight, but before she can think, the ref moves his hand in a sweeping motion, almost like the sign of the cross. She meets Angel in the middle for the customary fist bump, but Angel snubs her with a dismissive smirk.

"Stay focused, Adri," Boom yells over the clamor of the crowd. The audience seems to be feeding off of Angel's hostility because they shriek with glee when she lands the first punch.

If Max says anything, Adri doesn't hear it. Hannah, Rocco, and Eva are in a suite somewhere, either watching from their balcony seats or on a flat-screen television. It's almost midnight, but Adri knows Eva is wide awake and waiting.

Angel lunges forward, immediately going for a takedown, and Adri barely slips it. Boom was right—she wants the ankle pick. Only a few seconds pass before Angel tries it again, apparently wanting to finish Adri in record time. Adri manages to evade her again, but Angel doesn't let up.

After barely fending off two more takedown attempts, Adri feels herself panicking. Sweat slides down her neck and back. This isn't how she likes to fight—hurried, being pressured against the wall, with diminishing control—but Boom prepared her for this. Max did too. She remembers a technique he taught her a few days ago on the beach, a few miles from Hannah's house.

"You have to punish fighters like Sobo. They're relentless, so you have to make them hesitate." He lowered himself and wrapped his arms around Adri's waist to demonstrate. "After she tries to take you down a few times, nail her with an elbow, right here." He pulled Adri's elbow to the side of his head, showing her the perfect spot. *"She won't be so quick to try it again."*

When Angel dives in for her fifth takedown attempt, Adri takes his advice. Angel hits her with enough force that her back hits the cage, but Adri sends her elbow down in a short, blunt motion and feels Angel's grip loosen as she's momentarily stunned.

"Now, Adri!" Boom yells. "Bang, bang, bang!"

Adri starts throwing every punch she can, capitalizing on Angel's temporary shock, but then she feels a hand near her ankle again.

"Slip that!"

Angel's fingers close over her ankle, but Adri sprawls to break free. Angel reaches for her other foot, but Adri moves again and straightens.

"Thirty seconds left, Adri! You just have to hang in there for thirty seconds."

Adri tries to catch her breath as she moves around the cage, struggling to fend Angel off. Adri's moving more slowly now, and the sound of her own labored breathing rings in her ears as she darts away from Angel's grasping hands. Boom shouts something, but it's drowned out by Adri's own inner voice telling her to give up. Angel's too fast, too relentless, and Adri's too tired. She's too weak.

Adri hears a roar of fury escape her own lips. She can't listen anymore. She can't make another mistake. She can't lose. She can't be weak. She imagines Gemma's smug smirk and the possessive way she looked at Max. She thinks of Eva watching her with bright blue eyes, waiting for her win. She remembers Owen and all the damage he's done.

With ten seconds left, Angel goes for one more takedown, and Adri sees her last chance before exhaustion overtakes her. Praying for perfect timing, she raises her knee and feels it collide painfully with the side of Angel's face right before she crumples—not just shaken, but completely knocked out.

Stunned, Adri stares at her opponent's limp body as the crowd erupts, and the ref signals the end of the fight to the wide-eyed fight officials.

"Perfection!" Boom bellows. "Absolute perfection."

Heart pounding, Adri turns and finds him grinning. She can't help but look at Max too. He still hasn't said anything, but he's looking at her with an unfamiliar expression—almost like she's a stranger—as the referee lifts her hand in victory. A photographer asks for a picture of the three of them, but when Adri turns to face him again, her stomach sinks.

He's already gone.

Later, she and Boom join Rocco and Eva in the suite, where Hannah has prepared a four-course Thanksgiving feast to be eaten on flimsy Styrofoam plates. Eva is exhausted by the night's events, but she manages to stay awake for the final fight—Gemma Stone versus Lanie Ryan, a former Olympian wrestler turned mixed martial artist, one of the best in the business. Adri watches on the edge of her seat.

The fight begins, and the women exchange blows for a long time. For most of the first and second rounds, it looks like Lanie is wearing Gemma down, but then Adri watches, mouth open, as Gemma hits her with a perfect high kick, then finishes her on the ground with a barrage of steady elbows.

Adri's body tenses with every blow that Gemma lands. By

the time the ref calls the fight, Lanie's face is bloodied beyond recognition, and Gemma stands up to thunderous applause. An official hands her a microphone, and she smirks haughtily from the jumbotron.

"What do you think? How did I do?" she asks, as the crowd screams her name. "Not bad for a little foster girl from Modesto, right?" The audience cheers as Gemma smiles. She blows a quick kiss before she lifts the mic to her lips again. "I've just got one thing to say tonight, and it's for Adri 'Nobody' Rivera."

There's a wild mix of cheers and boos at the mention of Adri's name, and Adri's appetite vanishes. She can feel Boom and Hannah's eyes on the back of her head while Rocco and Eva stare at Gemma's face on the screen with round, wide eyes.

Gemma winks. "You can't hide forever."

Heart sinking, Adri hears her phone buzz on a nearby table and absently reaches for it. For a moment, she wonders if it might be a text from Max, but it's not. She frowns. A message glows from Owen.

19

ADRI LISTENS TO THE RHYTHM—three perfect thuds—as Skye executes a row of spinning hook kicks against her mitts. Her movements are quick and precise, and she lands them with impressive force.

"I'm ready," Skye says, breathless, to herself. Sweat glistens on her freckled forehead and neck. "I'm ready," she repeats.

"That's right." Adri nods along with her, keeping her voice light. "You're ready."

They're warming up in one of the pristine locker rooms inside the United Center in Chicago. After three months of insane, rapid-fire preparation, Skye is about to walk into her first professional mixed martial arts match with one of the sport's fiercest fighters. Adri glances at her. She looks as nervous as Adri feels.

While Skye finishes her warm-up with Enzo, Adri recalls Gemma's fight with Lanie Ryan in Miami. She's never seen so much blood spilled in two short rounds, but Skye is still determined to fight, despite Max's attempts to talk her out of it.

Enzo trained her in judo, Boom taught her his best groundwork techniques, and Max spent hours a day going over anything that might help her fend off Gemma. He even broke his weeks-long stretch of silence to ask Adri to be Skye's sparring partner. Adri agreed and did her best to help, but it was hard to watch. Max had showed Skye little mercy during their training sessions.

"I don't know if you get this yet, Skye, but Gemma Stone is good at everything." His voice was sharp with exasperation and concern. "You're a phenomenal kickboxer, but Gemma is good on her feet, on the ground, and everywhere in between."

Tears sprang into Skye's eyes as he talked, but he refused to be softened.

"No, no tears. No breaks. No excuses. You took this fight, so now you need to train like your life depends on it." His face darkened, no doubt recalling Gemma's brutal tactics. He led her back to the ring, where Adri was waiting. "This time, don't retreat when Adri advances. Fight back harder."

Skye took his words to heart and trained with more determination than Adri had ever seen, but now, as she watches Skye sink to the ground, dressed in a light blue sports bra and shorts emblazoned with the Lyons logo, Adri can't help but think that three months to prepare for Gemma Stone seems like a suicide mission.

Enzo sits down behind Skye and massages her back. He presses hard near her shoulder blades, then more gently around her neck. Adri watches as he glances at the door and scowls. "I'm going to kill Max if he doesn't show up soon," he grumbles.

Skye shushes him. "No, we can't be mad at him about anything ever again. I took the fight without asking him, and he's gone above and beyond—"

"He always made the same stupid excuse! 'You're too young, Skye.' Well, guess what? You might be young, but you're a good fighter. Max can deal," Enzo interjects, his temper rising. "And he passed you up for—"

"Hush, Enzo. I don't want to get into it now," Skye says, flashing him a fierce look while purposefully avoiding Adri's gaze. "I need to focus."

Adri gives them both a small, understanding smile, awkwardly aware that she's the one who Max passed Skye up for. "If it makes you feel any better, he's still giving me the silent treatment," she says, sighing. Besides her sparring sessions with Skye, he still avoids her like the plague.

Enzo's face softens. "Is he still mad about the Owen thing?"

She shrugs. "I guess so." Her tone is purposefully light, but truthfully, Max's silence hurts, especially since their blowup in Miami has proven to be so unnecessary. Ultimately, all Adri did was agree to let Owen talk to Eva on the phone once a week. So far, he'd dutifully stuck to their agreement. Sometimes he even sent Adri links to different training videos, saying that the instructor reminded him of her. Seeing his number and hearing his voice still gives her a slightly uneasy feeling, but Eva looks forward to their conversations every Saturday morning.

"Guys, I feel weird." Skye's shaky voice draws Adri back to the present. "Like . . . I feel really lightheaded. And not good."

Skye's already fair skin turns even paler as Adri grabs her water bottle. "Here, take some small sips," she says, keeping her voice as calm as she can. She exchanges nervous glances with Enzo as Skye drinks, both of them sensing that she might be on the brink of a panic attack.

"You're good, babe," Enzo says, as Skye rests her head against his chest and breathes slowly. "You got this."

Adri hears a hint of worry in his voice as he helps Skye stand up and stretch. Her fight is only a few minutes away now, and Adri desperately wishes Boom were here. He couldn't make the trip with Rocco, but they could all use his calming presence. Finally, Max steps into the locker room.

"Dude!" Enzo glares at him, his face uncharacteristically fierce. "Of all the days to be late to something, this is the one you pick?"

Max ignores him and focuses on Skye. "Are you good?" The words are barely out of his mouth before she rushes to hug him. His eyes widen as she clings to him, but then he puts his arms around her and hugs her back.

"Did you see my mom out there, Max?" she asks, looking up at him.

He nods. "She's in the second row, with Hope." He glances over Skye's shoulder at Adri. "Roman's here too."

"Adri, your uncle is so sweet." Skye turns to her with watery eyes. "Mom was worried about how they were going to get here since Hope can't drive yet, but Roman came to the rescue." She wipes her eyes, trying to hide her tears from Max, but he doesn't chastise her. Instead, he pulls her aside, almost out of earshot.

"Skye, I need you to listen to me, okay?"

She nods.

"This is going to be the hardest thing you've ever done."

She swallows.

"But you've done everything you possibly can to prepare for it." He puts his hands on her shoulders and steadies her. "I was so mad that you took this fight, and I still kind of am, but I'm also really proud of you." As he pulls her in for another hug, Adri hears her exhale against his shirt.

"Now, go show everyone else how much you wanted this."

Ready or not, the three of them follow Skye to the tunnel and wait for her cue. Her song, "Cosmic Love" by Florence and the Machine, is an unusual choice, but it fits her perfectly as she walks to the cage, her face resolute. Max's words seem to have steadied her. Enzo kisses her gloved hand as she steps into the cage, and slick voices boom overhead.

"It seems that Skye Nolan, a young boxer from Philadelphia, wants to follow in Adri Rivera's footsteps and earn a big win, despite being a new name in the sport. In fact, Nolan has Max Lyons and Rivera in her corner tonight, with Rivera coming off two impressive wins herself against Sabine Renux and Angel Sobo—"

"And a lot of folks are hoping for a bout between Rivera and Gemma Stone in the near future, Cam."

"Oh, definitely, Ray, and no one wants that more than Stone. She's been adamant for the last three months that Rivera is avoiding her, saying that Rivera prefers her leftovers, since Rivera's been tapped to fight Chloe Valentine."

Adri scowls at the reminder of Gemma's taunting words. She's also aware that *leftovers* refers to more than just her potential opponents, all of whom have been beaten by Gemma. Beside her, Max listens too, but his face is unreadable.

When it's Gemma's turn to enter, she half walks, half dances to the cage, dressed in slinky black and silver, mouthing the words to a lusty Beyoncé song. Inside the cage, she barely glances at Skye, looking past her to Adri, then to Max. She winks.

The next few minutes move in slow motion—the referee's warning to keep things clean, his signal, Skye and Gemma meeting in the middle of the ring, no fist bump. Adri inhales. Her own heart is thudding, so she can't imagine what Skye's feeling.

The crowd cheers as Skye and Gemma move around each other, Gemma obviously the faster and more at ease of the two. After a few more cautious steps, Skye swings first, but Gemma easily dodges it and lands multiple blows to Skye's face. Max shouts instructions, while Enzo watches with a pained expression.

"Come on, babe," he mutters, not taking his eyes off her as she moves around the octagon.

Skye struggles to protect herself from Gemma's rapid-fire strikes, while the crowd screams for more.

"Skye!" Max yells, as he bangs on the side of the cage. "Use your feet!"

It takes a few seconds, with Gemma still landing hard punches to Skye's face, but Skye manages to put some distance between them and land a solid kick that knocks Gemma backward. Adri's breath catches in her throat as Gemma almost hits the ground, and the crowd falls eerily silent. For the first time in Gemma Stone's career, she was almost knocked off her feet—and by a "nobody."

Adri hears Enzo roar with pride, and Max yells something, but Gemma recovers quickly and counters with a jab that makes Skye's nose bleed, then shoots in and takes Skye to the ground. Max shouts for her to get up, reminding her of every technique they practiced, but it's clear that she's panicking.

Adri can't help but look at Hope, Skye's teenage sister, who's seated a few rows away, her face pale as paper. Beside her, Skye's mother watches with her hands pressed against her mouth. The blood from Skye's nose smears across her lips and chin as Gemma hits her with those sharp elbows.

"Come on, Skye," Max yells hoarsely, his voice getting desperate. "You've got to do something. You can't stay there."

Gemma stops throwing punches long enough to trap Skye's arm and bend it back at an awful angle. There's a collective gasp from the crowd as Skye's slender elbow momentarily looks inverted.

"Tap, Skye!" Max pleads, hitting the cage. "Tap now—" Adri's heart plummets as she hears a wail of pain and sickening crack as the referee pushes Gemma away.

Skye gasps. The mat beneath her is smeared with her blood, and her chest rises and falls as she stares at her arm, in shock, as people storm the cage. "I think it's broken. I think . . ."

Enzo gets to her first, but the medics push him away while they examine her. Max is right behind him, his face darkening as Skye whimpers in pain. Adri manages to get close enough to touch Skye's cheek and she feels Skye's gloved fingers close over her hand. Adri's anger burns so hot her vision blurs.

Rather than show any kind of contrition, Gemma dances on her side of the cage as her song booms overhead, reveling in the raucous applause and boos. Her win is announced as the medics carry Skye away, cradling her mangled arm. Enzo and Max follow them, but Adri lingers, waiting until Gemma's eyes meet hers.

Gemma barely feigns sympathy. "Sorry about your little friend."

Adri inhales, but she doesn't respond. It takes all her strength not to lunge for Gemma now, as cameras surround them. She knows Gemma would love that. Gemma strides toward her until she's close enough that Adri can smell her sweat and perfume.

"Poor girl." Gemma clucks her tongue. "She doesn't even know when to tap."

"How about that kick, though?" Adri says.

Gemma's eyes flash, and Adri smirks, pleased to see Skye's kick embarrassed her. She turns to follow the others, but Gemma calls after her.

"Hey, I heard about your little spat with Max. Does that mean you're ready to fight me now?"

Adri keeps walking, her emotions warring with each step. She hears Gemma laugh.

"I don't think he's going to save you this time."

Skye looks even younger in her hospital bed. A nurse scrubbed away all the blood, so now her face is covered in freckles and fresh bruises. Her left arm is in a long thick cast, which Enzo is treating like a canvas as he replicates her tattoo with a blue Sharpie.

Adri leans against a wall, watching him draw, fighting her own exhaustion. Skye's mom and sister occupy the only chairs. They look worn down, but occasionally Enzo gets them to laugh. Adri glances at her phone. "Boom says he's praying for you, Skye."

Skye's face splits into a wide smile. "I love Boom. He's so cute and nice—"

"Hey, hey, hey," Enzo interjects. "I've been praying for you too. And I'm drawing the Mona Lisa over here—"

"I know." Skye pulls him closer. "I love you too. I love you more, actually."

His cheeks redden as she kisses him full on the mouth, apparently unfazed by her mother's presence.

Hope glances at Adri and giggles. "I think the pain meds are working."

Thankfully, there's a knock on the door, and Skye releases Enzo. "Come in," she says in singsong voice, and Roman enters with a bouquet of orange carnations. "Oh! Hi, Roman."

"How you feeling, kiddo?"

Skye sighs and looks down at her arm with a glum expression. "Well, it's broken in two places, so I won't be able to use it for twelve weeks, which sucks." She smiles weakly. "But at least Enzo is making it look pretty."

Roman sighs sympathetically. "Well, honey, you put up a heck of a fight."

"I know I should've tapped, but I thought I could get out of it." Skye shrugs in defeat. "I just wanted to do something amazing, you know? Of course you know." Her eyes fill with tears. "You're Roman Rivera."

Skye's mother rises from her chair to let Roman take it. He sits and takes Skye's other hand. "You did do something amazing, Skye. Fighting is brave, regardless of if you win or not."

Skye sniffles as Enzo kisses her forehead, but she quickly changes the subject. "Could someone please get me a pink Gatorade? They actually have that flavor here—"

"I'm on it," Adri volunteers. She quickly slips out of the room, thankful for an excuse to leave Skye with the others, who are in far better spirits than she is. As she searches for the break room, her mind wanders back to Gemma's cold laughter, and her anger burns hot.

She spots a laminated sign and enters a room full of vending machines, worn leather couches, and a small television. To her surprise, Max is sitting on one of the couches, his head in his hands. His mouth is moving, but no sound is coming out.

"Hey," she says quietly, giving him a warning in case he wants to flee.

His head snaps up. "Oh." He frowns. "Hey." He sounds as exhausted as Adri feels. They've been in and out of the hospital for the last few hours with little sleep between them. She waits, but he doesn't say anything else.

Sighing, she turns her back to him and fills a Styrofoam cup with coffee and buys Skye's Gatorade. She's almost made it to the doorway when he clears his throat.

"Adri . . . can we talk for a minute?"

The invitation surprises her, but she takes it. "Sure."

"Cool." He motions to the cushion next to his. "Sit, if you want to."

She joins him on the couch, careful not to spill her coffee on either of them. "Were you praying when I came in?" she asks.

For a moment, embarrassment flickers across his face, but then it fades. "Yeah, I was," he says. He straightens and turns his face slightly, so they almost face each other, but his eyes linger somewhere near her knees. "Sorry I freaked out on you in Miami," he says, each word coming out with some reluctance.

His quiet apology shocks her, but she keeps her face smooth as she takes a sip of coffee.

"I mean, I still think what you did was really messed up . . ."

As he goes on, she braces herself.

"But . . . I know you have your reasons, even if I don't like them."

Relief washes over her. And guilt. "I'm sorry too. I shouldn't have kept it from you."

He laughs. "Well, if you'd told me, I would've stopped you. Or killed him." His face darkens again, but his eyes soften when he looks at her.

Adri smiles faintly. "Friends?"

"Yep. Friends." He rubs his eyes wearily. "Can I have some of your coffee?"

She hands him the cup, and he takes a long drink.

"You missed it earlier," she says, giggling. "Skye told Enzo she loves him." She giggles harder, remembering the look on Hope's face. "And then she made out with him in front of her mom."

Max laughs into her coffee cup. "Will she remember any of that tomorrow?"

"Probably not, but I'm sure Enzo will."

He smiles, but it holds a hint of sadness. "Well, love is weird, I guess. It makes you do stupid things."

Adri's heart races as she glances up at him, and his eyes meet hers. She's still wearing yesterday's makeup, and her unwashed hair is tucked inside a baseball cap, but somehow the way Max looks at her makes her forget about that. No man—not Owen, not anyone—has ever made her feel the way he does.

She nods. "You're right. Love is weird."

20

ADRI BECKONS BOOM TOWARD HOT ROLLER'S PINK-PAINTED DOOR. "Mentally prepare yourself."

He frowns. "For what?"

"The color pink. And some creepy cats."

He laughs as she pushes open the door. "I'm ready."

A bell jingles as they step inside the salon, followed by the sound of hair dryers and whirring massage chairs. Boom raises an eyebrow. The walls are painted black, white, and pastel pink, and every inch of the place, aside from a row of vintage salon chairs, is crammed with her Aunt Dalila's porcelain cat figurines. The air is heavy and sweetly scented thanks to Sudden Beauty Super Hold, Yvonne's favorite hairspray. Overhead, a Sinatra song warbles through a few speakers, and an ancient television is playing a daytime talk show.

"Wow," Boom says before coughing. "There is a lot of pink."

"Told you."

"I'm just glad the cats are fake."

Adri smiles. The décor in Hot Rollers isn't her style, but she dearly loves the place. Whenever she's there, it feels like her aunt is still around but just temporarily out of sight, like she could just be finishing up a manicure before appearing around the corner with a smile on her face.

She gives Boom a quick tour, and they find Yvonne at her station, wearing her usual uniform—a snug pink dress with a loose black jacket embroidered with her name. Her aunt had one just like it.

Yvonne brightens up when she sees Boom. "Do I get to cut your hair too?" she asks.

He laughs nervously. "Not today, ma'am."

She eyes his top bun and looks disappointed. "Just here for moral support, then?"

He settles into the chair beside Adri's and grins. "I guess so."

"We needed a break from the gym," Adri explains as Yvonne drapes a slippery pink cape around her shoulders. "It's insane in there. We can barely get any training done."

Yvonne listens as she combs out a few tangles. "Are they done filming yet?"

Adri shakes her head. "No, not even close. They're still setting up." The producers of Coronet Cage Battle Tournament want footage of her training with Max and Boom, so they sent a demanding director and a fleet of cameramen all the way to Sparta. "And Skye and Enzo are interviewing instructors today." She sighs and sinks farther into the chair, thankful for a moment to sit down. All of their lives have been a roller coaster ever since they returned from Chicago, and sometimes Adri wishes she could get off the ride and let her feet touch the ground again.

Yvonne smiles at her exhausted reflection. "Well, big things are happening, honey. But that was always bound to happen with you, wasn't it?"

Adri smiles weakly. It's been a month since she agreed to the Coronet tournament—and two months since Skye's fight with Gemma—and she's still trying to catch her breath.

"I haven't seen Roman so happy in a long time," Yvonne continues. "You going after your dreams just puts the skip back in his step." She runs her fingers through Adri's hair and smiles. "So thick. Just like Dalila's . . ." Her smile fades for a moment, and Adri understands. Her aunt would be just as excited for her as they are. "Anyway, what are we doing today, hon? Just a little trim? Getting you ready for your big television debut?"

"Actually . . ." Adri bites her lip. She's been dreading this moment all morning, but she knows it's time for a change. "I want to do something a little different this time."

Yvonne raises a perfectly waxed eyebrow. "Oh?"

Boom looks surprised too.

"I think I want it . . . shorter."

"We could easily cut off three inches, and you wouldn't miss a thing."

Adri's heart races as Yvonne chatters. Since Adri was old enough to talk, her mother made her swear that she would never "ruin" her hair. Owen did too. Now, her own voice warns her not to do it, but this time, she ignores it. "Can you just . . . cut a lot of it?"

Yvonne stares at her reflection for a long moment. "How much?"

"Like . . . just long enough that I can still pull it back when I'm fighting?"

Yvonne looks like she might faint. Since Adri's hair is so long, that entails chopping off at least eight inches. Thankfully, Boom looks ready to catch Yvonne if she does pass out.

"Are you sure?" Yvonne asks, clearly hoping that she isn't, but Adri nods.

Her hair has been her security blanket for a long time—which is part of the reason why she wants to let it go.

"Well, honey, that is different." Yvonne's face falls slightly as she runs her hands through it one last time. "But I suppose different is good sometimes."

Relieved, Adri settles in while Yvonne searches for her sharpest pair of scissors. While she and Boom wait, the other long-time stylist—Franny Morrison—enters the salon. Franny's followed by her client—a woman with a round, scowling face and tortured hair. Adri frowns. She looks vaguely familiar, but Adri can't place her.

The woman glances admiringly at Boom, but his eyes are on the television. He nudges Adri. "Look who it is."

She looks up and sees Melissa Medlock, a prolific, recently retired UFC champion, talking with the show's host. They laugh together silently.

Yvonne notices Boom's interest and quickly looks around for the remote. "Franny, turn the volume up, would you, please?"

Franny begrudgingly obeys, and Adri and Boom listen.

"So, Melissa, besides a new show out in April, you've got another exciting announcement to make, don't you?"

Medlock beams for the camera. Her smile is blindingly white against a vibrant blue background. "That's right, Jen. I'm thrilled to announce that I'm hosting this year's Coronet Cage Battle Tournament. Eight fierce female fighters are going to Las Vegas, and one woman will walk out of the cage with the Coronet Strawweight Championship title and fifty thousand dollars—"

Yvonne spins the chair around so that Adri faces her instead of the television. "Are you and Max still coming to dinner tonight?" she asks, pulling Adri's hair back.

Adri nods. "Yep. We'll be there." A smile touches her lips before she can stop it. Since Chicago, she and Max have fallen into an unexpected weekly routine—no doubt helped along by some careful plotting by Roman and Yvonne, and maybe even Boom. Yvonne started inviting Max to her usual Saturday night dinners, but she insisted that he pick up Adri and Eva since she needed Roman's help beforehand. Never mind that Adri could drive herself.

To Adri's surprise, Max accepted Yvonne's request without hesitation, and for the last month and a half, he's shown up every Saturday evening at 5:45 on the dot, dressed sharply enough to rival Roman. He comes earlier than he needs to so the three of them can stop at the German bakery and Eva can pick out a tin of cookies for dessert. Adri's heart flutters in her chest as she thinks about those sweet, simple moments when it's just the three of them, which have become the highlight of her week.

He even broke the vow he made in Albany and went to church with them a few times the following Sunday mornings. His face is usually set and serious as he listens, but Adri can tell he *is* listening—and she's thankful for that. The electricity between them still crackles beneath the surface, but lately he seems just as determined as she is to not give in to it.

Boom, too, has noticed the changes in Max, but, like her, he's cautious. "He's come a really long way, Adri. . . ." he said the last time they spoke about it. "But he's still got a few things he needs to sort out. Keep giving him time."

She desperately wanted to press him for details, aware that Max confided in him, but she forced herself to be content with Max's slow but steady progress.

Yvonne's frown breaks through her happy thoughts. "Roman mentioned you're still talking to Owen," she says, making a few careful cuts. "How's that going?"

Adri frowns. Yvonne's displeasure, like everyone else's, is obvious. "It's going fine," she says flatly. "I just let him talk to Eva once a week. That's all." She doesn't mention that Owen's been a little less consistent over the last month, sometimes calling too late or too early to talk to Eva. She knows that will just make Yvonne even more uneasy.

Hushed laughter fills the room, and Adri glances in the direction of Franny and her client. She catches bits and pieces of their conversation.

"I guess her husband was bad news. . . ."

Adri finally recognizes Franny's client—Lexi Arden. They went to high school together. She was the cheerleader who followed Max everywhere.

"She had her kid out of wedlock, I think," Lexi adds. "She—"

"That's right," Adri says loudly, sitting a little straighter in Yvonne's chair. "I married my ex after we had Eva. We're divorced now, but I'm sure you already knew that."

Lexi falls silent, but her cheeks turn tomato red. There's a stunned pause as Yvonne throws Franny dagger eyes while Boom fights back a laugh.

"Just ignore that nonsense, honey," Yvonne says, frowning. "Jealousy comes in all kinds of different flavors."

Adri nods, but Lexi is already slipping from her mind. As she watches Melissa Medlock on the screen, her thoughts drift back to Coronet. Out of the tournament's eight fighters, Adri's ranked eighth. Gemma Stone is ranked number one.

Yvonne bundles her hair into two low ponytails and picks up her scissors. "Let's do it."

Adri feels a rush of anxiety as the blades get closer, but she reminds herself that it's okay to cut away old, too-heavy things. Yvonne hesitates for a moment, but then she cuts the first pony-tail, then the second, with four soft snips. As her hair falls into Yvonne's palm, Yvonne spins the chair around so Adri can see the full effect. The cut reveals the small, intricate crown tattoo on the back of Adri's neck. Yvonne hands her the silky severed ponytail as Boom stands up to take a closer look.

"What do you think?" Adri asks, ignoring her racing heart.

He smiles. "I think it's nice to finally see you."

Yvonne continues cutting and shaping while they listen to Med-lock's voice narrate the tournament details, spliced together with a montage of the eight female fighters and their coaches. Roman briefly appears with Adri, holding mitts for her in Max's gym. His face is as determined as hers is as she lands rapid-fire punches.

"I think I understand it now," Yvonne says, interrupting her thoughts with a small smile. "Why you and your uncle like fight-ing so much."

Adri gives her a curious look. "Why?"

"I think maybe it's because you come from a family that knows what it's like to lose everything." Her face falls, no doubt remem-bering Dalila's stories about the dangers she and Roman faced before they fled Cuba as young adults. That was part of the reason why Roman took the fight with La Cruz despite everyone expecting him to lose—he desperately needed the money.

"You know how that kind of loss feels, too, in your own way," Yvonne adds, as her eyes meet Adri's in the mirror. "It seems like it either breaks people or it turns them into fighters."

Adri inhales softly, surprised by the emotions that Yvonne's insightful words stir within her. She waits as Yvonne finishes up with a few more careful snips, until what's left of her hair perfectly frames her face.

"Do you feel a little lighter now, honey? That hair was *heavy*."

Adri stares at the unfamiliar woman in the mirror. For the first time in her life, she can't hide behind a dark, shiny curtain, but that doesn't scare her anymore. As she lifts the ponytail in her lap and feels its weight, it sinks in just how far she's come. "I do."

"Do you think this one's too much?" Adri holds a sheath dress against her torso. It's made out of a metallic material that looks like liquid gold and is undoubtedly the fanciest dress she's ever owned. The tags still dangle from the sleeve.

Roman studies it for a moment, then shakes his head. "It's for a big occasion, isn't it?"

She runs her fingers over the expensive fabric one more time, still unsure, but then she carefully folds the dress and adds it to her suitcase. She feels wildly out of her league as she looks over what she's packed for Coronet. Max surprised her with three beautiful brand-new fight uniforms. One for each fight—assuming she advances every round.

"When do you land tonight?" Roman asks.

She zips up one of her bags. "Pretty late." She, Max, and Boom fly out this evening to start her training camp before the tournament begins. Roman and Yvonne will bring Eva and join them a few weeks later.

She watches as Roman's eyes drift to the photos above her bed—the ones he pinned to the wall almost a year and a half ago now, when Adri first arrived in Sparta. He smiles, and Adri knows why. The young woman in the photos looks a lot like the woman standing in front of him and less like the one who showed up with bruises on her neck and a wounded look in her eyes.

"I'm sure you know this already, Adri, but I'm so proud of you."

She looks down at the carpet, trying to keep her emotions in check. The mounting pressure of the tournament has kept them a little closer to the surface than usual. "Thank y—" she starts to say, but she falls silent as her phone chimes on the nightstand. She glances at the number and frowns. "Oh. . . . One second."

Roman nods, but concern clouds his face.

"Hi," she says quietly into the phone as she moves toward the door.

"Hi." Owen's voice is cheerful on the other line. "Is this a good time? Can Eva talk? Or you, if you want to?"

Roman's eyes are on the photographs, but Adri knows he's listening. She pretends she didn't hear Owen's last question. "I'll get Eva for you."

"Okay, sounds good."

She leaves the room and finds Eva in the kitchen, drawing penguins. She and Rocco have been exchanging artwork for the last few months. Adri lowers the phone. "It's Daddy."

Eva takes it eagerly and presses it to her ear. "Hi, Daddy."

Adri can still hear Owen's voice through the phone as she steps away.

"Hi, beauty. What are you doing—"

Adri exhales as she reenters her room. Roman is sitting at the foot of her bed with his arms crossed. He sits rigidly, almost like he's ready to spring up and fight if necessary, but the look in his eyes is more troubling. He looks defeated.

She sits beside him. "I know you don't like that I'm taking his calls." She sighs, aware that her decision unsettled everyone. She thinks of Max, who disappears whenever Owen's name is mentioned. Boom, too, falls silent and his brows crease. "I just think Eva should have the chance to know her dad, if she can." She can't hide the hint of bitterness in her voice as she says it. Because even as much as Roman loved her, her own father's lack of love still hurt. "I've been working with a lawyer on a formal visitation plan, I've just been so busy—"

Roman raises one of his hands, silencing her. "I get it, kiddo. I do. I just . . . I'm praying he doesn't hurt you again. That's all."

"I won't let him."

He nods, but worry is etched into his face.

"Uncle Roman?" Her heart races as he waits for her to find the words she's been trying to say for months. So far, what she's come up with doesn't feel like enough. Roman was her uncle and her coach, but he was also her first real friend. She takes his hand, which is as callused as hers but softer with age.

"Thank you," she says simply. She used to be someone who never let anyone see her cry, but that part of her, like so many others, is gone. "Without you and Aunt Dalila, I wouldn't really know what love is like."

His eyes are wet, too, before he briefly turns away.

"I made a lot of mistakes, and I know some of them hurt you," she continues, steadying her voice. "And I'm sorry for that."

His face softens. "I forgive you, Adri." The words fill her with unexpected relief as he squeezes her hand. "Love is never free of pain, my dear. You know that as well as I do."

21

ADRI AND BOOM STARE OUT THE WINDOW, both mesmerized by the beautiful shimmering lights of Las Vegas below them. Max sits beside them on the plane, but his eyes are on the notebook in front of him. "Look," Adri says, nudging him. "You're missing it."

He gives the city a cursory glance before turning his attention to his notebook again, his expression serious. She frowns. Danny had one just like it, but he only fished it out for the toughest wrestling matchups. It's a simple leather book with lined pages filled with Max's neat handwriting. In bold letters at the top of the page, he'd written,

3. *Rivera vs. Kuniku*

2. *Rivera vs. Rimes*

1. *Rivera vs. Stone*

Her nerves surge as she realizes those are his predictions. She's been so focused on her first fight that she's hardly thought about the others, but Max's matchups remind her that she has *three* difficult fights ahead of her—unless one loss derails them all.

After the plane lands, they gather their luggage and arrive at the Bellagio Hotel well after midnight, but the lobby is bustling. People talk and laugh and lounge on velvet couches, but Adri is most intrigued by the ceiling, which is covered in thousands of gleaming glass flowers.

"Hey! Rivera!"

Adri turns and finds a curly-haired young woman grinning at her. She immediately recognizes her even though they've never met—Diana Kostas, a fellow Coronet fighter and the first to square off with Gemma. She's dressed in a short white dress and followed by a small crowd. They look sheepish and excited as they approach Adri.

"They want a picture with us," Diana says. "You okay with that?"

"Sure."

The group cheers as they crowd around Adri and Diana while one of them fumbles with the camera on his phone. Their interest in her surprises Adri until she remembers that Coronet is a massive promotion for female fighters, so being included automatically makes her a more recognizable face—for now, at least. That'll change if she loses against Jiayi Kuniku.

Max observes from a safe distance away, but Diana pulls Boom into the picture too. "Good to see you, Boom," she says with a coy smile. "You never texted when I was in New York."

"Oh, yeah, sorry about that." Boom awkwardly clears his throat. "I meant to, but . . . life got busy, you know?"

"Uh-huh." Diana flashes a wide smile for the camera between their conversation. "Well, I'm here for a few weeks. Maybe you'll find some time."

He smiles, but it looks a little forced as they pose for more photos together. When the group eventually disperses, Diana throws him one last look before turning to Adri.

"Good luck with Jiayi next week. She's tough." She grins cockily. "I'll knock out Gemma for you. Who knows? Maybe it'll be us two in the final fight."

Adri nods, but Max shakes his head sadly when Diana saunters away. "Yeah, there's zero chance she's going to beat Gemma." He glances at Boom. "She seems nice, though. Why didn't you text her back?"

Boom sighs, his embarrassment growing.

"Yeah, Boom," Adri says, teasing him as the three of them wait for an elevator. "Why didn't you?"

He scowls. "You, too, huh?" When the door slides open, he's the first one inside. "Look, Diana's a lot of fun, but she's just . . . in a different mindset. I'm looking for someone a little more serious."

Max smirks. "What, like a nun?"

Boom laughs. "No, dude, nuns don't date. That's like . . . a huge part of being a nun."

"Oh yeah." Max presses the button for their floor. "Because they're dating God or whatever, right?"

"No, that's not it," Boom says, throwing him a weary look. "They don't think God is their boyfriend or something. They just want to focus on building their faith and helping people."

Max's brows knit. "You can do that and love someone, can't you?"

Adri frowns, uncomfortable with the turn in conversation.

"Sure, but it's just harder." Boom looks between them with a slight smile. "Love can be pretty distracting."

As soon as the elevator doors slide open again, she's the first one out, eager to escape. Boom and Max follow behind as they walk through a hallway decorated with ornate mirrors and boldly patterned carpet. "This is us," Boom says, flashing a card in front of a door's card reader.

Adri steps inside and stares in disbelief. The two-bedroom suite is more luxurious than anything Adri's ever seen. The massive living area is filled with heavy cream-colored furniture and floor-to-ceiling windows with an incredible view of the city. The bedrooms feature huge canopy beds draped with green satin curtains. She claims one and looks around, still totally in awe.

"Nice digs, Miss Rivera," Max says, smiling at her shocked expression. "You must be a big deal or something."

"I don't mind taking the couch," Boom says, nodding toward one of the windows, where the Vegas lights blink and glow against a deep blue-black sky. "It's got the best view."

Max joins him in the living room and flips on the razor-thin television. A smooth, familiar voice fills the room.

"Eight women have converged on the city of Las Vegas for the Coronet Strawweight Championship to find out who has the skill. Who has the will? Who's worthy of the Coronet Crown?"

Max glances up when Adri joins him on one of the couches.

"This year we've got fighters from all over the world, which is something we always like to see," the voice continues. "From Jersey City, first-timer Diana Kostas joins us with a track record of eight wins and one loss—"

"Hey, Boom, your girlfriend's on," Max says.

Adri laughs as Boom throws a pillow at him. "You two are insufferable tonight," he mutters.

Max smirks. "That's a fancy word."

"Yeah, it means annoying." Boom rises and grabs a steel bucket off the marble countertop. "I'm going to get some ice. Make fun of me while I'm gone and get it out of your system."

"We'll try," Max says. Adri laughs again, but they both fall silent as the door shuts behind him, leaving them alone in the suite. Max clears his throat, and they quickly turn their attention to the television again.

"Jiayi Kuniku from Tokyo made the Coronet semifinals last year and has been on an untouchable winning streak ever since. She's going to face off with our tournament underdog Adri Rivera first—"

Adri springs from the couch when the narrator mentions her name. She can't watch another edited montage of her training sessions spliced with awkward interviews. Most of the footage included Max, too, and neither of them have addressed the strangeness of watching themselves on a screen yet.

Alone in her quiet, beautiful bedroom, the fatigue of travel and training sets in. She starts to get ready for bed but pauses for a moment when she sees a small diamond-shaped chocolate wrapped in gold foil on her pillow.

"Look what I found," she says, reappearing in the doorway. "On my pillow."

Max turns his attention away from the television and squints at the chocolate in her hand. He grins. "Welcome to the big time."

She laughs. "I can eat it, right?"

"Sure, knock yourself out. You look amazing."

Color fills her cheeks.

"I mean . . ." His own face flushes as his eyes drift to the floor. "In training. You look amazing in training. And your weight is on track, so . . . yeah."

"Thanks." For a brief moment Adri considers bringing up Owen, but the commentator interrupts them.

"Hailing from Oakland, California, Tosha Rimes is ready for the win. She's coming into Coronet with fourteen professional wins, and she's a *brutal* striker—"

For months now, Adri's wanted to tell him that she's been talking to a new lawyer, and they've been working on a formal visitation plan that she was close to getting Owen to sign.

"And, of course, we had to get Gemma Stone in this tournament. She burst onto the scene a couple years ago, and she's been dominating the sport ever since. For a lot of folks, she's the favorite—"

More than anything, though, she wants to tell Max that she's not being weak—or, at least, she's trying her very best not to be. But, as usual, the words stay stuck in her throat, even when he glances at her curiously.

"Everything okay?" he asks.

"Um . . ." Her determination fades the longer he looks at her, partly because she knows there's a chance he still might not believe her—and that would hurt too much. "Yeah, everything's okay. Good night."

As she shuts the door between them, she hears the sound of her own voice coming from the television. Someone—a cameraman or a producer, she can't remember now—had asked her what it would feel like to win Coronet. She hears herself sigh before she answers him.

"Honestly? I just have to take it one fight at a time."

"Good. Again, just like that."

Adri lands a perfect kick against Boom's kick shield, her third in a row. They've been training in the official Coronet Training Center—a gleaming top-of-the-line gym covered with black-and-white photos of past champions and colorful sponsor flags—for the past week. They share it with the other fighters and coaches, so their time is almost up.

"One more," Boom says, and she kicks him again in a seamless motion before finishing with a flurry of strikes until Max calls time. They both look impressed, and that gives her a much-needed boost of confidence.

"Let's work with clubs again real quick," Max says, jogging over to the well-stocked equipment room. Adri groans when he returns with two small steel clubs in his arms.

"I'm so bad at these."

He smirks. "That's exactly why we should practice with them." He hands her the twenty-five pound one and keeps the heavier one for himself. "Plus, you're a lot better than you used to be." His smirk softens into an understanding smile. "Give yourself some credit."

She nods reluctantly, and Boom leaves them to it. Adri waits for Max's instruction, but to her surprise, he doesn't give her any. "Just go over what we did last time," he says, and this time he's the one who waits. "I'll follow you."

She lets out her breath slowly, simultaneously annoyed by his coaching and thankful for it. She knows what he's doing by putting her on the spot. It's another small way to prepare her for the cage, for that moment when everyone's expectant eyes fall on her and the loudest voice is the one in her own head.

She grips the club tightly with both hands, keeping it upright, and then attempts to mimic the sequence he showed her the day before—a series of squats and lunges, plus swinging the club in smooth, uninterrupted motions around her head. She feels ridiculous as she does it, but she does her best to focus on the club and nothing else.

"That's pretty good," Max says, copying her. His movements are much more natural than hers, and his face is reassuring. "See? You're doing better than you think."

"Who came up with these again?" she asks miserably, as her shoulder muscles start to burn.

"Persian and Indian strongmen," he answers.

She laughs between labored breaths. "That's so random."

"What? You didn't know that?"

"Literally no one knows that."

He smiles but keeps moving, easily swinging his club in unison with hers. Adri grits her teeth. It feels heavier and heavier with every second that passes, but she doesn't let go.

"Those Persians were some of the best wrestlers in the world," he adds, clearly trying to take her mind off some of the pain. "Using clubs are good for grip strength, since it pulls away from you, just like an opponent would." His face turns more serious as his eyes meet hers. "If you get ahold of Gemma, you definitely don't want to let go."

"Do you think I should go for the takedown?" Adri asks, unsure. "Or stand with her?"

"I think you should trust your own instincts," he says firmly. "You've been training for that moment. You'll know what to do once you're in there."

Adri frowns. He's right, of course, but she *doesn't* trust her instincts yet, not fully. Her confidence is growing, but it isn't totally restored. She knows why. Five years with Owen did a lot of damage—much more than she's been willing to admit, even to herself. Some of those lingering doubts still spill over into other parts of her life unless she fights them off.

"Here, take this one."

She nods wearily as Max hands her the heavier club. She can barely keep it upright now, thanks to her worn-out shoulders, but she grips it with all the strength she has left and tries the sequence one more time, ignoring her shaking muscles as she swings. She imagines Gemma is in front of her, draining her strength and pulling away, so she hangs on tighter.

Right as the club starts to slip from her fingers, Gemma's face is replaced by her own. Adri digs in, still not wanting to let go and lose herself, but the weight is too much for her. Her shoulders slump as the club sails toward the ground, but thankfully Max reaches out just in time and steadies her hands.

"Thanks," she says quietly as he takes it from her and hands her a water instead.

"Your endurance is much better," he says. "That'll be the key with Gemma. Tomorrow night is about speed, though. Kuniku is fast."

Adri nods as unwelcome nerves briefly rise to the surface. Her first fight is tomorrow, and truthfully, she doesn't feel ready. Although her muscles burn from endless training and her mind isn't as clear as she'd like, she's resigned herself to fighting her heart out, no matter the circumstances. Too many people have worked too hard for her to get in her head now.

She and Max make it back to the hotel just before the first fight of the tournament begins: Kostas versus Stone. Adri wants to shower away the day's sweat, but she can't tear her eyes away from the television screen as Gemma walks through the tunnel and into the Coronet Dome to deafening applause. She's obviously one of the fan favorites. Next, the camera zooms in on Diana, who smiles good-naturedly from the other side of the cage. Gemma doesn't.

"And we're off, folks," says a smooth-voiced commentator. "Stone is so bloody fast! Kostas has to seriously pick up the pace if she wants to make it through the first round—"

Adri watches as Diana, known for her quick takedowns, struggles to escape one of Gemma's harder blows. When one of the punches draws blood, Diana instinctively lifts her hand to stem the flow— and that's when Gemma pounces. She lands three more dizzying blows that drop Diana to the ground, where Gemma pummels her.

"Wait . . . is she done?" Even the commentator sounds stunned as he sits mere feet away. The referee drags Gemma off while her fans scream for more. "She's done, folks! Kostas is done already! It's over just like that." He lets out a long, low whistle. "Truly a decisive win for Stone. She's going to be a tough act to follow, isn't she?"

Stomach sinking, Adri glances at Max out of the corner of her eye and finds him chewing on the inside of his cheek. Boom, too, looks disappointed. He watches, frowning, as a coach helps Diana up. Her eyes are filled with tears, but she defiantly wipes them away as the cameras hover near her face.

When the camera refocuses, it zooms in on a grinning Kenny Archer, President of Coronet Cage Battle, who stands near the judges' table, dressed in one of his usual flashy suits. He passes a microphone to Melissa Medlock, who has the black-and-silver championship belt draped over her shoulder.

"How about that for a first fight?" she asks as fans scream and cheer behind her. "The next matchup is martial artist Jiayi Kuniku versus striker Adri Rivera. Rivera has the fewest professional wins of anyone in our lineup, and Kuniku is a seasoned veteran, so a lot of people are saying this will be a tough test for Rivera—"

"So, you're betting on Kuniku?" Archer interrupts, wiggling his eyebrows.

"Well, she's definitely the safer bet, but . . ." Medlock gives the camera a small, knowing smile. "If I've learned anything from fighting, it's that you should never underestimate an underdog."

Adri rubs her hands together and listens to the soft, scratchy sound of her gloves brushing against each other. She makes herself listen to that sound instead of all the others that compete for her attention. Otherwise, she'll get lost in the overwhelming noise as she walks through the tunnel.

The last twenty-four hours have felt like a strange dream. The kind of dream where you wake up, then fall asleep again, and your mind is still racing, unsure of what happened first, or how things will end, or if it was even about you or someone else. Adri blinks, letting her eyes adjust as she walks from darkness into the light.

Roman and Yvonne arrived at the Bellagio yesterday with Eva, who raced to Adri through the bustling lobby and ran her fingers through Adri's cropped hair, her new favorite thing to do. After their reunion, which involved sparring with pillows and a gondola ride at the Venetian, Adri was back on schedule again, training with Max, then Boom. Every night ended with an ice bath, then falling into sweet, deep, exhausted sleep. Her phone hasn't stopped chiming with missed messages from Owen, but she hasn't had time to respond.

Now, in the cage, facing Jiayi, Adri rubs her hands together one last time and feels the heat between her palms. Jiayi Kuniku is a lightning-fast Brazilian jujitsu artist, and her young, enigmatic face has a tranquil quality that's more unnerving than a cocky smirk or snarl. Adri exhales. Max's voice is somewhere behind her.

"Don't wait for this win, Adri. Just go after it."

She nods. He's right. She can't wait. Not with so many people watching who are sure that she's not even supposed to be here, that she hasn't earned her place.

The fight starts, and Adri lunges forward to throw the first punch, surprising Jiayi, who barely steps back fast enough. Jiayi throws her own combination of punches and kicks, one of which scrapes painfully against Adri's cheek, but Adri ignores the sting. She watches as Jiayi turns, intending to land a roundhouse kick. After so many hours spent training, her mind moves faster than ever before, and she sees her opportunity. Jiayi's back will be exposed for the next millisecond as she finishes her kick. Adri and Boom went over this a million times.

"Get her right after a kick, when her guard is down."

In a burst of speed, Adri pushes Jiayi against the cage. For the first time since the fight began, sounds from the crowd break through her concentration as gasps and cheers fill the room.

Faster, faster, faster, Adri tells herself. Jiayi tries to escape her pinned-in position, but Adri keeps her in place and throws her favorite combination—a heavy right hook, followed by a jab. The jab lands near Jiayi's temple, where Adri intended it to, and Jiayi staggers. She tries to grab onto the cage and stay standing, but her fingers slip, and she falls.

"Ouch, that was a *hard* hit by Rivera," a voice says, somewhere. "That one might've done Jiayi in. Let's wait and see."

Adri waits, buzzing with anticipation, as the referee hovers over Jiayi, giving her a few seconds to recover. Boom makes a celebratory sound, but Max stands still and silent, watching Jiayi closely. She tries to stand again but stumbles, her dark eyes are still far away. Finally, she pulls herself up. Her face is even more determined than before.

Adri exhales, disappointed, but she braces herself for the second round. She and Jiayi spend the next few minutes circling each other, both of them more careful now that they know what the other can do. Adri ignores her nerves as the minutes drag on, aware that every moment in the cage with someone as fast as Jiayi is one that can change in an instant.

Thankfully, the buzzer sounds again, and they both retreat to their corners. Adri sits heavily on her stool and catches her breath while Boom pours water into her mouth.

"You almost had her with that jab," he says.

Adri feels her face fall. He means to be encouraging, but his words have the opposite effect. She has the nagging feeling that she missed her chance.

"Stop talking yourself out of your win," Max says sharply.

She looks up. He looks down knowingly, then kneels, taking over for Boom.

"You still know what she's going to do, Adri. Lots of fancy kicks, followed by a textbook takedown. And you still know what she's *not* going to do, which is stand and throw punches with you. Make her do what she doesn't want to do." The buzzer sounds again as he squeezes her shoulder. "But, please, for the love of everything, be quick about it."

Adri stands and nods, steadied. She and Jiayi meet in the middle, both of them steeled and ready for the third round. Max was right; Jiayi throws an impressive sequence of kicks, some of which land painfully against Adri's legs or arms, though none of them hit their true mark. Adri lets her go on until she feels her own muscles tensing painfully, tight from blocking so many blows. She has one small comfort—if she's tired, then Jiayi must be exhausted.

When Jiayi momentarily lowers one of her hands, Adri throws the hardest jab she can and feels her fist collide with Jiayi's mouthguard with a loud crunch. Jiayi stumbles back. Blood trickles from somewhere near her nose or mouth.

"Another one, just like that!" Max yells, gripping the cage.

Jiayi recovers and retaliates, but the punch clearly shook her. Adri bobs quickly as she avoids Jiayi's powerful kicks and searches for one more chance. She shoves Jiayi's leg away, tired of her swirling, complicated kicks, and sees it. Jiayi poises herself to shoot in, sensing Adri's growing fatigue, but when does, Adri throws a hook with so much force that Jiayi's head snaps back and she falls to the ground—this time down for good.

Adri watches, exhausted, as the referee slices his hands through the air, signaling the end. Warm relief floods her as she sinks to the ground, letting her mind and body rest.

"It's over, folks!" Kenny Archer bellows in his microphone, wiping sweat from his brow with a striped handkerchief. "And our underdog lives to fight another day in the cage."

The referee lifts Adri's hand in victory, and she's so happy she feels like she could float up and touch the lights swirling above her head. After the announcement, Jiayi gives her a tight hug, followed by a small bow. Disappointment is etched all over her face, but her eyes are resolved as she bows to her fans before leaving the cage.

Adri glances in Max's direction, and his smile makes her heart soar even higher. He makes a quick motion with his finger like he's checking something off a list. She grins. She can't hear him over the crowd, but she can read his lips.

Two to go.

22

ADRI PAUSES FROM RUNNING TO REST AGAINST A TALL, wild-looking Joshua tree. As she leans back to study the barren landscape, the tree's rough, puzzle-like bark scratches the back of her neck. "I feel like I'm in a movie or something," she says between heavy breaths.

Roman chortles. An old straw hat shades his face as he sits in a rickety lawn chair a few feet away—a "checkpoint" created by Max. All around them, hundreds more of the gnarled, towering trees fill the desert. "I think a movie would be a lot more glamourous than this." He looks down at her clothes, which are drenched with sweat and dusted with red dirt. "You'd just pretend to train, and you'd have your own little air-conditioned trailer somewhere."

"Not going to lie, that sounds pretty good right about now." She sighs as she stretches her stiff muscles. Max drove them all out west of the city that morning for her final training session before she faces fellow brawler Tosha Rimes. The desert terrain is much more challenging than Adri expected, but she's also thrilled to be out of the gym for a few hours.

She and Roman wait patiently until Max finally appears over one of the hills. He's been running, too, but at a slower pace, apparently not as impatient to finish as Adri is.

When he joins her by the tree, he smiles at her weary expression. "You're almost done. Only six miles left."

She groans inwardly but nods.

"Come on," he says, motioning toward the rough trail in front of them. "Don't forget to breathe."

Roman tips his hat, and they start running together again. As they run along the winding packed-dirt path, Max makes the occasional comment about Rimes—her record, her reach, her coaches. He's always been a runner, so his words come out smoothly as he runs, unbroken by his footsteps or breathing. "Rimes is the most like you," he says, kicking a stray branch out of Adri's way. "She's gritty, and she likes to hit hard. Not a pretty fighter. A little reckless, but in a good way."

As he carries on, Adri's mind drifts to Gemma's last fight—the one that knocked Hayden Port, a beautiful boxer from South Africa, out of the tournament. The commentators were breathless with excitement.

"*This has to be one of our best matchups to date. These women aren't holding anything back. It's all on the table for Gemma and Hayden tonight.*"

Adri's nerves resurface as she runs. The commentators were right. Port put up the best fight against Gemma of anyone Adri's ever seen, but Gemma still managed to corner her. Max cursed as he watched it.

"*Port's got to get out of there!*"

It was too late, though. Gemma landed an uppercut, then a gut shot, then another uppercut, and Port turned into a rag doll against the cage. Gemma almost took her to the ground, but the referee stopped the fight before she turned it into her usual bloodbath.

"*That's it! A brutal combination from Stone, and Port, one of the tournament favorites, is finished. She's done. That means our next matchup is Adri 'La Tormenta' Rivera versus Tosha 'Powerhouse' Rimes—*"

"Rimes is the only thing standing in your way, Adri." Max's voice breaks through her thoughts again. "You have to think of it that way. She's just one last obstacle, and then you're right where you're supposed to be. In the cage, with Gemma, fighting for your title—"

"Has anyone ever told you that you're weirdly good at pep talks?" she asks between heavy breaths. "Maybe you should write a book or something."

He doesn't answer, but she catches his smile.

They slow down a little when they reach a steep hill littered with loose rocks. Max goes first, more comfortable with the landscape. Apparently, he discovered this path during his first training camp in Nevada for one of his big fights. "Almost to the finish line," he says, peering over the rocks.

Adri wipes her face with the edge of her sweat-soaked tank top and follows him up the hill with a few careful steps. "I like this place."

"Yeah, it's cool, isn't it?" he says, kicking a few more rocks to clear the path. "Also kind of eerie, though."

She looks around, noting the dense blue-green junipers growing in thick clusters and the clear skies above, contrasted with crumbling rocks beneath their feet and dusty Joshua trees bent over with age. She nods. "It's sort of like heaven and hell combined into one. Alive and dead at the same time."

He thinks for a moment. "That's a good way to put it." He smirks. "Maybe you should write my book for me."

They finish their climb and find Boom at the top of the hill, sitting on the hood of a rental car. As he grins at them, it dawns on Adri that Boom has a lot to do with Max's steady progress. Boom talks about his faith more openly than anyone Adri's ever met, but the way he does it doesn't seem to bother Max. Max asks more questions now, like he did that night in the elevator.

"Your prize," Boom says, when Adri reaches him. He ties a red bandana—something cheap and touristy—around her forehead like a crown. "I got you one, too, Max. Wouldn't want you to get jealous." Boom tosses him a matching bandana and Max ties it around his wrist. "All right, for your last station, we'll keep it simple." Boom grins. "Push-ups till you die."

Adri relaxes slightly, glad for something familiar. "I thought I was going to have to chase a coyote or something."

Boom laughs. "Do you want to chase a coyote?"

"Not particularly."

"Then push-ups it is." He points to a small patch of grass with less brush. "Max, you in?"

"Sure." Max smiles weakly. "Solidarity, right?"

He and Adri lower themselves to the ground, their bodies only a few feet apart. Boom gives them the signal, and they start their push-ups in unison, keeping a steady tempo. Max matches her pace until she starts to slow down, but he looks surprised when she's still going a minute later—fatigued but steady.

"Good job, Adri. Keep going."

She looks at him. When he looks back at her, it hits her just how much she loves him. She loves how disciplined he is, how hard he works, how loyal he is, how so much power and gentleness mingle together beneath the surface of his hard exterior. She loves him so much that her heart feels heavier as she breathes in the smell of dirt and juniper.

She finally lets her torso sink down to the ground. "Okay." She exhales shakily. "I'm dead." She winces as her muscles burn.

He joins her in the dust. "I'll be dead, too, then."

She smiles tiredly as Boom leaves to fetch their water bottles. Above them, a bird sings. "How'd you get that scar?" she asks Max, her curiosity getting the best of her. She recalls the first time she noticed it at Coralou's—that's one of the few parts of that night that she can still vividly remember.

He frowns. "The one by my eye?"

She nods.

"It's from my last fight. It was over fast, but Furi got in one good shot and almost blinded me." He smiles wistfully and traces the faint circle with his finger. "But I'm honestly kind of glad he got the shot. It kept me a little more humble than I probably would've been otherwise."

"Relatively humble," Boom interjects as he returns.

Max laughs as Adri smiles. More than anything, she wishes she could've seen his last fight. She wishes she and Danny could've seen it together instead of Max fighting it alone. She wishes she'd been in his corner the way he is in hers now. She sighs inwardly, aware that some things can change—but the past isn't one of them.

Later, the four of them pack up and pile into the car to head back to the hotel, but to everyone's surprise, Max drives them farther into the desert.

"We're not going back yet?" Adri asks. Her fatigue is setting in in full force now. "I want to do another ice bath."

Max shakes his head. "I've got something better."

Boom gives him a curious look, but Max doesn't offer any more details as he drives them into the red-orange canyons. Roman does what he does best and fills the silence with stories. Apparently, he visited Willy La Cruz in Vegas decades ago, after their famous fight in Miami.

"Willy had a mansion out here back then, lots of gold and marble statues and such. Not really my taste, but it suited him." Roman smiles faintly for a moment, remembering. "He'd heard about Tomas getting sick, so he wanted to take my mind off it. He tried everything—golf, parties, race cars, gambling."

Adri laughs, trying to imagine her strict, straitlaced uncle partying and driving race cars with a man like Willy La Cruz. "What did Aunt Dalila think of that?"

Roman chuckles. "She didn't mind too much, to my surprise. I think she wanted it to work too." His face darkens. "None of it did, but at least he tried, you know? A lot of people had bad things to say about Willy, but he was a good guy—"

"How did Tomas die, Roman?"

The air turns heavy as Roman turns to face Boom, who sits in the back seat with Adri. Her stomach tightens. Good ol' blunt Boom. His eyes are full of warmth, but Roman's face still crumples, and Adri wants to answer for him—just a few short words—but her uncle beats her to it.

"Tomas got sick. He was three. Dalila wanted to take him to

the doctor, but she worried a lot. Sometimes so much it made her sick too." Roman sighs heavily and briefly glances down at the dark veins in his hands. "It just seemed like a bad cold to me, so I said we should let him sleep it off. . . ."

Adri's throat tightens, waiting for the rest.

"But . . . Dalila was right to worry that time. Tomas went to bed and never woke up. Some kind of rare pneumonia. Extra bad for kiddos." Roman hangs his head. "She never blamed me, though. Can you believe that? She never once said it was my fault."

Sadness fills Adri as she remembers the few times her aunt and uncle talked about Tomas. Most of the time they didn't, because even just the mention of his name made her aunt lose her appetite for days, while Roman turned hard and silent before he slipped away to the gym. The few times that they did talk about him, though, their love was palpable. They loved him with the same kind of deep, unrelenting love that they showered on her ever since the day they found her standing on their porch seventeen years ago.

"Were you mad at God, Roman?" Boom asks, cutting through the silence as Max shifts uncomfortably in his seat.

Roman makes a soft scoffing sound. "Of course I was mad." His voice is sharp but not harsh. "For a long, long time. Raging mad. Not anymore, though."

"Why not?" Max interjects.

Surprised, Roman turns to him. "Well . . ." He thinks for a moment. "It took me a long time to figure this out, but Tomas was a gift. He wasn't mine with a capital M. . . . And he's not gone forever."

"That's true," Boom says. "He's—"

"That doesn't make it any better, though," Max snaps, interrupting them again. "If God exists, that means he took your son away. Or it means he's too weak to stop—"

"We all know he exists, Max," Roman says, gently cutting him off. "And, yes, he gave me my son, and then he took him, and he's got him now. Obviously, it's not what I would've done, but I don't know everything that God knows."

Max shakes his head in frustration. Adri can see his shoulders stiffen as he drives.

"If he's real, then why?" he asks. "All the pain you and Dalila had to deal with? All the—"

"*Pain* is just more proof that he exists," Roman says firmly. "It means that what we're going through is temporary, and this temporary life isn't what we're made for. If death and randomness and survival is all we're about, we wouldn't love each other so much. Things wouldn't hurt so bad. Evil wouldn't matter. Good wouldn't matter either." Roman looks him in the eye. "But it does, doesn't it?"

Max doesn't challenge him, but his face is still hard as he turns sharply onto a gravel road. The car struggles over dips and slopes.

"Good things can grow out of pain," Roman adds softly. He seems to be talking to himself now, more than to the others. "We all know that from experience as fighters, don't we? Pain inspires us to change something. That inspiration leads to discipline. Discipline leads to growth. Growth leads to glory, eventually—"

"We're here," Max says brusquely, slowing the car and parking in front of a large shadowy formation of sun-bleached rocks.

Roman falls silent. Adri can tell he wants to keep pressing, but like a good coach, he knows when to stop.

They get out of the car and follow Max toward a crystal-clear pool of water in a basin at the base of the rocks, fed by a nearby rushing stream. "It's called Ice Box Canyon," he explains. "The water stays cold because of the spring."

A cold breeze ruffles Adri's hair as she approaches the edge of one of the rocks. She slips off her shoes and socks, both of which are coated with a thick layer of dust, and dips her sore feet into the freezing water. She gasps.

Max smiles at the blissful look on her face. "Kind of a nice change from another ice bath, right?"

She nods happily. "Yeah, it is." Beyond the rocks, rolling green hills touch the sky and a few birds pierce the clouds. "It's beautiful."

The men leave her to soak and go off in different directions—Max one way, Roman and Boom another. Alone, she strips down to her sports bra and shorts and carefully slips into the water. The cold stings at first, but the numbing sensation is a relief to her overworked muscles.

A few minutes later, she stretches out on one of the smoother rocks, leaving her face in the sunshine while letting her legs float. Eventually, her mind drifts to God again. And Max. She frowns.

God, help him forgive you. . . . She pauses from her prayer, realizing it's not quite right. Max doesn't need to forgive God. It's the other way around. *Help him understand*, she prays. *Help him trust you. Help him be free.* She sighs, wishing she knew exactly what to do or say to help him, but she knows from her own strange journey that the truth will either sink in—or it won't.

She stays on the rock for a long time, almost asleep but not quite, thanks to a perfect mix of sun and shade, until she hears footsteps approaching. She sits up on her elbows and squints. Boom and Roman aren't very far away, sitting on weathered rocks, talking in low tones, and the footsteps are Max's as he walks toward the two of them.

23

THE LIGHT IS PAINFULLY BRIGHT as Adri walks toward the Coronet cage a second time, dressed in deep red this time. She sees the animated faces of fans, some cheering for her, others against, as if they were snapshots frozen in time.

At first, it almost sounds like they're underwater, but the volume gradually increases and sharpens as she gets closer. Boom cheers beside her and grins for the many phone screens flashing in their faces. Max squeezes her hand, then lets go. For the first time in years, Roman stands beside her too. Adri can feel his excitement and nerves. She sets the pace, and the three men follow.

"This is it for Tosha Rimes and Adri Rivera, folks, the final frontier for these two. This is the fight that determines who's going all the way to the end."

A commentator's voice booms behind her and shakes the cage.

"Rimes has a huge reach advantage, but Rivera's been known to surprise us. . . ."

As they speak, Tosha enters to a bouncy Azealia Banks song, followed by a fleet of coaches. Her black-and-red braids are wound into a high, thick bun, and she wears a striped bra and shorts set that shows off her incredible abs.

Adri exhales. Of all of her opponents thus far, Rimes is the most unpredictable, and Adri's still feeling the effects of her fight against Jiayi. Her only consolation is that Tosha fought a brutal first-round bout against Kat Simenon and barely won. Like Adri, she looks a little battered.

"All right, ladies. Let's fight!"

The fight moves faster now that Adri has spent some time in the cage already. As she and Tosha circle each other, their movements almost mirror images, Adri focuses on her strategy.

"I don't want you to stand with her for three rounds," Max had said, when they were still out in the desert. *"That's way too risky with Rimes. She hits too hard."*

Instead of striking, Adri's preferred weapon, Max and Boom wanted her to put on a kick clinic. It was risky, but not nearly as risky as taking a few big blows from a striker like Rimes.

Adri barely dodges a deadly hook in the center of the cage and goes for her first kick. She lands a decent blow to Tosha's shin, but Tosha looks totally unfazed by it. When Tosha shoots in again with another heavy combination, Adri sidesteps it and throws her second decent kick, harder this time. As the first round goes on, Tosha gets in a few good, dizzying punches, but thankfully Adri manages to evade the deadlier ones.

By the middle of the second round, Adri's energy starts to fade fast from dodging so many blows, just as Tosha starts to fall into a rhythm—something Max said she might do if she got tired enough. After another drawn-out minute of dancing around each other, Adri catches the pattern.

"This time, Adri!" Max yells, his thoughts in sync with hers.

"You know what's coming now, kiddo! Let her have it!"

Adri hears Roman's voice as Tosha throws a hard jab, which Adri narrowly slips. Seizing the moment, she takes a wide step backward with her left foot, turns, then kicks her right foot high and hard, aiming for the center of Tosha's face. It's a wild, unconventional kick—like the one Boom almost accidentally knocked Max out with years earlier—but to everyone's amazement, Adri's foot makes contact with Tosha's chin, and she hears a loud crunch as Tosha falls backward before hitting the ground with a heavy thud. The referee rushes to her, anxious for her to stand again, but she struggles to recover.

"Wow!" the commentator roars as the crowd explodes. "Did you see that, Ray? That was almost like a reverse round kick, wasn't it? Now that's a kick you don't see every day, folks, and Rivera executed it perfectly for this win. . . ."

Tosha does her best to shake it off, but she staggers slightly when she lets go of the cage, obviously still too dizzy to continue. Her face falls as the referee signals the end of the fight, but she dutifully joins Adri in the center as he announces her win.

She gives Adri a hard thump on the back. "Good kick, Mama. I'd rather lose to another mama anyway." She grins and points up at the suites. "I'm going to go hug my girl now. You should go hug yours."

Adri smiles gratefully. "I will." She watches as Tosha disappears into the commotion with her coaches, who envelop her with hugs and pats on the back. Suddenly, a familiar voice fills the Coronet Dome.

"In a truly unexpected turn of events, Tosha Rimes just couldn't recover from that crazy kick—which means Adri Rivera is going to the finals!"

As Adri listens, she feels something heavy and warm on her shoulders. Surprised, she turns and finds her uncle draping his old title belt on her shoulder, his eyes shining under the bright lights. Max, too, arranges one of his light heavyweight belts on her other shoulder. Boom places a third belt across her back, his middleweight championship title, as tears fill her eyes. Each belt gleams under the spotlights, and they all say the same thing in bold letters—*Champion*. Cameras flash as they pose together, their smiles as big as hers as the voice booms overhead again.

"Who will Rivera face to earn a belt of her own in three weeks? Will it be Lila 'Blitz' Hoanu, or the current tournament favorite, Gemma Stone?"

The arena buzzes with anticipation.

"Tune in tomorrow and find out."

Hours later, Adri and Max sit in front of the Bellagio fountains. It's late, but the weather is cool, and bright lights make the water shimmer as it soars hundreds of feet into the air before cascading down again. An electrifying song blares from hidden speakers, in sync with the fountains, and Adri is giddy as she eats a scoop of cookie dough ice cream—her first cheat meal in months.

Max laughs as she takes another enthusiastic bite. "Slow down, woman." He tries to take the container from her, but she moves too fast. "You're going to jack up your stomach—"

"Worth it," she says, spooning out the last chunk of cookie dough and savoring it. She can't remember the last time she felt so good. "Because I'm going to the final fight!" She pumps her fist wildly in the air, making him laugh harder.

"I knew you would," he says, smiling. He almost looks as happy as she does.

She sighs. It's one of those rare, perfect moments—the glittering colors of the fountain, the lingering sweetness on her tongue, the leftover adrenaline from her fight, the double armada kick, Roman's belt on her shoulder. And Max. Max laughing and smiling and believing in her.

They watch the fountain together until the music fades.

"I love Las Vegas," she says.

"Really?" His brows scrunch. "I could live without it."

"That's because you were made for Sparta."

"What's that supposed to mean?"

She grins at his defensive tone. "It means you like the simple life. You really should run for office. They'd make you mayor in a heartbeat."

He smirks. "Yeah . . . I think I'll pass on that."

Not far from them, a street performer starts to strum a guitar, playing something slow and familiar. Max glances at his buzzing phone. "Enzo just texted me. He says Skye didn't stop screaming until the end of the fight, then she ugly cried."

Adri laughs.

"He also says they're proud of you."

She smiles, missing them, but she's also thankful for the moment alone with Max, away from the noisiness of gyms and press conferences. The mood between them is light, but she knows she should ask the question that's been on her mind for months. "Max . . . are we *really* friends again?"

His head tilts in surprise. "That's a weird question." He smiles faintly. "Maybe you've been hanging out with Boom too much."

She smiles, too, but she waits expectantly for a serious answer.

He sighs. "I mean, we'll probably always be friends, won't we? Whether we want to or not."

She frowns. That's not the response she was hoping for. She watches as his eyes meet hers, then drift to the water again.

"We have too much history not to be friends."

"So . . . do you forgive me?" Her heart races uneasily when he doesn't look up. "For leaving Sparta the way I did," she adds, surprising herself with her own sudden bluntness. Color fills her cheeks. Maybe she *has* been spending too much time around Boom.

Max thinks for a long time, then lightly cracks his knuckles against the railing. "Yeah, Adri, I forgive you. You were ready to get out of Sparta, and I wasn't. I can't hold that against you." He sighs again, more heavily this time. "But . . . I don't know if I forgive you for choosing Owen yet." She hears the hint of bitterness in his voice and wonders if it will ever fade. "I mean, after everything we had . . . you picked *him*."

Her heart sinks with regret, and she covers her face with her hands.

"Why are we even talking about this, though?" His face softens. "It's pointless—"

"I made the wrong choice."

"Adri . . ."

She feels his hand on one of hers as he gently moves it from her face, revealing her tears.

"Oh crap." He wipes one away. "Come on, Adri. Please don't

cry. Not tonight, of all nights." He tips her chin up. "I forgive you, okay? Does that help?" When she doesn't stop crying, he pulls her against his chest. "You're just tired. Tonight was crazy, and—"

Max stares down at her, stunned. "Why are you telling me this?"

"I . . ." She frowns, not even sure of the reasons herself. "I guess because it's the truth, and I . . ." She sighs, too tired and too close to him to think clearly as her heart hammers inside her chest. "I don't know, okay? It just seems like the right time, maybe? Because we're friends again, and you forgive me? Or at least you're pretending like you do." She shakes her head, overwhelmed by her wild emotions. "And I just . . . love you. I just do."

As he looks down at her, his face is a mix of shock and desire. A moment passes that feels like an eternity, with the broken past and uncertain future hanging heavily between them, but when his mouth meets hers, fanning the flame that never stopped burning between them, time stops and stands blissfully still. His hand cups the back of her head, bringing her even closer, but just as quickly, he pulls back.

"Don't look at me like that," he says, responding to the crushed look on her face. "I'm going to do this right for once." She watches, confused, as he takes both of her hands in his. "Adri Rivera . . . I love you too."

Her heart leaps.

"So . . ." He clears his throat awkwardly before a small smile touches his lips. "Would you like to go out to dinner sometime and talk about God and other serious things?"

She bursts out laughing at his somber tone, and his smile widens as the fountains reach up to touch the sky, in sync with a new sweeping song. His question touches her almost as much as the hopeful look in his eyes.

When her phone starts buzzing, Adri fumbles to find her phone on the nightstand to silence her morning alarm. She's just about got it, but Eva beats her to it, expertly hitting the snooze button and snuggling deeper into the covers. Adri smiles to herself. Her daughter has never been a morning person.

Adri yawns. She wants to sleep in the hotel's massive, pillow-filled bed, but a sliver of light is already creeping through the curtains. That, and sleep has been evading her since she and Max returned to the hotel late last night after watching the fountains. On her phone, four messages glow, unread.

When should I call?

Is Eva with you yet?

Call me. Please.

They're from Owen, whom she's barely been able to respond to since she arrived in Vegas. There's one from Max.

Making coffee if you want some.

She smiles. He sent it a few minutes ago. Quietly, she gets out of bed, careful not to wake Eva, and reaches for a sweatshirt. She winces as she pulls it on. The numerous bruises on her torso are just a little reminder of Tosha's impressive punches.

In the living room, she finds Boom snoring on the pullout bed surrounded by throw pillows, his hair splayed wildly over his forehead. Max, shirtless, smiles at her from the kitchenette, and her stomach flips. She joins him and watches as he fiddles with the coffeemaker.

"How did you sleep?" he asks, keeping his voice quiet. Adri can't help but giggle as he pours her coffee. "What?"

"I don't know. . . . That just seems like a funny question to ask."

"Why?" He gives her a quizzical look when she laughs harder. They both freeze when Boom stirs on the couch, but thankfully he continues to snore.

"Ignore me. I'm just sleep deprived," Adri says, aware that she's running on fumes after such a surreal night. She groans softly as she shifts on the barstool, feeling every punch all over again.

Max notices her discomfort and frowns. He rummages around

until he finds a plastic bag in one of the drawers. She watches as he fishes a few ice cubes out of the ice bucket and drops them in. "What's hurting the most?" he asks.

"Hmm . . . I don't know. Maybe my face? Or my hands? Or my ribs? Or—" She exhales as he lightly presses the homemade icepack against her cheek. "Thanks," she whispers, savoring the relief. When she takes over, he makes a second one and drapes it over her swollen knuckles.

"Are you excited for our date tonight?" he asks.

She grins at the playful look on his face. "It involves food, right?"

"Yep."

The soft crunching of springs fills the room as Boom abruptly sits up and turns to face them. "What?" He pushes the hair out of his eyes and squints. "Did you say you guys are going on a date tonight?"

They both stare at him, stunned.

"Are you?" Boom repeats.

Adri's cheeks redden. "Were you only pretending to be asleep?"

Boom ignores the question and turns to Max. "Seriously? You asked her on a date?" He looks at her next. "And you said yes? And it's happening? No more ping pong?"

When Max nods, Boom cheers loudly, shocking them both.

"Finally! Thank *God*," Boom says, raising his fists in victory as Max bursts out laughing.

"What, have you been praying for that or something?" he asks.

"I sure have, brother." Boom throws Adri a smile that she returns. "I guess miracles really do happen."

24

ADRI STARES AT THE PAINTINGS IN FRONT OF HER, her heart racing slightly from what Max just told her. The canvases are coated with thick acrylic paint and displayed on heavy black easels. She shakes her head. "No. Sylvester Stallone did not paint these. No way."

Max laughs at her skepticism. "Yes, he did." The two of them are in a private room of a beautiful rooftop restaurant in the heart of Vegas, and he looks even more handsome than usual in a perfectly cut suit. He points to a little placard next to the paintings.

"No, he didn't," she insists, unable to believe it.

"Yes, he *did*. Read it."

Her eyes widen when she spots Stallone's wild signature. Her eyes shoot back up to the paintings again, awestruck. "So, wait . . . he really did? Seriously?"

Max laughs harder. "What do you think, Adri? You think I painted them or something?"

"Wow." It's all she can say as his words sink in. "That is just so . . . *cool*. And weird."

"They are really weird, aren't they?" Max tilts his head to study them with her. Neither of the paintings are conventionally beautiful, but there is something powerful about them. One features a swirling abstract portrait of Superman in bright blues and muddy yellows. The other is called *Woman*, and that one—with its splattered orange and black lines against a deep red background—captivates Adri's attention.

"But if he actually painted these, then how are we looking at them right now?" Adri frowns. "Shouldn't they be in a museum or something?"

"A *museum*? I know you love the guy, but he's not exactly Picasso."

She laughs as he tears her away from the paintings and leads her to their table, hand sliding easily from her shoulder to her waist in a way that makes her pulse quicken. "A friend of mine bought them a while ago," he says, pulling out her chair for her. "I thought you might like to see them."

Adri exhales as he sits down across from her, amazed and a little overwhelmed. They're the only ones in a beautiful room with a view of the city, and their personal sommelier brings Max a leather-bound wine list. Stallone's paintings rest on easels against the far wall, and she smiles as a Heart song plays from the hidden speakers. "This is one of the nicest things anyone has ever done for me, Max."

He looks relieved. And happy. "I'm glad you like it."

She grins as he scans the wine list and orders something French-sounding.

"I've never seen Fancy Max before. I like him."

He laughs, but a hint of embarrassment touches his face. "There's no such thing as Fancy Max, unfortunately. I'm pretending like I know how to be romantic."

"Well, you're doing pretty good."

He smiles at her over the menu, and her heart races. No man has ever made her feel so desirable with just one look. She toys nervously with one of her chandelier earrings—Yvonne said they went best with the gold sheath.

The next hour passes in a happy blur as they talk about the little things over salads and steak—updates from Enzo and Skye, their training schedule, the tiresome Coronet camera crew, Boom's teasing about their date, which went on for the rest of the afternoon and into the early evening and only stopped when he left to meet Diana for dinner somewhere.

Adri briefly brings up Owen and her new arrangement with him—some communication, no custody, and supervision at all times. Max isn't terribly happy about it, but to her relief, he understands. Her lawyer warned that if Owen fought back even just a little, there was a small chance he might be able to overturn the default custody ruling.

She takes a long sip of wine when their conversation hits a lull. "So . . . should we talk about God now?" She laughs at the surprised look on his face. "I wonder how many people say that on their first date."

Max laughs into his wineglass too. "I don't know. Probably not that many." His face gradually turns more serious. "But yeah, we should talk about God. And the future. And Eva."

She inhales, thrilled and overwhelmed at the same time. "Okay."

"The last time we talked about this, I was kind of a jerk."

She raises her eyebrows. "Kind of?"

"Okay, fine. I *was* a jerk. I finally figured out why." He sighs, obviously regretful. "I've been mad at God for a long time."

She nods slowly.

"But I don't want to be anymore," he says.

"So . . . you believe he exists?"

He nods, finishing what's left of his wine. "I never really thought he didn't. That was just a good excuse to ignore him. But Boom helped me realize some things. And Roman too." His eyes meet hers. "And you, obviously."

Adri smiles. As she listens to him talk about his budding faith, a heavy weight falls from her shoulders. Everything she prayed for—that Max would listen and learn and understand—has been happening for the last few months.

"Christianity makes a lot more sense to me now," Max continues. "Not *total* sense, but more sense than anything else I can come up with, so I want to keep learning about it." He smiles. "With you."

She exhales happily. "I want that too."

He reaches for her hand. "And I want this—us—to be serious. I don't want to date anyone else, and I want to work toward being Eva's dad . . . if that's what you want too."

She stares at him as his words sink in. "That's exactly what I want, Max."

"Okay. . . . Good." He lets his breath out slowly before laughing. "Man, it feels really weird to be so straightforward, but it's also kind of nice."

Adri laughs, too, understanding. Ever since she left Owen and took her first leap of faith, she's grown increasingly tired of worrying about what's right or cool or weird or not weird. She just wants the truth. "I like it," she says, as his eyes meet hers.

"Me too."

Her pulse quickens as she shifts in her seat, her bare leg accidentally brushing his, and a long, loaded moment passes between them.

He clears his throat. "And all of that said . . . I think we should take things slow."

She nods in agreement, inwardly torn.

"I mean, relatively slow," he adds quickly. "Not *super* slow."

She laughs at his indecision. "What does 'relatively slow' mean?"

He leans in. "I can kiss you, right?" He takes her smile as a yes, and Adri melts into him. When he releases her moments later, his fingertips still grazing her neck, she sighs. Part of her wishes he'd never stop kissing her, but another part is glad because his kisses make her want to do anything except go slow.

Hours later, they leave the restaurant to walk back to the hotel in the warm summer air, but they stop inside a busy sports bar to catch Gemma's fight with Lila Hoanu. A few drinkers recognize them and stare, and one drunk guy points in their direction and shouts something, but thankfully no one approaches. Max pulls her closer as the fight begins.

"Do you think Lila has a chance?" Adri asks, leaning into him.

"Everybody has a chance, but . . ." His frown tells Adri everything she needs to know. They watch as Lila, a twenty-nine-year-old Hawaiian kickboxer, grins at Gemma from across the cage.

She's been on a hot winning streak for the last two years, but Gemma looks totally unfazed.

She and Max watch, hope rising, as Gemma struggles in the first round and takes a slew of hard hits. Adri's heart races as Lila lands more blows and the occasional kick, but the tide quickly turns when Gemma surprises her with a leg sweep that knocks her to the ground in a stunning upset. The audience roars, along with the bargoers. Max scowls.

Gemma, now mounted on top of Lila, hits her hard in the face. Lila almost manages to break free, but Gemma subdues her with her signature elbow. Lila can't escape, and like so many of Gemma's opponents, she's beaten bloody until a referee intervenes. Adri sighs as Gemma steps carelessly over Lila's body, eager to claim her victory.

"That's it, then. Rivera versus Stone," Max says quietly in her ear. "This is what we've been working toward."

Adri nods, although her sudden doubts unnerve her. She desperately wants to fight Gemma and finally earn the title she's wanted since she was seventeen years old—but she also knows it'll be the hardest fight of her life.

25

"ARE WE FORGETTING ANYTHING?" Boom asks.

Adri and Max stand in the middle of the ring and ponder Boom's question, their faces tense with fatigue and anticipation. There are only a few more hours before Adri's press conference with Gemma, and the Coronet Training Center is eerily quiet. Max throws her a reassuring smile, but her nerves make it hard to smile back.

"We covered takedown stuff, ground and pound, kicks." Boom ticks the strategies off on his fingers. "Your wrestling is looking really sharp—"

"You just can't let her get the mount, Adri," Max says firmly, interrupting him. His face turns darkly serious. "That's where she always finishes fights, so you just need to make her stand and face you the whole time. She's a good striker, but you can take more hits than she can."

Adri nods, but she must look nervous because both Max and Boom frown back at her. "I'm good, guys," she says, drawing a shaky breath. Her mind searches for anything else she could do to prepare, but a resigned feeling fills her chest. She's as ready as she'll ever be. "You've both done everything you can," she says, looking between them. "Now it's up to me."

Boom smiles. Like her, he looks exhausted after weeks of near-constant training, but his eyes are bright and clear. He puts one of his hands on her shoulders, and the other on Max's. "Let's pray." They close their eyes, and Adri exhales gratefully. "God, thank you," Boom prays. "Thank you for Adri's opportunity to fight again. . . ."

As he prays for her, Adri recalls all the small, seemingly unimportant decisions that led her to this moment, like when she chose to walk into an old limestone church where no one knew her name because Owen pushed her to her breaking point. That strange decision led to another, then another, and now she's *here*—with Boom, her dear friend, and Max, the love of her life, and a title fight less than twenty-four hours away. She sighs softly and feels Max squeeze her hand. When she opens her eyes, she finds him smiling.

Almost over, he mouths, and her heart pounds because he's right. Her fight with Gemma will either crown her a champion, or she'll leave in defeat—a possibility she can't bear to think about now that she's so close.

Instead, her mind briefly drifts to Owen and his undetermined role in Eva's life. She silently adds that to Boom's list of prayer requests.

". . . make Adri the champion, if that's your will for her. Thank you for fighting for us and with us. Amen."

"Amen," Max repeats.

Adri's nerves fade slightly. "Amen."

Boom packs up and heads out first, leaving her alone with Max in the gym. It's almost evening, so what's left of the late afternoon sun is fading fast when he pulls her in for a long kiss. She wraps her arms around his neck and kisses him back.

"Don't forget about your kicks," he says, his lips still touching hers. "You've got some good ones." He starts to kiss her again, then stops. "Oh, and—"

Adri laughs as she lightly pushes him away. "Okay, that's enough. You're still in coaching mode." She sighs sadly, already wanting to pull him close again. "And . . . we should probably keep it that way for a while. I have to focus."

He looks disappointed, but he nods. "I'll see you tonight."

"Any final tips?" she asks, as he walks her to the elevator.

He shrugs. "No, not really. She's a good fighter. So are you. It's going to be a close one."

As they wait for the doors to slide open, her stomach twists nervously. "Do you think I can beat her?"

"Yes," he says firmly, sensing her fear. "Do you, though?" When she doesn't immediately respond, he gives her a quick kiss on the forehead as the elevator opens. "You can, Adri." She smiles and waits for him to join her, but he shakes his head. "You take it. I've got a meeting here in twenty minutes."

"Oh, okay." The door starts to close between them when he catches her attention again.

"Hey, Adri?"

"Yeah?" she says, looking up.

He grins. "I love you."

She's sealed behind the doors before she can respond, but her heart soars happily. Only a few weeks have passed since their "date," but her feelings for Max grow by the day.

When the door slides open to reveal the main entrance of the Coronet Dome, Adri walks across the long stretch of gleaming tile and pushes the exterior doors open, stepping out into the cool evening air. She walks briskly toward the hotel, anxious to get ready for the press conference and get it over with, but she slows slightly when she hears quiet footsteps behind her.

"Adri?"

The familiar voice gives her goose bumps. Turning sharply, she sees Owen, and her pulse quickens. He must've been stand-ing somewhere in the shadows, waiting for her. He flashes her a small, apologetic smile.

"Sorry to surprise you like this, but . . . I've been trying to get ahold of you." He takes a cautious step forward. "I know you've been busy." For a moment, she's too shocked to respond, so he takes a few more steps, quickly closing the space between them. "Can we talk about Eva tonight? It won't take long at all."

Her breath catches in her throat as she glances down at her phone. Sure enough, there's a text from him. He sent it earlier that morning.

In Vegas for a fight. Can we talk?

She looks up again and searches his eyes. He's sober, with a fresh haircut, and dressed in clean clothes, but she still looks around uneasily, more out of habit than anything else. He smiles patiently as he waits for her answer, her doubts mounting.

The supervised visitation agreement is drawn up and ready— the only thing missing is his signature. Once she has that, she can finally close another uncertain chapter of her life.

"Sure," she says. "Let's talk."

26

M AX WAITS WITH ROMAN AND YVONNE in the crowded lobby of the Bellagio. Eva looks grown-up in a blue-and-white dress embroidered with silk butterflies, but she squirms as Yvonne tries to fix one of the pins in her hair.

Roman checks his watch again and frowns. "My goodness, they really cram it all in, don't they?"

Max nods. He and Adri have been running to events all week. He scans the lobby one more time, but there's still no sight of her.

"She's going to need to rest up," Roman adds, glancing at him. "You'll make sure of that, won't you, Max?"

He nods again. "Today was our last training session."

"Did she seem okay?" Yvonne asks, her motherly eyes searching his. "I just can't imagine the pressure she's feeling."

"I think she's nervous, but that's to be expected." Max recalls the doubtful look on her face on the elevator and feels a pang of regret. He wonders if he should've said more to ease her fears.

Yvonne's concern grows as the minutes tick by. "Maybe I should go check on her? It's not like her at all to run so late. . . ."

"I'll go up," Max volunteers, already eager to see her again—and to make sure she's not in her head. He knows she has a lot on her mind. "Want to come, Eva?"

Eva nods excitedly and takes his hand, and they head for the elevators, only slowing their pace when someone bumps into Max with surprising force. Surprised, he turns and finds Gemma Stone smirking up at him.

"Max." His name rolls off her tongue like honey. She's dressed in a clingy, flesh-colored dress that enhances every curve, but he tries to keep his eyes on hers. She looks down at Eva, then back up at him with pitying expression. "Babysitting?"

He ignores the remark but catches the flash of anger in her eyes when he lifts Eva into his arms.

"She's just using you, Max. Isn't that obvious yet? She's letting you be the hero now, but once she loses, she'll go crawling back to what she's used to." She glances at Eva, who turns to Max with an uncertain expression. "She's just that type of girl," Gemma adds, not softening. "Some people are just weak."

Her words make his temper rise dangerously close to the surface, but he forces himself to stay calm as he faces her. "Look, Gemma. You clearly don't know anything about Adri—or me," he adds pointedly, with as much disdain as he can muster. "So stop acting like you do."

A small, furious sigh escapes her lips, but he turns, disappearing into the crowd with Eva before she can retort.

Once they're in the elevator, Eva looks up at him. "She was being mean, wasn't she?"

"Yes, she was," Max says, gently setting her down when they reach the room. "And we don't have time for mean people." He knocks on the door, surprised by the long moment that passes with no answer. He considers digging out his key card, but finally Adri opens the door.

Alarm fills him. Her face is pale and tense, and she's still in the clothes she trained in that afternoon.

"Daddy?"

Eva's hopeful voice interrupts his thoughts as she squeezes by him and races into the suite. Confused, Max looks past Adri. Before he realizes what's happening, Eva runs to someone sitting in the living room. Max watches, stunned, as Owen Anders stands up and barely takes a step before Eva wraps her arms around his legs. He falls to his knees and hugs her, tears streaming down his face. Max watches in disbelief.

"What . . . what is he doing here?" His voice comes out in a harsh whisper. When he looks at Adri's face again, jealousy claws at his heart.

"He was waiting for me by the dome."

Max's eyes widen. "He's . . . stalking you?"

"No, no," she says quickly, but her voice is strangely shrill. She turns from him to look at Eva, who still clings to Owen. "He just wanted to talk about seeing Eva."

Max's frustration boils over. "You had to do that *here*? Alone?"

"He was in Vegas for another fight," Adri explains, but she's clearly distracted. They watch as Owen cups Eva's face and kisses her forehead. Eva's crying too. Max fights the urge to pry her from his arms.

"He said he was coming," Adri adds quickly. "I just didn't see his text this morning."

Max stares at her blankly, not understanding why she's making so many excuses for Owen, of all people. Suddenly, it dawns on him that she might be making those excuses for herself, and his distrust deepens. "Did he sign the agreement?"

She shakes her head slowly, like her thoughts are cloudy. "No . . . not yet."

Max grits his teeth in frustration. He wants to pull her aside to talk more privately, but he feels a pair of eyes on him.

"Hey," Owen says coolly, meeting Max's gaze when he turns to face him. His tone is light, aside from a hint of coldness, but Max glares at him. The strong, bitter taste of jealousy fills his mouth as his mind unwillingly drifts to what could've been happening five seconds before Adri opened the door.

"Sorry if I made Adri late," Owen adds, though his tone is barely apologetic. "I was just getting ready to go." He gives Eva another long, tight hug, but when he takes a step toward the door, she won't let go of him. "I'll come back soon, beauty," he says, patting her head. He glances up questioningly at Adri. "If Mommy lets me."

Predictably, Eva starts bawling and begging him not to go, but he just raises his hands helplessly. Max considers dragging him out, but Adri's eyes plead with him not to.

"Mama, please don't make Daddy leave!" Eva wails. "Please!"

The torn look on Adri's face is like a slash to Max's own heart. She takes a step toward Owen and Eva, then pauses. She glances at Max again and lingers near the door. "We have to go now, Eva. Me, you, and Max," she says firmly, finally meeting his eyes. "But . . . hopefully you can see Daddy again soon. We'll see."

Jaw clenched, Max watches as she pulls Eva away from Owen and struggles to soothe her sobs. Max exhales angrily as Owen doesn't help her. Instead, he just stays where he's standing as Adri glances up at him apologetically.

"I'll call you later, okay?" she says.

Owen lingers for another moment—for far too long, in Max's opinion—then nods and heads for the door. He ignores Max's protective stance as he stops to look at Adri and Eva one more time. "Thanks for talking to me tonight, Adri. I don't deserve it, but I appreciate it." He smiles weakly. "I hope the fight goes well."

Adri nods politely, but her eyes move uneasily between the two of them. "Thank you."

As Owen walks out, he keeps his eyes straight ahead, but Max catches his small smirk. He watches him with narrowed eyes until he slips into an elevator.

"I'll meet you down in the lobby in ten minutes." Adri's voice breaks through his turbulent thoughts. "Will you tell everyone I'm sorry? But please don't mention Owen, okay? I don't want Roman and Yvonne to worry." She looks overwhelmed as Eva continues crying against her shoulder, but Max's anger keeps him frozen in place.

"You let him in here, Adri?"

She glances up sharply at his cold tone. "I wanted him to sign the agreement." Her voice breaks at the look on his face. "Please don't be mad at me, Max. I can't deal with that right now."

"What am I supposed to feel right now, Adri? I just found you and Owen alone in the hotel room—"

"Oh my . . . Are you being serious?" Her eyes narrow in disgust. "We were *talking*, like I already told you. He hasn't seen Eva in over a year—"

"I know exactly how long it's been," he snaps, cutting her off. He softens his voice when Eva cries harder, but it's a struggle to keep his emotions in check. The sight of Owen standing so close to Adri, after all the ways he hurt her, reignites his anger. "Have you forgotten what he did to you?"

She groans in exasperation and shifts Eva to her other arm. "Look, I don't want to fight with you about this right now. I *can't*." Her eyes move anxiously toward the clock. "I haven't forgotten anything, I just—"

"He wouldn't sign it, would he?"

She stiffens, and Max's distrust sharpens. She glances down at Eva, whose sobs have quieted as she looks between Adri and Max with round, concerned eyes.

Adri gives him a pleading look. "Why are you so angry? He was going to sign it; we just ran out of time. You knew I had to talk to him eventually, Max. We have a daughter—"

"Why are you still making excuses for him? Where's the woman who's ready to move forward? Where's the woman who knows what she wants?" His frustration with her mounts, but he stops himself from cursing. Partly because of Eva but also because no matter how much Adri's decision infuriates him, he doesn't want to be like Owen. Adri deserves so much better than that, even if she still doesn't see it.

"I just . . . I don't know who you are sometimes," he says, sighing heavily. Sometimes he feels like he knows her better than he even knows himself, but other times, like now, it's like she's a stranger again.

Tears fill her eyes, but he doesn't want to be softened by them.

"You *do* know who I am, but you're still mad about who I used to be."

He knows there's some truth in what she's saying, but he wrestles with it. He *has* forgiven her. He *does* want to move forward. Isn't she the one pulling them back? Gemma's words replay in his head.

"She's just using you. When she loses, she'll go crawling back to what she's used to."

As he stands there in silence, the wounded look on her face feels like a blow to his own heart, but he ignores the pain and turns from her, heading for the door. Once alone in the stairwell, he finally lets himself curse, though it does nothing to relieve the tension that's building up inside him.

As his voice echoes back to him, it reminds him that he had to walk away from his feelings for Adri once before. It was the most painful thing he's ever done, but if he has to, he'll do it again.

27

ADRI'S HEAD POUNDS as voices fill the room around her. Gemma sits at the same long table she does, but she feels miles away. Max, Boom, and Linc sit between them, fielding questions from a crowd of murmuring reporters and guests. In the audience, Eva listens, her head resting on Yvonne's shoulder, clearly exhausted from the night's events. Her tears have subsided, but she watches Adri with a solemn expression.

Boom nudges her. "You good?" He frowns as he looks her over, and Adri knows why. Unlike Gemma, who's dressed in a sexy designer body-con dress, Adri wears a wrinkled black dress and minimal makeup to hide her red-rimmed eyes. She barely had any time to get ready after Max left.

"I'm fine," she says, but her voice falls flat as she glances at Max two seats away. He hasn't looked at her since she arrived, and his face is hard as he offers short, brusque answers to the crowd's questions. Adri's heart sinks when she catches a glimpse of Gemma. She looks calm and confident. Linc does too.

"What are you expecting tomorrow night, Gemma?" a reporter asks.

Gemma flashes him an amused smile. "I expect to win. Decisively."

A few reporters raise their eyebrows while others laugh.

"That's a stupid question," Linc adds smoothly. "Given Gemma's record, tomorrow is a done deal. She'll leave the champion, and that'll be that." Linc smirks in Adri's direction. "She's already fought much better opponents. This one's for fun."

Adri watches as Max's eyes narrow, but he says nothing.

"What about you, Adri?" The same reporter turns to her. "Are you as confident as Gemma?"

"I . . ." It's difficult, but Adri forces herself to focus on the questions instead of Max, who looks as far away as she feels. She considers feigning confidence, but she's too worn down. "No, I'm not." She shrugs as a few people murmur in surprise. "I can beat her, but I don't know how *decisive* it'll be. She's a good fighter."

Linc snorts derisively. "She's more than 'good.' She's a professional."

"Yeah, and she's going up against Adri for the title," Boom retorts sharply, surprising her. "Doesn't that make them *both* professionals?"

"Nope." Linc throws Adri a dismissive smirk. "She's lucky, that's all. She's gotten more than a few favors. That's the only reason why she's here tonight.

Boom's face darkens, but Adri touches his hand before he can retort. "It's okay." She smiles weakly. "Let's save the fighting for tomorrow."

Another reporter stands up to ask a question. "Gemma, is it true you wanted to work with Max Lyons before he started training Adri? But he turned you down?"

The room grows quieter as Gemma sighs into the row of microphones in front of her. "I wanted to work with a lot of people." She shrugs coolly. "I briefly considered Max." She tries to hide it, but there's a hint of bitterness in her voice. "He and I met when I was still a new fighter, and I was impressed by him." She smiles coyly for the crowd. "I think he was impressed by me too."

Adri keeps her eyes straight ahead as her stomach churns, not wanting to see Max's reaction. There's a rustle among the reporters as Gemma continues.

"I approached him about coaching me, but he said he wanted to focus on his little gym, and then I guess he decided to make Adri his pet project." She tosses her glossy straight hair over her shoulder. "That's his loss, as far as I'm concerned."

Adri looks up, unable to help herself, but Max's face is still unreadable.

"Any response to that, Max?" someone asks.

"No, not really," he says in a bored voice. He turns his head to look Gemma in the eye. "Other than I'd make the same decision a million more times."

Adri smiles faintly as Gemma's face turns to ice.

"Adri, is that true?" another reporter interjects. "Did Max make you his project?"

"No." She scowls, irked by the question, but she keeps her voice as light as she can. "I'm the one who asked for his help. Max and I . . ." She trails off, unsure how to describe their relationship now that Owen's driven another wedge between them. "We . . . grew up together." She can feel Roman's questioning gaze on her. Of course, he knew something was wrong when Adri joined the others in the lobby before the press conference, but he didn't have time to press her for answers.

"That's cute and all," Linc says, cutting her off. "But if Lyons was smart, he'd want to work with the best. Someone who doesn't quit—someone who's dedicated." He looks pointedly at Adri with his snake-like eyes. "Gemma's never quit. She's fought for everything. She *earned* it."

A hush falls over the room as Adri's anger simmers under the surface. But the longer she considers his words, the more she feels an unexpected calm.

"Adri, any response to that?" someone asks.

She turns to look at Linc, who scowls back at her. "Yeah, I do have a response." Her eyes slowly drift across the crowded room illuminated by chandeliers and the occasional flash from a camera. Her heart races. "He's right. I did quit after I had my daughter." Eye and cameras turn sharply onto Eva in the front row, who looks up shyly. "I wanted to fight again, but I didn't, so I let a lot of people down, including myself." Adri glances at Roman, then at Max—but he still doesn't look at her. A wave of regret washes over her, but she breaks through it. "But I'm here now, right? I'm at this table with Gemma because I earned my place too."

Roman smiles proudly.

"My uncle always told me that every day is a new fight, and that I don't have to fight it alone. That's why I'm thankful for all the people who helped me get to this table." Curious faces pivot between her and Max, but his eyes stay fixed ahead of him. She sighs, ignoring the pierced feeling in her heart. "Tomorrow night is my second chance, and I'm taking it."

Finally, she turns to face Gemma, who looks back at her with pure spite. As they stare at each other, ignoring the clicks and flashes all around them, Adri feels the fire that Roman helped to ignite so many years ago. Her dream is right in front of her, and Gemma's just in the way.

28

ADRI PACES IN THE SUITE, far away from the music and gambling floors below her. She's listening for any sound that might signal Max's return, but so far there's only silence. The guilty knot in her stomach tightens as she remembers the betrayed look in his eyes when he saw her with Owen, but she tries to keep her thoughts on the present moment. She has to, otherwise she'll fall apart.

Kicking off her painful shoes, she sits down, choosing the chair in her bedroom, although she quickly regrets it. A silver silk robe embroidered with gold letters spelling out her name hangs over the door—a beautiful gift from Max for her fight tomorrow. As she stares at it, another cold wave of regret rolls over her.

She remembers his stony silence, and anger and shame fill her at the same time. Anger, because Max doesn't trust her, despite all the progress they've made, and shame because she understands why. As much as she didn't want to admit it earlier, it *was* foolish to talk to Owen alone. She knew that deep down when she agreed to talk to him here, but part of her—the part that desperately hopes he really has changed—ignored her instincts. And that decision might've cost her Max. She covers her face with her hands and draws a tired breath.

She hears a sharp knock on the door and sits up straighter. Her heart picks up its pace. For a moment, she almost doesn't believe she really heard it, but then there's another, and another. Hope rising, she stands up and rushes to open it, expecting Max to be on the other side.

"Oh." Her heart sinks heavily as her eyes meet Owen's. "What are you doing here?"

When he doesn't immediately answer the question, a familiar panic fills her. Confused, she watches as his eyes dart past her to scan the empty suite. Adri moves fast, intending to slam the door between them, but he pushes his way inside before she can.

Max walks the Las Vegas Strip, along with hundreds of other people, pressed in on all sides. Unlike him, most of them are laughing or drinking or celebrating, but he's silent as he moves in no particular direction, walking fast for a while, until he finally slows down. He wants to quiet his mind and think clearly, but the heaviness in his heart is clouding his judgment.

The press conference didn't go as he expected. He thought Adri might return his iciness, but she didn't. Instead, she was warm and composed, despite Gemma's provocations. Max could feel Adri's pleading eyes on him more than once, but he made his heart cold, still reliving the shock and jealousy of seeing her alone with Owen in their hotel suite. Now her words, spoken softly and sincerely, haunt him.

"It's my second chance, and I'm going to take it."

She said it with so much hope and conviction—more than he ever had when he was fighting. Her words made him realize how much he doubted her. Has she just been using him for her second chance? Is she actually strong enough to leave Owen behind? Should Max really trust her again? He desperately *wants* to believe her love for him is real. Her eyes tell him it is. Sometimes the way she looks at him fills him with so much warmth that he can barely pull himself away from her—but those sharp, nagging questions can still chip away at everything they've rebuilt.

He briefly manages to force his mind elsewhere. Boom has been texting him nonstop ever since the press conference, so Max silenced his phone. And Adri . . . who knows? Maybe she's waiting for him to return, but his jealous mind goes places it shouldn't.

He passes the Coronet Dome. A towering, larger-than-life-size poster hangs in front of it, featuring Adri. Her arms are crossed in front of her chest, and her face is beautiful and determined. Ever since she cut her hair, there's a new vulnerability to her revealed features, but she looks powerful and intimidating as she stares down at him—undoubtedly ready to fight for what she wants. His heart races faster as he stares at it, full of regret.

"So . . . what do I do now?" It still feels strange to talk to God, but it feels less strange than it used to. Over the last few months, he's become increasingly aware of a voice that he can't describe. It's neither audible, nor is it his own, but it gently pushes him out of his darker thoughts. "How do I stop doubting her?"

He rests his arms against a nearby railing and lowers his head, waiting for an answer. Everything in him wants Adri—to love her, to take care of her, to be there for her and Eva—but he's still been holding her at arm's length, afraid that she might hurt him again.

He sighs, conflicted, as his mind replays the last year with its vivid highs and lows. The longer he thinks about the woman she's become right before his very eyes, along with his own gradual transformation, the less power his doubts have over him. For years, he felt so trapped whether he was locked into the cage or not, but Adri showed him something that finally set him free.

As fresh resolve fills him, what's left of the heavy weight that's been draped across his shoulders for so long feels like it's slowly slipping off as his mind clears, and he gets the answer he's been waiting for.

29

IT ALL HAPPENS FASTER THAN ADRI EVER THOUGHT IT COULD—faster than any fight she's ever been in, faster than waking up from a nightmare.

All of her fragile hopes that Owen and Eva could have a relationship are shattered like glass when his fingers close around her throat. Instinctively, she rips his hand away before he can tighten his grip, but he grabs her arm and drags her back. She screams, but he roughly covers her mouth. When she bites down, he slaps her with his other hand, dizzying her, but she stays conscious. He manages to pull her down, and they struggle on the floor.

"Stop fighting, Adri," he growls. He hits her repeatedly in the face, trying to subdue her, but she doesn't stop trying to wrestle him off. He smells like sweat and alcohol, and it's such a familiar smell that she almost vomits. His hand still covers her mouth, so she screams prayers in her head as her mind goes into survival mode.

The room turns silent and bright as everything around her freezes—the only thing that moves is her body against Owen's. Her back digs painfully into the wood floor, pressed down by his weight, but she barely notices the pain. She's too focused on his hands—the one on her mouth, and the other reaching under her dress. In a burst of panic and rage, she yanks her face to one side, and his hand momentarily slips off, unbalancing him. She captures that hand with hers and uses all of her weight to roll, reversing them.

For a moment, he's too stunned to react, so she rises and runs to the door. Her fingers almost brush the knob just as he grabs at her ankle and pulls her back. She turns and kicks his hand away, but he grabs at her again, unwilling to let go. Desperation fills her as he rises swiftly and lands a hard punch to her side. When she crumples to the floor, dizzy with excruciating pain, he climbs on top of her again. She claws at his eyes until he pins her arms down.

He scowls as he looks down at her with dark, vengeful eyes, but she returns his gaze with a silent message that he isn't used to—that she's not going to stop fighting unless he knocks her out or kills her. It's going to take one or the other before she quits. She braces herself, aware that he's probably willing to do either.

His hands move to her throat and press painfully against her skin until she can barely breathe. She wrenches at his fingers, but her vision starts to blur and her body feels lighter, but her mind briefly registers a nearby sound—a quick click, then a soft creak. Is she imagining it? She doesn't know. Her mind is moving slowly as she tries to keep her eyes open, and her ears are ringing with a deep, hollow sound.

Dizzy, she catches a glimpse of Owen turning his head as his face collides with a fist. She gasps as her burning lungs fill with oxygen again as he falls back with a hard, heavy thud against her numb body. Another moment passes before Max drags him off, completely freeing her from his weight. When her head stops spinning so violently, she sits up. Eventually, her eyes refocus on Max, and her mouth parts. His hands and elbows are bloody as he drives them into Owen's face.

"Max!" She thinks she says his name, but he doesn't stop or turn around. His eyes are fierce as he slams his fists down over and over again, rattling the nearby furniture. Owen isn't moving anymore. "Max!" she says again, and he finally turns to her.

The sorrowful look in his eyes pierces her heart as he steps over

Owen and moves toward her. He slides his arm under her neck and gently pulls her to him, and she feels his chest rising and falling against hers. As she relaxes into him, she tries to keep her eyes open. Even though she can't really hear him, she knows from the look on his face that he's apologizing. She opens her mouth to say she's sorry, too, but the room turns black.

30

ADRI DOESN'T KNOW HOW MUCH TIME PASSES IN THE DARKNESS, but it's interrupted by a faint shimmering light. And noise. A familiar noise, but she can't quite place it. As her senses sharpen, a door opens, then closes, and there's quiet footsteps. Something warm rests on her right hand. Finally, she opens her eyes.

Eva's face is the first thing she sees, and she smiles. She realizes the light is from the crack in the drawn curtains in her hotel room, and the noise is Eva's soft, steady breathing. Her small hand rests on Adri's.

Tears fill Adri's eyes. "Hi, butterfly."

Eva blinks up at her. She looks fearful but relieved as she turns to someone on the opposite side of the bed. Adri tilts her head and winces from the sharp pain in her side, but it subsides when she sees Max. He stands on the other side of her, and his hand covers her other hand.

"Hi," he says quietly.

"Hi."

Someone taps on the door and slips inside. When Yvonne looks at Adri, her worried face breaks into a relieved smile. "Thank goodness. I'll tell Roman he can stop pacing now." She approaches the bed to smooth Adri's hair. "Oh, honey."

Adri smiles weakly as the memories of last night resurface. The last thing she remembers is seeing Owen's lifeless body and looking up into Max's eyes before she passed out—but then more images float to the surface. At some point, she must've regained consciousness because she remembers briefly answering a police officer's questions before Max took over. She glances at him again and frowns. A streak of blood stains his white dress shirt, and his knuckles are bandaged.

Yvonne looks between them and puts her hand on Eva's shoulder. "Come with me, sweetie. You'll see your mama again soon. Let's let her and Max talk for a minute."

Eva starts to follow Yvonne, but Adri doesn't let go of her hand. She can see the lingering fear in Eva's eyes and desperately wants to make it disappear. "Everything's going to be okay, Eva," she says, making her voice calm and steady. "You're a very strong girl."

Her little face still holds a hint of uncertainty, but she nods. "You are, too, Mama." When she departs with Yvonne, leaving Adri and Max alone, a heavy silence fills the room.

"Hi," she says again, overwhelmed and unsure where to begin. He smiles sadly. "Hi."

"Well . . . you were right about Owen."

He curses softly. "I didn't want to be right, Adri."

"I know," she says, cutting him off with a sigh. "But you were. I should've listened—"

"No, don't think for a second that it was your fault." His hand gently tightens around hers. "He's the one who . . ." His voice trails off bitterly, too consumed with anger to go on. Eventually, he softens again as he sighs. "Sometimes you do your best with someone, and they still blow it."

As he hangs his head, she senses his deep regret for the night before, and his eyes are apologetic as they meet hers. She touches his cheek and brings his face to hers. "I love you," she whispers, as their lips brush. The words spill into his mouth before she kisses him deeply—her own unspoken apology. He only pulls away when they hear a quiet knock on the door, and Roman steps inside.

Adri's heart breaks. Somehow, he looks a decade older. His eyes—so bright with excitement yesterday—are heavy with grief.

He shakes his head as he sits in the chair abandoned by Eva. "I'm sorry, kiddo. I'm just . . . I wish I would've . . ."

"Not much point in wishing, is there?"

He frowns at hearing one of his many sayings repeated back to him.

"I'm still standing, Uncle Roman." She smiles reassuringly. "That's something."

His eyes shine as he grips her hand tightly. "Yes you are, my dear. After everything, you're still standing."

As her uncle studies her, her mind drifts back to the evening's nightmarish events. "Where's Owen?" she asks.

Her uncle's face darkens. "Gone."

The finality in his voice alarms her. "*Gone?*"

"He was arrested last night," Max explains, his face hardening all over again. "He's in the hospital now, but then he's going to jail."

Shock fills her as his words sink in, followed by a deep wave of relief—until she glances at the alarm clock on her nightstand and realizes what time it is. "Am I still fighting Gemma tonight?" she asks, sitting up quickly before gasping at the searing pain near her rib cage.

Max hurries to her side. "No way, Adri. Your side looks really bad. And your face is . . ."

"What? What's wrong with my face?" She looks around for a mirror until he reluctantly brings her one. Her heart sinks as she examines every angle of her face, taking in all the new bruises and cuts. Her right eye is badly swollen, and everything aches, but her rib hurts the most.

"I'm going to tell them to put in Tosha," Max says quietly.

"*What?*" Her head snaps up. "No!"

"They're not going to let you fight without a physical—"

"Then schedule one," she demands, giving him a fierce look. "I'm fighting tonight."

He groans. "Adri . . ."

"Please, Max." She sits up straighter and almost gasps again but presses her lips together, hiding the pain. She lightly pushes her hand against her side, searching for the most sensitive part. It burns with pain, but she presses harder, testing how much she can take. "Can one of you help me up? I need to walk around."

Max tries to protest, but she's adamant, so he helps her slowly stand. At first, she feels off balance, but she gradually regains her footing. She catches a glimpse of herself in the room's massive gilded mirror and frowns at her reflection. She doesn't look terribly intimidating with her battered face and crumpled black dress, but she's determined. As she throws a few punches, she notes the way her torso throbs as her arm extends and retracts. Thankfully, the more she throws, the less she notices the pain. It won't be easy, but she can still fight.

"Please." She looks pleadingly at Max. "Schedule the physical. I'll pass it."

"Adri . . ."

"Please, Max." On some level, he must've sensed that she would still want to fight, otherwise he would've wasted no time calling for a doctor. She looks at Roman next, hoping that he'll back her up. He looks uneasy, but he doesn't try to stop her. They both look at Max next, waiting for his answer. "What if it was your fight?" she continues, her voice starting to break. "This is it. This is my chance. Don't let Owen take it away—"

"Okay," he says finally, as her heart leaps with hope. "I'll schedule it." But concern is etched all over his face. "I would be lying if I said I wanted you to fight like this, but . . ."

She smiles faintly. "You know I'm going to anyway?"

He sighs and gently pulls her to him. She winces, but she pushes the pain away as she looks up at him. His eyes are full of doubt, but the doubt seems to fade the longer he looks at her.

"Just win, okay?"

31

THE CORONET DOME is lit up like never before as fans pack the seats. Electronic music shakes the speakers and sends a shiver of adrenaline up Adri's spine as she watches everything from the television screen in her locker room. Clips of her and Gemma—both looking their fiercest—replay endlessly on the jumbotron, high above a fleet of commentators seated near the cage. Adri listens as they discuss her personal life like it's just another highlight reel.

"In a shocking turn of events, Rivera's husband, Owen Anders, a former fighter, was arrested last night—"

"Her ex-husband, actually," someone quickly corrects him.

"Oh, right, her ex-husband, my apologies." He clears his throat and glances down at something on the table before continuing. "Yes . . . Owen Anders, once a prolific fighter from Miami, was arrested last night after an altercation that left Rivera injured, though not seriously."

"Thank God," Melissa Medlock adds, seated nearby.

He nods. "Absolutely, but obviously these aren't ideal conditions for Rivera as she enters the cage tonight, especially against a fighter like Stone."

Boom steps in front of the television, blocking Adri's view. "That's enough of that. Time to warm up." Adri nods, and they fly through her best combinations. Owen almost fractured her rib, so her abdomen is wrapped with gauze and tape, but the tape keeps unraveling the more she moves. Boom notices and frowns. "You're going to protect that rib for me, right?"

As she toys with the loosening tape, her heart sinks. Both Boom and Max want her to leave it wrapped, but she knows it won't make a difference. Gemma will go after her injury whether it's taped up or not. She faces Boom in her fighting stance and signals to her rib cage. "Try to hit me."

Max's face darkens as Boom cautiously goes for a light punch near her rib. Adri blocks that one, then another, but the tape scrapes against her skin as it continues peeling off.

She sighs. "I just need to unwrap it, guys." She looks to Max, and he reluctantly unwinds it, slowly revealing the large welt blooming against her skin. Even just his light touch stings, but she ignores the pain.

"Are you sure?" he asks.

She nods, scared but sure. He nods back, his face still uncertain.

When an official knocks on her door to let them know that it's almost time to go, Boom hugs her tightly. "Rocco told me this morning that you're his favorite fighter," he says. "He said he likes you even more than Cyrus Saber, so that's a pretty big deal for him."

She smiles and turns to Max next, and he holds out her robe and helps her slip it on over her gold sports bra and shorts. *La Tormenta* shines across her back. "Thank you," she says quietly.

He hugs her, too, and Adri lingers in his arms, listening to the steady beat of his heart, which momentarily slows her own. "Rocky Balboa would be proud," he says against her hair, making her laugh. "Danny Lyons would be proud." Her laughter softens into a sad smile. "Dalila Rivera would be proud too." Tears fill her eyes as his arms tighten around her before he turns her toward the door. "Let's go." She can sense that he doesn't really want to let her go, but eventually he does.

As the three of them walk down the narrow hallway, toward her tunnel, the sounds from the dome get louder and louder. Elaborate purple and white lights swivel, illuminating the cage and the crowded seats, where thousands of fans hold signs and shout her name as cameras glide around them, capturing everything. When they reach the opening, Adri's walk-in song—"The Final Bell"—rattles the walls, and she loves it as much as she did the first time she heard it as a little girl watching *Rocky* for the first time.

As she makes her way to the cage, she pauses to look up at the suites. She can't see anyone, of course, but she knows they're all there—Roman, Yvonne, Skye, Enzo, Rocco, and Eva. Eva is probably waving furiously at her while Roman watches through the glass, his mouth moving in a silent prayer.

Adri draws a shaky breath. Gemma walked out first, so she's already waiting in the cage, dressed in a dark metallic set that glitters under the moving lights. Her eyes move over Adri's bruised face and linger near her torso before she smirks coldly. Suddenly, Adri remembers what she said about Skye so many months ago.

"I'm going to finish her in the first round."

Her stomach tightens with fear. Gemma has the same vindictive gleam in her eye now, but Adri's falling confidence is bolstered when she realizes the crowd is clearly on her side. They're still cheering for her, and some are even on their feet.

Gemma notices, too, and scowls. Linc stands behind her, in her corner along with a team of coaches, and he stares menacingly in Adri's direction.

"This is it, folks, this is the moment." A familiar voice fills the dome, narrating the night's events. "For the win, for fifty thousand dollars, for the title of Coronet Strawweight Champion . . . Who will take it all? Who has the will to win tonight?"

In the few seconds remaining before the fight begins, Adri's mind races to the night before, the day before, the weeks before, the months before—every moment of torture, of training, of progress. She imagines Owen, finally locked away in a cage of his own and feels a twinge of pity mingled with satisfaction. In some ways, she almost understands him and the rage that fuels him. Without

Roman and Dalila's guidance, she might've grown up to be cruel and controlling too. Adri frowns. Unlike her, Owen never discovered the incredible power of love and forgiveness. She prays one last time as she waits for the referee's signal, but she doesn't pray to win. Instead, she just offers up a silent, sincere thank-you for her freedom.

When the referee takes his place in the center, it feels as if everything is moving in slow motion until she and Gemma tap their gloves together. Then, in an instant, time speeds up again, and Adri's senses sharpen as Gemma throws fast, hard punches, immediately making her move around the cage. Adri tries to fend her off, but Gemma moves around expertly, easily anticipating what Adri will do next.

"This is an unexpected matchup if there ever was one, folks. Our number-eight seed is fighting the number-one seed, and it's showing. Rivera's holding her own out there, but this looks personal for Stone. She's got Rivera on the run—"

"Shots to the body, Gemma!" Linc barks, in unison with her coaches. "Body! Body! Body!"

Gemma doesn't listen to them, though. She's enjoying keeping Adri on the defense, throwing constant jabs at her face and trying to pull her down every chance she gets. Adri's chest rises and falls as she tries to catch her breath and find an opening, but Gemma is relentless. Panic fills her as the first round drags on.

"Just take her down, Gemma!" one of her coaches screams. "Don't stand with her!"

Gemma shoots in and almost manages to take her down, but Adri sprawls just in time, gritting her teeth as Gemma claws at her side.

"Hang in there, Adri!" Boom yells. "You've got another ten seconds!"

Adri does everything she can to keep Gemma from getting the mount that she so desperately wants, but her side throbs painfully as Gemma tries to yank her off balance. Max's warning rings in her ears, filling her with dread as she shoves away her grasping hands. If Gemma gets her on the ground, even for a just a few seconds, Adri knows it'll be over.

Finally, the buzzer sounds, signaling the end of the first round, and the referee pulls them apart, but not before Gemma gives her a quick, hard shove. Adri's anger bubbles up as the crowd responds with cheers and grumbles, but Adri doesn't react. Instead, she just retreats to her own corner, where Max is waiting for her. She doesn't have any extra energy to waste.

Adri sits down heavily as he splashes cool water on her face. "She won that round," she says glumly, wanting him to disagree, but he nods. Her confidence deflates until she notices the small smile playing on his lips.

"What?" she asks, as he discreetly applies ice to her abdomen, helped by Boom, who blocks them both from Gemma's view. They don't need to give her any more reasons to attack Adri's injury.

"Did you hear what her coach said?" Max asks.

She frowns, trying to remember, but her mind and body are too overwhelmed with adrenaline and fatigue.

"He told her not to stand with you for much longer. Apparently, she can't handle a real striker." He looks her squarely in the eye. "We already knew that, but it's nice to know that they know it too."

Adri exhales, encouraged but still intimidated. She wanted to throw more punches in the first round, but she was too afraid of opening herself up to more takedown attempts.

"Commit to the plan and follow through, Adri," Max says firmly, capturing her attention again. "Faith or fear—you pick. You're taking a big chance either way."

She nods, understanding, as he helps her up again. She can keep retreating, or she can trust the power inside of her and advance.

She begins the second round with fresh resolve, but Gemma seems equally determined. Her punches and kicks land hard, numbing Adri's already battered body, but Adri throws just as many as she does this time, countering every punch with one of her own and landing some powerful ones, much to the delight of the crowd.

Behind her, Max and Boom scream for her to keep going, their voices growing more hopeful as the round goes on. A few more minutes in, Adri feels the momentum building in her favor—until Gemma lunges forward, surprising her. She rams her body against Adri's, purposefully throwing all of her weight against her injured torso as she tries to take her down again.

A gasp of shock and rage escapes Adri's lips as pain overwhelms her senses, but she moves instinctively thanks to her training, bearing down just in time so Gemma can't pull her to the mat. Clearly frustrated, Gemma drags her to the side of the cage instead and pins her there. Adri realizes what her plan is and panics—Gemma's going to throw her signature elbow strikes there instead of on the ground, with Adri's face and torso trapped between her and the cage door.

Adri barely dodges the first elbow, but Gemma immediately follows up with a brutal punch to her abdomen, as close to her injury as she can get. Adri doubles over in pain as the crowd gasps, and the referee hovers over them, ready to end the fight if Adri can't recover quickly enough. She sees tiny silver stars as she forces herself to straighten again, but she manages to stand tall despite the staggering pain.

As Gemma keeps her trapped in place, throwing more elbows and jabs, Adri feels her victory slipping away like sand in an hourglass. When Gemma lands another solid punch to her torso, tears run down Adri's cheeks, but she barely notices them now—she's too numb. There's a strange high-pitched whistling sound in her ears as she takes more blows.

She knows Max and Boom are probably yelling at her to break free, and that the crowd is screaming for her to fight back, and that her uncle and Eva are likely praying with their faces pressed against the glass, but her body feels temporarily paralyzed with pain even though the still, small voice in her head urges her not to quit.

Gemma's eyes narrow when she survives yet another heavy hit to her rib, and, in that moment, Adri forgets that she's losing and throws a heavy punch of her own. The crowd roars when it makes impact with Gemma's chin, stunning her long enough that Adri pries herself free from her grasp. By then, there's only a few seconds left in the second round, so she finishes it with everything she has, landing a steady stream of punches that make Gemma's coaches spring up and bang on the cage as they shout new, frantic instructions at her. When the bell finally rings, they both retreat to their corners, equally rattled this time.

"Adri, listen," Max says, his voice deadly serious as he quickly tends to her wounds. "This next round, she knows she can't stand with you, so she's going to do *anything* to take you to the ground." When his eyes meet hers, she can see the fear in them. And hope. "You have to finish it, okay? Finish it now."

Adri's heart races as the pressure mounts, but she knows he's right. Gemma's desperation is written all over her face when they meet in the center again for what Adri knows will be the final round. Every move that they make in the next five minutes will determine who leaves the cage a champion tonight.

"Gemma, take her down!" Linc shrieks as the round begins. "Finish it!"

Gemma obeys, roughly grabbing Adri around the waist, but, after so many attempts, Adri is ready for her this time. She sends her elbow down, slamming it against Gemma's temple. The crowd erupts when she stumbles backward, and Adri gets her with a hook before pushing her against the cage. Gemma fights back, but Adri releases a stream of blows to her face.

"Gemma, focus!" one of her coaches screams. "Cover up and get out of there!"

Gemma covers her face and manages to sneak in a sharp upper-cut to Adri's injured torso—her hardest one yet. She smirks through her mouthguard as Adri staggers. "You feel that one, Rivera?"

She's about to pull Adri to the ground, but Adri surprises her with a sudden burst of counterpunches, one of which hits Gemma squarely in the face with a sickeningly loud crunch. Adri watches as blood pours from her opponent's broken nose, and a heavy hush falls over the dome as Gemma touches her face, clearly stunned.

Adri looks her in the eye. "Feel that one?"

Gemma's face contorts with rage as they exchange more blows, both more determined than ever now. Adri's body burns all over, but she doesn't stop punching, not for one second. Eventually, she manages to force Gemma to one side of the cage, near where Max stands.

"Finish the fight right here, Adri," she hears him say. "It's yours."

His voice fans the flame inside her as Gemma doubles over, trying to protect herself from Adri's relentless strikes. All Adri can hear is the sound of her own labored breathing as more blood continues to pour from Gemma's nose, covering them both.

"Get away from her, Gemma!" Linc screeches. "Get away!"

Gemma tries her best, but she can't escape, so she stays hunched over but continues clawing at Adri's rib, doing whatever she can to inflict the most pain. For a brief moment, she's reminded of Owen. For years, Owen found all the things that mattered most to her—her passion for fighting, her freedom, her love for Eva—and those were the things he used to inflict the most pain. Now, Gemma is the one trying to use that pain against her . . . but Adri can use it too.

She inhales, drawing fresh determination to finish the task in front of her, still aware of her weaknesses but even more aware of her growing strength. When Gemma sends another vicious punch toward her rib cage, Adri blocks it, shocking everyone. Thinking fast, she uses that split second of surprise to throw her most powerful hook yet, hoping it'll be her last. The crowd gasps in unison as Adri's fist makes contact and Gemma's head snaps in the opposite direction. The Coronet Dome falls silent—then explodes—as her body falls gracefully to the mat, landing with a soft thud.

Adri's heart races as she waits, while her thoughts move quickly between the power of the punch she just threw, the vivid red color of Gemma's blood mingled with her own, and a strange, unexpected memory. In the very first scene of *Rocky*, a large somber-faced portrait of Jesus hangs in the gym where Rocky fights, watching over him as he struggles. The rest of the film makes no mention of God, so the viewer is left to make their own connections between the true "Man of Sorrows" and the bloodied but victorious hero at the end of the movie.

Adri hovers anxiously over Gemma's motionless body, pressing one hand against her wounded side while keeping the other one ready to strike again if Gemma springs back up before the final seconds tick by. Thankfully, she doesn't, and the referee cuts his hands through the air, signaling the end of the fight as warm relief—and shock—washes over Adri.

"That's it, folks!" a commentator screams, clearly as stunned as she is. "That's it! It's done! Stone's done! Stone is out cold! Adri Rivera knocks out Gemma Stone with a stunning hook—"

As he rambles on, Adri falls to her knees, completely overwhelmed. Her body is numb, the applause is deafening, and the lights are blinding, but her mind and heart are calm and quiet as she watches the tumult all around her.

"The underdog takes it all, folks! Adri Rivera is your Coronet Strawweight Champion!"

She watches as commentators and reporters flood the cage, just as Gemma finally pulls herself up. They swarm Gemma, but she pushes past them, hiding her face from the cameras. Her fans howl and clamor for her attention as she heads for the tunnel, but she doesn't give them a second look. Her coaches hurry behind her, followed by a scowling, sweating Linc.

"Adri!"

Adri turns, heart racing, at the familiar voice.

"Adri!" Max yells again, as he enters the cage and makes his way through the sea of people. A smile breaks across her face as she waits for him.

She imagines Eva first, God's greatest gift to her, seated high above all the chaos and noise, watching as Adri's dream unfolds in living color. She remembers Roman and Yvonne, too, of course, and her aunt, and Boom—every faithful soul who kindled the fire in her soul and prayed for moments like this, even when Adri didn't believe in them anymore.

When Max finally reaches her in the middle of the chaos, the look on his face thrills and steadies her at the same time. Love and pride are mingled together in his dark, warm eyes as he lifts her into his strong arms, and Adri lets herself hold on tightly as he carries her from the cage.

Acknowledgments

I'd like to say thank you to everyone who believed I could be a writer before I ever had a book to show for it.

My devoted parents and in-laws,

my hype-team siblings and extended family,

my incredible husband, Jeff, and our ridiculously adorable children,

Jessica Schmeidler, my fabulous agent and fellow Kansas underdog,

the observant teachers and mentors who gently or not-so-gently pushed me to keep writing,

and my very first readers, Haley, Lacey, Elizabeth, Miranda, and many more.

The list goes on and on and on.

It's easy to be excited for someone *after* their book is published, but it takes a special kind of commitment to support a struggling wannabe writer, and I couldn't have asked for a better group of family and friends.

I also want to say thank you to everyone who helped make *After She Falls* a real-life book:

Dave, Jen, Amy, Noelle, Brooke, and many others at Bethany

House, thank you for believing in Adri's story, and in me. And thank you, Rachel Hauck, for the kind words that probably inspired at least a few people to pick up a Christian MMA romance novel and give it a try.

Finally, I want to thank my amazing readers, who are the reason why I get up early and stay up late to write. Thank you to every woman wise enough to love God above all else and brave enough to fight the good fight. I hope Adri's story inspires you as much as your stories have inspired me.

Yours in the fight,
Carmen

Discussion Questions

1. Adri, despite being a former fighter, finds herself in an abusive relationship. Does this surprise you? Why or why not?
2. Roman often refers to the "fire" he sees in Adri. What do you think he means by that?
3. Max, despite all his success, still struggles to feel content with his life. What are the limits of success? Why doesn't it seem to keep us satisfied for long?
4. Adri, like so many people, has a love-hate relationship with her hometown. Why do you think that is?
5. When relationships fall apart, children often suffer the most. Do you think Adri was right to try to include Owen in Eva's life? Or was she being "weak," as Max claimed?
6. Yvonne says that relationships work best when you find someone "who makes you feel off the charts in love but also someone who helps keep your feet on the ground." Is she right?
7. Boom mentions the controversial Christian subculture within MMA circles. Why do you think so many fighters wrestle with questions of faith?

8. MMA is a highly contentious sport. Some say it's an impressive discipline, while others think it's just unnecessary violence. Do these characters make you see professional fighting in a new way?

9. What was your favorite quote or passage from the book?

10. If the book were being adapted into a movie, who would you want to see play what parts?

Carmen Schober (www.carmenschober.com) is a debut novelist, wife, full-time mother to two daughters, avid boxer, and *Rocky* enthusiast. A graduate of Kansas State University, where she earned a master's degree in English literature and creative writing, she currently lives in Manhattan, Kansas. She has published sports fiction in *Witness* magazine and *Hobart Pulp*, and she regularly blogs about faith, family, and fighting.

Sign Up for Carmen's Newsletter

Keep up to date with Carmen's news on book releases and events by signing up for her email list at carmenschober.com.

You May Also Like . . .

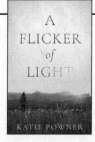

Widower Mitch Jensen is at a loss with how to handle his mother's odd, forgetful behaviors, as well as his daughter's sudden return home and unexpected life choices. Little does he know Grandma June has long been keeping a secret about her past—but if she doesn't tell the truth about it, someone she loves will suffer, and the lives of three generations will never be the same.

A Flicker of Light by Katie Powner • katiepowner.com

More Contemporary Fiction

Molly McKenzie has made social media influencing a lucrative career, but nailing a TV show means proving she's as good in real life as she is online. So, she volunteers with a youth program. Challenged at every turn by the program director, Silas, and the kids' struggles, she's surprised by her growing attachment. Has her perfect life been imperfectly built?

All That Really Matters by Nicole Deese
nicoledeese.com

When pediatric heart surgeon Sebastian Grant meets Leah Montgomery, his fast-spinning world comes to a sudden stop. And when Leah receives surprising news while assembling a family tree, he helps her comb through old hospital records to learn more. But will attaining their deepest desires require more sacrifices than they imagined?

Let It Be Me by Becky Wade
A MISTY RIVER ROMANCE
beckywade.com

After her dreams of mission work are dashed, Darcy Malone has no choice but to move in with the little sister of a man who she's distrusted for years. Searching for purpose, she jumps at the chance to rescue a group of dogs. But it's Darcy herself who'll encounter a surprising rescue in the form of unexpected love, forgiveness, and the power of letting go.

Love and the Silver Lining by Tammy L. Gray
STATE OF GRACE
tammylgray.com

⬦BETHANYHOUSE

More from Bethany House

Left to rue her mistake of falling in love with the wrong man, Maisie Kentworth keeps busy by exploring the idle mine nearby. While managing his mining company, Boone Bragg stumbles across Maisie and the crystal cavern she's discovered. He makes her a proposal that he hopes will solve all their problems, but instead it throws them into chaos.

Proposing Mischief by Regina Jennings
THE JOPLIN CHRONICLES #2
reginajennings.com

After promising a town he'd find them water and then failing, Sullivan Harris is on the run, but he grows uneasy when one success makes folks ask him to find other things—like missing items or sons. When men are killed digging the Hawk's Nest Tunnel, Sully is compelled to help, and it becomes the catalyst for finding what even he has forgotten—hope.

The Finder of Forgotten Things by Sarah Loudin Thomas
sarahloudinthomas.com

When a renowned profiler is found dead in his hotel room and it becomes clear the killer is targeting agents in Alex Donovan's unit, she is called to work on the strangest case she's ever faced. Things get personal when the brilliant killer strikes close to home, and Alex will do anything to find the killer—even at the risk of her own life.

Dead Fall by Nancy Mehl
THE QUANTICO FILES #2
nancymehl.com

BETHANYHOUSE